SOPHIE
WAS
HERE

BOOKS BY KATHRYN CROFT

The Girl With No Past
The Girl You Lost
While You Were Sleeping
Silent Lies
The Warning
The Suspect
The Lie
The Wedding Guest
The Girl in Room 12
Two Mothers
The Last One to See Him

The Lying Wife
The Neighbour Upstairs
The Other Husband
The Mother's Secret

SOPHIE WAS HERE

Kathryn Croft

bookouture

Published by Bookouture in 2025

An imprint of Storyfire Ltd.
Carmelite House
50 Victoria Embankment
London EC4Y 0DZ

www.bookouture.com

The authorised representative in the EEA is Hachette Ireland
8 Castlecourt Centre
Dublin 15 D15 XTP3
Ireland
(email: info@hbgi.ie)

Copyright © Kathryn Croft, 2025

Kathryn Croft has asserted her right to be identified
as the author of this work.

All rights reserved. No part of this publication may be reproduced, stored in any retrieval system, or transmitted, in any form or by any means, electronic, mechanical, photocopying, recording or otherwise, without the prior written permission of the publishers.

ISBN: 978-1-83618-619-9
eBook ISBN: 978-1-83618-618-2

This book is a work of fiction. Names, characters, businesses, organizations, places and events other than those clearly in the public domain, are either the product of the author's imagination or are used fictitiously. Any resemblance to actual persons, living or dead, events or locales is entirely coincidental.

For my wonderful Mum
Thank you for nurturing and inspiring my love of books
x

PROLOGUE

Mud sticks to her feet, slowing her down as she runs deeper into the forest. Rain has fallen relentlessly all day, and the sky is a dark blanket of murky grey – foreshadowing what this evening will bring. She turns around and glances at the farmhouse, an ominous shadow against the sky. If those walls could speak.

Shivering in her thin satin T-shirt and loose jeans, she stops and surveys her surroundings. This should be far enough. She listens, but all is silent. She's sure she is alone, no one has followed her, but her heart thuds in her ears – a trick of the night.

To her right, there's a sprawling oak tree – that will do; she's not going to venture any further. Although she knows this place as if it's her own garden, at night it becomes a different creature, devoid of any soul.

This is it.

There's no going back once she's done it. She hesitates. She doesn't think about what she's doing, her body carrying out actions her mind won't let her process.

Taking out the shovel she's brought with her, she begins to dig.

ONE

Sometimes there are things you do for love that go against your instinct. And what Charlie's doing for me is one of those things. He doesn't want to leave London, to head back home to the place that years ago he vowed to leave behind. But this is the right decision for us, it's what we need to do to save ourselves – eventually he will see that.

'What are you thinking about?' I ask.

Charlie keeps his eyes on the road, his fingers gripping the steering wheel. He reaches across and briefly places his hand on my thigh. 'It feels weird leaving London behind,' he says.

'I know. It does for me too – I've lived there my whole life. But we both agreed it would be a good move for us. And with my mum gone...' I turn and stare out of the passenger window; the blur of trees makes me dizzy. The truth is, Charlie won't say it, but the main reason he's going along with this is because a few months ago we were on the brink of falling apart, and this is what it will take to repair our fractures. A new life. A fresh start.

'I just worry you might not like the village,' Charlie says. 'Life will be completely different. Can you imagine what it's like being somewhere with so few people that everyone knows your business? It's not like London, Emmie. What if you hate it?'

London is now far behind us, and an unfamiliar landscape awaits. An unrecognisable life. 'I'm ready to make the best of it.' I place my hand on his knee. 'This is what we need.'

'It's not too late,' Charlie says. 'Just say it and I'll turn the car around, call my parents and tell them we're putting the house up for sale.' He smiles, but behind it I sense the conviction in his words. 'I don't need it,' he says. 'I've got you.'

'Charlie, that's insane! Your parents have given us a five-bed farmhouse for *nothing*!'

'You've only seen it in photos, Emmie. And look how much work needs to be done. I just want you to be prepared for that.' He drums his fingers on the steering wheel – a nervous gesture that doesn't escape my notice. It touches me that he's so concerned about how I'll feel about the house.

I haven't admitted to Charlie that I, too, am nervous. I've been so tied up with work that there hasn't been a chance to visit the house. Our landlord had only given us a few weeks' notice on our rental flat, and the unwanted attention I'd been getting from our neighbour meant I was only too happy to leave London behind. It had started on our neighbourhood WhatsApp group – private messages that unnerved me. Charlie had dealt with it, but the more miles I put between me and that man, the better.

But this rush to leave means I don't know what state the farmhouse is in, or how we'll make it work for us. But as Charlie says – we've got each other. And it was too good an opportunity to turn down. Everything has fallen into place, as if it was the final draft of a script – no more amendments, filming is about to begin.

Everything was further cemented when I was made redundant from the job I loved on the same day Charlie's parents called him with the news that they were giving us the house.

They'd wanted to give their three children as much as they could, to avoid inheritance tax where possible, and while Vanessa and Myles got a lump sum of cash, Charlie got the house. Whether it's fate or chance, this is where we're meant to be. I'll find another job, and in the meantime there's a house to work on, a project for me to throw myself into. 'We'd never afford a house like this in London,' I remind Charlie. We've had so many conversations like this over the last few weeks that no thought goes into my words, I just churn them out, say all the right things to reassure him.

'That's true,' Charlie admits. 'And at least we're far away from that arsehole who was harassing you.' He falls silent for a moment, throws me a flicker of a glance. 'But aren't you nervous about meeting my parents in person for the first time? There's that too, remember?'

For the last sixteen years, Charlie's parents have lived in Dubai, so in the year we've been together, I've only met them over FaceTime, attempting to bond over a screen and miles of ocean. 'No,' I say, 'because they're lovely.'

'You do realise that Myles and Vanessa will be there too? Everything's happening at once for you. A new home, new family to be part of. I just don't want you to—'

'Please stop worrying about me. You know I'm used to change. I adapt easily. I can do this. And Peaslake isn't too far from London. I'm sure I'll love it.'

Charlie nods, but keeps his eyes on the road. 'And will *we* be okay?'

'Of course. If we both want to be.'

He nods. 'I definitely want to be.'

'Don't you have good memories of growing up in Peaslake?' I ask, changing the subject.

'Yes... course.' A shadow flickers across his face, and he falls silent. 'Will it ever be our house?' he says quietly. 'It might always feel like my parents'.'

'We'll make it ours,' I assure him. 'It will look completely different by the time we've finished with it.' I turn to him. 'The paperwork *has* all gone through, hasn't it? It's definitely in both our names now?'

'Yep. It's all ours. Let's just hope Mum doesn't turn up every day to interfere with the renovations.'

'She just wants to help, don't be hard on her. And she assured me that she'd leave everything up to us,' I say. 'Remember? They really want us to have this house. But it's weird that they didn't sell it when they moved to Dubai.'

Charlie shrugs. 'It's been in the family for decades, and they didn't want to let go of it. They're very sentimental.'

'But they left it empty all those years,' I say. 'Nearly seventeen, wasn't it?' Charlie has told me all about how his dad, a top surgeon, was offered a position at a prestigious hospital in Dubai, so I understand the part about them having to leave in a hurry. 'Couldn't your mum have stayed and rented it out?'

'She wasn't about to leave Dad. They've always done everything together. As a team. Anyway, they've rented property before and had a nightmare with tenants. Mum couldn't bear the thought of going through anything like that again. Vanessa went with them, so she couldn't help with the house. And Myles was supposed to be keeping an eye on it, but he never seemed to have time. I think he didn't want to leave his wife and kids up there and travel down here on his own.'

'It's just such a shame. Couldn't you have helped out with the house?'

Charlie sighs, weary of my questions. 'I was starting uni in London, remember? I wasn't about to leave. I was only eighteen, Emmie.'

I nod, staring out of the window once again, silent now.

I don't see it, but I sense Charlie glance at me. 'Are you having second thoughts?'

'No,' I assure him. This is where we need to be.

'Do we need to talk about what happened with us?' he asks.

'No.' I don't want to think about that now, or it's likely I'll tell him to stop the car and let me out to find my way back to London. Back to my creepy neighbour. But just as Charlie is doing this for love, I am giving this relationship a chance for love.

'We'll be there soon,' Charlie says. 'And we'll have time to look around the house before we meet everyone at the restaurant. I guess there's no going back now. We made our choice. We'll have to just try to make the most of it.'

We drive on in deafening silence.

My first thought when we pull into a large gravel driveway is that this must be a mistake. I knew from the photos that the house would be large, but now I'm right in front of it, it's hard to believe the enormity of the farmhouse, when I'm used to our one-bed flat. Nine long rectangular windows adorn the front of the house, and the wide front door is flanked by thin white pillars. The overgrown front lawn is twice the size of my childhood back garden, and enclosing it, trees stretch to the sky. I gasp.

'Like it?' Charlie asks.

It would have been a fabulous family home sixteen years ago, and I can see what it could become now, but there's something stark and forlorn about it that will never be masked by renovations. 'It feels different to the photos.'

He nods. 'I did warn you. Also, there's something else.' He points to the adjoining garage. 'Mum said that's crammed full of junk. I wouldn't even go in there until it's been cleared.'

Still staring at the house, I nod. 'Nothing we can't sort out. Let's go in.'

Charlie hesitates, but then opens the car boot and pulls out our overnight bags. The removal van isn't due until tomorrow afternoon, so we've got a chance to see what the house looks like empty. Not that we've got enough furniture to fill this place – our small rented flat in Clapham could fit in this house at least six times.

Charlie unlocks the door, but hesitates before he steps inside.

'We'll have to try to only see the potential,' I say, taking his arm.

My stomach sinks when I take in my surroundings. If the outside looked neglected, then the interior is far worse. We're in a dark, narrow corridor, and the magnolia wallpaper is stained with mould. Under our feet, the terracotta floor tiles make it even darker. A pungent damp smell assaults my nose, and gets worse as I follow Charlie through the house.

As we examine each room, I try to talk animatedly, telling Charlie what I think all the spaces could become.

'Mum said she left some essentials in the fridge for us,' Charlie says, when we get to the kitchen. 'I'll make coffee.'

I glance around. It's not too dated compared to the rest of the house, and I remember Charlie telling me they'd had it done before they moved to Dubai.

'Not sure where we'll sit, though,' he says, pulling open cupboards.

I shrug. 'On the floor? Like we're students again. It'll be fun!' I push away my distaste at sitting on the cold, mouldy floor, and remind myself it's better than having a stalker neighbour.

'Perfect,' Charlie mutters.

The moment I remove my denim jacket, goosebumps erupt on my arms.

'It's summer, and it's freezing,' Charlie says. 'I forgot how cool it always was inside, even in the summer.'

'Nice on sweltering days, though,' I say, silently noting that one of the first things we need to do is get the insulation sorted.

'I still don't get why your parents let it get into such a bad state.'

Charlie wipes dust from the worktop with his sleeve. 'They were busy people. It wasn't a priority, and then when they were going to Dubai, I guess they put it out of their minds.'

I almost point out that only people with excessive amounts of money would do that, but stop myself. I want to make this move easier for him, not make him feel bad. 'How about *I* make that coffee?' I say.

His phone rings, and he pulls it from his jacket pocket. 'It's work,' he says. 'I'd better get it.'

While he takes his work call out in the garden, I search the box of groceries Heather left for us, watching Charlie from the window as I wait for the kettle to boil. A lock of his dark blonde hair falls across his face, and he flicks it back, turning to me, his smile lighting up his large hazel eyes. I feel a rush of excitement. Even after a year together, I still find Charlie as attractive as when I first saw him.

The garden stretches endlessly, wrapping around the sides of the farmhouse, and there's a large summer house at the end of it, with a field beyond that.

I walk around the kitchen, trying to get a feel for what it could become, and notice there's a door leading off – probably a store cupboard. I try the handle, but it's locked. Scanning the kitchen, I assume the key must be in here somewhere, so I rummage through dusty kitchen drawers until eventually I find a box full of keys in the utility room.

The kettle finishes boiling, but I ignore it, determined to find out what's behind the door. Strange that Charlie didn't mention what it was. It takes me several minutes to find the right key, and when I finally get the door open, I'm stunned to see a stone staircase leading down to a basement.

My legs freeze beneath me; I'm unable to move. The last thing I want to do is go down there. Charlie should have told me there was a basement. But then... what would I have done? Refused to come?

Eventually, my breathing steadies, a silent mantra playing in my head. *It will be okay. I can go down there.* With a deep breath, I flick the light switch and tentatively make my way down, the air turning even chillier as I descend.

The basement is huge, with ugly grey walls scarred with cracks. There's not much in here – a few boxes and an old sofa.

We could use this room for storage while we're renovating, and I will send Charlie to fetch anything we need. I'm about to go back up when my eye is drawn to the bottom of the bannister, where something is carved into the wood.

Moving closer, I read the words.

PLEASE HELP ME

And underneath, a dark red smear that looks like blood.

TWO

'Charlie!' I rush up the stairs, almost stumbling in my hurry to get out of the basement.

In the back garden, he finishes his call and slips his phone in his pocket before making his way inside. 'What's going on?'

'I found something...' I'm breathless, aware of how hysterical I sound. This isn't like me. I force a deep breath to calm myself. 'There's something you need to see.' I gesture to the basement door. 'You didn't tell me there was a basement.'

He rushes over and throws his arms around me. 'I'm so sorry. I... I didn't think. I'd forgotten all about it. It's been sixteen years since I lived here. Are you okay?'

I nod. 'Yeah. But I found something down there.' Taking his arm, I lead him to the door, forcing myself to take the lead down the stairs. When we reach the bottom, I point to the bannister. 'Look at that.'

Charlie frowns. 'What is it? I know it's grim down here. We can shut it off – we never have to come—'

'No, look at that carving in the wood.'

Charlie leans down and examines the words. *'Please help*

me,' he reads, frowning. 'Don't know what that is.' He glances at me and shrugs.

I peer at the carving again. 'It looks like blood – underneath the words.'

Charlie kneels down to study it more closely. 'I think that's just paint, Emmie.' He stands up and pulls me into him, resting his chin against me. 'Look, I know it must be difficult for you to... be down here... but I think that's probably something we did as kids.'

'I'm not some vulnerable damaged person who can't think straight, Charlie. You didn't warn me there was a basement, but I still came down here, didn't I?'

'Sorry. I should have told you, I just forgot about it.'

'It doesn't matter.' The truth is I'm grateful Charlie didn't tell me – it would have made this move more difficult. I stare at the carving again. *Please help me.* 'Strange words for a kids' game, though. And wouldn't you remember something like that?'

'Look, remember we're getting this place done up,' Charlie says. 'We can even block off the basement if it helps you feel comfortable.'

I nod. 'Let's see.'

He leans down to kiss me. 'We need to get ready if we're going to make it for dinner.'

I watch him head upstairs, then lean down to study the writing again, running my fingers over the blood stain. '*It's not paint,*' I whisper to the empty basement.

From the farmhouse, The Ivy restaurant is a twenty-minute drive, and we arrive early. It's still warm outside, and I pull my sunglasses over my eyes as we get out of the car. Although Charlie talked non-stop on the drive here, filling what would have been silence, I have barely listened, my mind instead wandering to the message in the basement. *Please help me.* A kids' game, Charlie had insisted. Perhaps he's right; it's no wonder I'm always quick to assume the worst. Yet that was blood, I know it.

'I get that you're nervous,' Charlie says, placing his arm around me as we walk across the car park. 'But you've already met them on FaceTime, and they all love you.' This is important to him, and I want to make a good impression with Charlie's family. The stakes are high, and I'm fully aware that the Hollingers live in a different world to the one I inhabit. This choice of restaurant is proof of that. I don't want them thinking I'm using Charlie for his money; that's why I'm insisting on paying for all the renovations myself, using all my savings to do so.

Whenever I've spoken to his family on FaceTime, it's always been from the comfort of my own home, my territory, where I felt in control. It was Charlie who moved into my flat, not the other way around. But this place – the Surrey Hills – is far from my comfort zone.

We're led to a table, with ten minutes still to go before everyone is due, yet Charlie's eyes dart to the door every time it opens. I'm not the only one who's nervous.

'Are you okay?' I ask. 'You're close to them all – aren't you looking forward to seeing them?'

He nods too many times. 'Of course I am. It's just been a long day.'

'I know. And that message in the basement was creepy.'

Charlie stares at me, but doesn't respond.

'I wonder if Myles or Vanessa might remember carving it?'

'Emmie, it was just a silly kids' game. Do you think you're blowing this out of proportion because of—'

'Don't say it. This is *not* because of what happened to my dad.' I've spoken so loudly that people turn their heads, silence falling across the restaurant.

'I'm sorry,' Charlie says. 'I shouldn't have said that. I'm just... That call I had earlier. There's stuff going on with one of my clients, and it's a bit of a nightmare. They could lose the business they've spent years building. And I need to work out how to help them.'

I know very little about corporate law, but I do know how hard Charlie works for his clients. 'Hey, you'll sort it out. You always do, right?'

He nods. 'Yes. Sorry.'

The restaurant door opens, and Charlie's parents walk in, smiling and waving as they spot us.

Immediately I feel at ease. This isn't much different from talking to them online. 'Darling!' Heather Hollinger says, holding out her arms to Charlie. 'I can't believe we haven't seen you for... what is it now? Two years?' She looks far younger than sixty-two, and her stylish dark hair is cut in a short bob, emphasising her youthful features.

Charlie's face reddens. 'Sorry, Mum. I would have flown out to see you but... work has been full on.'

'My darling, no need to apologise. Life gets in the way, doesn't it?' She turns to me. 'Emmie! Finally, we get to meet you. I've been so looking forward to this.' She folds me into a hug and squeezes me tightly.

Edwin pats Charlie on the back then pulls him into a hug. 'Good to see you, son.' He's far taller than he appeared in video calls, at least six foot, the same as Charlie, and I'm surprised by how alike their facial features are too. They have the same dark blonde hair and large hazel eyes. He turns to me and smiles. 'Wonderful to finally meet you properly, Emmie,' he says, giving me a hug as enthusiastic as his wife's.

'Yes, it is,' Heather says. 'Nothing like meeting in the flesh. We can't wait to get to know you better. FaceTime's just not the same thing, is it?' She smiles. 'Edwin and I are thrilled that we'll all be living so close. The house we've bought is only in the next village.'

'Where are Myles and Vanessa?' I ask. 'Charlie said they were coming too.'

'They're just looking for a parking space,' Heather says. 'Myles drove us. It's terrible for parking around here.'

I glance through the window, and as if on cue, Charlie's brother and sister walk past, deep in what seems to be a heated conversation. Vanessa shakes her head, then Myles grabs her arm but she pulls away from him and rushes inside.

Strange. Charlie has always spoken of the close bond the three of them share. Rarely arguing, more like friends than siblings. I will ask Charlie about it when we get home. *Home.* The word feels alien.

'Well, that was a nightmare,' Myles says, glancing at Vanessa. 'Should have got a taxi.'

Heather smiles. 'You're here now. Let's just all sit down and enjoy this meal. How wonderful that we're all together again!'

Vanessa sits in the empty chair beside me, offering a brief smile then quickly looking away, reaching for her menu.

'Hi,' I say. 'It's nice to finally meet you properly.'

Vanessa nods but keeps her eyes on the menu. She has the same dark blonde hair as Charlie, but her eyes are a mix of grey and blue. Like her brother and father, she's also tall, but her body looks frail and thin.

I glance at Charlie, shocked by Vanessa's reticence. When Charlie and I had video calls with his parents, Vanessa had often hovered in the background, not saying much at all, but I'd assumed she just didn't like being in front of a camera, and that when I finally met her in person, she would be warm and talkative, more at ease.

'You'll have to excuse our sister,' Myles says, giving me a hug before he sits beside Charlie. 'She seems to have lost her manners.' He glares at Vanessa.

Unsure what to say, I smile and ask Myles how it feels having his family back in the UK. Myles has darker hair than the others, but the sibling resemblance is strong.

'It's nice, but a bit strange,' he says. 'I'm used to being the only Hollinger here.'

'Um, hang on a minute,' Charlie says. 'I've been in London the whole time. It's not that far from Leeds.'

'Two hundred miles,' Myles says. 'Far enough, brother.' He turns to me. 'Sorry we haven't had a chance to meet in person.' He looks down. 'I've been going through a bit of a hard time.'

Charlie has already warned me about Myles's divorce. It's still recent, so I'm sure he doesn't want to go into details. 'What made you move to Leeds?' I ask. Charlie's already told me this, but it feels like a safer topic.

'I went to university there,' Myles says, lifting the jug of water and offering it to me. 'And just never came back.' He glances at Heather. 'Much to the annoyance of my mother.'

Heather rolls her eyes. 'Of course I'd want all my children around me. I'm a mother. What about you, Emmie? We want to know all about you.'

Under the table, Charlie takes my hand as I tell the Hollingers all about my career. I've never been comfortable talking about myself, but I'm ready for them to ask lots of questions, to get to know the girl that Charlie has made a commitment to. Though I sense that this evening will be harder than I anticipated. 'I'm a child behavioural therapist,' I say. 'My job in London was helping teenagers through animal therapy.'

'What a worthy cause,' Heather says, beaming. 'I'm sure you'll find a new job soon.'

The waiter comes to take our order, and I notice Vanessa only orders soup.

'So, Emmie,' Heather says, 'what do you plan to do with all your spare time?'

I glance at Charlie. 'Well, we thought that while I'm looking for a new job, I could make a start on the renovations. Organising it all. Doing what I can myself. It will keep me busy. I've worked solidly since I left university.' I place my fork down. 'Thank you, by the way. We really appreciate your kindness.' I turn to Charlie and smile.

'We wanted the house to stay in the family,' Heather says. 'We're delighted Charlie wanted it.'

'It's a beautiful house,' I say. 'Actually, I found something—'

'Anyone for wine?' Charlie says, holding up the bottle, his eyes sending me a silent message.

'Not for me – I'm driving,' Myles says. 'And I need to Face-Time the kids when I get back to the hotel. Don't want to be slurring my words when I talk to them.' He forces a laugh.

'You have some,' I say to Charlie. 'I'll drive home.'

'If you're sure?' Charlie says. 'Thanks.' He fills everyone else's glasses, and Vanessa grabs hers immediately and takes a long gulp. 'I have every faith that Emmie will get snapped up soon,' Charlie says, again urging me with his eyes and steering the conversation back to my career.

I turn to Heather and Edwin. 'Can I ask why you didn't want to move back into the house? It was your family home for years.'

Heather smiles. 'Yes, we did love that house. We just don't need all that space now. And it wouldn't be the same without the kids there. It's a family home, Emmie, and should be filled with people and laughter. We've found a much smaller place. It's only recently been built, so we won't need to do anything. Just enough space for us.'

I turn to Vanessa. 'Where will you be staying?' I ask.

Vanessa stirs her soup but doesn't lift her spoon.

'Vanessa?' Heather says.

'I don't know,' she says, not looking up.

'Oh, Vanessa's staying with us,' Heather says. 'Just until she finds somewhere.' She glances at her daughter, who pushes her bowl away and folds her arms. 'We know you'll love that house as much as we did,' Heather says, turning back to me.

'I'll be glad to get out of the hotel,' Edwin says. 'Need my creature comforts.' He laughs. 'Old age makes us set in our ways, Emmie.'

'You're not old,' I say. 'Anyway, isn't it a five-star hotel?'

'Still,' Heather says, 'nothing like being in one's own home, is there?' She turns to Charlie. 'I hope that's how it felt walking into the farmhouse today?'

'Yes,' Charlie says. 'It felt just like coming home.'

Silence falls across the table, and beside me, Charlie squirms in his chair. They don't know that he didn't want to move into the house, I'm sure of that now. But why? They seemed such a close-knit family, so why would he keep this from them? And clearly Charlie doesn't want me mentioning the writing I found in the basement. Charlie will say I'm just being paranoid and mistrusting because of what happened to me. But I know it's more than that. I *feel* it under my skin. 'Would you like to come and see the house tomorrow?' I ask.

Edwin smiles. 'We'd love to, but maybe another time. We've got some things to sort out with the solicitor for the new house.' He smiles. 'We'll let you get settled first. You'll love living in Peaslake. It's a fabulous place.'

Heather pats his arm and smiles, turning to me. 'You know, Edwin was a bit of a celebrity in the village. A renowned surgeon. He couldn't walk down the road without people fawning over him.'

'Then you must come back,' I insist. 'Surely some of the same people must still live there.'

Edwin smiles. 'That's true, and we'll see them all at our housewarming party next Friday. It will be wonderful to catch up with old friends.'

'The Curtises still live there,' Myles says. 'Still running the pub. They'll never leave.'

It's a relief when the food arrives, and I eat silently, listening as Myles talks about his dental practice, and Heather and Edwin reminisce about their time in Dubai.

And Vanessa sits silently, barely touching her food.

Back at the farmhouse, Charlie and I lie on the old mattress that's been left behind, covering ourselves with the duvet we brought with us. It still smells of our old flat, and a wave of homesickness washes over me. Followed by sadness and regret.

I've opened the window in the bedroom, but no amount of cool night air smothers the lingering damp odour that's leached so deeply into the walls that I wonder if it will ever leave.

'I thought tonight went well,' Charlie says, stroking my hair.

'Why did you cut me off when I was about to mention the message in the basement?'

He frowns. 'I'm sorry. Everyone was having such a nice time, I didn't want them to think we were complaining about anything.' He kisses me. 'Mum really liked you – I could tell. She can be very protective over all of us, wary of welcoming just anyone into the family, but she seemed at ease with you.'

'Well, I'm glad she approves of me. But you are an adult. She'd have to accept whoever you choose to be with.'

He gently prods me. 'I'll remind you of that when you're vetting our daughter or son's partners.'

I laugh. 'I will not be *that* kind of mother.'

'We'll see.'

'Is Vanessa okay?' I ask. 'She was so quiet.'

'She's... not very sociable. She just keeps to herself. I should have warned you, but I didn't think she'd be *that* bad. I thought she'd at least make an effort.' He sighs. 'Mum was telling me she's been getting worse, but I hoped being back here would... I don't know. Spark some joy?'

'Getting worse? What's wrong?'

Charlie yawns. 'Emmie, it's really late, and we've had a long day. Mind if we talk about this another time?'

I'm tempted to mention the argument I saw Myles and Vanessa having outside the restaurant, but then I recall how stressed Charlie was feeling earlier about work; I don't want to add to his burden. It can wait.

I wake in the night and turn over to face Charlie, who is sleeping soundly next to me. Pulling the duvet aside, I slip my bare feet into my slippers. Using my phone torch to light my way, I head downstairs to the kitchen, stopping outside the basement door. Steeling myself, I push it open and switch on the light. It takes another moment, a huge force of will, but I make my way down the stairs, stopping when I reach the bottom.

The carving on the bannister isn't there.

Confused – I know it was right at the bottom – I check the rest of the bannister but there's nothing. It looks like the same chipped wood – the only difference is there's no writing carved on it. No bloodstain.

'What the hell?' I whisper to the silent room. I know what I saw. And Charlie saw it too.

Rushing upstairs, I nudge Charlie awake. 'The writing's gone!'

Charlie rubs his eyes. 'What? What's going on? Are you okay?'

'I've just been down to the basement, and that message has gone! All of it! The carving in the bannister and the bloodstain!'

Charlie sits up in bed, staring at me. 'What do you mean?'

'I don't know what's happened, but it's not there any more – there's nothing written on the bannister!'

'Emmie, just calm down.' Charlie places his hands on my shoulders. 'I don't understand. What message? What bloodstain? I have no idea what you're talking about.'

THREE

Streaks of sunlight stream through the windows, forcing me awake. Something feels wrong, and I jolt upright, taking in my surroundings. The dusty wood floor, bare windows. It all crashes back to me.

There's an empty space beside me where Charlie should be. I call his name, then hear the shower running in the en suite. It's only four minutes past six, too early for him to be up when he's taken the next few days off work.

I pull myself up from the mattress and knock on the bathroom door. 'We need to talk.'

The shower stops. 'Yes,' he says from behind the door. 'But I didn't want to wake you. Can we talk about this later? There's been an emergency at work – I need to go in and prevent a business from breaking the law. They're about to lose everything.'

Although I don't know a lot about Charlie's work as a corporate lawyer, I do know how hard he works, and how much he loves it. He'd even warned me when we first met that he was addicted to his job. How I'd laughed, thinking it was a gross exaggeration, but it wasn't – he was simply being honest. Which means there's no point trying to talk him into staying at home –

I wouldn't even want to, especially when I'll only be confronting him about that message.

'I showed you that message carved into the bannister,' I insist. 'You *saw* it, Charlie.' He opens the door, standing there with his hair damp and a towel wrapped round his lower body, a torrent of steam flowing out of the bathroom. 'Emmie, please don't take this the wrong way, but I think maybe you had a bad dream? It could be the stress of moving, or of being made redundant. Or... what happened to your dad.' He wraps his arms around me. 'We just need to focus on making this house our home now. This is a fresh start for us. I know I didn't want to come here, but I can see the life we could have here. Once this house is sorted.' He kisses me. 'I think... being in that basement freaked you out, and who knows, maybe that made your mind conjure up—'

'No! I didn't dream it. Or conjure it up!' It's hard to keep my voice measured.

'I'm so sorry, Emmie. I really have to go.' He walks to the wardrobe and pulls out one of his suits. 'The removal van's due today, so I've messaged Myles. He was more than happy to come and help out.'

'I'll be fine,' I insist. 'I don't need any help. And the removal team will be here.'

Charlie winces. 'Can you just do it for my brother, then? Please, Em? He pulls on his trousers and blue shirt, then stands in front of the cracked wall mirror to put on his tie, all the while avoiding eye contact. 'It will do Myles some good to come and help,' he says, sitting on the bed to put on his socks and shoes. 'Since his divorce he's been really down. He misses them all. And Victoria's moved the kids away, so he barely sees them. This will be good for him. Having his family around him so he can find his sense of purpose again.' He pulls me towards him, and strokes my hair. 'So will you let Myles help? For his sake?'

'Fine,' I say. It will give me a chance to get to know Charlie's brother away from the rest of the family.

After a hot shower and toast, I try to focus on the plans to make this our home, and to put the blip we experienced behind us. But it's hard to ignore Charlie's lie – I know he saw that message as clearly as I did, and only he can be the one who made it disappear.

Outside, I scan the area. The huge front lawn is disorienting, even without the weeds and overgrown bushes. And it's strange not to see any other houses around. I long for my bike, but it won't arrive until late this afternoon.

I rarely walked in London, preferring to cycle everywhere, to enjoy that sense of freedom of being on my bike among all the concrete and brick. Here, though, the backdrop of Hurtwood Forest will make for more pleasant strolls.

Birdsong accompanies me as I walk, and I breathe in the air, forcing myself to focus only on what's good. I encounter so many different shades of green, and only two cars pass me on my way to the centre of the village.

When I get there, I'm surprised to see there's only a pub – the Hurtwood Inn, which also appears to be a restaurant and hotel – along with a village store and a bike rental place attached to the pub. This is alien to me – I've never lived outside London, where you're never more than a few metres from a supermarket or coffee chain. I take a deep breath. I will adjust; I just have to give it time. And find out what that message meant, and why Charlie is lying to me.

I push through the door of the Peaslake Village Stores, not surprised to hear a bell jingle to alert the owner to my presence. What's next? A disgruntled shop manager, annoyed that someone from out of town has dared to move in and disrupt the status quo? I'm being unfair, but this place – as picturesque as it is – is starting to unnerve me.

A middle-aged woman stops stocking shelves and looks up, flashing me a bright smile. 'Morning. Going to be a beautiful day according to the Met Office.'

I return her smile, grateful to be proved wrong in my assumptions of how she might react to me. 'We do seem to be having a lovely summer.'

'Can I help you with anything?' She studies me. 'Biking or hiking?'

'Hi. Um, neither.'

She frowns. 'Oh. Most people I don't recognise are here for the bike trails. We're renowned for it. Didn't you know?'

'No... I'm... I just moved here from London.' I hold my breath, waiting for the woman's manner to change. 'It was all in a bit of a hurry, so I didn't have time to check the area out.'

'Ah, I see. Well, in that case, welcome to Peaslake! You've probably worked out by now that we're the only shop in the village. But we do most essentials as well as fresh coffee, bread and pastries.'

I scan the shop; there are no tables and chairs, only rows of crammed shelves.

'It's takeaway only, I'm afraid. But most people take it to the bus stop just outside and sit there.' She points to the window. 'Especially in this beautiful weather.'

'Okay. Thanks for the tip.'

'But if that's not for you, or the weather's bad, then the Hurtwood Inn does teas, coffees, food – whatever you need.'

'Thanks,' I repeat. 'I'm just going to pick up some bits.' I grab a basket by the till and browse the shelves, getting bread and other essentials to last until I can go to the supermarket. Heather has left us some things, but not nearly enough.

The woman smiles at me as I take it back to the till. 'If you don't mind me asking,' she says, scanning the bread, 'what house did you move into? I don't remember any being for sale recently. Or for rent. Need a carrier bag? I won't charge you for it. Don't believe in doing that.'

'Thanks. It's actually my partner's parents' house. They were kind enough to gift it to us. The old farmhouse?'

'Oh, yes! The Hollingers' place. How generous of them – that's one huge property. Mind you, it's been empty so long I dread to think of the work that needs doing. I imagine damp is the least of your problems.'

I nod, and a vision of the blood stain and carved words flashes into my head. 'Yep, it's going to be a challenging summer.'

The woman holds out her hands. 'I'm Cassie. Owner and manager of this place, and most of the time the only person who works here. I do get students to help out in the summer, but whether they show up or not is another matter. Can't say I blame them – they're not as invested in this place as I am.' She smiles, and rests her elbows on the counter. 'My mum used to own it and I'd help her out. Then when she died, I thought about selling but couldn't bring myself to do it. So here I am!' She studies me. 'So you're from London?'

'Yep. Born and bred.'

'Ah, then you might not know what it means when a place is as much a part of you as your own skin? That's what Peaslake means to me. To everyone who's from here, I reckon.'

'Do you know the Hollingers well?' I ask, curious to find out more about Heather and Edwin.

'For sure. Everyone around here knows them. They were an important family in the community. Mum absolutely adored Edwin – as did everyone else. And Heather did so much for the community. Did you know she was instrumental in setting up the school in the village? It's around the corner from here so you may not have noticed it tucked away. But the school means kids can stay local for their secondary education instead of having to get a bus or lifts to the schools in Guildford. I'm sure you know Heather's father used to own an international hotel chain. She worked with him until she married Edwin.'

Charlie has told me none of this, but I nod.

'She gave it all up to do philanthropic work. You're lucky to have her as a mother-in-law.' Cassie smiles.

'Charlie and I aren't actually married.'

'Ah, don't worry, love. I'm sure he'll ask you one day.'

I fight back the urge to scream. 'Actually, I've never been bothered about getting married. Happy as I am. My mum always taught me to be independent and never rely on anyone.'

Cassie nods. 'Smart woman. Does she live in London too?'

'She died a year and a half ago. Cancer.'

'Oh, I'm so sorry. Well, not that anyone can replace your mum, but Heather Hollinger will be a wonderful second mum for you.'

I nod. 'I had no idea she did so much for the community.' Charlie has never mentioned this.

'Yes, Heather was always campaigning for some cause or other. We were all gutted when the Hollingers suddenly left for Dubai. I know it's beautiful there, but still – it was a bit of a shock. Some people thought it was because—'

The door opens and a young man walks in, dressed in a postal worker's uniform. 'Morning, Cassie,' he says, with a nod.

Cassie smiles, pointing to a large grey sack behind the till. 'In case I didn't mention it, we're also a post office,' she tells me. 'If you've got any parcels you need to send.' She turns away. 'Thanks, Alfie. See you later.'

As soon as we're alone again, I ask Cassie what she was about to say before he came in.

She frowns. 'I'm not sure. Brain like a sieve these days. Shocking what menopause can do to you. Although you're a long way off that. You can't be more than thirty.'

'Thirty-three.'

'Ah. Enjoy your youth.'

'You mentioned something happened here years ago?' I ask, trying to hide my frustration that Cassie didn't finish what she was about to tell me.

'No point dwelling on the past, is there? Peaslake is a wonderful place to live. Clean air and a wonderful house. You really have got it all, you lucky lady.' She taps something on the till. 'And what is it you do for work?'

'I'm a children's behavioural therapist. But I was made redundant, so I'm looking for a new job. Not sure there's much around here.'

'You should advertise on my noticeboard,' Cassie says, pointing to the door, where a large corkboard hangs, filled with cards and flyers. 'You'd be surprised how many people check it on their way out,' she explains. 'Oh, I know what you're thinking – who needs local community noticeboards when everything's online now, but what have you got to lose?'

'Okay,' I say. 'I'll give it a try.'

'Great.' Cassie packs the carrier bag. 'That's ten twenty-five for this lot, and then I'll get you a card to write your advert on.

'Can I pay on my phone?'

She chuckles. 'Course you can. We're not some backwards village shop with no technology.' She turns to get a piece of card from a pile at the back of the counter and hands it to me with a pen. 'Just a few details about the role you're looking for and maybe list your qualifications. And your contact number, of course.'

Thanking her, I write on the card, then hand it back to Cassie.

'Perfect,' she says, without glancing at it. 'Have a lovely day!'

Outside, as the morning sun wraps me in warmth, I contemplate going back home. But the thought of that empty house, and the basement, fills me with dread.

And Charlie's lie sits heavily in my stomach.

Cassie in the shop had been about to tell me something, and I need to find out what it was. Glancing across the road, I make my way to the Hurtwood Inn, where she'd told me I'd be able to get lunch.

The interior of the pub is more modern than I'd imagined. The dark oak tables and red fabric chairs look comfortable and inviting, and floor-to-ceiling glass doors lead to an expansive beer garden at the back. Other than an elderly couple sitting at a table by the window, the place is empty. Behind the bar, a dark-haired man around my age is rearranging bottles of spirits. He turns around and smiles as I approach. 'Hey, what can I get you?' He has a friendly face, and I immediately warm to him.

'Your lunch menu, please.'

'Sure.' He pulls a menu from the pile on the bar. 'D'you mind ordering here and then I'll bring it over? I'm unexpectedly on my own today, which makes it difficult to do table service. Hoping not to get a big rush. Although that's not good for business!'

I smile. 'Let me guess – casual summer staff?'

'Actually, no, Marta's been with us for years, but she had a family emergency today. Anyway, something to drink?'

'Just a coffee, thanks.'

He laughs. 'Okay. One coffee.'

I study the menu. 'And I'll try a tuna and mayonnaise baguette, please.'

He nods. 'It even comes with fries. Take a seat, I'll bring it all over.'

I choose a seat by the window overlooking the village centre, and while I wait for my food, I contemplate what to do about Charlie's lie. I should have taken a photo of the bannister, but I had no idea I'd need to. It makes no sense. Why would Charlie get rid of that message? I'm not even sure how he did it, or when.

Myles is due at the house in a couple of hours – Charlie won't like me mentioning what I found in the basement to him, but I have every intention of bringing it up.

When the barman brings my food over, he asks if I'm here for the bike trail.

'Nope. But I do love biking, so I'll definitely do it when my bike arrives. I've just moved into the Hollingers' farmhouse.' It feels strange saying these words.

He raises his eyebrows. 'Is that so? And I thought I knew everything that went on here.' He smiles. 'Today is full of surprises. I'm Liam Curtis – welcome to the village. My parents have owned this hotel for decades. I'm helping them out for a bit until they can get someone else to manage it. They're not in the best of health, so they can't manage it themselves any more. Didn't realise the Hollinger place was up for sale.'

Taking a deep breath, I explain for the second time this morning how I came to be living in the farmhouse. And as I talk, the warmth fades from Liam Curtis's face.

'Charlie's girlfriend,' he says, as if he finds the words distasteful.

'Last time I checked, at least.' I laugh, hoping I'm just being paranoid.

But the atmosphere has shifted, and Liam's face hardens. 'I know Charlie. We went to school together.'

I hold out my hand. 'Well, it's nice to meet an old friend of his.'

Liam leaves my hand lingering and screws up his face. 'Yeah, I wouldn't say that. Charlie Hollinger is the *last* person I'd call a friend. Enjoy your sandwich. And don't forget to pay at the bar.'

FOUR

Back at the house, I try to brush off Liam's comment. It probably doesn't mean anything – there are plenty of people I went to school with who wouldn't consider me a friend.

I call Charlie's mobile, but it goes straight to his voicemail. A swell of panic surfaces in my gut, and I end the call without leaving a message. I'm the one who pushed for this move, yet now it feels as though everything is unravelling. Just like before. Only far worse.

When my phone rings, I grab it from the table, expecting to see Charlie's name, but it's Heather.

'Hi, Emmie. How is everything? I was trying to get hold of Charlie, but he's not answering.'

'He had to go to the office. An emergency with a client.'

'Oh, that's a shame. I wanted to let him know that our house purchase completes on Monday. Such good news. It's so wonderful that we'll all be back together again. But how are you? Settling in okay? Do you need anything?'

All together apart from Myles. 'Isn't Myles going back to Leeds?'

'Yes. Such a shame. But he knows he's welcome to come and

stay with us whenever he needs to get away. And I do miss my grandchildren. Libby and James are such sweethearts. Just promise me one thing – you'll never do to Charlie what Victoria did to Myles.'

'I'm not planning to,' I assure her. 'And we're a long way from having children.'

'Well, just don't leave it too long, Emmie – women can have all sorts of trouble conceiving if they delay trying. I... it took me a few years to have Myles. We'd begun to give up hope. I'd just hate to think of you and Charlie having to go through what we did.'

'I'm so sorry. I didn't know.'

'Please don't apologise. It all turned out fine in the end – I've got my three wonderful children. Couldn't wish for anything more. Well, let me know if you need anything at all.'

It's nearly three o'clock when the removal team finally arrive, with our belongings crammed into a medium-sized white van.

'Sorry we're late,' one of the men explains. 'Busy today. Had some issues. And those roadworks on the M25. Nightmare.'

I scan the road behind them; there's still no sign of Myles. 'You're here now, though,' I say, vaguely directing them to the living room. 'I think all the boxes can go in there for now. And obviously the sofa and TV cabinet.'

'Don't worry,' the other man assures me. 'We have done this before.'

It takes less than an hour, and then they're gone – leaving me alone, staring at the basement door. I can't get my head around it. Or Charlie's lie. There'll be an explanation – I just have to find it.

At four o'clock, when I'm making up the bed, I hear what sounds like a door slam downstairs. I freeze, and listen out. It's nothing. Old houses make noises. I'll need to get used to that.

But here, in this secluded village that feels like it's cut off from the rest of the world, it's hard not to panic.

I make my way downstairs, stopping short when I see Myles standing in the hallway.

'Oh. What—'

'I'm so sorry, Emmie. Didn't mean to scare you,' he says. 'I let myself in.' He holds up a key. 'Hope that's okay. Mum gave me her set. Not to use, but to give back to you.'

I rush down the rest of the stairs. 'You scared me to death.' My hand rests on my chest. 'I thought someone was breaking in.'

'Jesus, I'm so sorry,' Myles says. 'I'm a complete idiot.' He throws his head back and stares at the ceiling.

'No... it's fine. It's not like I didn't know you were coming.'

Myles looks around. 'Hard not to still think of it as our family home.' He smiles. 'Looked a bit different then, of course.'

Myles drops the keys into my palm, once more glancing around the house. 'So weird being back here. As if I never left.' He's mumbling, as if he's talking to himself.

'Thanks for coming, but I don't think I need any more help. The removal men have done it all.'

'That's good,' Myles said. 'I could help you unpack. As I'm here now.'

I'm about to tell him it's fine, when I remember that he probably needs to talk to someone, anything to take his mind off his divorce. 'How about coffee? At least there's a table to sit at now.'

He nods. 'That would be great. Thanks, Emmie.'

We sit at the round glass table from my old flat, which is far too small for this humungous kitchen. I'd loved it in that flat, now it feels wrong and out of place, just like I do.

'So it's crazy how you and Charlie met,' Myles says. He picks up his mug then places it straight back down. Perhaps I should have warned him it was instant. 'Did he really knock you off your bike?'

'Yes. When I was cycling past his work.'

Myles's eyes widen. 'What exactly happened?'

'I'd been on a training course in central London and was heading home. Those roads really aren't great for cyclists. Cars and bikes competing for limited space. I was bound to have an accident sooner or later, the amount I cycled. I'm just lucky I wasn't hurt.'

Myles frowns. 'But... how did you end up *together*?'

'I was totally fine, but Charlie felt so bad, he called me the next day to apologise. He'd insisted we grab a coffee to sort out getting me a replacement bike. We just hit it off and started seeing each other. You know the rest – he moved in with me after a few months.'

Myles's eyes are on me, but seem to be staring through me, as if he's somewhere else. 'That will be an interesting story to tell the kids,' he says. He looks down at his hands. 'You should definitely have kids. I love being a dad...'

'Oh, we're nowhere near that stage,' I say. 'We've only been together for a year. You should bring the kids and come and stay,' I offer.

'I'm sure it's not too far on the horizon. You'll want to fill this house, won't you? Make use of all those rooms. Victoria and I couldn't wait to have kids. I think we'd only been together six months.'

'I'm sorry to hear about your divorce,' I say.

'Thanks. Yeah, it's been tough. But at least I've got my kids. Nothing will change the fact that I'm their dad.' He reaches into his pocket and pulls out his phone, scrolling through it. 'Here. Libby and James. My greatest accomplishment.'

I take his phone and look at the picture he's showing me. Libby and James with their arms wrapped around him.

Matching smiles on all three faces. 'They look just like you,' I say.

'Yeah. Victoria resents that, I think. A constant reminder of me whenever she looks at them.'

Myles leans forward, resting his elbows on the table. 'Did Charlie tell you what happened?'

'Not any details,' I assure him. 'He only said you and your wife had separated just before I met him.'

Myles stares at his hands for a moment. He still hasn't touched his coffee. 'And now we're divorced. She left me for some guy she works with.' He looks away. 'It happens, doesn't it? No such thing as happily ever after.'

'Your parents have managed it. They seem really close, and they've been together all these years.'

'There's still time.' Myles finally lifts his mug and drinks. 'Life isn't a fairy tale.'

'Did you ever use the basement in this house?' I ask, desperate to get him off this topic, to stop him dwelling on his situation.

'What? Why?'

'I didn't even realise there was one – Charlie forgot to mention it.'

'We hardly used it. It was more of a dumping ground, really. Why? Is something wrong?'

In the few minutes I've sat here with Myles, it's clear to me that he's not the person I should be talking to about what I found down there. He's got his own issues to deal with, and I doubt he has the headspace to take my concerns seriously. 'There's no problem with it,' I say. 'I just wondered what you all used it for when you lived here. I'm trying to work out what we should do with it.'

Myles shrugs. 'Like I said, it was mainly for storage. We hardly went down there. Pointless room.' He takes another small sip of coffee.

'Is Vanessa okay?' I ask. 'It's just that I saw the two of you outside the restaurant last night, and it looked like you might have been having a disagreement. Then she was pretty much silent for the whole of dinner. I hope I haven't upset her in any way.'

His eyes narrow. 'No. Vanessa's issues are nothing to do with you, trust me.'

'I just wondered if maybe she wasn't happy with Charlie and me being given the house.'

'I doubt that. Vanessa would never have wanted it. She was always desperate to escape Peaslake. Besides, our parents gave us all equal amounts of money; Charlie just got his in the house. And as for her being quiet – that's just Vanessa. We weren't arguing, Emmie; I was just... telling her not to ruin the dinner. And that she should make an effort with you because you're a big part of Charlie's life.'

'It just seemed more serious than that.'

'Vanessa's a drama queen,' Myles says, his voice louder than it's been since he got here. 'You'll soon learn that.' He stands, taking his coffee to the sink and pouring it down, with no apology or explanation. 'Better get going. Just be sure to tell Charlie that I offered my help.'

'Thanks for coming,' I say to his already retreating back.

I'm in the back garden, tackling the lawn with an old lawnmower I found in the garage. The thought of all the jobs that need to be done in the house is overwhelming; the lawn seemed a manageable place to start. Plus it gives me a sense of satisfaction as the scruffy lawn transforms into neat rows.

I don't hear the doorbell, and don't realise I've got company until I turn around and see Heather standing by the back door, waving.

I turn off the mower and wave back. 'Hi... sorry, I didn't realise you were coming.'

'It was a last-minute decision. I was passing and thought I'd stop by and see how you're getting on. I did knock, but no one answered. So sorry, but I heard the lawnmower, and the side gate was open, so I came around. You don't mind, do you? I don't want to intrude.'

'It's fine. Would you like coffee?'

'No, thank you. I know you're busy in here, so I won't stay. 'I wanted to bring you this.' She holds up a carrier bag. 'It's lasagne. Charlie's favourite. I thought you'd be too busy to think about dinner. And clearly you are. Mowing the lawn and everything. I'm impressed, Emmie.'

'Thank you.' I take the bag from her. 'Charlie does love lasagne. I do too! So kind of you, Heather.' My first date with Charlie had been to an Italian restaurant where he'd devoured his lasagne. 'Are you sure you won't stay for coffee? Or tea?'

Heather places her hand on my arm. 'Another time, definitely. Edwin and I are off to visit the new house. Check where we'll put everything. I can't wait to get out of that hotel. Living out of a suitcase just doesn't sit well with me. And I'm sure you'll want to get on.' She smiles. 'And tell Charlie I said mowing the lawn should be his job. You know, no matter how busy Edwin was with work, he always mowed the lawn himself. Refused to have a gardener. He loved being out here.' She sighs, glancing across the lawn. 'So many memories.'

'I'm honestly happy doing it, Heather. I need to keep busy.'

'I understand. I hope you find a new job soon – it's not good to be at home too much. Gives us too much time to dwell and overthink things.' Heather turns to leave.

I reach for her arm. 'Can I ask you something?'

'Anything.'

'I need to plan what to do with the basement. What did you use it for?'

'The basement? I never went down there. It gave me the creeps. Sorry. I hope it doesn't put you off the house. It was locked most of the time. We only used it to store wine and the kids' old toys. I'd always send Edwin down if we needed anything.'

From Heather's light-hearted tone, it's clear that Charlie hasn't told his family about what happened to my father. And to me.

'I'll be off, then. See you soon.' Heather hugs me, then disappears, the overpowering scent of her perfume wafting behind her.

Charlie is held up in meetings and still isn't home by dinner time, and when my stomach begins to growl, I heat up Heather's lasagne and sit down to eat it by myself, putting the rest back in the oven to keep warm for him.

Worn out from unpacking, I consider going to bed. But as I get up from the table, my eyes are drawn to the basement door.

Once again, I take a moment to prepare myself, then turn on the light and make my way down the cold stone stairs, ready to examine every inch of that room.

The door slams shut, and my stomach lurches. I rush up the stairs, turning the handle, but the door won't open. 'Hey!' I scream, pounding on the door, so hard the flesh peels from my knuckles. 'Who's there? Let me out! Let me out!'

Seconds tick by, and my chest pounds, my throat constricting until I feel all the air slowly draining from my lungs and I'm struggling to breathe normally.

And then as suddenly as it slammed shut, the door opens, and Charlie is standing there. 'What's going on? What are you doing?' he asks. 'What's happened?'

I gasp for breath. 'I... I came down here and... someone slammed the door shut and locked me in!'

Charlie pulls me towards him and holds me tightly, stroking my back. 'But the door wasn't locked, Emmie. I just turned the handle and it opened.'

FIVE

Charlie and I spend the weekend cleaning and sorting out the house, throwing ourselves into our tasks so we don't have to air our thoughts. I scrub the terracotta kitchen floor tiles until they gleam, and Charlie cleans out the cream farmhouse-style cabinets. Neither of us mentions me getting trapped in the basement, yet I know that door was locked – I'd tried the handle several times.

But Charlie insists I panicked and only thought it was locked, and by the time Sunday rolls around, doubt gnaws at me, and I wonder if he's right, that my blind panic caused me to believe I was locked in – a physical manifestation of my fear.

'But how did the door slam?' I ask Charlie, breaking the silence as we strip ugly, faded wallpaper from the living room walls.

He keeps his eyes on the strip of wallpaper he's just loosened. 'A draught?' He shrugs. 'The windows were open, Emmie. You've been leaving them open since we got here.'

This is true – my desperate attempt to mask the pungent smell of damp. But even if this is what happened, Charlie still lied to me about the bannister.

'Do you know what I think?' Charlie says, putting down his wallpaper steamer. 'I think what happened to your dad has made you paranoid about the basement. And that's totally understandable.'

'I was only three. But I get flashes of those men breaking in that night. I couldn't even see them clearly; I was sitting on the stairs, too scared to move. And sometimes I don't even know if they're real, or if I'm making them up. Did I really see them or am I just remembering from what people told me after?'

'Even if you couldn't remember,' Charlie says, 'it would affect you subconsciously. All your life you've had to live with knowing your dad was murdered in his own basement. It's bound to have affected you – both consciously and subconsciously. It's no wonder your mind has filled in the gaps.' Charlie crosses to me and folds his arms around me. I nestle into him, and let his body reassure me. 'And you were left upstairs on your own for hours, wondering where he was. That's traumatising in itself.'

'I'm okay,' I say, my eyes prickling because I don't want his sympathy. I squirm out of his hug. 'Let's just finish these walls.'

He sighs as he picks up his wallpaper steamer again.

'Did I tell you I met Cassie from the shop on Friday?' I say, when the silence is too much to bear.

Charlie smiles. 'She's still there? I thought she would have been long gone by now.'

'I also met Liam at the Hurtwood Inn.' I turn to him, studying his face. Sometimes Charlie can be hard to read.

His smile disappears and his eyes narrow. 'And what did *he* have to say? He's another one who never planned to stick around. Yet there he is.'

I jump to Liam's defence, even though I barely know him, and his manner was abrupt after he learned I'm Charlie's girlfriend. 'He said his parents aren't in good health, so he's helping them out. That's the reason he's still here.'

'Still. If you'd heard him talking when we were at school—'

I pull off a large shred of wallpaper and throw it in a black bag. 'He told me you weren't friends. I get the impression that's an understatement.'

There's a flicker of something in Charlie's eyes, almost undetectable. 'No, we weren't on good terms. I can't even remember why. Kids' stuff. No big deal.'

'Oh? Now I'm intrigued. Like what? Surely you can remember. It wasn't that long ago, Charlie.'

He climbs down from the stepladder and wipes his brow with his hand. 'Why is this starting to feel like an interrogation? I'm getting a coffee. Want one?'

Charlie doesn't wait for my answer, and I watch him disappear to the kitchen. Clearly, I've hit a nerve.

On Monday, when Charlie has left for work, I feel a crushing swell of loneliness and isolation. I remind myself why we're here, hoping it will spur me on. I had to leave London behind. This is where we're supposed to be. But my eyes keep flicking to the basement, and I know that's a large part of why I'm so unsettled. And it's not just because of what happened to my dad.

Desperate to escape these walls, I throw on leggings and a hooded top and ride my bike into the village, securing it outside the Village Stores with my heavy-duty bike lock. This isn't London, where bike theft is rife, but I'm not taking any chances.

'Hey, Emmie!' Cassie says, when I push through the door. She gestures to my bike helmet. 'Let me guess – trying the bike trail?' She chuckles. 'Nothing gets past me.'

I smile. 'I thought I'd give it a go.'

'Then you should definitely go and see Liam at the Inn. He's the expert, and he'll tell you everything you need to know.'

I stay silent about already meeting Liam, and how I might not be too welcome there since he found out I'm Charlie's girlfriend. 'Thanks – I'll do that. I just wanted to ask you something.' I glance around the shop. 'And to buy some water,' I add, reaching into the fridge for a bottle. I don't want Cassie to think I'm taking advantage.

'Ask away,' Cassie says, scanning the bottle.

'When I was in here the other day, you mentioned that something had happened in the village.'

Her smile fades. 'Oh, that. That was such a long time ago. No point troubling yourself with things that happened in the past.' She flashes a smile. 'That will be one pound fifteen. I mean, stuff can happen anywhere, can't it? Especially in London. Believe me, you're much safer here.'

I hold my phone to the scanner. 'Safer? From what?'

Cassie sighs, and hands me my receipt. She bites her lip and shakes her head.

'Please, Cassie. I'm just curious. I love knowing the history of places. And this is my home now.'

She lowers her voice, even though we're alone in the shop. 'Did Charlie not mention it, then? I'm surprised.'

'No, he didn't mention anything.' I don't add that he also didn't want to move back here.

'Look, I don't like gossiping.' Cassie leans on the counter. 'But... it must have been in 2008 or 2009. A teenage girl disappeared. Sophie. She left her house one evening to meet someone in the village and never came back. She was a pupil at Peaslake School. Everyone knew her. She's never been found. Lots of people were worried, and I did wonder if that's what helped the Hollingers make their decision to leave. When something like that happens on your doorstep... well, it's hard to think of the place in the same way. And Vanessa wasn't much older than the girl who vanished – they must have been worried for her safety too. And Heather. Well, she adored her children. She would have done anything to keep them safe, even moving across the world.'

'That's awful. Charlie never said anything.' This surprises me, given that Charlie would have said anything to keep us from moving here.

Cassie studies me for a moment, frowning, and I wonder if she's going to clam up and stop talking. 'Maybe it's too difficult for him to talk about?' she suggests. 'Why don't you talk to him about it? The girl was in his class at school. All the kids knew each other. Look, I don't feel right gossiping – please, just ask Charlie about it.'

I nod. 'So he knew her.' Now I'm even more shocked that Charlie didn't mention this. Although, given that he's already lied to me about the basement message, this shouldn't be a complete surprise. Clearly, I don't know him as well as I'd thought.

Cassie scans the shop, lowering her voice. 'Everyone knew her. Liam Curtis was a friend of hers too. Took her disappearance badly. But if you go to see him about the bike trail, please don't mention I was talking about this. I don't want him to think I'm gossiping. Don't want to open old wounds. I know it was a long time ago, but things like that... well, they leave a scar on a place. And some scars are permanent.'

I promise her I won't mention it. 'What do you think happened to her?'

'Not for me to say. Some people think she ran away. But who can disappear without a trace and live life undetected? Not in this digital age. The police have kept the case open all these years, but nothing's ever turned up to help them work out what happened.' Cassie pauses. 'Look, I've said enough already. Is there anything else you needed?'

'No. Thanks for telling me all this.' I grab my bottle and leave the shop.

Outside, the heat is already suffocating, and it's not even ten o'clock. The last thing I want to do now is ride into the forest, even though it will be cooler in the shade of the trees.

But it gives me an excuse to speak to Liam. It's information I need, and if Charlie won't be forthcoming, then I'll find people who are. Cassie clearly hadn't wanted to talk about the missing girl, and I need to be prepared that Liam might be the same.

Stepping inside the Hurtwood, there's no sign of Liam behind the bar, and no customers either. 'Hello?' I call, my voice echoing into the eerie silence.

After a few seconds, he appears from the kitchen, placing his phone in his pocket. 'Hi there. Back again? That baguette must have been good. I'll have to tell the chef.'

He seems to have forgotten that he shouldn't like me. 'No... I mean, it was lovely, but I'm not here for lunch.'

'Well, that's a relief. It's only ten o'clock. If you wanted lunch now, I'd have to wonder what's wrong with you.' He laughs. 'Just kidding. If you do want a sandwich then I'm happy to make it myself. Chef's not in for another hour.'

'I'm actually here for the bike trail, and Cassie tells me you're the person I need to speak to before I venture out.'

His shoulders relax. 'Now *that* I can easily do.'

Leaning across the bar, Liam spends ten minutes giving me advice about the trail; I'm only half listening, despite my passion for biking – I'm desperate to find out what he knows about the girl who went missing.

When he's finished, I thank him and take my opportunity. 'I'm sorry if I caught you off guard the other day. I understand if you and Charlie weren't friends. We can't like everyone, can we?'

He nods. 'Isn't that the truth.'

'But can I ask you something? I heard that a girl went missing here in 2009.'

Liam's eyes narrow. 'Charlie tell you about Sophie, did he?'

Sophie. I offer a vague nod, an acceptable version of a lie. 'It's just awful. And they never found her. That kind of thing shocks communities like this. It can never be forgotten. It rewrites the history of a place.'

Liam nods. 'Peaslake is a good place, with good people. Nothing like that has ever happened since.'

'I'm sure you're right. But it must have been hard. Especially for you. I know you went to school with her.'

He nods, then straightens up, filling a glass with tap water. 'Yeah, she was a good friend of mine. One minute she was there, large as life, and then she was... just gone. There's no way she ran away. She just wouldn't have done that to her mum. Sophie and Lynette had the closest relationship. Always supporting each other. No way she would have just left her mum to suffer.'

'What do you think happened?'

Liam shrugs and glances around, even though we're alone. 'She had a phone call the night she disappeared. It was from a payphone that used to be outside the Village Stores. She told her mum she was going out to meet someone – a friend, she'd said. And she never came back. No one saw her again.'

'And there's no chance she ran away?'

Liam shrugs. 'Well, I guess anything's possible, and that's what the police seemed to think. But what did she do for money? Look, I know this will sound like a cliché, but Sophie really wasn't the type to do something like that. She was smart. Going places. Out of all of us, she was the one who would have gone on to live an exciting life away from here. She was so determined and excelled at everything. There aren't many people you meet who are just naturally good at *everything*. Maths. Science. English. She was scientific as well as creative. Her drawings were outstanding. Her plan was to be a doctor and help disadvantaged people in other countries.' He sighs. 'That's the kind of girl she was.'

Sophie sounds too good to be true, but then I understand why, when someone goes missing or dies, people who knew them only want to remember the good. 'That's really sad,' I say. Useless, futile words.

Liam nods. 'Yep. And sixteen years later, still no answers.' He finishes his glass of water in one go. 'And time has made her fade from people's memories – no one who lived here at the time even talks about her any more. Apart from her mum and sister, that is.'

'So she would have been sixteen when she disappeared?'

'Just turned seventeen. Same age as I was. And *Charlie*.' He says Charlie's name as if it's left an awful taste in his mouth.

'What exactly is your problem with Charlie?' I ask. 'You were just school kids. Why have you held onto this grudge? Charlie says he can't even remember why you two didn't get along.'

'Is that right?' He raises his eyebrows. 'Some people have very short memories.' He leans forward on the bar again. 'Not sure how—'

He stops short when an elderly man appears in the doorway behind the bar. 'Hey, Dad,' Liam says. 'This is Emmie. She's just moved here. Charlie Hollinger's girlfriend.'

Liam's dad shuffles over to me, holding out a trembling hand. 'Hi, I'm Walter. Just came down for some juice. How are you finding Peaslake?'

The truth would be that it's better than being stalked by my neighbour in London, but my positive feelings towards this sleepy village are rapidly beginning to wane. I spare Walter this detail, though, nodding and smiling instead. 'It's lovely.'

'I could have brought that up for you, Dad,' Liam says.

'Don't fuss!' Walter says, flapping his hand. 'Lovely to meet you, Emily.'

I glance at Liam. 'I was just about to go on the bike trail. Your son's been very helpful with tips and advice.'

Walter smiles. 'That's our Liam. Could be I'm biased, but I've never met a single person with anything bad to say about him. You enjoy your bike ride,' he says, shuffling back through the door.

Liam shrugs. 'Sorry he got your name wrong. Dad's not the man he used to be. It's hard to watch.'

'I don't mind at all. He's not the first person who's called me Emily.'

Liam nods. 'Well, enjoy the trail. See you around then, Em*ily*.'

I laugh. 'What were you going to say about Charlie?'

'Look, it's not right for me to go shouting my mouth off. The Hollingers are a good family. Well, the rest of them, at least. Just... be careful.'

Outside, Liam's words crash around my head. Deciding to abandon the bike ride, I cycle back to the house. There's still wallpaper to strip, but I'd rather avoid the farmhouse right now. Instead, I plan to sit in the garden with my laptop and hunt for jobs before I end up going insane.

As I approach the house, I consider calling Cassie in the shop to ask if she needs any help until I can find something else. It will get me out of the farmhouse, and I can question her more when I'm there.

Inside, the cold draught encroaches around me, and I shiver. I make my way to the kitchen, where I know I left my laptop, but when I get there, the closed basement door catches my eye. Taking off my bike helmet, I check every room in the house, just to make sure I'm alone. Back in the kitchen, I glance again at the basement door. Despite my fear of being locked in again, I need to go down there, check the whole place once more. And just in case Charlie *was* right and the door slammed shut, I drag a heavy box I haven't unpacked yet from the living room and wedge it in front of the door, checking to make sure it can't be easily moved.

Heading down the stairs, with my heart thudding heavily, I

check the bannister again, but there's still no sign of the carved writing: the plea for help.

For the next half-hour, I check every inch of the basement, but I find nothing other than dust and grime. Back in the kitchen, I close the basement door and check to see if the lock jams. But it's fine – opening and closing easily when I turn the handle. Unlike last night. Pulling it open again, I check the other side of the door, and there, right at the bottom, there's another carving. I stoop down to read it.

SOPHIE WAS HERE

And the grooves of each letter are filled with what looks like blood.

SIX

MARCH 2008

Sophie sits at the bus stop, shivering in a light blue denim jacket that's too thin for this weather. An eternal winter, her mum calls it. By now there should at least be a glimpse of Spring, but every day is dark and grey, the sun yet to make an appearance. It doesn't bother Sophie too much; she's convinced her mum has seasonal affective disorder – her mood plummets in winter, and in summer she's a phoenix rising from the ashes, full of life.

Across the road, Liam Curtis comes out of the Hurtwood Inn, tentatively raising his hand in a wave. Even from this distance she can tell his cheeks are red. Sophie smiles. She hasn't spoken to him much; she only started at the school in January – a claustrophobic place where there's no room to breathe. Still, she's making the most of it and will be off to university in a few months. Sophie's got it all planned out, and nothing's going to stop it happening.

She'll take Mum and baby Orla with her, wherever she ends up. She won't let them fester in this tiny village; as picturesque as it is, there's a whole world out there to explore. Sophie's mind is bursting to be filled with more than this place will allow.

'Hey,' Liam says, sitting beside her. 'Going somewhere?' He gestures to the bus stop sign.

'Nope. Just taking a moment before I head home.' She doesn't tell him that she often sits here alone with her thoughts, planning her life and taking a moment to herself. As much as she loves her mum and baby sister, it can be hard sharing such a small space, living on top of each other.

Liam smiles. 'Maybe I should try it. The pub's always loud and busy. Sometimes it's hard to think straight. Anyway, just don't go in the shop.' He nods towards it. 'Mum's just been in there and said Vanessa Hollinger is kicking off.'

Sophie frowns.

'Have you met her? Charlie's sister. *Everyone* around here knows who she is. She got kicked out of the private school they went to, which is why their mum helped set up the village school.'

Sophie does indeed know who Vanessa is but has never spoken to her. Vanessa's a couple of years older, so she left the village school two years ago. 'Why is she kicking off?' she asks. 'What's happened?'

'Mrs Oberman just fired her. Accused her of raiding the till.'

Sophie scrunches her nose. 'But why would she? The Hollingers are loaded – she doesn't need to steal. Charlie's mum doesn't even have to work.' Sophie thinks of her own mum, how she has three part-time jobs and still manages with the baby. A surprise she wasn't expecting after having Sophie so long ago.

Liam shrugs. 'I don't think it's as black and white as that. Sometimes people steal for the thrill, not because they actually need anything.'

He has a point. They both turn towards the shop, but with posters and adverts covering most of the windows, it's impossible to see what's going on inside.

'I was wondering,' Liam says, clearing his throat. 'If you

want to... I dunno... do something together sometime? Maybe the ice-skating disco? It's on every Saturday night. My mum wouldn't mind dropping us there.'

Sophie inclines her head, appraising Liam. Has he just asked her out on a date? She's been out on dates before at her old school, but they just happened without anyone officially *asking* her. It feels so formal, so chivalrous, and she quite likes it. And Liam is cute, even if he is a bit shy. 'Yeah, maybe.'

His face brightens. 'Really? Okay. I'll need your number, then,' he says. 'If you don't mind?'

Sophie chuckles, then recites it for him, and watches as he carefully taps it into his phone.

There's a loud thud as the shop door is thrown open, and Vanessa stands in the doorway, flicking back her long blonde hair.

'I'm off,' Liam says, jumping up. 'That girl's a tornado. I'll call you.'

Sophie watches him walk away, and when she turns back, Vanessa is walking over to her, taking the seat Liam just vacated. She pulls out her phone; it's an iPhone – a phone Sophie's never known anyone to have. She thinks of her old BlackBerry, donated to her by her mum's ex, Roger. He was a kind man – Sophie has no idea why her mum ended things.

'Is he your boyfriend?' Vanessa asks, tapping on the screen.

'Liam? Er, no.'

'Really? Looked like he was really into you. His face was as red as a beetroot.'

Sophie feels a rush of heat to her own cheeks. 'He did just ask me out. Ice skating one Saturday. But we haven't arranged anything.'

'Why did you move here?' Vanessa asks, slipping her phone in her pocket and turning to Sophie. 'It's not exactly an exciting place to live. Nothing ever happens here, and if you want entertainment, you have to travel. Guildford's not bad, but London is way better. That's why I'm having driving lessons.'

'Our landlord kicked us out,' Sophie says. 'Well, he politely told us in a letter that he had family from abroad coming to live here and he needed the flat back. Our contract was about to be up so... here we are.'

'But why *here*? Of all the places you could have gone.'

'My mum said she was sick of London and wanted a change. Somewhere quiet and peaceful. She literally spent a whole month researching where we could go, and then she fell in love with Peaslake. Well, with the pictures, at least. But she still loves it now we're here. And we were lucky to have found somewhere we could afford.' Sophie's not ashamed to say this, even to the girl with the iPhone and loaded family.

'Well, good for your mum,' Vanessa says. 'Although I don't know what she sees in this place.'

Sophie shrugs. 'That's because you were born here. Anyway, I agree with you. I'm not planning to stay for long. Hopefully I'll live in student accommodation when I go to university next year.'

Vanessa stares into the distance. 'Dream big. I like that.' She grabs Sophie's hand and pulls her up. 'Come on, let's go back to your place. I don't want to go home yet. Any minute now my mum will be calling to find out why I'm not back. Then all hell will break loose because I've been fired from that crappy job. Brought shame on the family.'

Sophie feels a pang of sympathy for Vanessa – clearly, wealth doesn't mean you have no problems. But does she want Vanessa in her flat? 'There's really nothing to do at my place,' she says. Sophie pictures it now: the living room filled with clothes airers, with onesies and bibs dangling from the bars. Orla grizzling. Her mum looking frazzled and broken. 'On second thoughts,' she says, 'I suppose we can make our own fun.

Let's do it.' Sophie's not ashamed of their circumstances – people can take her for who she is or do one. If Vanessa Hollinger doesn't like it, then she can do one too.

By the time they've reached the flat, Sophie feels as though she's known Vanessa for a lifetime. There's something refreshing about her honesty, her refusal to conform. Her *take me as you find me* persona.

Lynette opens the door before Sophie's puts her key in the lock. 'Hi, love. I thought you'd be back before now. I was getting worried.'

'Sorry, Mum. I just went for a walk after school. This is Vanessa.'

Vanessa holds out her hand. 'Lovely to meet you, Sophie's mum.'

Lynette chuckles, and when she smiles, her face seems to light up. 'Lynette.'

'Well, welcome to the village, Lynette. How are you finding peaceful Peaslake?'

Lynette smooths down her crumpled maxi skirt. 'I love it! We haven't been here long, but it really feels like home.' She smiles, and Sophie's surprised that within a few seconds of meeting her, Vanessa has brightened her mum's mood. Lynette turns to Sophie. 'Sorry to ask this again, but would you mind watching Orla for a couple of hours? I just need to go and clean the Hurtwood.'

Sophie feels Vanessa's eyes on her. Is this when the judgement will come? 'Yeah, that's fine. Course I can.'

'She's down for a nap so won't be any bother,' Lynette continues. 'I'm sorry I have to ask, love.'

'Yeah, it's fine – you go, Mum.'

Lynette pats Sophie's arm. 'What would I do without you? By the way, I've just made cupcakes, if you girls want one?'

'I would *love* one,' Vanessa says. 'Thanks, Lynette.'

Lynette smiles and grabs her thick winter coat from the coat hook. 'See you girls later.'

When the door shuts, Vanessa wanders into the living room and sinks onto the sofa, stretching her long legs and resting her hands beneath her head. 'Nice flat,' she says.

'Really? I would have thought you'd find it a bit of a shoebox compared to your mansion.'

Vanessa rolls her eyes. 'It's not a mansion, it's just a farmhouse.'

'Oh yeah? How many bedrooms?'

'Five.'

Sophie lifts her hand. 'I rest my case, Your Honour.'

Both girls laugh, and Sophie feels as if they've become connected somehow. Two girls who couldn't be more different.

'I'm serious, though,' Vanessa says. 'I love what your mum's done with it. She's made it feel so... homely. All the ornaments and plants. It feels so warm and lived in.'

'I guess. I've never thought about it that way.' More proof of how much her mum loves it here. 'Come in the kitchen and have a cake before Orla wakes up and takes all of my attention,' Sophie says.

'Do you *always* have to look after your baby sister?' Vanessa asks, following Sophie and hoisting herself onto the kitchen worktop.

'Mum never *makes* me. I offer. She always feels terrible to rely on me. She tried to get a babysitter, but I told her it's a waste of money. She'd end up paying out whatever she'd just earned from cleaning.'

'Yeah, that kind of sucks. She's lucky to have a daughter like you.' Vanessa sighs. 'Don't think *my* mum would ever think that she's lucky to have me.'

'Why not?'

Vanessa bites into her cupcake, crumbs cascading down her

light blue flounced-sleeve top. 'They think I'm a big disappointment. Because I refuse to conform. And also because I don't want to follow in Daddy's footsteps and be a doctor. Or the next best thing – a lawyer, like Charlie's planning to be. Or a vet like Myles. All highly respectable professions.' She rolls her eyes.

'Hey, nothing wrong with being a doctor,' Sophie says. 'That's exactly what I want to do.'

Vanessa chews slowly, watching Sophie until she's finished her mouthful. 'Yes, but at least you're making that choice for yourself, not having it forced upon you. *Don't let the family down. Don't bring shame on us. We have an image to uphold.*'

'The trials and tribulations of a rich girl,' Sophie says. 'My heart bleeds.'

Vanessa glares at her for a moment then bursts into laughter. 'Yeah, I do sound like a spoilt brat. But...' She puts down her cupcake. 'You don't know what it's like to be in that house. Mum's overprotectiveness, and Dad being this perfect human we all have to live up to.' She rolls her eyes. 'Yeah, I know – I'm a walking cliché. My parents don't understand me, blah blah blah.' She falls silent. 'Your mum seems great.'

'Yeah, she is. Life's been tough for her but she soldiers on and never complains. She had me when she was nineteen. My dad was in the army, and he was posted overseas not long after I was born. I don't even remember him.' Sophie glances at the door.

'What happened to him?'

'He died serving his country.'

'Sorry,' Vanessa says. 'I don't believe in war. I'm totally against it. Maybe one day I'll find a way to end human conflict, and we can all live in peace and harmony.'

Sophie stares at her. 'Yeah, well—'

'I'm just kidding. Kind of. I don't think that's my life path, but I hope someone manages it. So people like your mum won't have to lose their husbands.'

'I hear her crying sometimes,' Sophie says. 'She'll never let me see, but I know she struggles. That's why I'm determined to get us all out of here. One day soon.'

Vanessa nods. 'I often dream of escaping. But then I realise that our baggage follows us wherever we go. So I'm just going to live my life and make the most of it. Have fun while I still can. Live hard, love hard. Sod everything else.'

'What happened in the shop?' Sophie asks. 'Why did Mrs Oberman sack you?' Now that she's met Vanessa, Sophie definitely can't picture her being a thief.

'Old dragon. I messed up with what I charged someone and the books didn't balance. She accused me of stealing ten pounds! Can you believe that? If I was going to steal, which I wouldn't, I'd take a hell of a lot more than that.' She shakes her head. 'She's never liked me. She only gave me the job because my mother had a word with her. Probably promised Mrs Oberman she could go to Dad with any health issues and he'd try to sort her out. But that's dumb. Dad's a heart surgeon, that's what he specialises in. No way he'd be able to diagnose things the way a GP does.' She smiles. 'When you're a doctor and you get married, make sure to tell your husband that.'

Sophie nods. 'Will do.'

'Anyway,' Vanessa says, jumping down from the worktop, a spray of crumbs shooting to the floor. 'What are you going to do about Liam?'

'I guess I'll go ice skating with him,' Sophie says, shrugging. 'He seems nice.'

'Hmm. Liam's okay. Looks-wise. But there's something about him... I can't work out what. I just don't trust him. And the way he looked at you. I think you should think about someone else if you want a boyfriend.'

'I don't want a boyfriend, he just—'

'Come to my house after school tomorrow. I like you, Sophie Bower. And Mum's always saying I'm too much of a loner. She'd like you. Might get them off my back if they think I've made a decent friend.'

Sophie doubts this. The Hollinger family live in a world so far removed from anything Sophie's ever known. But she finds herself agreeing to Vanessa's request, because there's something about Vanessa she likes.

'Great!' Vanessa says, placing her hands together in prayer. She wanders into the living room and plonks herself on the sofa, once again putting her feet up.

'What about you?' Sophie asks. 'Are you seeing anyone?'

Vanessa sits up, her eyes narrowing as she appraises Sophie. 'Can I trust you?'

'Yeah, course you can.'

Vanessa narrows her eyes. 'People always say that. But hey-ho, I'll take a chance. There *is* someone I'm seeing... but you can't tell anyone. Not one single person. If my family found out, they'd never let me see him again. And I can't let that happen. I really love him.'

'Who is he? Oh God, please tell me it's not a teacher?' Sophie says, sickened by this thought.

'Ugh, no way. But he *is* a little bit older than me.'

Sophie considers this. 'Well, you're nineteen. You're technically an adult, so I guess that doesn't matter too much.'

'No, it's not really the age thing that would bother my parents.'

'Then what?' Sophie is intrigued now. 'Tell me.'

'All in good time. Just make sure you come to my house tomorrow.'

A loud cry erupts from upstairs, and Sophie springs up. 'I'd better get Orla.'

'That's my cue to leave,' Vanessa says. 'Babies hate me – all they have to do is look at my face and the tears erupt. Tomorrow, then? I'll meet you at the school gates.'

Sophie agrees and sees Vanessa out. She's intoxicated by the secrecy shrouding this girl. It will certainly make life more interesting around here.

But while part of her is excited to find out why Vanessa's being so secretive, the other part of her can't help feeling that she might be better off not knowing.

SEVEN

From the living room window, I watch Charlie climb out of his car. He's already undoing his tie as he walks up the drive – he'll be the first to admit he prefers jeans and T-shirts to suits, but I know he loves how powerful they make him appear to the outside world.

I rush to the door and yank it open, grabbing his hand. 'I need to show you something. Come with me.'

He sighs. 'Oh, Emmie. Can I just have a minute?' He stops when he realises I'm leading him to the basement. 'I thought we agreed—'

'I found something else,' I say, flicking on the light and closing the door behind us. 'Look at the bottom of the door.'

Charlie crouches down and examines the writing carved into the door. Seconds tick by, and he doesn't speak. Then he reaches out to touch the carving, running his fingers over it. 'I never knew that was there,' he says quietly.

'I know she went missing,' I tell him. 'When you were seventeen. Why didn't you tell me?'

He pulls himself up. 'There was no reason to mention it. It's... it's been a long time.'

'When did she write this, though?'

'I don't know. Probably when she was over one time. She was really good friends with Vanessa. And stuff like that is just what kids do.'

'Maybe *young* kids. But why would a seventeen-year-old do that? Why? What if this is something to do with her disappearance, Charlie?'

'That's a stretch, Emmie. She was probably just messing around. Leaving her mark. Soph was always saying that's what she was determined to do.' He opens the door and heads back upstairs.

But this time I've got a photo, just in case it disappears, replaced with a new door, and Charlie tries to say he didn't see it.

I follow him up the stairs. 'But I don't get why you didn't mention it when you knew we were moving here. Especially when you didn't want to come here. You could have said it was too painful for you.'

'Emmie, it was sixteen years ago. She ran away. She never wanted to live in this village. She wanted bigger things. Have you eaten? Shall we get a takeaway?'

'I've already made dinner for us,' I say, gesturing to the oven. 'It's shepherd's pie.'

'Sounds like just what I need,' Charlie says. 'Thanks, Em.'

I grab the oven glove I've hung on a hook by the wall, and open the oven, standing back from the blast of heat. 'But what makes you think she ran away?' I say as I dish up the food. 'She's never been found.'

Charlie shrugs. 'I really don't know, Em. I've had a long day. I don't know what else I can tell you. No one knows where she went, or why she left. End of story. Why are you going on about this?'

I don't tell Charlie that I've already googled it, so I know the scant details. 'There's blood on that writing,' I insist. 'If you look closely. In the grooves.' I pull out my phone and zoom in on the photo. 'Look!'

Charlie barely glances at it. 'I think that's probably paint, Emmie. Come on, let's eat before it gets cold.'

'It was the same with the other message,' I continue.

'There was no other message, Emmie. Otherwise, it would still be there.'

'It was blood,' I insist.

Charlie sighs. 'I've had a really long day, and I just need to switch off.'

He is hiding something, and although I want to keep pushing him, I also know that he's reached his limit. While we eat, I talk about anything that doesn't involve our move to Peaslake or Sophie Bower. Coming here was supposed to help heal our relationship, yet from the minute we got here, there's been tension between us. And now something worse.

By the time he's finished eating, Charlie has visibly relaxed. 'I'm sorry about snapping,' he says. 'We're okay, aren't we?'

I nod. 'We can get through anything, remember?' This is what he'd said to me when our relationship began to crumble all those months ago, when he'd told me he needed a break, to sort his head out. It wasn't me, he'd assured me; I was perfect. He was the one who needed to work on himself. And I'd let him go. I wasn't about to beg and plead – I have too much pride for that. If it was meant to be, then he'd come back to me, I'd reasoned. And here we are.

The doorbell rings, and we glance at each other. 'I'll get it,' Charlie says, checking his watch. 'I hope that's not Mum. I love my family, but there's only so much I can take of them.'

Silently, I agree. And while Charlie goes to the door, I clear away the leftover shepherd's pie, wishing we had a dishwasher that worked. I hear Charlie greeting someone – a male voice – but I can't make out their words.

And then Charlie is rushing into the kitchen, followed by a

young man around the same age, with black hair and smooth light brown skin. 'Emmie, this is Khalid,' Charlie says. 'We were best friends in school. He lives in Boston now, so I haven't seen him for years!'

Khalid steps forward, holding out his hand. 'Nice to meet you, Emmie. I've heard all about you from Charlie's dad. Feel like I know you already. He speaks very fondly of you!'

I glance at Charlie, who's still staring at Khalid. 'I can't believe you're here! Dad didn't say anything.'

'I wanted to surprise you,' Khalid says.

I step forward. 'It's lovely to meet you. Please come in.'

We head to the kitchen, and Charlie roots through the cupboards. 'Have we got any wine?'

'There's that bottle your mum got us,' I say.

Charlie finds the bottle and pours three glasses. 'I can't believe you're here,' he says again, raising his glass. 'I had no idea you and Dad were still in touch.'

'Yeah, we have been for years,' Khalid says. He turns to me. 'I owe that man everything. He's the reason I'm a surgeon.' He lifts his glass. 'To Edwin.'

Charlie and I repeat the toast in unison.

'When I found out they were moving back here, I had to come and visit. Then Edwin told me the great news that you were moving here too. I never thought that would happen!'

'How long are you here for?' I ask.

'Just a flying visit. Here for a week. I'm staying at the Hurtwood. Can't believe Liam's running it now.'

'If we had the house sorted, then you could have stayed here,' I say. 'You're still welcome to. Isn't he, Charlie?'

'Khalid's always welcome,' he says.

'Thanks, but it's fine,' Khalid says. 'I wouldn't want to get in the way. But while I'm here, there'll be plenty of time to catch up.' He smiles and sips his wine.

We move into the living room, and I study Khalid as he

talks, regaling us with stories of life in Boston. I soak up every word, trying to get the measure of him. And I observe Charlie too, his relaxed body language, and the way he attentively listens, and come to the conclusion that he's genuinely excited to see his old friend. 'Do your family live here?' I ask, when there's a break in their conversation.

'Not in Peaslake,' Khalid says. 'But I have family all over the UK. My dad's in London. I'll be seeing him this week, but to be honest, the Hollingers always felt more like family than my own.' He smiles. 'When I was struggling with my confidence – with girls – Heather had a long chat with me and really helped me. Told me to stop trying to be someone I'm not to impress other people. She made me realise that people need to take me for who I am. Maybe I wasn't sporty, but, well, Heather showed me how to embrace my inner geek!' He laughs.

'Harvard Medical School,' Charlie says, patting Khalid's back. 'The boy did good.'

'Thanks to your dad,' Khalid says. 'He believed in me when I'd all but given up.'

Charlie nods. 'Although I'm not sure how you didn't believe in yourself when you sailed through school. Oh, other than that one time you got an A instead of an A star? Yeah, I can see how that would be a real blow to your confidence!' Charlie laughs.

'Ah, come on,' Khalid says. 'You don't know the pressure I was under. When everyone has high expectations of you, anything less than perfect feels like you're letting people down.'

'The only person you should care about letting down is yourself,' I chime in, taking another sip of wine; it's far too dry, but it's taking my mind off the writing on the basement door. *Sophie was here.* I turn my attention back to Khalid. 'So, I'm guessing you knew Sophie, then?' I ask, feeling Charlie's eyes bore into me.

The atmosphere in the room instantly shifts, and Khalid

glances at Charlie. 'Sophie. That's a name I haven't heard for many years. Sophie Bower.' He shakes his head. 'That was so sad.'

'More wine, anyone?' Charlie asks.

'I'd love another,' Khalid says, seeming relieved that the conversation has been interrupted. He hands his empty glass to Charlie. 'Good job I'm only staying at the Hurtwood and can walk back.'

Charlie holds out his hand for my glass. 'Not for me, thanks,' I say. 'Think I'll call it a night soon.'

He nods and heads to the kitchen, his phone ringing as he gets into the hallway. Probably work again.

'Is he all right?' Khalid asks. 'He shut that conversation down pretty quickly.'

'He doesn't seem to like talking about Sophie,' I explain. 'I only found out about her today. What exactly happened?'

'Everyone loved her,' Khalid says, shaking his head. 'She was just one of those girls who never rubbed people the wrong way. She was strong, but also kind. And so intelligent. She wanted to be a doctor too. There was a lot of friendly competition between us. You know, who could get the highest grades in whatever test it was that week. She pushed me to be better. I talked about owing Edwin Hollinger a lot, but I could say the same for Sophie.' He sighs. 'She was one of a kind.' He says this so quietly, I wonder if he meant to keep it in his head.

'Sounds like someone had a little crush,' I tease, emboldened by the wine.

Khalid's head jolts up. 'What? No. Not at all. There's no way I would have even entertained that idea.'

'Sorry, it just sounds like you were really close. It makes sense that you might have got together.'

Khalid stares at me. 'You mean he hasn't told you?'

My pulse races. 'Told me what?'

'Listen, I don't know what's going on, and I really don't want to get in the middle of it. So please don't say it was me who told you. But Sophie was Charlie's girlfriend. They were inseparable.'

EIGHT

I'm awake and downstairs long before sunrise, while Charlie sleeps on. I need this time to gather my thoughts; the more lies he tells, the more I distrust him – this man who claims he loves me.

I sit on the sofa with a mug of coffee and open my laptop, searching for anything I can find on Sophie Bower. Sophie's picture flashes up – a stunning girl with chestnut brown hair and striking green eyes. Missing from home since the fifteenth of August, 2009, right before she was due to start university. A conscientious student, just as Liam Curtis had described. No reason to run away from her life. A cold case now; it's doubtful that anyone other than her mum and sister is still looking for her.

Upstairs, I've just finished in the shower, and I'm in the bedroom towel-drying my hair when Charlie's alarm goes off. He stirs and sits on the side of the bed. 'Hey. You okay?'

'Yeah.' I force myself to smile because if I look at him now, then I will never be able to stay with him in this house.

'Drinking on a school night doesn't sit well with me,'

Charlie says, massaging his head. 'And I need to get to the office.'

'So much for that week off,' I say, but this could be a blessing; it will be easier if Charlie isn't here when I start digging around.

'How about I try to finish early?' he suggests. 'We could go out for dinner?'

'Sounds good,' I say, plugging in the hairdryer, still avoiding looking at him. 'I googled Sophie Bower this morning,' I say, testing the waters, pushing the limits of what I might get away with. 'Attractive girl.'

Charlie raises his eyebrows. 'Yeah, I guess.'

I wrap a section of hair around my brush and turn on the hairdryer. 'I bet she had a ton of boys interested in her. Was she seeing anyone?'

'No,' he says, too quickly. 'She wasn't interested in any of us. And there wasn't a big pool of boys to choose from at our school.'

His lie catches me off guard, even though it shouldn't, given what he's already lied about. The carving on the bannister. Getting rid of it. The basement door being locked when I was in there. And now this.

'Really?' I question. 'No one at all?'

Charlie grabs his robe. 'Why all the questions? Is this about that writing in the basement? I told you – Sophie was always at the house – she was Vanessa's friend. It was probably some game they were playing. Why are you reading so much into this?'

Because your ex-girlfriend disappeared sixteen years ago, and you're lying about everything. 'I'm just interested to know what happened to her,' I say, forcing myself to finally look at him.

Charlie crosses to me and wraps his arms around me. 'I get

it, Emmie, I really do. You've got... a lot of time on your hands at the moment. And moving home is stressful. Look, I'll see if we can get a renovation team in sooner. That might help?'

'I just need to be working,' I say.

He kisses my forehead. 'And you'll get something, I know you will. Let me jump in the shower and we can have breakfast together before I leave. Remember you're meeting Mum and Vanessa for lunch?'

'I know,' I say, but once again I turn away from Charlie, for fear of what I'll see in his eyes.

After he's left for work, I walk into the village. This time I barely notice my surroundings, the looming forest with all the secrets it must hold. All I can focus on is getting to the Hurtwood Inn. Inside, it's quiet once again, with only a group of cyclists sitting in the corner, engrossed in conversation.

Behind the bar, Liam looks up and smiles, waving me in. 'Nice to see you again,' he says.

I'm tempted to ask him about Charlie and Sophie's relationship, but there's someone else I need to speak to more urgently. 'Yeah, you too. Can you tell me what room Khalid Soto is in? I need to speak to him.'

Liam frowns. 'I'd love to help, but we can't give out guests' room numbers. Sorry.'

'Then can I call his room?'

Liam points to the reception area. 'If you ask Marta, she'll call his room for you.'

Five minutes later, I'm sitting in the pub garden waiting for Khalid. I pull out my phone and google Sophie Bower again. I'm fully aware that this is becoming an obsession, but I have good reason to be concerned. Why would Charlie lie about Sophie being his girlfriend? Why would that matter unless he had something to do with her disappearing? This thought chills my blood. People don't just vanish for no reason.

'Hot already out here,' Liam says, placing a cup of coffee on the table.

I frown. 'I didn't order this.'

'I know. On the house, as they say. While you wait for Khalid. Nice guy. Had a drink with him last night. It was great to catch up. I'll bring one out for him too when he comes down.' Liam pauses. 'Does Charlie know the two of you are meeting up this morning?'

Before I can respond, Marta appears in the doorway, calling Liam over.

'Um, gotta go,' he says.

Khalid appears in the doorway and greets Liam with a pat on the back before making his way to my table.

'Hi. Nice to see you again,' he says, holding out his hand. 'This is unexpected. Is everything okay? Is Charlie coming?'

I get straight to the point. 'No. He doesn't know I'm here. But I need to ask you something. I know we've only just met, but you've known Charlie a lifetime, and I'm really worried.'

Khalid pulls out a chair and sits, squinting in the bright sunlight. 'About Charlie? He's not ill, is he?'

'No. Nothing like that. But this morning I mentioned Sophie and asked him if she was seeing anyone at the time. He said she definitely wasn't, and that she hadn't been interested in any boys at school. I find it strange that he'd lie about this, when it was such a long time ago. I'm hardly going to care about a relationship he had as a teenager, am I?'

Khalid studies me, taking his time to answer. 'I'm sure that's true, but some people get funny about their partner's exes.' He holds up his hand. 'Not that I'm suggesting you're the jealous type.'

'Believe me, I'm not. But I need to know why Charlie's lying.'

Lines crease Khalid's forehead, like a crumpled sheet of paper. 'The thing is, I haven't even seen Charlie for a long time. Years. I know we were good friends, but I can't comment on what he's thinking or feeling right now.'

Liam appears and places a cup of coffee in front of Khalid. 'Enjoy,' he says.

I wait for Liam to leave before speaking again. 'Were Charlie and Sophie together for long?'

'About a year,' Khalid says.

'And they were together when Sophie went missing?'

'Yes.'

I take a deep breath. 'Please don't tell Charlie we've had this conversation.'

'I don't intend to,' Khalid says. 'Charlie...'

'What?'

'Nothing. I just mean that this is none of my business, and I really think I should stay out of it. I'm sorry, Emmie. Look, maybe Charlie just doesn't like talking about his past relationships. Not sure I do, either.' His eyes dart around and he shifts in his seat. He seems so different to how he was last night, when he was laid-back and relaxed. Now his shoulders are hunched, and he's jittery.

I take a sip of strong coffee. 'It just doesn't make sense that he'd lie about something like that. I need to find out why Charlie's lying about his relationship with Sophie. Especially as she went missing.'

Khalid stays silent, reaching for his coffee. 'I understand that,' he says. 'You've been together for what, a year?'

'Yes.'

'Some people are hard to know, even after all that time.' He glances around. 'Charlie's always... don't get me wrong – he's a good friend, but... he's very good at only letting people see what he wants them to.'

'I don't understand.'

'All I'm saying is... just... be careful.'

Liam comes back, checking everything's okay with our coffee.

'We're fine,' I snap, annoyed at the interruption.

'Just shout if you need a refill.'

As soon as he leaves, I lean closer to Khalid, lowering my voice. 'What exactly do you mean?'

'I just mean, Charlie changed after Sophie disappeared. And that's bound to have affected his subsequent relationships. Do you know about any of his other partners? I mean, after Sophie?'

'I know they never lasted long,' I say. 'He just didn't meet anyone he wanted to make a commitment to. But we don't dwell on the past. It's about us. Me and Charlie. Not the people we were with before we met.'

Khalid nods. 'That all sounds healthy, but we can't escape our baggage. I just meant be careful that Charlie's doesn't interfere with your relationship.'

'I can handle myself,' I say.

Khalid appraises me with narrow eyes. 'I have no trouble believing that,' he says.

I glance over at the bar, where Liam is chatting to a young couple. 'What happened between Charlie and Liam?' I ask Khalid. 'Clearly, there's no love lost there.'

He shifts in his seat and looks as if he'd rather be anywhere but here. 'What's the only thing that can get in the way of male friendships?'

'Girls. Sophie?'

'Let's just say Charlie wasn't the only person interested in her.'

Once again I look over at Liam. 'What happened?'

'Look, I really think you should talk to Charlie about this. I don't feel right going behind his back. And I think I've said enough already.' Khalid stands. 'It was nice to talk to you,

Emmie. I hope I'll see you again while I'm here.' He walks away, but then stops and comes back to the table. 'If you really want to know about Sophie, her mum still lives in the village. In one of the cottages on Colmans Hill. Number three.'

Following the directions Khalid has given me, I cycle to Lynette Bower's house. It's a modest white-fronted cottage, with ivy climbing every wall, and a garden of pink roses and white peonies. All of it could be a picture from a magazine. Taking a deep breath, I head up the path and ring the doorbell.

The first thing I think when the door opens is that the woman standing before me in leggings and a long navy T-shirt is far too young to be Lynette Bower. 'Hi, I'm looking for Lynette?' I say, glancing past her.

'That's me. Can I help you?' Her voice is soft, and she stares at me with large blue-grey eyes. Her light brown hair is tied back in a ponytail, and she's wearing slipper boots, despite the heat.

'Sophie's mum?'

Lynette jolts back. 'What's happened? Have they found her?' She spreads her hand across her chest.

'No, no, I'm sorry, it's nothing like that. I've just moved here with my partner.' I hesitate; I should have planned what to say more carefully instead of bolting here with no idea how to approach this poor woman.

Lynette waits for me to explain myself.

'Um, my partner is Charlie Hollinger.'

Her eyes widen, and without a word, she holds open the door and steps aside.

The cottage is as pristine on the inside as it is outside. Small bookshelves line the hallway, and two large rubber plants make the place warm and inviting. Lynette leads me into a small kitchen at the end of the hallway. The table in the middle of the room takes up most of the space, and it's cosy, bursting with character. Charlie would loathe it – not a whiff of anything modern or minimalist here, and barely an inch of free space on the surfaces. He wants us to completely modernise the farmhouse, to rid it of all its character and history.

'I was just about to put the kettle on. Would you like tea? Or coffee?'

'Actually, I just had one at the Hurtwood Inn.'

'I hear Liam's running it now,' Lynette says, boiling the kettle. 'I never go there these days. I used to clean there, for Liam's parents.' She pulls a mug from the mug stand, checking inside it before she places a tea bag inside.

'Did you always live here?' I ask. 'It's a beautiful cottage.'

'No. I only bought this place about ten years ago. It sounds silly, but I didn't want to leave the flat I was renting in case Sophie came back and couldn't find us.' She sits down and rests her elbows on the table, while behind her the kettle whirs loudly. 'That's ridiculous, isn't it? Sophie has my mobile number so she'll always be able to find me. I think I just used it as an excuse not to leave, because of the memories of Sophie. Again, that was stupid because we hadn't even lived there that long. If anything, I should have gone back to London. That's where Sophie grew up. That's where all the memories are.' She sighs. 'But still, that little flat around the corner was the last place I saw her. It was hard to leave, even for this place.'

'I totally understand that,' I say. 'My mum died a year and a half ago, and it was hard for me to leave London, because that's where she always lived.'

'Sorry to hear that.'

'But this is a lovely home,' I say, desperate to change the topic, because speaking about Mum feels too raw.

Lynette gestures around her. 'I know how lucky I am to have this cottage. And a mortgage. And it's all thanks to Heather Hollinger. She got me a job as an admin assistant at the village school, and I worked my way up to head teacher's PA. Before that, I had to work three jobs to pay our rent.' A tear meanders down her cheek. 'Sophie would be proud, I know she would.'

Reaching into my pocket, I pull out a packet of tissues and hand one to Lynette.

'Sorry, I'm going on and on. I haven't been asked about Sophie for so long. It's as if people just want to forget she disappeared. Wipe her out of existence.'

'Most people can't understand others' pain. It makes them uncomfortable.'

Lynette nods.

'You've done really well for yourself. And I'm so sorry about Sophie. I can't imagine how hard it was.'

'Yes.' She dabs her eyes. 'I only got through it because of Orla, my other daughter. She was a baby at the time and needed me. She's seventeen now, and that's hard because it's the same age Sophie was when she disappeared. I keep thinking the same thing's going to happen to her. But I know that's not logical. It's not how the world works.'

The kettle flicks off, and Lynette gets up to make her tea. 'So, you and Charlie are together. I'm assuming you know that he and Sophie were in a relationship? Is that why you're here?'

'I didn't know until we moved here,' I begin. 'We lived together in London for a year. I've lived there my whole life until now, so similar to you. But Charlie's parents offered us their old farmhouse and—'

Her face brightens. 'Ah, yes – I heard the Hollingers were back in the UK. I've been meaning to contact Heather. It would be lovely to see her again. Sorry, I interrupted you. You said they just gave you the farmhouse?'

I nod. 'All we have to do is pay for the refurbishments. It needs a lot of updating.'

'Yes, I imagine it does. I often walk past it going to work, and every time, I think what a shame it is that they just left it to rot. It was very strange. They didn't seem like the kind of people who'd just abandon their home. But then Edwin was offered a once in a lifetime opportunity to go and work at a top hospital in Dubai. It was great for his career, so I suppose they had to grab the opportunity. And they never had to worry about money.' She sighs. 'It's very kind of them to give you and Charlie the farmhouse. Doesn't surprise me – they were good people. Always looking out for others.' She frowns. 'But I'm not sure I understand why you're here?'

'Charlie's been lying to me since we moved here.' It's easy to be open with Lynette when I've got nothing to lose.

'What about?' she asks, leaving her tea bag in her mug and coming back to the table.

'To start with, he's never once mentioned Sophie. Not when we were living in London, or when we were planning to move here.'

'Oh. Well, that's hardly a lie. Maybe he found it difficult to talk about her? Her disappearance really affected him.'

'Yes, I get that, but when I found out Sophie had gone missing, he made out that he just knew her from school. He never told me they were together. He even said Sophie definitely hadn't been interested in any boys at school and didn't have a boyfriend.'

Lynette puts down her mug. 'I don't understand. That doesn't make sense. Why would he... Wait here.' She heads out of the kitchen, returning a few moments later clutching a photo album to her chest. 'It's an old cliché, but the camera never lies, does it?' She places the album on the table, and gestures for me to open it.

Holding my breath, I turn the cover. And there they are. Charlie and Sophie, smiling for the camera, arms around each other. There are many more photos of the two of them, all telling the same story of two people in love. I should feel something, but there's only a numbness that makes me feel as though I'm made of ice.

'I used to worry about them,' Lynette says. 'From the moment they met, they were inseparable, and I wasn't sure it was healthy. I wanted Sophie to focus on her studies. To not take the same path I'd taken.'

I frown.

'I mean, having a baby so young. I wouldn't change a thing – I loved Sophie's dad. But I didn't want that for her. She had big dreams.'

'She wanted to be a doctor,' I say. 'Khalid and Liam both told me.'

Lynette's eyes widen. 'Khalid? He's back?'

'Just for a visit,' I say.

'He was a lovely boy. Sophie thought very highly of him.' She sighs. 'After Sophie disappeared, her school friends rallied around at first, searching the woods for her. Then later, making sure everyone talked about her, keeping her memory alive – but that can't be sustained, can it? Eventually the initial energy fizzled out, and they all stopped coming to check on me and Orla. I think our pain was too much for them. I do understand that – they were young and had lives to live. Vanessa was the only one who kept coming, until she moved away with her parents.' Lynette pauses and sighs. 'I'm doing it again, aren't I? Talking too much and not letting you get a word in.'

But this is fine – I'm learning so much about Sophie, storing the information away because I know it will help me shed light on Charlie and those messages I found. 'I'm happy to listen,' I say.

'Well, like I said – I had my reservations about the intensity of their relationship, and how young they were, but Charlie adored Sophie, and I'd rather that than her be with someone who treated her badly. I figured, if it was meant to last, then who was I to stand in their way?' She appraises Emmie. 'Can't work out why he'd lie to you, though. Maybe he wanted to spare your feelings.' She pauses. 'I haven't thought about this for a while, but there was a time when I started to wonder if Sophie was mostly going round to the Hollinger house to see Vanessa. The two girls had become really good friends, even though Vanessa was a bit older. I liked Vanessa. She wasn't afraid to be herself, and I imagine being a Hollinger kid wasn't easy. All those expectations. She'd talk to me about it sometimes, when she was waiting for Sophie to get home from school. I'm assuming you must have met Vanessa?'

I nod. 'Only once in person, the other night at dinner. And she wasn't exactly friendly.'

Lynette nods. 'Go easy on her. She's been through a lot. I think losing her best friend like that maybe hit her even harder than it hit Charlie. She was never the same after Sophie disappeared. She seemed to lose her spark. She was always bursting with character. The life and soul, so to speak. But after Sophie, it's like everything was sucked out of her. She became quiet and withdrawn. Didn't want to socialise with anyone. Heather tried her best to support her, but nothing worked.'

As I digest this new information, I wonder how a girl like Sophie could have bonded with someone as stone cold as Vanessa. 'I found something in the house,' I say.

If Lynette is startled by my abrupt declaration, then her face gives nothing away, and she listens intently while I explain coming across the carved messages in the basement.

Then tears glisten in her eyes. '*Sophie was here.*' Her voice trembles. 'She was always at the Hollinger house. It was like a second home to her.' She pulls a tissue from her pocket and dabs her eyes. 'Funny that she'd write that. It's something we used to write as kids way before Sophie's time. Didn't think young people her age did that.'

'But it's the other message that's more disturbing,' I say. '*Please help me.*'

Lynette frowns. 'I've spent so many years hoping to find something that would lead me to Sophie. But I can't get my hopes up that this means something. I've done it too many times. Like I said, Sophie was always in that house. The police would say that was just a kids' game.'

'What if it's not, though? What if—' I stop short. I'm not sure what it is I want to say – I haven't yet given voice to the dark thoughts trawling through my mind.

Lynette's eyes widen. 'Do you really think... Did you take photos?'

'Not of the first one. I wasn't expecting it to disappear.' I flick through my phone and show Lynette the photo. 'I wasn't going to make that mistake again.'

'Sophie,' she says, running her fingers over the screen as if it's a photo of her daughter.

'You could come to the house and see it properly,' I say. 'Charlie's at work, so he wouldn't even know you're there.'

Lynette chews her bottom lip. 'I can't go to the farmhouse. Too painful.' She rests her elbows on the table and leans forward. 'Are you sure you saw that first message? Because on its own, *Sophie was here* isn't evidence of anything.'

Although I find it strange that Lynette is so doubtful when any clue – no matter how small – should have her running to the police station, it's clear that she's struggling to believe me. I am after all a stranger to her. 'I know what I saw. And I know that someone made it disappear. Charlie and I were the only ones in the house that could have done that. I think that part of the bannister was replaced.'

'But who would have replaced it?'

I've been asking myself this question. There wasn't a lot of time between me finding it and it disappearing. Charlie and I had gone to dinner, and it was when I woke in the night that I found it gone. I explain this to Lynette.

'Let me get this straight – are you suggesting that Sophie

was in the Hollingers' house before she went missing? Because—'

'I don't know what I'm suggesting, but something doesn't feel right about it. Why did Charlie lie about Sophie?'

Lynette silently studies me, but says nothing. This is not the reaction I was hoping to get from Lynette Bower.

'Well, let me put your mind at rest,' Lynette says eventually. 'Charlie wasn't even around when Sophie went missing. The Hollingers were away on holiday that week. In Wales. So if you're thinking Charlie had anything to do with Sophie's disappearance, then I don't see how that's possible.' She pauses. 'But you do need to show the police that photo. It could be nothing, but there's no harm in letting them have a look. And it might lead to something that could make them reopen the case. I suppose Sophie could have gone to the Hollingers' house while they were away. Maybe she stayed there for a bit because she knew they were away on holiday.' Lynette closes her eyes, shaking her head. 'I wasn't expecting this today – it's thrown me.'

I should feel relieved that Charlie wasn't in Peaslake when Sophie went missing. But part of me had hoped that his lies would help me find out what happened to Sophie Bower, and now those hopes crash down around me. 'I'll tell the police what I've found.' I pause. 'I hope you don't mind me asking this, but what do *you* think happened to Sophie?'

Lynette's eyes glass over. 'I don't think for one second that Sophie ran away. Someone must have taken her.' She turns away. 'But I'll never stop looking for her, even if the police gave up long ago. I set up a website back then – Find Sophie. But it rarely gets any visits. It's like she never existed.' Tears stream down her face and she turns back to me. 'Sophie had everything to live for. She'd just finished her A levels and was excited about her future, even though...'

'Even though what?'

'I don't know... I don't know if it's anything, but...' She dabs her eyes with her sleeve. 'I thought when Charlie went away on holiday, that Sophie would have been a bit lost without him. You know, missing him and just hanging around waiting for him to come home. It was summer, so there was no school to distract her.' She shakes her head. 'But she seemed... not just okay, but better than okay. Like she was really excited about something.'

I stare at Lynette. 'I don't understand.'

Lynette nods and looks away. 'I can't be sure, and she never told me anything, but that last evening I saw her, she had a phone call, then she said she had to go out. I asked who with, but she just said it was a friend. I thought it must be Vanessa or Charlie, but she said it wasn't. And they were in Wales, so it couldn't have been them. Then the baby started crying, so I got distracted and didn't pursue it. That was... the last time I saw her. I can picture her now, rushing out of the door. She looked so nice too. She was wearing a dress instead of jeans, and Sophie never wore dresses unless she had to. She lived in her jeans. Wherever she was going, she was excited to be heading out. I told the police all this, and it all came to nothing. It didn't help their investigation, so I put it out of my head.'

'I'm still not sure I understand what you're saying.'

Lynette looks distraught. 'Sophie was a kind girl. She always did the right thing. But... I just had this feeling that she was meeting a boy.'

'Are you saying Sophie was seeing someone else?'

'No, no, I'm not. I don't know what I'm saying.' She stares at her empty mug. 'When the police traced the call, it didn't come from any of her friends' phones. The phone call came from the old payphone outside the Village Stores.'

This confirms what Liam told me.

'But there was no CCTV, and Mrs Oberman didn't notice anyone in the phone box,' Lynette says. 'The police followed it up, but couldn't find any evidence of Sophie being involved with anyone else.'

'But you don't seem convinced.'

Lynette takes her time to answer, and when she looks up at me, her eyes have pooled with tears. 'Because a mother just knows. And maybe... I didn't know my daughter as well as I thought I did.'

NINE
JULY 2008

Sophie hasn't paid attention to how much time she's been spending at the Hollingers' house, until her mum pointed it out this morning. Lynette wasn't having a go at Sophie, or trying to make her feel bad – her mum never did that – instead, she'd patted Sophie's arm as if to say *I don't blame you for wanting to escape this tiny flat and the constant cacophony of baby noise and mess.* Her mum likes Vanessa, even though many people in the village consider her trouble because she says what she thinks, regardless of the consequences. Speaking your mind doesn't make you trouble, though, and at least Sophie knows where she stands with Vanessa. Other people can be snakes.

'Would you like a chocolate chip cookie?' Heather Hollinger asks, holding a tray of cookies under Sophie's nose. They're in the kitchen at the farmhouse, where Sophie has been waiting for Vanessa to get home for too long now. 'I know they're your favourite,' she says.

'Thanks, Heather. Really kind of you.' The smell of the chocolate sends a rush of dopamine to Sophie's brain, and she gazes at the perfectly rounded cookies. *How does Heather do it? She really is a superwoman.* Sophie smiles. 'I'd love one, thanks.'

She takes a biscuit and bites into it; it tastes just as divine as it looks.

'You must take some back for Lynette,' Heather says, placing four cookies in a plastic tub. 'Can't have my children pilfering them all, can I?'

Sophie thanks her again. 'Aren't you going to have one?'

'Oh, no. I've made these for all of you. And Edwin.'

Sometimes Sophie can't understand why Vanessa doesn't appreciate her mum more. Anyone can see that she'd do anything for her kids. Heather is thoughtful and caring, always putting everyone else first. Vanessa's words ring in Sophie's ear: *Yes, she does a lot for people, but the woman is also a control freak.*

'I'm not sure what's taking Vanessa so long,' Heather says, checking her watch. 'Her dental appointment was two hours ago – she should have been home by now. I knew I should have driven her, but she insisted on getting the bus. I'll try calling her again to see where she is.' She picks up the phone and dials, placing the receiver to her ear. 'Vanessa? It's Mum. Please call me when you get this. Sophie is waiting for you, and we're worried. Love you.' She puts the phone down and sighs. 'I do worry when she does this.' Her panic is palpable, and Sophie feels helpless.

'I'm sure she's okay,' Sophie says. 'Please don't worry, Heather.'

'Oh, you are a sweetheart,' Heather says, patting her arm. 'Yes, you're right. I'll try not to panic.' She smooths down her top and wanders to the back door. 'Why don't you sit in the garden, Sophie? It's too nice a day to be stuck inside.'

'Are you coming out too?'

'I wish I could. But there's the kids' washing and ironing to do.'

Sophie frowns; surely they're all old enough to do their own washing. She has been for years. 'You know, my mum always says if she could afford it, she'd totally get a cleaner to help out.'

Heather nods. 'Yes, that would certainly help. But it wouldn't feel right to let someone else do all the things I should be doing for my kids.' She shrugs. 'But that's just me!'

They hear footsteps in the hallway, and Myles comes into the kitchen. 'Hi, Mum.' He turns to Sophie. 'Hi, Sophie.'

Sophie's hardly seen Myles since she's been friends with Vanessa. He's quieter than his siblings, and when he's back from uni, he seems to prefer being out of the house than in it. 'Have you been baking again, Mum? Smells delicious.'

Heather offers him the tray, lightly smacking his hand when he tries to take two.

'I'm a growing boy!' he declares, laughing.

Outside, Sophie sits on a sun lounger under a large white parasol and wonders what it would be like to live in this house. The natural stone and timber cladding give it an elegant charm, and the wraparound porch seamlessly blends the house with the expansive garden. The whole place is warm and welcoming, and Sophie really feels part of the Hollinger family.

'Hey.'

She looks up, and Charlie is strolling towards her. He's tall, probably close to six foot already, and his floppy dark blonde hair falls across his forehead. He's striking, but Sophie will never let him know she thinks that. Not when every girl in their year is after him.

'Didn't see you at school today,' Sophie says. 'Are you okay?'

'Yeah, but had a bad migraine again. I've been getting them my whole life. People think they're just headaches, but they have no idea how painful they are.'

Sophie knows this. She makes it her job to soak up medical information, so that she can hit the ground running when she begins university.

'Did I miss anything interesting?' Charlie sits on the grass beside her sun lounger.

'Nothing much,' she assures him. 'Only Miss Tulley lecturing us about staying safe online. You don't send naked pictures of yourself to anyone, do you?'

Charlie laughs. 'Er, not that I can recall.'

'Then you'll be fine.'

'Where's Vanessa?'

'I have no idea. She told me to meet her here at three thirty, but your mum hasn't seen her. We've tried calling, and she didn't answer.'

'Strange,' Charlie says. 'But then, my sister is a law unto herself.' He snickers. 'Mum's always saying that. Right after she has a panic attack because she doesn't know where Vanessa is!'

'Why does Vanessa have a go at your mum so much?'

Charlie shrugs. 'Vanessa just hates anyone telling her what to do. Or caring about what she does. She thinks Mum is overprotective. Vanessa just doesn't see that there are far worse things a parent can be.'

'Do *you* get on with your mum?' Sophie asks. 'Heather's always so kind to me.'

'She's been a great mum,' he says. 'I don't always agree with her need to control everything, but she cares about us. *All* of us. We're lucky to have everything we have. And Vanessa's the last one who should complain. She's got both my parents wrapped around her finger.' He pauses. 'But I understand how Vanessa feels. She just wants... freedom to be herself.'

'You're really close, aren't you?' Sophie says, feeling a pang of sadness that she doesn't have a sibling closer to her age; by the time Orla is sixteen, Sophie will be in her thirties.

'Yeah, we are,' Charlie says.

'Well, I really like Heather. She's so kind to me. And she makes the best cookies!'

'I can't imagine anyone *not* being kind to you.' Charlie

strokes her hand, and even though Sophie feels a frisson of excitement, she pulls away. It was only last weekend that she and Liam finally went ice skating. He didn't kiss her or anything, but they had a nice time, and they've been talking on the phone, messaging constantly.

Charlie doesn't seem to notice, or care. 'I really like you, Sophie.' He smiles, and Sophie feels a flutter deep in her stomach. This has never happened to her before. She likes Liam, and gets on with him, but she has to admit there's no spark. She used to think people were making it up when they spoke about chemistry, but now, sitting here with Charlie, she thinks it just might be possible. 'I...'

'Is this about Liam?' Charlie asks. 'He's not right for you, Sophie. I think you know that, don't you?'

'That's presumptuous.'

'Sorry, you're right.' He holds up his hand. 'My dad's always saying that we should speak our minds freely – I think that's ingrained in me. I didn't mean to offend you. What I'm trying to say is – I really like you and think we could have fun together.'

Sophie raises her eyebrows. 'Fun?'

'I don't mean... Oh God, I'm not talking about *sex*!' His cheeks redden. 'I mean... Just let me show you what I mean. Let me take you out for dinner tomorrow night.'

Sophie wants to feel excited. Charlie could offer her experiences she's only dreamed of. But she won't choose him over Liam because of his wealth; she has principles. 'No, I can't. Liam and I are getting to know each other. I'm giving that a chance.'

'Have you kissed him yet?'

'What? No! Why?'

Charlie leans forward and kisses her. She wants to fight him off, but her body is ablaze and she doesn't want it to stop. After a moment, he slowly pulls away. 'Well, now you've kissed *me*, so if you go out with Liam again, then technically you're cheating on me.'

Sophie punches his arm. 'It doesn't work like that, and technically *you* kissed me. I did not reciprocate.' But her body did, and she'd be in denial if she said it didn't feel good.

Before she can respond, Vanessa flounces into the garden, rushing over to them, her thick blonde waves dancing around her shoulders.

'Tomorrow night, at the Hurtwood,' Charlie whispers, standing up and patting Vanessa's arm. 'Nice of you to turn up, sis,' he says. 'Don't worry, I've been entertaining Sophie for you.'

'Thank you, brother, but if you don't mind – girls only right now. Important things to discuss.'

'I was just leaving,' Charlie says, turning back to Sophie and flashing his charming smile. 'Nice chatting to you, Sophie.' He winks and walks off, turning around to soak her up once more before he disappears inside the house.

Vanessa sits in the sun lounger on my other side. 'Sophie? Your cheeks are red.' She frowns, glancing back at the house. 'Hang on a minute. You and Charlie—'

'What? No! We were just talking.'

'I know the signs! It's all over your face! You like him, don't you?'

Sophie winces. 'Um... I think I might. Maybe. A tiny bit.'

'Well, I never saw that one coming. I mean, I knew he liked you – I just didn't think you felt the same. Thought you'd be immune to his charms. And I thought you were into Liam Curtis.'

Liam. Guilt wrenches her body. Sophie's got some explaining to do. 'Nothing's happened with Liam. Or Charlie.' But she can still feel him on her lips. 'Can we talk about something else?'

'Yeah, we can,' Vanessa says. 'But just to say – you could do a lot worse than my brother. For all his faults – you know, that *I love myself* vibe he gives off – deep down, he's decent. Kind of cool. But hey, don't ever tell him I said that, okay?'

Sophie laughs. 'And where have you been, anyway? You said three thirty.'

'I was hoping you'd ask me that. I've been preparing for tonight.'

'What's happening tonight?'

'Tonight is the night.'

'Still confused, Vanessa!'

Vanessa looks back at the house and lowers her voice. 'I know we've tried to make it happen a few times, but *he's* finally ready to meet you. Tonight.'

Vanessa's mystery man, who, despite multiple arrangements for them all to meet up, Sophie still hasn't laid eyes on, and knows nothing about. It's dragged on for so long now that it's occurred to Sophie that perhaps this man is a figment of Vanessa's imagination.

'But it has to be late,' Vanessa says. 'Can you sneak out at around ten? Meet me outside the shop?'

'I can if Mum isn't working. Otherwise, I'll have to babysit Orla.'

'You have to come! Bring Orla. She's just a baby, she won't know anything.'

'I'm not bringing Orla out that late at night. She'll be sleeping. And you do know that babies come with a whole load of literal baggage: nappies, bottles, spare sleepsuits, teethers, not to mention—'

'Yeah, yeah – enough already, spare me the details, please.'

'And I don't even know where we're going,' Sophie says.

'That will only make it more exciting for you.' Vanessa springs up from her sun lounger. 'I've got to go and get ready. See you at ten!'

. . .

Her mum and Orla are both asleep when Sophie sneaks out of the flat. Lynette crashed early – worn out from a day of cleaning and looking after Orla, whose teething is keeping both of them up most nights.

Sophie feels a mixture of excitement and nerves as she throws a bottle of water and two bars of chocolate into her backpack; there's no telling what this night will bring. She's grateful she met Vanessa; her friend makes living here tolerable. You never know what each day will bring, and it's invigorating. Every moment with Vanessa feels like an adventure.

Sophie's phone vibrates – she hopes it's Charlie; she finds him intriguing, and every time she thinks of him, her stomach feels as if it's floating. She likes his whole family too.

Outside, the night air is muggy, despite the sun setting an hour ago, and Sophie makes her way to the bus stop, scanning the empty streets. It's as if there's no one else in the world but her. She'd never felt like this in London – even in the dead of night. But then, as she approaches the bus stop, she hears someone behind her. Turning around, she sees a male figure. Her pulse quickens. She reaches for her phone, just in case, but as the figure approaches, she realises it's Liam.

'Hey,' he says. 'What are you doing out so late?'

Still in shock, Sophie's defences are up. 'I could ask you the same thing. You scared the hell out of me, creeping up on me like that.'

Liam's face falls. 'Oh God, I'm sorry! I just saw you leaving your house and I wanted to check you're okay.'

'I'm fine. Apart from the shock of you being here.'

Again, he apologises. 'I did call out to you, but you didn't hear me. You were lost in your own world.' He smiles. 'What are you up to? Running away?'

'No, course not. I'm meeting someone.'

'Oh.'

'Vanessa,' Sophie says quickly.

'Really? Okay. Why so late?'

'What's with all the questions, Liam?' Sophie knows she's being abrupt, but she's still annoyed that he frightened her. 'Sorry, I didn't mean to be rude. But for a second, I thought... I don't know what I thought. I was just scared.'

'Can I make it up to you?' Liam asks. 'We could go bowling tomorrow? My mum said she's happy to drive us.' He smiles. 'She said it's about time she got to know you after all the time we spend talking on the phone.'

Now would be a good time to tell him about Charlie – it's not fair to keep Liam hanging. 'Actually, Liam, I'm... I'm kind of seeing someone.'

Liam's body stiffens, then his face seems to fold in on itself. 'But... I thought...'

She knows what he's about to say and wants to spare him the humiliation. 'It's all my fault. I thought we were just friends. We never actually said there was something else between us, did we? And nothing's ever happened between us.'

Liam's cheeks flame. 'No, but—'

'And what's going on here?' Vanessa's voice cuts through the icy tension.

Sophie hugs her as soon as she gets close enough. 'Nothing. Liam and I just bumped into each other.'

'Is that right?' Vanessa says, glancing at Liam before turning back to Sophie. 'Don't let Charlie find out.'

Liam stares at Sophie. 'Charlie?'

Vanessa nods. 'Yeah, didn't you know?' She grabs Sophie's hand. 'Come on. We've got somewhere we need to be, and we need to go *now*.'

I'm sorry, Sophie mouths to Liam.

But she catches the look in Liam's eyes before Vanessa drags her away.

Pure and utter hatred.

TEN

After leaving Lynette's, I sit at the bus stop outside the Village Stores, feeling the sun soak into my skin, and pull out my phone. At the shop window, Cassie looks up from the till and spots me, waving before turning back to the customer she's helping.

Doubts flicker in my mind as I call the police station. It's in Guildford, too far for me to cycle to and be back to meet Heather and Vanessa for lunch, and Charlie has taken the car to the train station.

I tell the officer who answers that I'm calling about a missing person from 2009. 'I think I've found something. It may or may not be important, but I think you should know.'

'Okay, can I take your name?'

'Emmie Jackson. My address is The Farmhouse, Old Farm Lane.'

'And what case is this relating to? Do you have a case number?'

'No. It was a long time ago. I've just moved into this house. But I found something, and I think it was the missing girl who wrote it. Sophie Bower.' I explain the carvings and ignore the officer's sigh. 'I know it doesn't sound like much, but I think someone should come and have a look.'

'Okay. I've taken down the information and someone will call you back.'

I end the call, already wondering if I'll ever hear back from anyone. Although I will send them the photo of the message on the basement door, the police need to see it for themselves, and analyse the reddish-brown substance that Charlie claims is paint, but I'm convinced is blood. With a surge of hope, I fasten my helmet and unlock my bike from the rack by the shop.

As I ride past the Hurtwood Inn, I see Liam out at the front, showing his mountain bike to someone. He nods to me, and I contemplate stopping to ask if he knows whether Sophie might have been seeing someone else. But he's busy with a customer, and I can't be late for this lunch.

The Gomshall Mill isn't far, and I make it with fifteen minutes to spare. This invitation from Heather had come out of the blue – Charlie only announced last night that his mum wanted to take me out for lunch. To get to know me properly, Heather had explained. That works both ways, I think now, as I lock my bike against a railing in the car park.

Inside, I'm shown to a table, where I'm surprised to see Heather and Vanessa are already seated. I thought I'd have some time to prepare for this.

'Did I get the time wrong?' I ask. 'I thought we were meeting at one?'

Heather stands to give me a hug, squeezing me tightly. 'No, not at all. I just like to be punctual. And I see you do too. Seems like we might have a lot in common. That's a good sign, isn't it?'

I nod, even though I'm not clear on her meaning. 'We're so happy to welcome you into the family,' she says. 'It's about time Charlie settled down.' She flashes a smile identical to Charlie's.

I turn to Vanessa, who silently watches our exchange. 'Nice to see you again, Vanessa.'

She nods. 'Yeah, you too.' She rummages in her bag and pulls out her phone. 'Sorry, I just need to message a friend.'

'Who's that, then?' Heather asks, picking up her menu.

'No one you know,' Vanessa says, without looking up.

Heather raises her eyebrows. 'Well, let's sit and enjoy a lovely lunch,' she says, sliding a menu towards Vanessa and handing one to me.

'Any news on the house?' I ask, after she's chosen what she'll eat.

'We completed yesterday. It's now our home. Oh, you and Charlie must come and see it. Did I tell you it's in Shere? The next village along. It's much smaller than the farmhouse, and it's very modern, but it will do us just fine at this time in our lives. We don't want anything high maintenance.'

'That's great.' I turn to Vanessa. 'Have you moved in too?'

Vanessa looks up from her phone. 'No.' She glances at her mum, then fixes her eyes back on her phone. 'I'm thirty-five. Not about to live with my parents. I'm staying with a friend in London. Until I find somewhere.'

I feel a swirl of homesickness, but it disappears as soon as I remember why I'm here. 'Which part?'

Vanessa looks up again, frowning. Clearly, she'd rather I didn't speak to her at all. 'Putney,' she says, glancing at Heather.

'I know it well,' I say.

'Are we ever going to meet this friend of yours?' Heather asks Vanessa.

Vanessa rolls her eyes. 'It's no one you know, Mum. And I'm not a teenager.'

Heather turns to me. 'When you have children, you'll understand. It doesn't matter whether they're five or fifty – they'll always be your babies.'

Vanessa stands up with such force that the back of her chair smashes against the wall. 'I'm going to the toilet.'

Tension lingers, even when Vanessa is out of sight. 'You'll

have to forgive her,' Heather says, keeping her voice low. 'I don't know how much Charlie has told you, but she's always had some... troubles. I was hoping it would all come good as she got older, but sadly that's not the case.' She puts on an expensive-looking pair of reading glasses and picks up her menu. 'Does Charlie talk about her much?'

'He actually doesn't talk about any of the family much,' I reply. 'He's normally so focused on work.' Numerous times I've attempted to get information out of Charlie about his childhood and family, but each time he's found a way to shut down the conversation. Only now am I beginning to see why. He didn't want me judging Vanessa. 'He did tell me that he was seeing Sophie Bower, though,' I say. 'The girl who went missing.'

Heather's eyes widen, and she peers at me over the top of her glasses. 'Sophie. I'd forgotten all about that. It was such a long time ago.' She glances in the direction of the toilets. 'Probably best not to mention it in front of Vanessa, though. She and Sophie were best friends. It was extremely hard on Vanessa when she disappeared.'

'I didn't know that,' I lie.

'In fact, she took it harder than anyone when Sophie ran away.'

This is exactly what Lynette Bower told me earlier. 'Is that what happened? I thought Sophie went missing?'

'Well, we don't know,' Heather says. 'That's what's so sad. No one actually knows what happened. We were on holiday in Wales at the time. I remember we came back, and Charlie went straight to her house to see her. She hadn't replied to his messages for a few days, so he was worried. That's when Lynette told him that Sophie was missing. Such a shock. She was a lovely girl. I just cannot fathom why she'd up and leave like that.' She sighs. 'Sophie really was part of the family.' Heather looks at me and smiles. 'Still, I doubt their relationship would have lasted.'

My ears prick up. 'What makes you say that?' This is similar to what Lynette had said.

'Oh, I don't know,' Heather says. 'Call it maternal instinct. I just don't think she and Charlie were right for each other. They were very different people. From different worlds.'

Again, Heather's words echo what Lynette told me about Sophie's phone call the night she went missing.

Vanessa returns to the table, her eyes swollen and red.

'Are you okay?' I ask.

Vanessa throws a cold stare at me. 'I'm fine.' She takes a sip of water, then looks at me again, her expression softer this time. 'Thanks.'

'Let's order, shall we?' Heather says, gesturing for the waiter. 'I think I'll have the mushroom wellington.'

'Just salad for me,' Vanessa says.

'I wish you'd eat more,' Heather says. 'I do worry you'll waste away.'

I order the same as Vanessa, and notice her face soften when I do.

Once the waiter's taken our order, Heather turns to me. 'So how are you settling in?'

'It feels like home,' I say, hoping they will swallow my lie. 'And I met Charlie's friend Khalid last night.'

'Khalid!' Heather says, clapping her hands together. 'I had no idea he was flying over! How wonderful – I'll have to let Edwin know. He'll be absolutely delighted. He might have retired early, but he still loves talking anything medical.'

Vanessa is silent for the rest of the meal, only nodding occasionally when Heather directly addresses her. When we've finished and the bill arrives, Heather scoops it up, despite my insistence on paying. I don't want to be accused of using Charlie for his family's wealth, and I'm conscious of Vanessa's glare on me.

'Nonsense,' Heather says. 'I won't hear of it. I've invited you out so it's my treat. It's been lovely getting to know you better, Emmie. And we mustn't be strangers – I'm sure there's still a whole lot more to know.'

'Not really,' I say, feeling a rush of heat across my body.

Before we leave, Heather excuses herself to use the bathroom, leaving me and Vanessa alone.

'I'm sorry if we've got off on the wrong foot,' I say, after a few awkward seconds of silence. As hard as it is to reach her, I need to get Vanessa talking.

She raises her eyebrows and tilts her head. 'We haven't.'

'I understand if it's hard for you,' I continue. 'I know you and Sophie were good friends, so maybe it's difficult for you to see Charlie with someone else.'

'He told you about Sophie?'

I shrug; it's better if Vanessa believes Charlie is being open with me, that there aren't dark secrets threatening to destroy us.

'Do you really think I care about Charlie being with someone else?' Vanessa snarls. 'That was years ago. They were just kids. Sophie would...' She stops and shakes her head, regaining her composure. 'Do you love my brother?'

'Yes. Very much.'

'Then you're a fool,' she snarls.

Before I can ask what Vanessa means, Heather comes back. 'Well, it was lovely to see you, Emmie. You and Charlie will have to come over for dinner at the end of the week. See the new house.'

We step outside into the glaring sunlight. 'What's Liam Curtis like?' I ask, when we cross the carpark to their hire car.

Heather frowns at my abrupt change of topic. 'Liam? Why do you ask?'

'I could be wrong, but I got the slight feeling that he and Charlie weren't on good terms?'

'His family are decent people,' Heather says. 'I can't imagine why Charlie and he wouldn't have got along.' She shrugs. 'Strange. Anyway, come, Vanessa, we need to get going for my hair appointment.'

Vanessa lags behind, and while her mum climbs into the driver's seat, she grabs my arm. 'Stop asking questions,' she hisses. 'You won't like what you find.' She jumps into the car and slams the door, leaving me staring after them as Heather drives off, waving.

A large white van is sitting on the drive when I get back to the house, next to a yellow skip. Charlie's BMW is parked in front of it, and I check my phone. It's only three o'clock, and I'm sure Charlie mentioned having to work late again this evening.

Dismounting my bike, I wheel it to the front door and fish my key from my pocket. But the door opens before I've even put it in the lock, and Charlie stands there, a wide grin stretched across his face. 'Surprise!' he says. 'The renovations have started! You've been so stressed, so I made a few calls and was lucky enough to find these guys who could start straight away.' He beams again. 'Sorry if it's a bit of a shock, but I really wanted to surprise you, so didn't tell you what I was up to. I've even paid myself, so you don't have to worry about using your savings.'

I stare at him, soaking up words that make no sense. 'But we haven't even finalised what we want done yet. We're not ready to start.'

'I know, but that's okay – they've started with the basement. That gives us time to figure out what we want to do next. And I know that place was giving you the creeps.'

I rush past him, heading straight for the basement, where I can hear the men have already begun work. I stop short when I get there – the door to the basement has been removed. The door with the carving in it, evidence I was taking to the police.

'Where's the door?' I shout down the stairs.

One of the men looks up, startled. 'Gone,' he says. 'Door is gone.'

'What do you mean gone? Is it in the skip?'

The man turns to his colleague and mumbles something in Polish, shrugging. 'Not understand,' he says, turning back to me.

I race outside, towards the skip, with Charlie following.

'What's the matter?' he asks. 'What are you doing?'

Ignoring him, I peer into the skip. 'It's empty! Where's the basement door?'

'The men must have removed it,' Charlie says. 'But it's fine – we're getting a new one. That one was rotting. I want to make the basement a nice space so you're not so anxious to go down there. I thought you'd be happy.'

'But the men didn't know anything about the door!'

Charlie takes her arm. 'They don't really speak English, Emmie. Look, what's going on, Em? Is this about that stupid carving? I've already told you – it doesn't mean anything! You've got to let this go.'

ELEVEN

Charlie's gone before I wake up the next morning, and I am alone again in this silent house. These walls hide secrets, mocking me because I can't even scrape the surface of the truth.

I know what Charlie is doing, leaving for work so early when he's supposed to have taken leave: escaping confrontation, just like he's done since I've known him. He hasn't learned from the last time we drifted apart, but there's nothing I can do to change him. And I don't want to. I want Charlie just as he is.

Outside, I hear a van crunch across the gravel. I rush to the window and peer out. It's the same white van, the same two men climbing out of it, ready for another day of destroying the basement, making sure there's no trace left of the original room. None of this makes sense; other than stripping wallpaper, Charlie and I aren't even ready to begin work on the house yet – we'd agreed to live in it for a couple of months first, to get a good feel for what we wanted the house to become, instead of rushing in and doing things we might later regret. Yet now it's full steam ahead, with no regard for it being my house too.

I pull on jeans and the same vest top I wore yesterday and rush downstairs, throwing open the door. The two men make their way up the path, hesitating when they see me already at the door. They seem unsure whether to greet me or run away.

'Morning,' I say, flashing a smile. 'Coffee?'

The men shoot a glance at each other, then the taller one nods. 'Yes. Please.'

I lead them through to the kitchen and flick on the kettle.

'We make lot of noise,' the other man says. 'Sorry.' He looks to be in his late forties, and his dark hair is flecked with grey. The taller man only appears to be around thirty, and I wonder if they are friends as well as colleagues.

'That's okay,' I say. 'Thanks for coming at such short notice. We were lucky you didn't have another job on.'

He frowns. 'No. No job. We book this months ago.' He turns to his colleague. '*O czym ona mowi?*'

The other man shrugs.

'But my partner just called you this week.'

'Sorry. No. We book in months ago.'

I'm about to protest, but it's all too clear now. More lies and covering things up. I can almost understand Charlie not wanting to bring up Sophie Bower's name, but to lie about the house renovations doesn't make sense. A chill slithers through my body, making me even colder in this kitchen.

'There's been a change of plan,' I say to the men. 'What more do you need to do in the basement?'

'Plaster walls and ceiling. Floor. Then ready for decorate.'

'And after that?'

The men glance at each other again. 'No after that. Nothing. We just here to do basement.'

'My husband booked you months ago to just do the basement?'

He nods, then shrugs before turning to his colleague again and talking in Polish once more.

'I'll bring your coffee down,' I say, as my heart hammers. 'I'm sure you want to get started.'

. . .

While the men work – whose names I have discovered are Andrzej and Cezary – I sit at the kitchen table with my laptop, googling Sophie Bower again, to see if there's anything about her online that I've missed.

Finding nothing, and without any concrete evidence to go to the police, there is little I can do until Charlie messes up and backs himself into a corner with his lies. He will just tell people that I am mistaken, that the stress of losing my job and moving to an unfamiliar place has got to me and affected my mind.

One way to counteract that is to find a new job as soon as possible. I can't spend my days in this house, which is rapidly beginning to feel anything but mine.

The village school is looking for a teaching assistant – I'm qualified to do this, even though it's not exactly what I'm after. At least it would be something. I've just submitted my application when my phone rings, with a number I don't recognise. I put it on speakerphone. 'Hello?'

'Hi. Emmie? This is Lynette Bowers.'

I turn my phone off speakerphone and clasp it to my ear. 'Hi, Lynette. Is everything okay?'

'Yes, yes. But... two things really. I wondered how you got on with the police yesterday?'

'I told them what I'd found. But I'm not sure how seriously they took it. I'm waiting for someone to call me back. I've sent them that photo too.'

'Well, don't hold your breath. I certainly won't be. They gave up on Sophie long ago, and it won't be the same people working there now.'

'I know, but we can't give up hope. I'll let you know when I hear something. What was the other thing?'

'I saw your ad on the noticeboard in the Village Stores.

And... I was wondering if you might be able to help my daughter Orla. I mentioned her when we spoke yesterday.'

'Yes, I remember. And yes, I can definitely help. Did you say she was seventeen?'

'Yes, last month. And she's been... acting out of character lately, and I'm worried about her. Do you think you could have a chat with her? See what you can find out? I've always wondered if she should have had therapy. Orla was a small baby when Sophie disappeared, so she doesn't remember her, but just knowing that she has a sister out there that no one knows what happened to... it's bound to have affected her.' She coughs. 'I'll pay you. Whatever it is you normally charge.'

'We can talk about all that,' I say, although I have no intention of taking any money from Lynette. 'Just keep in mind that I'm not a counsellor. Behavioural therapy is quite different. Normally I help young people with negative or harmful behaviour that's interfering with their learning or ability to work. But I'm happy to offer whatever help I can.'

'Well, something's definitely interfering with Orla's studies. She's been... off track.'

'Okay. When would you like me to come and see her?'

'Actually, do you think you could come right now? She's locked herself in her bedroom and won't talk to me.'

By the time I cycle to the Bowers' cottage, Lynette has somehow convinced Orla to unlock her door. But she still hasn't ventured out of her bedroom.

'Thanks for this,' Lynette says, pointing up the stairs. 'She knows you're coming, and she didn't protest, which surprised me. As academic as she is, Orla has a huge mistrust of authority. It takes a very patient person to get through to her.' Lynette smiles. 'I have a feeling that's you.'

Upstairs, I knock on Orla's bedroom door. It's slightly ajar, but I can't see inside. I put aside thoughts of finding out more about Sophie's disappearance – and how Charlie might be tied up in it – and switch to work mode. 'Can I come in?' I ask, peering around the door.

Orla is the image of her mother. And Sophie, from the photos I've seen. A thick curtain of long, dark hair frames her face, and she sits on the bed, her legs crossed beneath her. 'Hi, I'm Emmie.'

'I know,' Orla says, appraising me. Her fringe falls across her eyes and she tucks her hair behind her ear. 'Mum told me who you are. Are you going to come in, then, or talk to me from the door?'

I step inside, gesturing to the desk chair in the corner of the room. 'Okay if I sit down?'

'You don't have to tiptoe around me,' Orla says. 'I'm not some troubled kid who's about to erupt into violence if you say something wrong...'

'I know,' I say. I admire Orla's candour. 'I'm just being polite, that's all. I've made no judgements about you, I promise.'

'I don't *need* behaviour therapy,' Orla says. 'It's laughable.' She rolls her eyes. 'But I love my mum, and if this makes her feel better, then I'll go along with it. But I want to be clear – there's only one reason I'm talking to you now.'

'Oh?'

Orla springs up and closes the bedroom door. 'Because I needed to see what kind of woman would want to be Charlie Hollinger's girlfriend.'

I stare at her, momentarily lost for words. But I'm used to challenging situations, and I will rise to this one. 'I'm guessing now you've said that, I'm supposed to ask you what you mean?'

Orla shrugs. 'Do or don't ask – that's your choice.'

'How about this, then? I'll tell you all about me – and then you can tell me what's been going on with you? That seems fair, right?'

Through narrowed eyes, Orla studies me again. 'I suppose.'

'Right. Well, Charlie Hollinger is my partner. We've been together for just over a year. And as I'm sure you know, we've just moved into his parents' old house. That massive farmhouse that's too big for even large families. I'm from London. I *miss* London with all my heart.'

I wait for a reaction, but Orla doesn't flinch. I clear my throat, deliver a spiel that is easy to pretend is not my life story at all, but belongs to someone else. 'My dad died when I was three. We lived in America then. My mum brought me back to the UK, and we got through it. She was amazing. She was the one who made me everything I am today. She died not long before I met Charlie. Anyway, I'm very determined, and I never, ever give up on anything or anyone.' I let out a deep breath. 'There. Me in a nutshell. Over to you.'

Orla's eyes widen. 'Wow, I wasn't expecting all that. Sorry about your mum. Um... what can I say about me? Okay, well, I study hard. I want to be a doctor. To do what my sister never got the chance to do.' She pauses, and scrutinises me. 'I choose my friends carefully – not that I've got much choice at our tiny school. But even if it was huge, I'd be very careful who I spend my time with. It's precious, isn't it? Mum's always telling me that. She learned that the hard way.' Orla uncrosses her legs and moves forward so she's perched on the edge of the bed. 'I'm very determined when I set my mind to something.'

I nod. 'Thank you for sharing all of that. I—'

'Wait, I haven't finished. I'm... messed up about my sister. There, I've said it. I'm not stupid, I know what's going on in my head. I know I was a baby when she died, but I was doing okay, you know – in life. Until the Hollingers came back last week and opened up Mum's old wounds. Before that, I'd only ever heard about them. How wonderful they are. How much Sophie loved them all. How they accepted her as part of the family. All that meaningless waffle.'

I can't help but smile. 'Are you saying it's not true? Please know that you're free to speak your mind, even if I am Charlie's girlfriend.'

'I *will* speak my mind, don't you worry about that. I didn't think anything much about the Hollingers until the day I heard Charlie and his brother, Myles, arguing. It was a couple of months ago. They were in the Hurtwood. Didn't even notice I was watching the whole thing. I have a weekend job there, clearing glasses and boring stuff like that. Dull as dishwater. Hate it, but it allows me to hear things. See things.'

'Orla, I'm confused. Charlie and I only moved here a week ago. Charlie couldn't have been in Peaslake. We were in London.'

'Wrong! I'm telling you he was here, with his brother. They were having a drink and a very heated argument. It was busy in there that night, so no one would have even noticed. But *I* did.'

I try to process what I'm hearing. With Charlie's lies mounting up, it's possible he came down here one evening without telling me. He's always working late and I've never had a problem with that; I've never been one to question him about where he's been. 'What were they arguing about?'

'That's the problem. I couldn't hear all of it. It was noisy and I was working, so I only caught bits. But they were arguing about the house. Charlie was telling Myles he wanted to sell it and use the money to get somewhere in London, but Myles was mad at him. Told Charlie he had to take the house. That it had to stay in the family, it meant a lot to their parents. But Charlie said he didn't want to. Then Charlie got right in his face – I thought he was about to hit Myles, but then Myles said something, and Charlie sank back into his chair. It was as if all the fight went out of him.' Orla takes a deep breath. 'I was about to walk away – Liam was calling me to help him with something – but then I heard one of them say "Sophie".' She stops and lowers her head, peering at me from behind her long, dark fringe. 'My sister.'

'I know,' I say. 'I'm sorry.'

'I didn't understand it at the time,' Orla continues. 'And I still don't – but it got me wondering about my sister again.' She lowers her voice. 'Since then, I've been watching people. People in the village who would have known Sophie. I've been asking questions, but nobody wants to speak much about her. It's as if they've all put her out of their minds. They don't want their peaceful little village tainted. This is why Mum thinks I've been acting out of character. I have. But it's only because I think there's more to my sister's disappearance. I don't believe she ran away. Mum's always said that, and I have to trust that she knew Sophie better than anyone. So is my sister dead? If so, her body's never been found. It's eating away at me – I need to know what happened to her for Mum's sake. It's like there's this huge black cloud constantly hanging over us.'

'I want to know what happened too,' I say.

Orla stares at me. 'Why? You didn't even know my sister.'

'No, I didn't – but she was Charlie's girlfriend, and I need to know he had nothing to do with her disappearance.'

The two of us sit silently with our thoughts for a moment. Now that I've said it aloud to Orla, I realise this is what I've been feeling all along, that maybe Charlie knows what happened to Sophie.

Orla nods her agreement. 'Will you help me?' she asks. 'I need to know what happened to my sister. And you live with Charlie. If he knows anything, then you're the one person who could find out. Mum told me what you saw in your basement.'

There's an update on this story, but I have no intention of mentioning the sudden basement renovations to Orla yet. The fact that the evidence has now gone. Not when she's already struggling and I haven't even told her mother yet. 'I've told the police. I'm waiting for them to get back to me.'

Orla sighs heavily. 'Yeah, we'll see how *that* goes. It always comes back to Charlie. Do you see that?'

I nod. 'But he was on holiday in Wales with his family when Sophie went missing. He wasn't anywhere near her.'

Orla rolls her eyes. 'That doesn't mean anything. He could have got someone else to take her. To do something to her.'

'Orla! That's a serious accusation.'

'We need to be real, Emmie. People do terrible things, you know.'

Orla is right; people can do vile things when they're pushed to their limits. My dad was a victim of someone who had no moral compass. Someone who broke into our house and didn't hesitate to kill him when he tried to stop them burgling us. 'I'll see what I can find out,' I say. But you can't jump to conclusions and just assume Charlie is guilty of something. Not until we know for sure.'

'Mum told you she thinks Sophie might have met someone else? Well, that could have made Charlie jealous, couldn't it? What if he did something to her in a rage?'

My pulse races. 'The police didn't find evidence of that, though, did they? I'm guessing there were no messages on her phone or anything to link her to anyone.'

'Mum says they treated Sophie as a runaway and barely investigated. That's what's so infuriating. So much time has passed now, it's going to be so difficult even if they reopen the case. But we need to find something to force them to do that. And me overhearing Sophie's name in a pub isn't going to cut it. Someone knows something. And most likely, that's the person who hurt her.'

'*If* she was hurt.'

'Sophie had no money,' Orla protests. 'She wouldn't have been able to run away. What would she have lived on? And the police traced her bank activity – she didn't make any withdrawals.'

The alternative doesn't bear thinking about. 'Someone could have helped her. Given her money to leave. Maybe she was running from something. Or someone.' *Charlie?* 'Let's just keep an open mind. It's never good to make assumptions.'

'Fine,' Orla snorts. 'But in my gut, I *know*.'

'Do you know anything about Vanessa Hollinger?' I ask.

'Only that she was Sophie's best friend. And Mum said, after Sophie disappeared, Vanessa completely changed. She became quiet and withdrawn, when she'd always been vibrant and outgoing. It was like she had a lobotomy.' Orla clears her throat. 'Sorry. I know she's your sister-in-law.'

'Nowhere near,' I say. 'I suppose it's understandable that she'd change, given that her best friend disappeared without a trace. She must have been frightened.'

'Yeah, I guess. You must have met her – what's she like now?'

'Brusque. Distant.' Yet I'm determined to get through to her, to find out her thoughts about what happened to Sophie.

'And you want to be part of the Hollinger family?' Orla asks. 'Why, exactly?'

'I love Charlie,' I say, my throat constricting as I utter words that feel like knives.

Orla raises her eyebrows. 'So did my sister. At least at the beginning. All I can say is be careful. If there's any chance he did anything to my sister, then what's to stop him doing something to you?'

TWELVE
JULY 2008

'Where are we going?' Sophie asks. 'A heads-up would be good. I don't like surprises.'

Vanessa laughs. 'Just a little walk through the forest. Would I lead you into danger? You're the best thing that's happened to me in years.' Vanessa smiles. 'Actually, make that the second-best thing.'

Sophie stops and folds her arms. 'Are you saying this guy – whoever he is – means more to you than our friendship? I'm offended!' She laughs.

'You won't be when you see him. You will totally get it.'

They continue walking, their feet crunching on twigs they can barely see, and Sophie wonders if she is actually going to finally meet this mysterious man. It wouldn't be out of character for Vanessa to be carrying out some kind of hoax that she'll think Sophie will find funny eventually. But as she watches her friend, the way her eyes shine, even in the darkness, Sophie knows they're on their way to him.

Vanessa slows down. 'I have to know I can trust you, Soph. Not a word to anyone. It would ruin everything.'

'I give you my word,' Sophie says. 'Unless he's a teacher. Or a pensioner. Or anyone else who'd make me want to vomit!'

'No, it's not like that. And don't make it into a joke,' Vanessa says. 'I'm really serious about him.'

'But what are we doing in the woods? This is freaking me out. He can't live here.'

'It's the only place that's safe to meet.'

'I knew it! He's a teacher!'

'No!' Vanessa takes Sophie's arm. 'Will you stop saying that? Just come. Not far now.'

Linking arms, they continue through the wood. Vanessa hums quietly under her breath, and Sophie wonders if she's getting nervous.

'There,' Vanessa says, coming to a halt. She points into the distance, where all Sophie can see is what looks like a small grey tent. 'Right. Some ground rules. Don't ask him too many questions. He's a very private person.' Vanessa glances at the tent. 'Look, please don't judge me. Or him. You're the only person I can trust. I need you to be on my side. I really love him.'

'I am on your side,' Sophie insists. 'But why all the secrecy?'

'Okay, look, his name's Caleb, and he's... he's been in a bit of trouble in his life. With the police. He's from London, so he comes down here to get away from it all. To... hide, I guess.'

Of all the things Sophie has expected to hear, this isn't one of them. 'What do you mean by "a bit of trouble"?'

'Okay. He was kind of involved in some stuff. Gang stuff. Drug dealing. That kind of thing. Caleb doesn't take them himself – God, no – but he... Well, we've all got to make a living, haven't we? And not everyone can be born into money.' Vanessa screws up her face, as if she hasn't just described herself. 'And he's a little older than me, but not much. Twenty-nine.' She looks away. 'Nearly thirty. Actually, he's thirty-one.'

Twelve years older than Vanessa. Sophie stares at her,

trying to think of something supportive to say. 'Well... I think he's a bit old for you, but you must really like him.'

'I do. I love him, Soph. Wait till you meet him. He's nothing like you'd imagine. He's smart and funny. He just hasn't had a break in life. But he's really trying to turn things around. He got in with the wrong crowd at school and—'

'How about we just go in and I can take him for who he is?' Sophie suggests.

'Yes. Great. Let's do it!'

Sophie's never seen Vanessa so nervous, and it makes her friend all the more endearing. They approach the tent, and Vanessa calls out, her voice lacking its usual self-assurance. 'Caleb, it's me. And Sophie.'

Within seconds, the tent door opens, and a man Emmie can only assume is Caleb peers out. The first thing Sophie notices is how striking he is. Dark piercing eyes and longish hair falling across his forehead. Weeks of stubble cover his face. He's not Sophie's type, but she can understand what Vanessa sees in him.

'Babe,' he says, taking Vanessa's hand. 'You took your time.' He climbs out of the tent and turns to Sophie. 'And you must be Sophie. Vanessa doesn't stop talking about you, so I feel like I already know you. Weird, I know. This feels like a big moment finally meeting you. Come in, ladies. I've got food for us all. And beers.'

'You didn't have to do that,' Vanessa says, kissing him on the mouth. Her skin glows in the moonlight, and Sophie can't help but smile.

'What kind of host would I be if I didn't have food or drink?' Caleb says. 'Come in then, what are you waiting for? Is it because you've never seen such an exquisite palace?'

Vanessa laughs and playfully nudges him before disappearing inside.

Caleb looks around, peering into the forest, before he beckons Sophie into the tent.

The tent has enough space for all of them to sit, but other than a sleeping bag, pillow and a large sports bag, there's nothing else in there. 'Welcome to my humble abode,' Caleb says, grinning.

'Do you actually live here?' Sophie asks. 'Don't you get cold in the winter?'

Vanessa shoots her a glance.

'Sorry, no offence.'

'None taken,' Caleb says. 'I'm not ashamed of who I am, where I've come from. I'm a survivor, and I know that I can deal with anything people hurl at me. Let's just say I got myself into a tricky situation and there are people who don't want me to still be breathing. And actually, never tried camping in the winter. Hoping by then I will have moved on from this tent.'

Sophie gasps. 'I'm sorry. But if people want you dead, why don't you—'

'I hope you're not going to say go to the police? Ha, yeah, they love me, the police do. I'm sure they'd do anything to help a guy like me.' He laughs. 'But to answer your question, I wouldn't say I *live* here. I don't like to pin myself down to a fixed address. I have to be ready to leave at any second. No ties. You understand?'

Sophie nods. 'Yeah, I do. Vanessa says you're from London?' She sits down, surprised at how rough the ground feels beneath the tent floor.

Caleb smiles. 'Yep. Barking. And you're a Londoner too, am I right?' He flashes a smile at Vanessa. 'Told you it feels like I already know you.'

Sophie can't say the same for him. Before tonight she only knew that there was a guy Vanessa was seeing. Someone her friend had to keep secret. Still, anything is preferable to him being a teacher. 'Roehampton,' Sophie says.

'Ah, south. Not my territory. Been there a few times, but... always feels strange to venture out of the east side.' Caleb moves closer to Vanessa and takes her hand, lifting it up to kiss it.

Vanessa giggles and bats him away. 'What are you like?'

'Right, what can I get you ladies from my bag of goodies?' Caleb points to the sports bag.

'You're not going to offer me drugs, are you?' Sophie says. 'Because I'm totally not into that.'

For a moment, silence descends, and Sophie is aware of all eyes heavily upon her. Heat rushes to her cheeks. 'I just mean—'

'Chill out,' Caleb says, laughing. 'No, I'm not going to offer you drugs. I'm not into drugs – never taken them and never will. Both my parents died from drug overdoses.' He jumps up. 'All I've got in that bag is crisps and biscuits. Check it out if you don't believe me.'

'No, that's okay,' Sophie says. 'I'm sorry about your—'

'No need to apologise. Look,' Caleb says, 'even though I'm not proud of it, I'm not ashamed of what I do to make money. If that makes sense? It's not forever. I've got big plans, haven't I, babe?' He turns to Vanessa, who nods enthusiastically. 'And I won't take a penny from my girl.' He squeezes Vanessa's hand.

Sophie's about to respond – to tell Caleb that there are other options for him – but a phone rings before she can open her mouth.

'That's me,' Vanessa says, pulling out her phone. 'Shit, it's Mum. I'm not answering.'

'You should answer, babe,' Caleb says. 'She'll only worry. Just let her know you're okay. Do the right thing.'

Vanessa hesitates, then grabs her phone and takes it outside.

'I love that girl,' Caleb says, when he and Sophie are alone. 'But she really needs to treat her mum better. The woman's only worried about her daughter.'

'Have you... met her mum? I actually really like her.'

He inclines his head. 'Now, what do you think? Hardly suitable boyfriend material, am I? At least not on paper. But just because they wouldn't approve of me doesn't mean I don't know what's right.'

Sophie realises that, despite being determined not to, she has already made assumptions about Caleb. She needs to do better, take him how she finds him, like she always insists she does. 'But maybe if they got to know you—'

'Nah, that only happens in movies.' His hands form air quotes. 'Flawed hero overcomes challenges, and girlfriend's parents welcome him into the family with open arms.' He laughs. 'I wish life was that simple. But it ain't.'

Vanessa comes back in, shaking her head. 'I have to get home. Mum's panicking and asking too many questions about where I am. But don't worry – I have a plan. I'll show my face, wait until she's asleep and then I'll sneak back out.'

Caleb shakes his head. 'You don't have to do that, babe. Just stay at home.'

'No, I hate thinking of you out here on your own.'

'I'm totally at peace with my own company. You know that.'

'No can do.' Vanessa turns to Sophie. 'You'll stay and keep Caleb company, won't you? I know Mum will drop off to sleep as soon as she knows I'm safe in bed. That woman!'

'I'll come with you,' Sophie says, reluctant to be stuck in a tent in the middle of the forest with a stranger. 'You can't walk through the forest alone.'

'I won't. I'll get a cab, it will be quicker. And I'll get a cab back too.'

Caleb stands. 'This all sounds like a whole lot of bat-shit crazy to me.'

But Vanessa isn't listening, and she rushes from the tent before either of them can stop her.

'Stay here,' Caleb tells Sophie. 'I need to check she's okay.'

Left alone, Sophie helps herself to a bag of crisps, and when it's finished, she begins to panic. She needs to get home. If her mum wakes up to find she's not there, she'll be distraught.

Deciding she'll make her way home, even if she has to navigate the creepy forest by herself, Sophie crawls out of the tent, and straight into Caleb's legs.

'Woah, are you okay?'

'Sorry... I need to get home.'

'Vanessa will come back,' Caleb says. 'Have you ever known her not to follow through on a promise? She always finds a way.'

This is true – Vanessa's determination is admirable. 'I know, but I really need to get home.'

'Okay, how about this,' Caleb says. 'Give it an hour, and if Vanessa isn't back by then, I'll walk you home. She had her heart set on us getting to know each other – it means a lot to her.' He shrugs. 'Don't know what I've done to deserve that girl – I probably don't.'

Despite wanting to get home, Sophie agrees. What harm would an hour do? 'Fine. One hour, then.'

Back in the tent, Caleb opens the packet of chocolate Hobnobs and offers it to Sophie. She thanks him and takes one. 'The Hollingers are good people, you know,' she says, biting into her biscuit and dusting crumbs from her top. 'Look at me – I don't come from money, and they've accepted me into their lives.'

Caleb takes a biscuit and puts the packet on the floor between them. 'Oh, yeah. I heard you and Charlie have a thing going on.' He smiles.

'He just said he'd take me to dinner, that's all. It's not a *thing*.'

'Very posh. Is that what girls like? To be wined and dined?'

'Some, maybe. I don't know. Maybe we just want someone who can make us laugh. And be there for us. Give us their time.'

He nods. 'Not asking for much, then!' He laughs. 'Seriously, though, I see why Vanessa likes you,' he says.

Sophie smiles. 'Yeah, likewise.'

'Crisps?' Caleb asks.

'Already helped myself,' Sophie says.

While they wait for Vanessa, Caleb tells her how he became involved in a street gang when he was thirteen. 'I was disillusioned with school,' he says. 'Felt like it was smothering me. I just wanted to be free. Then I met a guy called Mikey. He was much older than me – introduced me to a life selling drugs. It seemed like the only way I'd ever dig myself out of poverty. But I don't hurt people. Never. That's not my code.'

'But do you ever think about doing something else?' Sophie asks, reaching for another biscuit. 'Then you wouldn't have to live like this.' She gestures around the tent.

'The whole reason I'm living like this is so I can save money and not waste it on rent,' Caleb explains. 'My plan is to buy a house outright for me and Vanessa to live in. And I'm doing it myself, not taking a penny of Hollinger money.' He smiles. 'I didn't believe in happily ever after until I met her.'

Sophie soaks up his words; she's warming to Caleb and can see how much he cares about her friend. 'How long?' she asks.

'What?'

'How long until you can save up enough? I'm just wondering how long Vanessa has to hide you from her parents.'

'I'm nearly there. Before I reach thirty-five, for sure. Whatever it takes.'

Caleb's phone rings. 'Hey, babe,' he says.

Sophie watches his face fall, thick creases forming on his forehead. 'What is it?' she says.

Caleb holds his finger up. 'Yeah, yeah. Okay. I'll call you tomorrow. Love you.' He hangs up, shaking his head.

'Vanessa can't come back. Her mum and dad are up watching a movie, and she says it's too risky to sneak out.' He snorts. 'I'm starting to think they know she's seeing someone. I told her to be careful. If they find out about me, then we don't stand a chance.'

'But she's nineteen,' Sophie says. 'She's an adult. They can't stop her.'

'They don't see her as an adult. And I'm way older than her. And they can cut her off. Use any means necessary to keep us apart.'

Sophie considers this. Nothing she's seen of Heather or Edwin Hollinger suggests they'd do anything like this.

Caleb reaches into his bag and pulls out two cans of beer. 'Well, what can you do? It is what it is.' He hands one to Sophie. 'Looks like it's just me and you, then.'

'I don't drink,' Sophie says. 'I'm not eighteen until next year.'

He smiles. 'A stickler for the rules, eh? Fair enough.'

'I have to go.' Sophie stands. 'My mum might wake up and wonder where I am. I have a baby sister, and she always wakes in the night. It's exhausting.'

'I'll walk you home,' Caleb says, reaching for his phone.

'No, I'll be fine. Stay here. Maybe Vanessa might find a way to get out of the house after all. Bye, Caleb. I'm glad we finally met.'

She rushes off, ignoring Caleb's protests for her to wait.

Walking through the forest by herself when she can barely see in front of her tests her to her limits, and it feels as though she's holding her breath the whole way, but now that her flat is in sight, Sophie wonders why she got so freaked out and rushed off like that. *We have nothing to fear but fear itself.* Another one of her mum's mantras.

She reaches into her pocket for her keys, just as a hand falls heavily on her shoulder. 'And what are you doing out so late at night?'

THIRTEEN

Charlie's car is parked in the driveway when I get home from the Bowers' house, and there's no sign of Andrzej and Cezary's white van. Even the skip has been cleared away.

Inside is silent as I open the door, and there's no response when I call out for Charlie.

Heading into the kitchen, I stop short when I see him sitting at the table, staring at me.

'What's going on, Charlie? How come you're home from work already?'

He folds his arms. 'I had to come. I got a call from the building company. They said you'd been interrogating their men about why they were doing the basement and who asked them to do it. Criticising their work. Emmie, this isn't like you – what's going on?'

I place my bag on the kitchen table. 'That's not what happened. I think it must have got lost in translation.'

Charlie sighs. 'What if *we're* the ones who are lost in translation,' Charlie says, shaking his head. 'Ever since we moved here you've been acting strangely – questioning everything I do, interrogating me. I don't get it! You pushed us to move here when I was reluctant. If you're having second thoughts about this move, all you have to do is tell me!'

'Did you visit Peaslake a few months ago? With Myles. Because you'd told me you hadn't been back here since you moved out and went to university.'

Charlie stares at me, a flash of defiance in his eyes and something I don't recognise, and not for the first time he feels like a stranger to me. 'No,' he says. 'Why would I have come back here? I told you I didn't even want this house.'

'I know you didn't want it. And I think Myles talked you into it – or forced you to accept it. Was it just to keep it in the family for sentimental reasons? Or is there something else?'

Charlie ignores my question. 'Emmie, I don't know what's going on here, but I think you need to talk to someone. You're acting—'

'I won't be gaslighted, Charlie.' I place my hands on the table and lean forward. 'Don't you know that about me? I'm not just going to play along with what you're doing. I know you saw that message on the bannister.' I pull out my phone and show him the photo of the carving on the door. 'I wasn't going to make that mistake again. And I know you were seeing Sophie. What I don't know is why you felt the need to lie about it.'

Charlie pushes my phone out of his way and scrapes his chair back, striding to the back door. He stares at the neatly mown lawn. Seconds tick by, more than enough time for him to come up with a story, one which I will never allow myself to swallow. 'The reason I didn't tell you about Sophie,' he begins, 'is because that relationship wasn't what it looked like.'

Of all the things I've expected Charlie to say, this is not one of them. 'I don't understand. What do you mean?'

He turns to face me. 'I mean... everyone thought we had this amazing bond, and that Sophie was this perfect person. But only I knew the truth. She was not who everyone thought she was.'

'What are you talking about?'

'It doesn't matter! It's in the past.' Charlie walks over to me and places both his hands on my shoulders, pressing down too firmly. 'You need to let this go, Emmie. Before something happens. Stop talking about Sophie. She's gone, and nobody wants to remember her. You chose to come here – I told you it was a bad idea, but you just didn't listen.' He lets go of me and moves back, then shaking his head, he disappears into the living room, slamming the door behind him.

All the breath has been sucked from my lungs. Was Charlie threatening me? I've never believed him capable of violence, even when he's reached the limit of his anger. Now, though, his chilling words. *You need to let this go... before something happens.* Then I think of Vanessa's warning to stop asking questions, that I won't like what I find.

The things Charlie said about Sophie are cruel if they're a lie. But it's possible not everything Charlie says is a lie.

I fill a glass with water and down it in one, then grab my bike helmet and leave the house without a word to Charlie.

I ride faster than I should, flying along unfamiliar roads, and although I'm an experienced cyclist, several times I almost lose control of my bike. But still, I keep going, to where I have no idea. And the whole time, Charlie's words ring in my ears. I don't know what he meant about his relationship with Sophie not being what people thought, but then I think of our own, and the parallels chill me to my bones.

Faster I pedal, jolting over twigs, flying through the forest, until once again I'm out on the main road. I'm so consumed with my tornado of jumbled thoughts that I don't hear the car behind me until it's too late and it's smashed into me, sending me hurtling into the air, thundering to the ground, violent fireworks of pain erupting all over my body.

And then everything fades to black.

. . .

'Emmie, can you hear me?'

I open my eyes, and Charlie's face peers down at me. Machines beep, and the bright yellow lights force me to squint. I'm in a hospital bed. I didn't die.

He grips my hand, so tight I want to yank my hand away, but I don't have the energy. 'Thank God,' he says, stroking my cheek. 'I've been so worried. Do you remember what happened?'

My throat is dry, and it takes all my effort to get any words out. 'A car hit me,' I manage to say.

'Did you see what car it was?'

'No. It happened too fast. Who hit me?'

Charlie shakes his head. 'I'm sorry, but it was a hit and run. There are some nasty people in this world. Thankfully, Liam was driving past and saw you lying on the ground next to your bike. He stopped and called the ambulance. I guess I owe him. He's been here since they brought you in. I told him he could go home, but he's still in the waiting room.'

I close my eyes. My head feels as though it's been crushed, and every inch of my body aches. 'I want to speak to him,' I say, my throat still hoarse. 'Can you tell him?'

Charlie's eyes narrow. 'Why do you want to see Liam? I'm here now.'

'Just get him for me. I want to ask him what he saw.'

'He's already told the police—'

'Charlie. Please just get him, or I'll climb out of this bed and do it myself.'

It takes him a moment, but finally, he gets up and leaves the room, shaking his head on his way out. The second he's gone, panic overwhelms me, and I'm back on my bike, speeding down a road that's quiet, with no other traffic. No reason why a car would need to get close enough to me to knock me off. I know the accident wasn't my fault.

Which means someone ploughed into me on purpose.

It's several moments before Liam comes in, standing in the doorway as if he needs my permission to enter. 'How are you doing?' he asks. 'I mean, not good clearly, but—'

I try to pull myself up, but the pain is too much, and I'm forced to stay lying down. 'I can put the bed up for you,' Liam offers. 'Might be more comfortable?'

I nod, and he quickly sorts the bed out for me. 'I know you must think it's strange that I asked for you,' I say. 'But I just wondered if you'd seen any cars around before you found me? Did anyone pass you on the other side of the road?'

Liam sits in the chair next to my bed. 'No. The roads were completely empty. Don't even know how long you were there for before I came along. I've told the police everything I know.'

'Thank you.'

'Charlie's in a state,' Liam says. 'He must be to actually have any kind of conversation with me. The paramedics said it was lucky you got to hospital when you did, otherwise you could have bled out.'

That cold chill again. Someone wanted me dead.

'I have to say,' Liam continues, 'I'm really shocked that someone would just leave you like that. They could have at least called an ambulance, even if they were scared of the trouble they'd be in for knocking you off.' He shakes his head. 'Can't be anyone local. I don't believe anyone in the village would do that.' Liam places his hand on my arm. 'Don't worry, though, the police will find who did this. I'm sure a knock like that would have seriously dented the car that hit you.'

'Thanks for calling Charlie for me.'

Liam frowns. 'I didn't. I'm not sure who called him. Probably the paramedics. He must have been at work, though, as he didn't get here for a couple of hours.'

'What? I thought he came straight away.'

'No, I'm the only one who's been here with you. Till Charlie came.

'Charlie was at home,' I say, almost to myself. 'I'd just left the house to go on a bike ride. Clear my head.'

Liam frowns. 'Are you sure? He said he'd come from work.'

'We were at home,' I say. 'I know we were.'

Liam's mouth twists, as if he's having trouble knowing how to respond. He probably thinks I'm concussed and confused about the details.

But there's nothing wrong with my memory, and I know Charlie was at home. So why did he wait two hours to come to the hospital? *Could he have been driving the car that ran into me?*

FOURTEEN
JULY 2008

'Liam. What are you doing here?' Sophie says. 'It's the middle of the night. And you frightened me. *Again.*' She wriggles free of his hand and takes a step back.

'I was worried about you. Going off with Vanessa like that so late at night. I know she does stuff like that, but I didn't think you would. I wanted to wait here until you got home safely. I wouldn't have been able to sleep otherwise. What were you doing in the forest?'

'That's just creepy,' Sophie says, indignation sweeping over her.

Liam steps towards her, and at least has the self-awareness to hang his head. 'I knew you'd think that, so I almost didn't come back. But then I weighed it up and thought, what if I woke up in the morning and heard that something had happened to you? It would be all my fault. Not that anything ever happens around here. Peaslake is too dull. But I just wanted to make sure you got in your house.'

Sophie shakes her head. 'And what would you have done if I hadn't come back? You didn't know where Vanessa and I were going. I don't need rescuing, Liam.'

'I know that. Course I do.' He nods towards the woods. 'But if you hadn't come home, I would have gone in there searching for you.'

Looking at his flushed cheeks, Sophie finds it hard to believe that Liam had any malicious intent in his stalkerish action. He's only looking out for her; she needs to stop being so cynical, mistrusting people before they've done anything wrong. 'I'm going inside,' she tells Liam. 'Before my mum wakes up and finds me out here.' She pulls her key out.

'Wait,' Liam says. 'Can we talk for a minute?'

Sophie sighs. 'Liam, it's late. I'm tired. I have to be up early to look after Orla.' She's exhausted after her unexpected night and wishes she hadn't agreed to meet Vanessa in the first place.

'Just for a few minutes? Please?'

This is the last thing she needs so late at night, but one look at the desperation painted on Liam's face, and she finds herself caving. 'Maybe just five minutes.'

'Thanks,' he says, smiling as if he's just won the lottery.

In the living room, Sophie shuts the door and perches on the arm of the sofa, to indicate that she's not about to get comfortable, and that their time here is limited. 'So, what's up? What did you want to talk about?'

He clears his throat. 'I know you'll come up with reasons why I'm saying what I'm about to say – but I need to tell you anyway.' He spreads his fingers and stares at his hands. 'Do you trust me?'

'What? Yeah.' She's never given this much thought before, but now that she is, she realises she does trust Liam.

'I feel like we're friends, aren't we?' he continues. 'I know I wanted more than that, but I get it. You're not into me like that. But I just have to say this.'

'What is it?' Sophie's getting unnerved now – why is Liam being so cryptic? 'Just say it.'

'Okay. You haven't known Charlie Hollinger long. But *I*

have. My whole life, in fact. And... he's not a good person, Sophie.'

'Right.'

'He... Oh, jeez. This is hard to talk about. Last year, he started... I don't know... like a hate campaign against me.'

'Why?'

'I don't think he's ever liked me, and then a year ago I was seeing this girl. Andrea. She moved away after what Charlie did to us, but—'

Sophie stares at Liam. 'What did he do to you?'

'Charlie liked Andrea. Had done for ages. He couldn't stand the fact that she was with me. He kept harassing her, begging her to go out with him, even though he knew we were together. Trying everything he could. But she was having none of it. Then, one evening, Andrea and I were in her garden, in the summer house. Just listening to some music. Chilling out. And suddenly something smashed through the window. It was a brick, and there was a cloth attached to it. It stunk of petrol. Next thing we knew, someone had thrown a match inside and the place was on fire.'

Horrified by what she's hearing, Sophie's mouth hangs open, but no words come out.

'I didn't see clearly,' Liam says, 'but I know it was Charlie. We heard someone run off, into the woods, and that was the way back to his house. Nobody else lived up by the farmhouse. It couldn't have been anyone else. It completely traumatised Andrea. Things ended not long after that, and then her family moved away.'

'But why would Charlie do that? It's... beyond evil.'

'Because he's used to getting what he wants. He's never been told no. So when Andrea rejected him, it was too much for him – he couldn't handle it.'

'But you have no actual evidence it was him,' Sophie says.

Liam lowers his head. 'No. But I told Andrea's parents it

was Charlie. Then, right before Andrea's family left, I went to see them, to check on her, and guess who was at the door, smiling and shaking hands with Andrea's dad? Edwin Hollinger. And the next thing I know, her family have moved away. Not hard to work out that Edwin probably paid them off to keep quiet about it.'

'But that doesn't prove it was Charlie,' Sophie says.

'In my gut, I know it was,' Liam says. 'And what kind of friend would I be to you if I didn't warn you.'

Sophie's head spins. She doesn't want to believe Charlie would do this, and she knows Liam is disappointed that she didn't get together with him, but it's better not to take any chances. After all, how well does she really know Charlie? 'Thanks for telling me,' she says. 'I think I need to get to bed now.'

For a moment, Liam doesn't move; he just watches her, and she begins to think she'll have to drag him out herself, but then he finally stands. 'Please be careful, Sophie. I'd hate it if anything happened to you.'

She sees him out, watching until he disappears around the corner, then she shuts the door and double-locks it. She pulls her phone from her pocket and sends Charlie a message.

Sorry, can't do dinner tomorrow. But thanks anyway.

That's as polite as she can make it, given what she's just heard. Even if Liam is wrong about Charlie, Sophie doesn't need this trouble in her life.

When she gets upstairs, Orla begins to wail. It's nearly one a.m. – Sophie can't let her mum see to the baby when she has to be up at five. 'Coming,' Sophie whispers, making her way to Orla's room, where she knows her mum will have a bottle of formula already waiting.

. . .

At school on Monday, Sophie keeps half an eye out for Charlie, but she doesn't spot him all day. He hasn't replied to her message either.

At lunchtime, she hears from another boy in their class that Charlie is off sick – another migraine. She contemplates sending him a message saying she hopes he's okay, but then an image of Liam running from a burning summer house forces its way into her head, and she puts her phone back in her bag. She's at peace with her decision.

When she gets home, she hears voices and then her mum laughing, and Sophie wonders if Vanessa is here. But when she opens the living room door, it's Charlie sitting on the sofa, apparently migraine-free, regaling Lynette with some story or other that's clearly amusing her.

'Hi, love – look who's come to see you.' Her mum beams. Charlie has won her over. Of course he has – he oozes charm and charisma.

'What are you doing here?' Sophie asks.

'Sophie!' her mum says. 'Why are you being rude? Look what Charlie has brought you.' She points to the coffee table.

On it is a large bouquet of pink and white roses.

The sight of it snatches Sophie's breath; she's never seen such a beautiful arrangement. She turns to Charlie, open-mouthed.

'Thought I'd surprise you,' Charlie says. 'Do you like them?'

'They're beautiful. Thank you.'

He nods, pleased with himself. 'Mum chose them for me. I've been in bed all day with a migraine but feel much better now.'

'I'll head off to work,' Lynette says, giving Sophie a hug. 'Orla's napping. Are you sure you don't mind looking after her? I'll be back by six.'

'It's fine, Mum.' Sophie smiles, so that her mum doesn't

spend the next two hours in a panic that she's had to rely on her daughter again.

'Well, I'll just be at the Hurtwood if there's any problem.'

'Orla will be fine, Mum.'

'I know she will. But you're my daughter too.'

'I can stay with Sophie and help with Orla,' Charlie offers, his smile stretching across his face. Yet somehow it doesn't manage to reach his eyes.

Lynette beams again. 'Thank you both. I'd better run. Help yourselves to anything in the fridge. There isn't much, but what's ours is yours.'

As soon as she's gone, the atmosphere immediately changes, and Charlie falls silent. Questions hang in the air between them, and it makes Sophie uncomfortable. She hadn't wanted him to turn up here; her plan had been to distance herself from Charlie.

'So why exactly didn't you want to go on this date with me on Saturday?' he asks. 'You didn't exactly explain yourself.'

'I—'

'Have I done something wrong?' His manner is gentler now. 'Because if I have, just give me a chance and I'll put it right. I'll do whatever I have to.'

'You haven't done anything. Not to me. But—'

'But what?' He takes her hand.

'Did you set fire to Liam Curtis's summer house?' Sophie believes in being direct; it saves a lot of time and hassle. 'And then your dad paid them off to keep quiet?'

Charlie screws up his face. 'What? No! Is that what he said? Jesus, Soph. And my dad would never cover for me even if I *had* done it. Why are you listening to Liam?'

'He didn't say anything. I just heard a rumour.'

His eyes narrow. 'I know you're good friends – it must have been him. And no doubt he spewed a load of lies about me and Andrea. What did he say?'

'Nothing.'

'If he told you I liked Andrea, he's lying.'

'I didn't say—'

'Look, do you like me?'

Charlie's eyes implore her, and Sophie finds it flattering. This is a guy who's probably never had to beg for anything, yet right now it feels as though he's begging for her. 'Yes,' she says. 'I do.' *But.* There a thousand buts she could list, but the words lodge in her throat.

He leans in and kisses her; it's gentle and tender and makes her feel as though she's floating. When he finally pulls away, his touch lingers on her lips. 'People always like to talk shit about me,' he says. 'Because of who I am. There's a lot of jealousy because of everything my family has. They see us as having this amazing life where we can do what we like. And do you know what's so unfair? My mum tries her best to do good in this village. She goes above and beyond for these people, and all the while, snakes like Liam shout their mouths off and try to blacken our family name.'

Sophie strokes his arm. 'We can go to that restaurant. This Friday?' She doesn't add that she'd be happy with a peanut butter sandwich – fancy restaurants and posh food don't mean anything to her. 'On second thoughts, how about a takeaway instead?'

Charlie's eyes widen. 'A takeaway?' He shrugs. 'If that's what the lady wants...'

Sophie giggles. 'It is.'

Charlie suggests they watch a movie, while Orla's still napping, and they trawl through her mum's DVD collection.

'All of these are so old,' Sophie says, wrinkling her nose.

'I don't care about the film,' Charlie says, pulling one out and slotting the disc in the DVD player. 'It's nice just being with you.'

And as they settle on the sofa to watch, Charlie's arm

draped around her shoulders, Sophie can't stop thinking about Liam and what he told her about the fire. As if her thoughts have summoned him, her phone beeps with a text message from him.

She slips her phone in her pocket and turns back to the television.

'And what does Liam want?' Charlie asks, staring at the TV.

Sophie shrugs. 'Don't know – haven't read it. Let's just watch the movie.'

'Yeah,' Charlie says. He pulls her in tightly, his arms pressing heavily around her.

FIFTEEN

'It's good news that you can go home today,' PC Marsden says, smiling at me.

I try to nod, but even that small gesture causes my neck to spasm, pain surging through my whole body.

'And your partner's picking you up – is that right?'

I'm fully dressed, sitting on the bed, itching to leave this place, even though the thought of going back to the farmhouse – cold and devoid of any soul – fills me with dread. 'Yes, he is,' I say, unsure how or why she even knows this.

'Well, I won't keep you long.' She glances around the room. 'I'm sure you just want to get back to the comfort of your own home. Nice that you got your own room here, though.'

The nurse had told me this morning that Heather had paid for it, insisting I should have my own space. I would never have agreed to this, but I was so out of it last night that it was taken out of my hands. 'Yep, I'm very lucky.' Again, I nod, bracing myself for the pain.

'Understandably, you weren't able to tell us much yesterday,' PC Marsden says. 'Can you talk me through what you remember?'

Despite the knock to my head, it's all clear until the moment I hit the ground. 'I was riding my bike. Going into the village.'

'Any particular reason?' PC Marsden tilts her head.

To get away from Charlie. 'Just to get some groceries. Get some fresh air. I love cycling. The next thing I knew, a car had ploughed into me. It seemed to come from nowhere – the roads had been quiet up until then.'

PC Marsden nods. 'Yes, you were very fortunate not to have broken anything, or worse.'

'It wasn't an accident,' I say. 'I was knocked off deliberately.'

'And what makes you think that?'

'Because that road isn't narrow. Nothing was coming in the other direction – there was plenty of space for that car to pass me without going anywhere near me. And before you ask, I didn't see what make it was. Or the colour. It happened too fast.'

'Someone could have just not been paying attention,' PC Marsden says. 'Maybe they were on their phone, and that's why they didn't stick around. Worried we'd find out they were texting. All sorts of trouble for that.'

This is possible, but I know it was deliberate, even if I'll never be able to convince the police of that.

'Either way, though,' she continues, 'it's a serious offence to leave the scene of an accident like that. Don't worry, we'll find out who did it.'

'Is there any CCTV?'

'Not on that stretch of road, but we're checking all the cameras further along.'

I glance at the door. Charlie was supposed to pick me up half an hour ago. 'Do you know what's happened to my bike?' I ask.

'Doesn't appear to be salvageable. I'm sorry. But we need to keep it for our investigation. Do you have insurance?'

'No,' I say. 'I've never needed it.'

'Well, when we find out who did this, they'll be liable to pay damages. I know it's easy for me to say this, but just try to focus on what didn't happen, rather than what did. You survived this.' PC Marsden stands. 'That's what matters. We'll be in touch, but if you do remember anything, please give us a call.'

Edwin appears in the doorway moments after she leaves. 'How's the patient?' he asks, stepping inside. 'Heather sends her love – she's got a doctor's appointment in London, but she sent me to make sure you're okay. What a worry!'

'I'm fine, thanks.'

'And are they looking after you here? If not, you let me know straight away. I have a lot of contacts here.'

'Thanks, Edwin.'

'Now, I hope that son of mine's on his way to take you home? If not, I can take you.'

There's a knock on the door, and we turn to see Khalid standing there. 'Okay if I come in?' he asks. He shakes Edwin's hand, then gives him a hug. 'Good to see you again.'

'Yes, shame about these circumstances. I can't believe people would do this. Accidents happen, but at least own up to them. It's sickening.'

I'm so shocked to see Khalid that it takes me a moment to answer. 'Hi, Khalid.'

'Good and bad news, I'm afraid.' He pauses. 'Er, Charlie's had to rush to an emergency meeting, so he asked me to pick you up. Hope that's okay?'

Charlie is avoiding me again. He must know I've been waiting to confront him about why he took two hours to get to the hospital last night. 'Thanks,' I say to Khalid. 'But Edwin's offered me a lift.'

Khalid smiles. 'Edwin, please let me. You've got a house to sort out, and I know Heather will want things perfect for the housewarming party.'

Edwin rolls his eyes. 'Yes, she's even written me a long list.

Just between us, I think being a surgeon is easier!' He laughs, then leans down to hug me. 'I'll leave you in Khalid's capable hands then. But you just call if you need anything at all.'

When he's gone, I tell Khalid that I can easily get a taxi.

'I'm afraid I'm under strict instructions to get you home safely. Charlie's orders. Besides, the hospital won't let you leave on your own, and because you've had head trauma, someone has to stay with you for twenty-four hours. In case...' He leaves that thought unfinished.

'There's no point arguing with you, is there?' I say.

'Nope.' He points to the bag that Charlie brought in for me. 'Let me grab that.'

Stepping outside, it feels as though I haven't breathed in fresh air for weeks, rather than just hours. Khalid opens the door for me, and I ease myself in, wincing at the pain even the smallest movements cause.

Khalid makes pleasant small talk on the way home, but I'm only half tuned in, until he asks me if I've spoken to Charlie this morning.

'Only by text. He didn't reply to my last one asking where he was. And he didn't let me know you were coming.'

Khalid frowns. 'When I spoke to him he said it was all kicking off at work.' He glances at me. 'I'm just a bit worried.'

'Charlie thrives on the stress of work. He never seems able to switch off. He'll be fine. I'd be more worried if he wasn't busy at work.'

'No, it's not that.'

I stare at Khalid, who keeps his eyes fixed on the road. 'What do you mean?'

'Last night, we had a drink at the Hurtwood. Well, a few drinks. Charlie just seemed to need it. He was really tense. Not surprising, when you were in hospital. But...' He turns to me again for a brief moment then focuses back on the road.

'Just say it, Khalid, please. What's going on?'

He drums his fingers on the steering wheel. 'He got a bit... let's just say paralytic. I've never seen him so drunk. But I didn't say anything because I knew how upset he must have been about your accident.'

Upset that I survived? I don't want to believe this. Is Charlie right, and my dad's attack has silently traumatised me? My breath catches in my throat, a hard lump blocking my airways.

'But when I questioned him about it – and please keep in mind that he was barely coherent – he was mumbling, almost talking to himself. He could hardly even focus on me. But... he kept mentioning... Sophie.'

The name shatters through the air like a bullet. *Sophie.*

'I asked him what he was talking about, and he just kept repeating her name. And that... he'd do anything to change things and be able to bring her back.'

I open the window and stick my head out, desperate for fresh air.

'Are you okay?' Khalid asks. 'Shall I pull over?'

'No... don't. Keep going. I just want to get home.'

'I've never seen him like that before,' Khalid says. 'He was like a different person. I know I haven't seen him for years, but still. It wasn't Charlie.'

'Alcohol brings the truth to the surface,' I say, staring ahead. 'What do you think he meant?'

'I don't know. I thought maybe coming back here just brought up all the memories of Sophie, but the way he phrased it just doesn't sound right. He'd do anything to change things and be able to bring her back. It just seems—'

'As if he knows what happened to her.'

Silence hangs over us, eerie and deafening. I've got nothing to lose now by telling Khalid what I found, and what I think.

By the time we've reached the house, he knows all about the messages carved in the basement that suddenly disappeared, the locked door that Charlie claims wasn't locked at all, and my suspicions about my bike accident.

He's silent for a moment, his mouth twisting as he tries to make sense of what I've said. 'I can't explain any of that,' Khalid says, 'But I owe the Hollingers everything. I wouldn't have pursued my career if it wasn't for their encouragement. I don't want to believe Charlie would do any of those things. But there was something in his eyes last night that... frightened me. They were... vacant – there was nothing there. No warmth, no heart. Nothing. Which was even stranger because he was talking about Sophie. The girl he loved.' He grimaces. 'Sorry.'

'You don't need to apologise. I have no issue whatsoever with Charlie having loved Sophie. Please believe me.'

'But now you're worried he did something to her?' Khalid asks.

'Aren't you?'

His shoulders hunch. 'I don't know what to think. One thing's apparent, though – I don't know Charlie any more. All these years we haven't seen each other have eroded our friendship.' Khalid stares at the house. 'So many memories in that place. And now I don't even know what's real.' He turns back to me. 'I brought him home in a cab last night – even came in the house to make sure he was going to be okay and didn't choke on his own vomit or hurt himself any other way. Then when I called him this morning, he couldn't remember anything. Said he remembers having a drink at the Hurtwood but nothing else. And he was so... *normal.*' He sighs. 'Told me he was really worried about you and asked if I could pick you up and stay with you until he got home. It made me start doubting myself. I can't bring myself to believe that Charlie knows what happened to Sophie, let alone that he actually did something to her. But now those doubts are back again, and I just can't reconcile the man I saw last night with the Charlie I know.'

'He's not the man I know either,' I say. 'And I think he's

trying to stop me finding out what happened to Sophie. Being knocked off my bike wasn't an accident.'

Khalid shakes his head. 'You think that was Charlie?'

'I don't know. I don't want to believe the man I love would try to hurt me. Or that he was capable of hurting Sophie. All I can do is work with what I know. And I don't think his relationship with Sophie was what everyone thought it was. Do you know anything about that?'

Khalid avoids looking at me, staring out of the window. 'I suppose no one really knows what goes on in a relationship when two people are alone,' he says.

And I know that more than most. 'At least you're getting out of here on Monday. Back to your life in America, far from all of this.'

He closes his eyes. 'But the Hollingers are family to me. How can I take all this stuff about Charlie with me and not tell them? Edwin and Heather deserve to know if there's even the smallest chance that Charlie...' He lets his sentence hang unfinished.

'There's no real proof of anything,' I say. 'Not yet. But I'll get it. And then everyone will know, including the police. Look, I'm going inside now – I need to rest before the housewarming party this evening.'

Khalid turns to me. 'Surely you're not going to that? Heather will understand – you've just been in hospital.'

'There's no way I'm missing it.' I need to see how Charlie behaves. Perhaps the best place to confront him is when he's with his family.

Khalid checks his watch. 'I suppose you've got some time to rest before it starts. Come on, then.'

'No, I'd like to be alone.'

'I'm not leaving you. You need to be with someone for twenty-four hours, remember? And I'm a doctor, so there's no way I'm—'

'Okay, but I hope you've got something to do – I need to sleep, and it will be a long afternoon sitting in that empty house on your own.'

Khalid reaches to the back seat of the car and pulls out a book. 'Never leave home without one,' he says.

My eyes shoot open, and I'm disorientated as I take in my surroundings. I should be used to waking up in this house – it's been a week now – but having to stay in hospital last night has thrown me off course.

Voices drift from downstairs, Khalid's and someone else's – female. I pull the covers off and slide my feet into my trainers, listening at the bedroom door. The female voice is too quiet for me to make out who Khalid is talking to.

I tiptoe downstairs, but then the voices stop, and everything falls silent. Nobody leaves the room, though, so I continue down, wincing in pain with each step.

Throwing open the living room door, I stare in disbelief as I take in what I'm seeing: Khalid with his arms wrapped around a woman, her head nuzzling into his neck, her hand spread across his chest.

Vanessa Hollinger.

SIXTEEN

Vanessa's head jolts up, her eyes wide with shock as she gapes at me. Khalid, too, looks shaken.

'Emmie... I'm sorry,' Khalid says, breaking the silence. 'We thought you were asleep, and... Vanessa just came over. We—'

'You don't have to explain,' I say, stepping into the room. 'But why the big secret?' As far as I'm aware, both of them are single.

'It's difficult,' Khalid explains, taking Vanessa's hand. 'As much as I love Heather and Edwin, when it comes to Vanessa, they—'

'They don't think I'm capable of making my own decisions,' Vanessa says, staring at her trainers. 'I'm a thirty-five-year-old woman, and I have to run everything by my parents. Where I live, where I go. What I do. Everything. They keep going on and on, trying to force me to tell them who I'm staying with in London. But I won't give in.'

'This is awful,' I say, trying to fit what I've seen of Edwin and Heather with this new information. It doesn't make sense.

'It's complicated,' Khalid says. 'Vanessa had a depressive episode a few years ago, and they just want to keep her safe.'

'Keep me a prisoner,' Vanessa says, this time looking right at me.

Khalid turns to her and strokes her cheek.

'It's okay,' Vanessa says, 'you can tell her.'

Khalid takes a deep breath. 'A few years ago, Vanessa tried to jump off a bridge in Dubai. It took a lot of people, and the police, to talk her down, and then she tried to run in front of a car. She was sectioned and spent some time in a private hospital.'

'Paid for by dear Mummy and Daddy,' Vanessa says, snorting. 'But I didn't need to be there – I just needed to be *heard*. No one would listen to me. Not then and not now.'

I sit on the sofa next to Vanessa. 'I'm sorry you've been through that.'

'They treat me like a child. Eyes on me all the time. It's hell on earth. Do you know what it's like to be watched all the time? By your own family? And now that we're back here, Myles and Charlie are just as bad.'

I glance at Khalid. 'But they like you,' I say. 'Why do you have to keep this a secret.'

'Sure, they like me as Charlie's friend, but if they knew Vanessa and I are seeing each other, they'd start looking at me through a different lens.'

'But—'

'It's true,' Vanessa says.

I've become so used to her reticence that when she actually speaks she's like a different woman.

'Khalid only got here a few days ago – have you only just got together?'

'I contacted Vanessa around a year ago,' Khalid explains. 'To see how she was doing. And we've been talking since then. Pretty much every day. And I flew to Dubai several times to see her – Edwin and Heather had no idea I was there.'

'I'm sure they—'

'You don't know how protective they are over Vanessa. Over all the kids really, but Vanessa more so.'

'Please don't tell anyone,' Vanessa begs. 'Khalid is the only good thing in my life, and I don't want anyone ruining things for us. Even Charlie and Myles can't know.'

'I've been sorting things so Vanessa can come and live in America with me,' Khalid says. 'And they'd never let her go if they knew. They just don't think she can be independent without them – but they're wrong.'

Even though Khalid is convinced of this, and I've seen another side of Vanessa now, I still don't understand how he can be so sure. 'Surely Edwin and Heather have had doctors check you?' I ask Vanessa.

'Yes, and they've all said the same thing – I'm not able to make decisions for myself. And I can't be trusted not to slash these.' She holds up her wrists and mimes slicing into them. 'But that incident on the bridge was years ago, and I've done nothing since then. I've been supporting myself too. I started painting in Dubai, and I'm quite good at it. I've even sold some of my paintings online. I don't make loads, but it's enough to live on. I don't want my parents' money – I never have. All I've ever wanted is to be left alone. To be allowed to be *me*.'

'I won't say anything to anyone. I promise. But I need something from you in return, Vanessa.'

Vanessa glances at Khalid, who places his hand on her shoulder. 'Okay,' she says, clasping her hands together. 'What?'

'I want to know the truth about Charlie's and Sophie Bower's relationship. And I think you're the person who can tell me what that is. I know you were good friends.'

Vanessa takes a deep breath, then looks up at the ceiling. 'I can't believe I'm saying this out loud,' she says. 'I haven't said it to anyone – not even Khalid.' She takes his hand. 'I've tried to bury it, pretend it's not possible that it happened.' She looks down at her feet again. 'I love my brother. We were always so close.'

Khalid frowns. 'What are you saying, Vanessa?'

She takes her time to answer, and when she finally speaks, her words come out with no hesitation. 'I heard them having an argument. It was a while before she disappeared. He was accusing her of all sorts of things. They were round the side of the farmhouse so didn't know I was there, but I'd just come home. I'd never heard him so angry. And... I think Charlie might have had something to do with Sophie disappearing.'

My body aches and is covered in mulberry-coloured bruises, but I manage to slip on a black midi dress. Heather and Edwin have gone all out for this housewarming party, and even though they've insisted that I need to stay home and rest, I'm determined to show my face. There will be others there, people who might know things about Sophie and Charlie.

I turn to watch Charlie picking out a tie from his vast selection, standing with his towel wrapped around him, ready to get in the shower. I can't help thinking dressing up this much is a bit over the top for a family housewarming party. I say this to Charlie; provoking him is the only way I'll expose the true man beneath his fake demeanour.

Since I was hit by that car, Charlie hasn't once mentioned the argument we had leading up to it, but the tension between us still simmers, threatening to boil over.

'It's not just family,' Charlie explains. 'My parents have got old friends coming too. This is important to them. I just hope Vanessa doesn't embarrass everyone.' He puts back the tie he's chosen and goes through them all again.

Vanessa had shut down after she'd dropped her bombshell about Charlie. Khalid and I questioned her, but she withdrew into herself, and the self-assured Vanessa I'd been talking to disappeared. Which makes me wonder if Khalid is right to trust that Vanessa's mind is healthy.

'Why did you take two hours to get to the hospital yesterday when I was hit by that car?'

Charlie doesn't flinch. 'I didn't. I came straight away.'

'Liam said you didn't turn up for two hours.'

'Liam?' Charlie turns to me, his face hardening. 'And why would you listen to him? He's probably just trying to cause conflict between us. Can't you see that?'

'Why would he do that?'

'Because he can't stand me.'

'All because of a girl you went to school with sixteen years ago.' I shake my head.

Charlie walks over to me and places his hands on my shoulders. 'Listen, Emmie, you had a nasty bump to your head. I think you need to rest. It's bound to have affected your memory, or how you're seeing things. Head trauma can cause all kinds of personality changes.'

'I'm fine,' I say. 'I've never seen things more clearly. And I know someone deliberately ran into me.'

Charlie stares at me. 'Emmie. We don't know that, there's no—'

'What did you do after I left?'

Turning away, Charlie walks towards the en suite, pausing in the doorway. 'I didn't do anything. I just had a glass of wine. I needed to calm down. It felt like I was being attacked... and we were falling apart. Like before.'

'This is not like before,' I say. *Because now I know I can't just walk away.*

'It feels like it,' he says, finally looking at me. 'And this time it's you who's pulling away from me.'

I step towards him, frustrated that my injuries mean I'm not as strong as I need to be right now. I'm so close to him that I can smell the aftershave he must have put on this morning. It's not his usual one – this new scent is as unknown to me as Charlie is.

'I can't trust you,' I whisper, even though we're alone.

'Emmie, please.'

And then with all the strength I can muster, I leave the bedroom.

Standing in the hallway for a moment, I wait until Charlie has shut the bathroom door and turned on the shower, and then I make my way to his study. He still hasn't unpacked anything, and five large boxes are stacked against the wall. Closing the door behind me, I open the first one, rifling through all the paperwork that doesn't look work-related. It's the house I'm interested in. Technically, this place is mine too – the house is in both our names – and if I leave Charlie now, I would be entitled to half the money we'd get from selling it. I don't want any money from any of the Hollingers, but I would give it to Lynette and Orla. It won't make up for their daughter disappearing, but if Charlie has got anything to do with it, then this would be the least I could do for them.

Anxious that Charlie could finish his shower any moment and come looking for me, I work faster, scanning file names until I finally find one labelled *HOUSE*. I rifle through it until I find the title deed. I've never bought a property before – I've always rented – so I'm unsure what I'll need to show to a solicitor, but this seems like a good place to start.

My breath catches in my throat as I flick through the document, scanning each page in case I've missed something.

But there's no mistaking it – this farmhouse belongs only to Charlie, and my name is nowhere on the title deed.

SEVENTEEN

Charlie and I barely speak on the way to Edwin and Heather's new house. It's in Shere, the next village, and Charlie speeds along winding, narrow roads, so close to the cars passing on the other side that I clutch the seat and grit my teeth. But I stay silent. I might have been able to dismiss as coincidence all the things that have happened so far, but not now. Now, I realise that Charlie has planned all along that we would never own this home together. Why, though? Why would he get me to move here, all the while pretending *he* never wanted to come back to Peaslake? What does he want with me?

My stomach tightens, and I wind down the car window, letting in humid air that does little to calm me.

I turn to look at him, and he smiles at me; the same charming smile he used on me the last time we fell apart. But this time everything is different.

There are already several cars parked outside the house when we arrive. It's a detached new build with a sprawling front garden. It's half the size of the farmhouse, and lacks character, but it's immaculate. Charlie grabs my hand tightly as we walk up the drive. I know it's for show – to prove to his parents that we are okay, although I can't work out why that's important to him. A few months ago he was ready to throw us away, yet now he's clinging to me as if his life depends on it. Our confrontation earlier must have unsettled him.

'Darling!' Heather opens the door, holding a glass of champagne. 'I thought you'd be here by now. Everyone's already arrived.' She looks elegant in a white embroidered maxi dress with angel sleeves.

'Sorry,' Charlie says. 'We just had to make sure Emmie was well enough to come.'

Heather takes my hand. 'My dear, you really shouldn't have worried about coming. Everyone would understand. You need to be resting. Charlie, you should have insisted Emmie stay at home to recover.'

'I'm fine, Heather,' I insist. 'It will take a lot more than being knocked off my bike to stop me living my life.' Almost imperceptibly, Charlie tightens his grip on my hand.

'Still, you must take it easy this evening.' She smiles. 'So many people are here. Do you remember the Fosters?' she asks Charlie.

'I think so.'

'Well, they've come all the way from Brighton.'

'Who else is here?' Charlie asks.

'Lots of our old friends. Come in and you'll find out,' Heather says.

Sensing Charlie's hesitation, I pull him forward, leading him into the house. It's modern inside, in complete contrast to the farmhouse.

'Well, what do you think of the house?' Heather says. 'We really want it to be a place where you and Charlie – and any little additions to the family – feel welcome.' She beams and squeezes my hand.

'It's lovely,' I say.

Heather smiles. 'I know it lacks character. But as soon as it's filled with plants and ornaments, it will feel more homely.'

Charlie makes a comment about being surprised Heather hasn't already bought up half of Harrods, but I'm only half listening as I spot Edwin at the end of the hallway talking to Lynette Bower.

Charlie notices her at the same time and stops talking. His face pales as he turns to his mother. 'Why is Lynette here?' he whispers.

'Your father ran into her the other day, so he invited her. Why don't you go and say hello – I'm sure she'd love to see you.' Heather ushers him forward, and I watch as Charlie takes slow steps towards Lynette, who still hasn't realised we're here.

'That's Sophie's mother,' Heather explains. 'The girl who went missing. So sad that we still don't know what happened to her.'

'I've met Lynette,' I say, my eyes still fixed on Charlie. Lynette is hugging him now, and even from this distance I can see her eyes well up, while Charlie looks frozen.

'Where?' Heather asks.

'Her mum answered my ad in the Village Stores. I'm working with her daughter, Orla.'

'How wonderful that you found some work,' Heather says. 'They're a lovely family.' She sighs. 'And Sophie was a lovely girl. We very much saw her as a daughter.'

Lynette glances over and waves, so I wave back.

'Well, I must mingle with the other guests,' Heather says. 'I'll let Charlie introduce you to everyone.'

She flounces off into the kitchen, and I make my way over to Charlie and Lynette.

'Lynette was just telling me you've already met,' Charlie says, grabbing my hand.

Lynette briefly registers his action, but she says nothing.

'Yes. I'm going to be working with Orla,' I say.

'You never mentioned that,' Charlie says.

'It's only just happened,' Lynette says, glancing at me. 'And you poor thing, Emmie, I can't believe you were knocked off your bike like that. Charlie just told me.'

'Emmie really shouldn't be here,' Charlie says before I can answer. 'She's supposed to be resting.'

Ignoring him, Lynette places her hand on my arm. 'Just take care of yourself. If tonight gets too much, then I'm sure Heather and Edwin won't mind you leaving. I can always drive you home.'

'Thanks, but no need,' Charlie says. 'I'm ready to take Emmie home whenever she wants to leave.'

'I won't be leaving early,' I insist. 'I've got people to meet. Peaslake is my home now, and I want to get to know everyone, whether they still live here or not.' I smile at Charlie.

'Orla's here somewhere,' Lynette says. 'I have to say – I don't know what you both spoke about the other day, but it's done her the world of good. She's really brightened up.'

'I didn't really say anything,' I say, pulling my hand away from Charlie's. 'It was more of a getting to know each other chat.'

'Well, whatever you said – thank you. Right, I'd better go and make sure she's okay.' Lynette turns to Charlie. 'It was lovely to see you after all this time,' she says. 'I hope you'll love living back here.'

As soon as she's gone, Charlie takes my hand again. 'You don't look well,' he says. 'You shouldn't have come here.'

'I wouldn't have missed it for anything,' I say, forcing a smile. 'That must have been strange for you – seeing Lynette again.'

He shrugs. 'It's been a long time, Emmie. You seem to be dwelling on it more than anyone who was around at the time.'

'Of course I am,' I hiss, keeping my voice low. 'After all your lies and what I found in the basement.'

Charlie ignores me, as if I haven't spoken. 'Will you at least go and rest?' he says. 'Your body can't be up to this. There's a sofa in Dad's office, and I can make sure no one disturbs you.'

I walk off without a word, and head to the living room where most of the guests are gathered.

Edwin jumps up from his seat and beckons me over. He looks dapper in his dark grey suit, and his hair looks freshly cut. 'Emmie, my dear. How are you feeling?'

'I'm doing okay.'

He gives me a hug. 'I still can't believe this happened.'

'I'm sure the police will track down whoever hit me,' I say.

He nods. 'Yes, and the sooner the better. That's the thing about life, isn't it – the truth always comes out in the end. But let's just be grateful that you weren't more seriously injured, or worse.'

'I am,' I assure him.

He pats my arm. 'I admire your strength of character, Emmie. The fact that you're here tonight for us. It means a lot to Heather and me.' He smiles, and for a moment I feel bad that my relationship with Charlie is teetering on the edge of a precipice. Edwin seems like a decent man, and he's not responsible for his son's actions. 'It's funny,' he says, 'but until he met you, we were all a bit worried about Charlie. Never settling down with anyone long enough for us to get to know them. He'd abandon women almost as soon as he met them. Not how I wanted my son to act. But I can tell it's very different with you. He's finally met someone he can see a future with.' Edwin pats my arm. 'Thank you – for whatever it is you do that makes him so happy.'

In my mind I see the farmhouse title deed, Charlie's name standing alone on the page. The sole legal owner. Yet I had signed all the paperwork – and I'd read through it meticulously, poring over every word to be absolutely sure. 'Can I ask you something, Edwin?'

'Of course. Anything. You're part of the family now.'

'What made you give the house to Charlie now? You could have done it years ago.'

'Because it's only now we see he's settled down. We didn't want just anyone owning it with him. It had to be someone Charlie was serious about.' He smiles again. 'I can't tell you how happy and proud it makes me to see you two together.'

'But it's not really my house,' I say. 'Not legally, I mean.'

'What do you mean?' Edwin asks.

'Charlie only wanted his name on it. I guess it was a precaution in case our relationship didn't work out.'

Edwin frowns. 'Well, that's strange. Heather and I thought it was for both of you. Well, you mustn't worry about that. It's clear that Charlie has every intention for your relationship to last'

I want to tell Edwin that he's wrong, but I'm still trying to make sense of why Charlie would lie to his parents about this. 'What about Myles or Vanessa? Couldn't they have had the house?'

'Myles didn't want to move from Leeds. Can't understand that myself, but I suppose he's made a life for himself there. And Vanessa...' He sighs, and then his shoulders sag. 'I think she's a long way off sorting herself out. But they got the equivalent value in money. We've always tried to be fair with the kids.'

'Don't underestimate Vanessa,' I say, the words slipping from my mouth with no warning.

Edwin frowns. 'What do you mean?'

'I just think sometimes people aren't who we think they are. They can be capable of so much more than we give them credit for.'

Edwin studies me for a moment before he finally speaks. 'I only wish that were true, Emmie,' he says.

'There you are.' Charlie appears beside me and takes my arm, leaning down to kiss my cheek. 'How are you feeling?'

It's all I can do not to wriggle out of his grasp. 'I feel fine,' I lie.

Charlie puts his arm around me, and there's no way Edwin will notice how tight his grip is.

'You're blessed to have this lovely lady in your life,' Edwin says, patting Charlie on the back. 'Don't mess it up.' He laughs, but I sense that it's just to mask how earnest his words are.

'I need some water,' I say. 'If you'll excuse me.'

On the way to the kitchen I bump into Orla coming out of the downstairs toilet. 'Are you okay?' she says. 'I wanted to come and see you, but Mum said I should give you some space. What happened, Emmie?'

'A hit and run.' At only seventeen, Orla is still a child, so there's no way I will tell her it was deliberate.

'This is why I hate people,' she says. 'I'm glad you're okay, though.' She scans the hallway to make sure we're alone. 'What about Charlie?' she whispers.

'He's not just going to tell me the truth. I need to find a way to make him talk. I think Vanessa might be able to help me.'

'Vanessa? But isn't she crazy?'

'Orla, that's not true. And she knows her brother better than anyone.'

Orla shrugs. 'If you say so. 'I was thinking – if Charlie was away when my sister disappeared, then he must have had help. Khalid was his best friend at the time – so he could easily know something.'

'Have you met Khalid?'

'Not until tonight. And I've been watching him – it's like he's part of the Hollinger family. Have you seen the way Heather and Edwin fawn over him? Like he's their son.'

'I think he *is* like a son to them. That doesn't mean anything.'

'It means Khalid is so close to Charlie that he could have easily helped him do something to my sister.'

I peer into the living room and see Khalid talking to Vanessa, looking like they're consciously trying to keep some distance between them.

'I don't know,' I say. 'I don't see it. But then it's good to keep an open mind.'

Lynette appears from the kitchen. 'I've got a bit of a headache, so I might head off now. Is that okay, Orla?'

'I might stick around for a bit. I'll get an Uber home.'

'I'd rather you came with me,' Lynette says.

I notice the fear in her eyes; she doesn't want to lose another daughter. Yet staying here any longer must be too painful for Lynette. 'I think you should go with your mum, Orla,' I say. 'Let's catch up tomorrow.' I give her a nod, hoping she'll understand how important this is.

'Yeah, think I'll come with you, Mum. This party's boring as hell anyway.'

I find the kitchen empty, and I fill a glass with tap water to try to stop the dull ache in my head. Someone taps me on the shoulder, and I spin around to see Vanessa.

'Sorry, I didn't mean to scare you,' she says, staring at me. She lowers her voice. 'I wanted to thank you for not saying anything to Charlie about me and Khalid. I know you didn't – he definitely would have questioned me about it.'

'I told you I wouldn't. But you shouldn't need their permission, Vanessa. You and Khalid love each other – that's nobody else's business.'

Vanessa pulls out a chair and flops onto it. 'I never thought I'd be capable of loving anyone again,' she says. 'After Caleb.' She lowers her eyes and runs her hands over the marble on the table. 'I'm guessing Charlie's never mentioned him?'

'No, he hasn't.' Intrigued to hear her story, I join her at the table.

'That's the thing about my brother. About all of them. They

seem to think the past can be erased if it's inconvenient and doesn't fit how you want to be perceived.'

'Who was Caleb?' I ask.

'He was the only man I've ever loved before now. I was nineteen and he was thirty-one. I kept him a secret from my family because I knew they wouldn't accept him.'

'Because of the age gap?'

She hesitates. 'No, because of his troubled background. He didn't come from money – the complete opposite, in fact. He basically grew up on the streets. But he was a good person, Emmie. I would never have fallen for him otherwise. Never. But to my family, it would have caused a huge scandal. Vanessa Hollinger dating an ex-drug dealer.'

'So what happened?'

'We kept it a secret, but I think my brothers must have found out and told my parents.' She glances at the door. 'I know I don't have proof, and they've never said anything about it, but I think they paid him to stay away from me.' She takes a deep breath. 'One day I got a text message from Caleb telling me he couldn't see me any more, that it wasn't fair on me.' A tear trickles down her face. 'I tried to call him back, but he switched his phone off, and then he must have changed his number. I never heard from him again.'

I frown. 'But what makes you think they paid him off?'

'Because I know he loved me... and money was the only thing that could have tempted him. He didn't really have a home, and all he wanted was to be able to buy his own place. They probably set him up in a huge house somewhere far from me.' Her tears fall faster now.

'I'm sorry that happened,' I say. 'And not having any answers makes it even harder to deal with, I'm sure. But you have Khalid now – just focus on that. You'll be with him in America soon.'

'We leave on Monday, and I'm never looking back,' she says.

And for the first time since I met Vanessa in person, there's a glimmer of peace in her eyes. 'You need to get away from here too,' she says.

I pause, still unsure how much I can trust what Vanessa is telling me. 'I know, but first I need to find out what happened to Sophie.'

Vanessa stares at me. 'Sophie? Why do you care?'

Before I can answer, the kitchen door opens and Khalid appears, glancing behind him. He smiles at Vanessa, then shuts the door. 'Charlie's looking for you, Emmie,' he says.

'Actually, I think I need to get home. My head isn't good. I'll get an Uber. Can one of you let Charlie know I've gone? I don't want a big fuss.'

'I'll drive you,' Khalid says. 'I haven't been drinking tonight.'

'No, it's fine, honestly.'

Vanessa shakes her head. 'You don't know Khalid. There's no way he'll let you make your own way home, so you may as well accept his offer.'

Khalid shrugs and pulls out his car keys. 'Shall I go and let Charlie know?'

I glance at Vanessa. 'No. Not yet. Can we just go now?'

'You can slip out of the side door,' Vanessa says. 'He won't see you leave.'

In the car, I question Khalid about everything Vanessa has just told me.

'I know all about Caleb,' he says. 'I didn't at the time, but Vanessa told me when I went to see her in Dubai. It really messed with her head.'

'Do you really think the Hollingers paid him off? You know Edwin and Heather well. It seems a bit extreme.'

Khalid shrugs. 'Please don't tell Vanessa this, but I don't think they would have done that. I could be wrong, but it's possible Vanessa struggled to come to terms with her relationship ending. Maybe it helps Vanessa to believe her version of events? And if that's what she needs, then I'm not going to try to convince her otherwise. It was sixteen years ago – it's in the past.'

'And is Sophie in the past? Best not talked about? Why is everyone so quick to ignore what happened? She was seventeen. Basically a *child*.'

'No... that's not what I'm doing. I really cared about Sophie. But if the police couldn't work out what happened to her, then how can anyone else?'

Orla's words ring in my ears. Could Charlie have involved Khalid in Sophie's disappearance? I don't know him – am I foolish to trust him?

We arrive at the farmhouse, and Khalid tells me he thinks he should come in with me.

'I'll be fine.'

He unclicks his seatbelt and gets out of the car, coming around to my side and opening the door. I'm touched by his gesture, even though I don't want or need help. 'Let me give you my number,' he says. 'And if you're worried about anything at all you can call me. I'm around until Monday. I'm counting the days until I can get Vanessa away from here.'

He walks me to the front door, and we exchange numbers.

'What are you going to do about Charlie?' Khalid asks.

'I'm going to get the truth from him,' I say, opening the front door. 'About everything.' Before I step inside, I turn back to him. 'Are you sure Vanessa is... okay? I know you're a doctor, but—'

'I've never been more certain of anything,' he says. 'And it's not because I'm blinded by love or anything, although I do love her. I see the real Vanessa, the person she never shows to her family because she's terrified they won't accept her, or believe that she's okay. Yes, she's had some troubles. Sophie disappearing like that threw her life into turmoil. She'll be fine once we're away from here and she can have some breathing space. America will be a fresh start for her.'

I admire his faith in her and hope it works out for them.

'Well, I'll get back to the party before someone notices I've gone,' he says. 'I'll pop in tomorrow and check on you. Goodnight, Emmie.'

Once I've shut the door on the outside world, the farmhouse feels cold and sinister. I make my way to the basement and stare down at the brand-new flooring and walls that have replaced the room it used to be. Eradicated its existence. I'm not safe in this house, yet I can't leave. There is unfinished business, and I'm determined to find out what happened to Sophie Bower. And whether Charlie is responsible. Vanessa blurted out that she thinks Charlie had something to do with Sophie disappearing, but even after this first strange and unsettling week in Peaslake, do I really believe I've been sleeping with a murderer?

Shutting the basement door, forcing out images of my father bleeding to death in his own basement, I make myself a cup of camomile tea and take it up to bed, keeping my dressing gown on as I slip under the covers. This house will never be warm, literally and metaphorically, and I need to make sure I'm not still living in it when winter comes.

I read for an hour, until my eyes begin to feel heavy, and just as I put my book down, a WhatsApp message comes through from Charlie.

Had a bit too much to drink. Will spend the night here. Sorry. Love you. See you in the morning.

I should be annoyed with Charlie for not coming back home when I've just been knocked off my bike, but all I feel is relief. When he's not here, I don't have to pretend, or worry about what I'm saying. I'm comforted by this thought as I drift to sleep.

. . .

I shoot up, my eyes struggling to adjust to the darkness. It must still be night; there's no sunlight streaming through the windows. There's a shadow in the bedroom doorway – someone is watching me. I jump up, reaching for the bedside lamp – the only thing I can use to defend myself.

Then when I turn back to the door, I realise who is there, watching me.

Vanessa.

EIGHTEEN
NOVEMBER 2008

Every morning when Sophie stands in front of the mirror, staring at her reflection as she cleanses her skin, she's annoyed that she's let herself fall into this relationship with Charlie. She does like him, and they definitely have strong chemistry, but she feels trapped, worried that she'll never be able to leave Peaslake now that they're together. But she's going to university soon, and she changed her application so that she'll be in Manchester, far away from here. Far from London, even. She hasn't told her mum yet, and Sophie knows she'll be devastated. But she'll let her mum know soon – just not yet. Maybe she can even convince her mum to move with her.

On the sink next to her, Sophie's phone pings with a text message. It's Charlie. It has to be.

Hey. What are you doing? Couldn't sleep last night because we didn't talk.

It's become a habit – Charlie calling her every night, staying on the phone until he falls asleep. He insists that hearing her voice is the only way he can drift off, but Sophie wonders just how true that is. Is it more about him checking she's at home in bed? Sophie nudges that thought away. Charlie's a good person, despite his confidence, which borders on arrogance. He loves her – she knows that. Her mum is always telling her that love is the only thing that matters.

'Are you okay?' Lynette asks, striding into the bathroom and grabbing her moisturiser from the cabinet.

'Yeah, I'm fine.'

'You looked deep in thought. Care to share? You know I'm always here to listen. I know I've been so busy, but—'

Sophie shrugs. 'Nothing to share, Mum. Honestly.'

Lynette hugs her. 'I know you're missing all your friends in London. Which is why I've organised a surprise for you.' Her face lights up. 'I've been saving up so we can go to London and stay in a hotel for a night. It's nothing fancy. Not the Ritz or anything like that.' She chuckles. 'Just a Premier Inn, and we'll have to share a room. But I thought we could go to a show. I've booked *Chicago*; you've always said you'd love to see it. It's taken me months to save up. Sorry – the seats are the cheapest ones, but won't it be amazing?' She searches Sophie's face.

'It will, Mum. Thank you.' Sophie hugs her mum tight. 'But you could have used the money for something important.'

'This *is* important. You and Orla mean everything to me – I don't care about material things. I'm in a place that I love, with my two girls – what more could I want?' She smiles and turns to the mirror, dabbing some moisturiser on her cheeks.

'Will we take Orla?' Sophie asks, already trying to picture how they'll manage that.

'No, I've arranged for Heather Hollinger to babysit Orla – she was happy to do it. I don't think Orla's ready for the theatre yet!'

Sophie flings her arms around her. 'Oh, Mum. That's amazing. Thank you.'

'Saturday night. Don't make any plans.'

'I won't,' Sophie says, her spirits lifting. A night in London with her mum.

They're lying on Charlie's bed, their arms wrapped around each other, when Sophie tells him what her mum has done for her. It's dark outside now, but Charlie's curtains are open, letting in a soft glow from the street light across the road. As she speaks, Sophie's body swells with happiness, her words cascading from her mouth.

She expects Charlie to understand her joy – he knows how hard her mum works, and how little time Sophie gets to spend with her, but his face is stony, his eyes unblinking as she speaks. 'When?' he asks, pulling away from her and staring at the ceiling.

All the joy she'd felt a moment ago instantly evaporates. 'Saturday.'

'But I'd planned a surprise for us this weekend.' Charlie doesn't look at her. This is what he does when he's sulking.

'Why? It's not my birthday.'

'Does it have to be your birthday for me to do something nice for you?' He glares at her. 'Why has your mum got you theatre tickets?' He sounds like a petulant child.

'Because she can never afford to get me much when it *is* actually my birthday. She's been saving for months for this, planning it for ages.' Sophie folds her arms. 'I don't want to fight about this.'

'Don't go,' Charlie says. 'I worry about you going to London. It's not the safest place, is it? What if something happens to you?'

'I'm *from* London, Charlie! I'm totally comfortable there. Just because you—'

He grabs her wrist, so hard her skin burns. 'If you go, we're over. I told you I've got something planned for us, and if you're selfish enough to throw it back in my face, then I don't want anything to do with you.' He lets go and pushes her away.

Sophie jumps off the bed. 'Fine with me. Have a nice life, Charlie.' She storms out of his bedroom, her whole body on fire. How dare he behave like this when she hasn't done anything.

As she walks past Vanessa's room, she knocks on the door, hoping her friend is at home. Vanessa and Charlie are close, but she's sure her friend will be on her side. When there's no answer, she opens the door and peers into the empty bedroom. Vanessa must be with Caleb somewhere; Sophie will call her when she gets home – for now, she just needs to be as far away from Charlie as possible.

Outside, when the cold winter air assaults her, she realises she's left her coat in Charlie's bedroom. No way she's going back in there to get it. Folding her arms across her body, her feet crunch along the gravel driveway so loudly she doesn't hear someone calling to her until she gets to the gate.

'Wait!'

She turns around and sees Myles rushing toward her. Dealing with Charlie's brother is the last thing she needs. 'I'm going home,' she says.

'On your own? In the dark?'

'I have no problem with that.'

'Where's Charlie?'

'In the house.'

'And he's letting you walk home by yourself?'

There's no point trying to make an excuse – besides, Sophie no longer cares; she's done with Charlie. 'As of two minutes ago, we're not together any more. Bye, Myles.'

Myles grabs her arm, scrunching his face. 'I'm sure that's not true. Charlie loves you.'

'Apparently not,' Sophie says, pulling away. 'Oh, well, that's life. Got to go.'

'I can't let you walk all the way to your place this late. Let me go with you. I'm heading to the Hurtwood for drinks with some friends anyway, and it's the same direction.'

'My flat's nowhere near the Hurtwood.'

He shrugs. 'I like walking. Happy for the extra steps. Are you coming, then? I'm already late.'

As they walk, an awkward silence surrounds them. Even though he's always been polite enough, other than staring at her all the time, Myles has never had much to say to Sophie, so his offer to walk her home is a surprise.

'Let's take the shortcut through the forest,' Miles says, glancing at his watch. 'I hate being late. And if I'm walking you home—'

'I told you, you don't have to. Anyway, I'd rather stick to the road,' Sophie says.

Myles stares at her. 'Suit yourself.'

But his face remains stony as they continue, making Sophie once again pleased that she doesn't have to have anything to do with Charlie or his brother again. Vanessa, though, is not like them, and she would hate to lose her as a friend. But she knows how close Vanessa is to Charlie, and seeds of doubt begin to implant in Sophie's head. Vanessa might not want to maintain their friendship now. After all, she'd been the one who encouraged Sophie to get together with Charlie.

'So why exactly did you and Charlie break up?' Myles asks, keeping his eyes on the path ahead.

'It just wasn't working out,' Sophie says.

'Really? I thought you two were solid. You've been inseparable since you got together.'

Sophie wants to explain that was Charlie's doing, not hers, but instead she says, 'C'est la vie,' trying to keep her tone lighthearted.

'Not sure Charlie will see it that way.'

'Actually, he's the one who ended it.'

Myles stops. 'What? Charlie did this?'

'Yes.' Sophie keeps walking. They're at least twenty more painful minutes from her flat.

A smile spreads across his face. 'Well, I'm glad to see he finally came to his senses.'

Sophie stops walking and stares at him. 'What?'

'Let's face it – you're not right for him, are you? And don't you think it's important to be with someone who's... on your level? Socially, I mean. No offence, but you have absolutely nothing in common.'

Sophie shakes her head, anger swelling inside her. 'This isn't that bloody *Titanic* movie. What planet are you living on?'

'I'm not the one who's deluded,' Myles says. 'Look, you seem like a nice person – you're just not right for my brother. And I'm sure soon enough Vanessa will grow bored of you, like she always does with people. Like I said, you're from a different world.'

Instinctively, Sophie slaps him across the face, surprised when he lurches backwards and trips, falling to the ground.

'You little bitch!' he shouts, pulling himself up, his face bright red.

Sophie turns and runs, never once glancing back to see if Myles is coming after her.

She doesn't stop running until she passes the Hurtwood, where she stops to catch her breath, grateful for the floodlights in the carpark. She's tempted to go inside to see if Liam's in, until she remembers that Myles is meeting some friends in there. The look of hatred on his face when she'd slapped him is ingrained in her mind. He would have hit her back, she's sure of it. Sophie hadn't intended to slap him, but his insults triggered a rage in her she didn't know she was capable of.

Before she can make her mind up where to go, a voice calls to her, then Caleb steps out of the shadows. 'Are you okay?' he asks. 'I saw you running, and it looked like you were in trouble. Has something happened?'

Relieved that it's not Myles, Sophie's body relaxes a fraction, but she looks past Caleb, expecting Myles to turn up any second. Unless he was lying about meeting his friends. 'I'm fine. Where's Vanessa?'

'I just walked her home. Well, most of the way. Once we get to the edge of the woods I have to let her go on her own in case anyone sees us.'

'Screw that family!' Sophie says. 'Except Vanessa. She's not like her brothers.'

Caleb raises his eyebrows. 'Sounds like you need to tell me all about it. Come on, I'll walk you home and we can talk on the way.'

'Thanks,' Sophie says. Normally, she would have told Caleb she doesn't need anyone walking her home, but she doesn't trust Myles, and he's still out there somewhere.

They head down the road, and something makes Sophie turn back. There, standing by the Hurtwood, watching them, is Myles.

NINETEEN

Vanessa stares at the bedside lamp in my hand. 'Emmie... wait... I'm sorry I scared you. But I needed to see you.'

I glance at the clock – it's ten past three. 'Couldn't it have waited until morning? And how did you get in?'

She holds up a key. 'I took it from Charlie's pocket. He was so out of it he didn't even notice.'

'Has something happened?'

Vanessa slips into the room and perches on the edge of the bed. 'I'm really worried. Khalid didn't come back to the party after he dropped you home, even though he promised me he would. And it was still early, wasn't it? I've been trying to call him all night and his phone just goes to voicemail. It doesn't even ring. What happened when he dropped you off? Did he say anything?'

'Not really. He definitely said he'd better get back to the party before he's missed.'

'See! Something's wrong – I know it!'

I sit beside her and put my arm around her bony shoulders. 'Vanessa, please try to stay calm. He gave me his number when he dropped me off – let me try and call.' I grab my phone from the bedside table, and there's an unread message from Khalid. 'He's messaged me,' I say.

Vanessa leans across and peers at my phone. 'What does it say?'

'It says can I call him straight away. There's something important he needs to tell me and it can't wait. That's it.' I read the message again, hoping it will reveal something I might have missed, but his words are too vague.

'Call him!' Vanessa begs.

I dial his number and put my phone to my ear instead of on speakerphone. It goes straight to his voicemail without ringing.

'Why isn't he answering?' Vanessa cries, jumping up and walking to the window. 'What did you talk about in the car? What happened?'

'We just talked about... Sophie. And Charlie.'

She peers out into the back garden. 'It doesn't make sense,' she says, clutching the sides of her head. 'Khalid wouldn't ignore my calls. He knows how much I worry. And he's a light sleeper, so even if he decided not to go back to the party, then his phone ringing would wake him up! I'm going to the Hurtwood. I know what room he's in.'

'Won't the doors be locked?' I ask, pulling on my jeans. 'How will we get in?'

Vanessa's eyes widen. 'You'll come with me?'

'I'm not letting you wander around out there in the dark on your own.'

She offers me a thin smile, and behind it I sense her pain.

We stand outside the Hurtwood, which at this hour has no floodlights on, and I marvel at how uninviting the place looks bathed in darkness.

'His rental car's not here,' Vanessa says, her shoulders

sagging. 'I don't suppose you've got Liam's number? That's the only way we'll get in.'

'Actually, I do. He gave it to me when I was asking him about the bike trail.' I pull out my phone and call, prepared to explain myself. I'm not too worried about Liam's reaction; he's been okay after our initial meeting when he learned that I'm Charlie's partner.

'Hello?' His voice is groggy.

'Liam, it's Emmie. I'm so sorry to bother you, but it's an emergency.'

'What's happened?' He's alert now, and I can hear the rustling of his bed sheets. 'Are you okay?'

'I'm fine, but... I'm with Vanessa Hollinger, and she's worried about Khalid. She doesn't know where he is.'

There's a brief pause. 'Khalid? Why is Vanessa looking for him?'

'I promise I'll explain everything, but can you just let us in? We're outside the Hurtwood.'

There's a brief hesitation, but then he agrees. 'Just give me a minute.'

A minute feels more like an hour before Liam unlocks the door and lets us in, wearing his dressing gown. 'Nice to see you again, Vanessa,' he says.

Vanessa keeps her eyes fixed on the wooden floor. 'You too.'

'I don't think Khalid will be too impressed with being woken up at three in the morning,' Liam says. 'I hope you don't think I can just knock on his door?'

Vanessa glances at me, then gives a small nod.

'It's okay,' I explain. 'Vanessa and Khalid are together. But the family don't know, so please don't say anything.'

Liam's eyes widen, but he quickly composes himself. 'Well, I'm happy for you,' he says to Vanessa. 'He's a good guy, but I'm still not comfortable with this.'

'He's not answering his phone, and his car isn't parked out the front,' Vanessa says, grabbing his arm. 'I need to find him!'

Liam sighs; I can tell he's grappling with the ethics of letting Vanessa check Khalid's room. He shoots me a glance, and I nod, even though this has to be his decision. 'Come on, then,' he says, heading towards the stairs.

Vanessa clutches my arm as we walk, and although I'm touched that she trusts me, her vulnerability worries me. I also don't know what to believe about her state of mind.

'Room eight, here we are,' Liam whispers when we reach a door at the end of the corridor. 'We need to be quiet, though – we're fully booked this week and I don't want to disturb the other guests.' He raps his knuckles on the door, and I hold my breath, praying that Khalid will open the door.

But there is only silence, and beside me, Vanessa's leg twitches. 'Something's happened to him!' she says. 'I know it has!'

'He must be asleep,' Liam says. 'I'm sure he's fine.'

'His car's not outside,' I remind Liam. 'We need to go in to check. And if Khalid's in there, he won't mind us waking him up to put Vanessa's mind at rest.'

With a heavy sigh, Liam pulls out a key card and slots it into the door, calling out to Khalid before he opens it fully.

It's dark inside until Liam flicks the switch, lighting up the empty room. The bed is neatly made, and there are no clothes or personal items anywhere.

Vanessa stares at the bed, then rushes to check the bathroom, as if he might somehow be hiding in there and this is some sort of mistake. 'Where is he?' she asks.

'This is strange,' Liam says, opening the wardrobe and finding it empty. 'He didn't check out. Do you think he had some sort of emergency and had to fly home?'

'He would have told me,' Vanessa says. 'He wouldn't just leave. I know he wouldn't do that to me.'

Liam glances at me. 'I don't know what to tell you. None of his things are here, so he's clearly not coming back.'

'Maybe he decided to stay with your parents for the last few days?' I offer, even though in the pit of my stomach, I know this isn't true. Vanessa has just come from their house, so she'd know if Khalid was there. And only a few hours ago Khalid had left me an urgent message saying he needed to tell me something, so why would he then leave?

'No,' Vanessa says. 'Not when we were...' She glances at Liam and lets her sentence evaporate.

'I think we should all get to sleep,' Liam says. 'We can see what happens in the morning. I'm sure he'll turn up with an explanation. He's already paid his full hotel bill so he wouldn't have needed to see me.'

'But did he give his key card back?' I ask.

'We have a box downstairs that guests can pop their cards in if they need to leave, and there's no one on reception,' Liam says. 'I can check.'

Vanessa rushes out of the room, and we follow her downstairs, where she's already emptying out the box on the reception counter. Only one card falls out, and she holds it up. 'Is this Khalid's?'

Liam takes it from her and goes round to the computer, scanning it in. 'No, that's another guest's.'

'Something's happened to him,' Vanessa wails, clutching her stomach and sinking to the floor.

Liam rushes to her and helps me pull her up. 'Don't think like that,' he says. 'Khalid can take care of himself. I'm sure he'll turn up in the morning with an explanation.'

I nod, though my instinct tells me this isn't likely. 'I don't think there's anything more we can do tonight,' I tell Vanessa. 'Why don't you come and stay with me at the farmhouse?'

Her shoulders tense, but she manages to nod.

'Thanks for your help,' I say to Liam.

'No worries. I'll call you in the morning.'

But he's frowning as he watches us leave.

We're yet to buy a spare bed, so I offer Vanessa ours, telling her I'll sleep on the sofa. She thanks me but says she'd rather sleep downstairs.

I make us both a mug of hot chocolate, and can't help feeling that I'm babysitting a child. But despite this, I know that the real Vanessa is buried deep within, and looking at the pitiful woman on my sofa, I'm determined to bring her out of herself.

'We'll find Khalid,' I say, and as I utter these words, it occurs to me that he might not want to be found. Has his relationship with Vanessa all got too much for him and he's run from her? But he didn't strike me as the type to do that – he seemed solid and dependable, even in the brief conversations we've had. And then I remember the message he left me, and I know without a shadow of a doubt that Vanessa isn't the reason he's gone.

Vanessa stares at me. 'Missing people don't always get found. Sophie never has been.'

I take her hand. 'I promise you, no matter what – I will find out what happened to Sophie.'

She frowns. 'Why do you care so much about her? You never even knew her.'

'No, I didn't, but I hate injustice. And I think there's more to her disappearance, and that someone knows what happened to her, even if the police don't. Why would a seventeen-year-old girl who loved her mum and baby sister, a girl who was heading to medical school, run away.'

'She wouldn't have,' Vanessa says. 'I told everyone that when it happened but nobody would listen to me. Even Charlie. We used to be so close – I could tell him anything. We were inseparable. But everything changed after Sophie disappeared.' She takes a sip of hot chocolate. 'I know *I* changed – I'm not stupid. Depression got the better of me after Caleb left me, and then my best friend disappeared. It was too much. Before that I was... a different person.'

'You can be that person again,' I say. 'She's still in you.'

She looks up at me with large blue eyes. 'I don't know how to be that person any more.'

'Do you trust me?' I ask.

Vanessa takes a moment to answer. 'I suppose as much as I can trust anyone. Which isn't very much.'

'Then that will have to do. There must be someone around, other than your family or Sophie's, who remembers her? Someone I could talk to about Sophie?'

'There's Liam. And his parents. Well, Walter, at least. My mum said his wife has dementia, so she probably won't be able to tell you anything. Not sure there's anyone else still around.'

Walter Curtis. Of course.

'Let's get some sleep,' I say. 'Tomorrow we'll find Khalid.'

'Why are you doing this?' Vanessa asks when I get to the living room door. 'You could get far away from here and go back to your life in London. You don't need to be here.'

'I'm here because I love Charlie,' I say.

I leave Vanessa with those words and head upstairs. Sleep will not come easily for me tonight.

TWENTY
NOVEMBER 2008

It's been two days since she's spoken to Charlie. At school, he walks right past her as though she doesn't exist, even if they are the only two in the narrow school corridor. Sophie should be relieved that he wants nothing to do with her, but instead it unsettles her; deep in her gut she knows that Charlie hasn't finished with her yet.

And then there are the anonymous text messages. Hundreds a day, all of them calling her a whore, telling her she doesn't deserve to live. Instead of letting it shrivel her up, dent her self-worth, Sophie deletes them and puts them out of her mind, throwing herself into her studies. She needs to get top grades in all her A levels – her place at university depends on it. She hasn't told her mum yet that she's applied to Manchester; she'll deal with that when she gets an offer letter.

She's sitting at the bus stop outside the Village Stores when Vanessa appears. Her friend looks furious. Sophie hasn't heard from Vanessa since she and Charlie split up, and she's fully expecting her wrath.

'I know what you're going to say,' Sophie says. 'But Charlie and I just aren't right for each other.'

'That's not what I was going to say,' Vanessa throws herself onto the seat next to Sophie. 'When have you ever known me to be predictable?'

Normally they would both smile at this, but their relationship has silently shifted, morphing into something unfamiliar, something Sophie doesn't like. 'What did you want to say, then?' she asks.

'I trusted you,' Vanessa says. 'I took you to meet Caleb when nobody else knows about him, and this is what you do.'

Sophie frowns. 'What has me and Charlie splitting up got to do with you and Caleb?'

'I know you were with him that night Charlie dumped you. Myles saw you with someone, and the person he described could only be Caleb. I know it was. Don't lie to me, Sophie!' Vanessa's face reddens. 'Don't you dare lie!'

'I bumped into him and he offered to walk me home, that's all.'

'You were all over each other – Myles told me everything!'

Horrified, Sophie grabs her friend's arms. 'Vanessa – I would never do that to you. Or anyone else! Myles is lying because I... I slapped him in the face and humiliated him. He's been sending me nasty text messages...' Sophie trails off; she doesn't actually have any proof that it's Myles who's sending those messages. It could just as likely be Charlie, or Vanessa.

'What messages?' Vanessa asks.

'It doesn't matter. I don't care about those. What a pathetic way to try to get to someone. I will never be a victim, Vanessa.'

Vanessa frowns. 'Myles wouldn't do something like that,' she says. 'It's not his style. If he doesn't like someone, then they know it. He wouldn't hide behind a screen. He likes to think he's above all that.'

'Charlie, then.'

Vanessa shakes her head. 'Never. Charlie wouldn't do that to you. He's in bits about your break-up, moping around the house. And he's refusing to believe what Myles told him about seeing you with someone else. Honestly, I've never seen my brother like this before.' She pauses. 'That's actually why I was looking for you. Charlie asked me if I'd speak to you. He doesn't know that I've been mad at you for two days – you know I can't tell anyone about Caleb. He wants me to ask you if you'll meet up with him.'

'No,' I say, the word erupting from my mouth before I've given any consideration to Charlie's request. 'I'm sorry, but I'm done with Charlie.'

Vanessa silently studies my face. 'It's that easy to walk away, is it? Charlie's a good person.'

Sophie wants to point out that Vanessa really doesn't seem to know her brother, or at the very least that she sees a different Charlie to the one Sophie has had to deal with, but knowing how close they are, she stays silent.

'I know how stubborn you are, Sophie Bower. But humour me. Will you at least meet up with him and let him say what he wants to say. It sounds like he's really sorry and wants to apologise. Pretty please?' Vanessa flashes her charming smile.

Sophie's about to repeat her answer, but reconsiders; if she's willing to at least hear Charlie out, it might help repair her friendship with Vanessa. 'Okay. I suppose talking can't hurt.'

'Great! I knew you'd see sense.' She pulls out her phone. 'Can you come over tonight? Mum and Dad will be in London at some surgeon's dinner in honour of Dad.'

'No. I'm not going to your house,' Sophie says, remembering how out of her depth she always feels in that sprawling place. 'I have to look after Orla tonight, so if Charlie wants to talk to me, then he'll have to come to me. Eight thirty.'

Vanessa raises her eyebrows. 'Okay. Any other demands?'

But Sophie's relieved to see that at least her friend is smiling.

Only as she walks away does Sophie realise that Vanessa

had a different phone, not her normal iPhone, but an old flip phone. She calls after her friend. 'Is that a new phone?' she asks, pointing to Vanessa's hand.

Her cheeks flush. 'What? Oh, yeah. I lost my iPhone. Using the same number, though. Anyway, see you!' That charming smile is back on Vanessa's face, but it's not enough to put Sophie at ease about the phone.

As Vanessa walks off, Sophie takes out her BlackBerry and calls her, but the phone in her friend's hand doesn't ring.

Sophie studies herself in her mum's full-length mirror. She's wearing old jeans and an oversized sweater this evening – perfect for showing Charlie that she has no interest whatsoever in restarting anything with him. Although Heather and Edwin have treated her as one of their own, she's never been able to blend in with his family. Sophie's felt as if she's been holding her breath the whole time, unable to come up for air.

But now she can breathe again.

The doorbell rings at eight thirty-two, and Sophie takes a deep breath before she opens the door. Charlie stands there, holding up a bag. 'This is for you,' he says. 'I was an arsehole to you and I'm so sorry.' His smile chips away at her resolve, but Sophie can't let herself crumble – she needs Charlie out of her hair because he's not good for her.

'Aren't you going to take it,' he says, holding the bag towards her.

'What is it?'

'A new iPhone. I thought it was about time you upgraded from that old BlackBerry.'

Sophie stares at him. 'No... I can't. I love my old phone.'

'I'm just trying to say sorry, Soph.' He waves the bag.

'I just don't think this is a good idea, Charlie.'

His hand drops to his side, the bag brushing against his

jeans. 'Can I just come in for a minute? We need to clear the air. I hate what's happened to us.'

'All your doing,' Sophie says. She regrets it the second the words spill out. She doesn't want Charlie to think she's bitter about him ending things. 'I mean – you're the one who wanted to end things.' Another mistake. Now Charlie will definitely think she wants him back. 'But it's all fine,' she adds. 'No hard feelings.' She pats his arm, as if they're nothing more than buddies.

'Yeah, no hard feelings,' he says, staring at her. 'So, are you going to let me in, then? I could do with some water. I ran all the way here – thought I was going to be late. Myles offered me a lift but I told him to stick it. After what he said about you, he'll be lucky if I speak to him again.' He steps inside, even though Sophie hasn't invited him to.

'Come in, then,' she says.

Charlie ignores her sarcasm and wanders into the kitchen, where he helps himself to a glass of water. He pulls out a chair and sits at the table, ignoring the water and staring at Sophie. 'You know, my mum told me we wouldn't work out. She warned me not to get involved with you.'

With a sharp intake of breath, Sophie tries to make sense of his words. Heather has always been so lovely to her, welcoming her into their home and treating her like a daughter. Even showing her more kindness than she appears to show Vanessa.

Charlie takes her hand. 'But I didn't listen to her. And I'm not listening to Myles now. I'm my own person, Sophie. And I want what I want, regardless of my family.'

'We're over, Charlie,' Sophie says. 'So I don't care what any of them think of me.'

He ignores her. 'I know Myles is lying about seeing you with some random guy. He has a vindictive streak, and he's just saying it because he wants you for himself. At least in secret. Myles would never have the guts to—'

'To what? Lower his standards and date someone whose mum cleans houses for a job?'

Charlie recoils at her anger. 'Your words, not mine.'

Sophie folds her arms. 'I think you should leave now.'

Again, he carries on as if Sophie hasn't spoken. 'I've invested such a lot into us,' he says. 'My pride. My reputation.'

'What are you talking about? I think you're going a bit over the top.'

'You don't get it, do you?' Charlie yells. 'The Hollinger name means something around here! It carries weight. We have a reputation. I can't have anyone thinking that you didn't want to be with me.'

'You're the one who left me,' Sophie insists. 'That's all anyone will know. And I couldn't care less.'

'Yes, I ended it. And now I've changed my mind.'

'I'm not interested, Charlie. Just tell people you left me – I don't care. Do you think I give a shit about what other people think? I hold my head up high and no one can make me feel ashamed.'

Charlie stares at her for a long time and then laughs, a loud and hollow sound that Sophie can tell is forced. Charlie is acting, just as he's done from the moment she met him. And she's furious that she let herself get swept away. Charlie grabs her wrist, twisting it so tightly her skin burns. 'You're not leaving me, Sophie. We're meant to be together, don't you see that?'

'Get off me!'

'I know you're angry with me for what happened the other night, so I'll put this all down to you being upset. But you're *mine*, Sophie – and that's the way it's always going to be.' He lets go of her and her hand smacks against the table.

But Sophie won't give him the satisfaction of seeing her react. Instead, she looks him straight in the eyes. 'And how do you think you'll get away with lying to everyone? If anyone asks me, I'll tell them the truth, Charlie.'

He sits back in the chair and folds his arms. 'I don't think you will.'

She almost doesn't want to ask, but Sophie needs to know what she's up against. 'What are you talking about?'

He flashes a smile laced with menace. 'Your mum likes living here, doesn't she? She told me how much her life has changed for the better being in Peaslake. Said this is the place she wants to grow old in. Says it's really lifted her spirits being here in such a supportive community. She's never had that before, has she? Living in London her whole life.'

Charlie is right – her mum has settled here so easily, as if this was her home town.

'You do know my parents own this flat, don't you?'

Sophie stares at him. 'No. You're lying. Mum would have told me.'

'Not if she didn't know. The letting's all done by the estate agent, so there would have been no reason for your mum to know.' He smiles.

'I don't believe you.'

'It doesn't matter whether you believe me. Just imagine if they decided to sell up or find a new tenant.'

'We'd find somewhere else.'

Charlie snorts. 'Okay, how about if your mum lost her job because people found out she was... I don't know... stealing, perhaps? Or something much worse. All it takes is one whisper to ruin someone's reputation. To make sure they never find work around here. And then she'd have to move. Start all over again somewhere. That would be a shame, wouldn't it?' He leans forward and rests his elbows on the table. 'Or I could make worse things happen. That's the thing when you have money – it really does buy you anything you want. Maybe there's evidence that she's been neglecting the baby, or harming it. Wouldn't take much for social services to whisk Orla away. How would your mum deal with that?'

It's all Sophie can do to stop the avalanche of tears that threatens to erupt; Charlie is despicable. And it sickens her that people with money can hold so much power.

Heavy silence surrounds them, and Sophie's fear turns to anger. She hates Charlie Hollinger for bringing her mum into this, more than she's ever hated anything in her life.

Upstairs, Orla begins to wail.

'Think I'll leave you to it,' Charlie says, kissing her on the mouth. It feels strange, and vile, and Sophie can't believe she once enjoyed his touch. 'Saturday night is Myles's birthday party at the farmhouse,' he continues. 'I'll pick you up at seven.' He smiles at her as if the conversation they've just had didn't happen.

Sophie makes sure he's gone before she rushes upstairs to feed Orla. And through the bedroom window she watches him stride down the road, smug and satisfied that he's got her trapped.

But Charlie Hollinger is wrong if he thinks Sophie will let him do this to her family.

TWENTY-ONE

Despite not feeling as though I've slept much, it's almost eight o'clock when I wake up. Bright shards of sunlight filter through the blinds, and dust motes dance in the air. I check my phone, but there's still nothing from Khalid, and when I try to call him, his phone remains switched off.

My body still aches as I make my way downstairs, where I find Vanessa in the kitchen, sitting at the table, her phone in her hand. 'He's still not answering,' she says, searching my face expectantly as if I can offer her some hope.

'I tried too.'

Her breathing quickens. 'It's like Caleb all over again. My family have done this. They must have found out about him and made sure he left. They don't want me having my own life in America.'

I join her at the table, recalling how Khalid was sure Heather and Edwin wouldn't have forced her boyfriend to leave her. 'I'm sure your parents wouldn't do that, even if Charlie and Myles would.'

'You really don't—'

The sound of the front door opening stops Vanessa in her tracks.

'That must be Charlie,' I whisper.

Vanessa stands up. 'I don't want him to find me here. He always... he always tries to control me. Just like the others. I need to go before he sees me.'

But it's too late, and Charlie is in the kitchen doorway, shaking his head. 'Vanessa! What are you doing here? Mum and Dad have been worried sick about you. They've been out searching for you all night!'

'I asked her to come,' I say. 'Because I didn't want to be left alone after my accident. Don't blame Vanessa.'

Charlie stares at me. 'You should have let my parents know, then.'

'Vanessa's not a child! She's a thirty-five-year-old woman!'

'There are things you don't know, Emmie. Family stuff. I'm sure Vanessa hasn't told you any of it.'

'Where's Khalid?' Vanessa says. 'He wasn't supposed to go until Monday. Do you know where he is?'

Charlie walks to the sink and fills a glass with water. 'I have no idea.'

Vanessa gets up from the table. 'You found out we're together. And you don't want me going to America with him! What did you say to make him leave?'

Charlie scrunches his face. 'Vanessa, you know that's not true, don't you?' He walks over to her and places his hand on her shoulder. 'You and Khalid aren't together. I'm sorry. I think being back here has messed you up and brought back painful memories. Maybe we need to get you to the doctor. Have you been taking your pills?'

'Vanessa's telling the truth,' I say. 'I found out yesterday when I saw them both together. And Khalid confirmed it.'

Silence descends on us as Charlie grapples with this information, his face draining of colour. He moves away from

Vanessa and stands right in front of me. 'Why didn't you say anything?' he asks.

'Because it's no one else's business.'

Charlie turns to Vanessa. 'Can you please leave now? I need to talk to Emmie.'

Without a word, Vanessa grabs her jacket from the back of her chair and brushes past us.

Charlie waits until she's gone before he addresses me again. 'I think it's probably best if we don't spend too much time with Vanessa. I feel like she's heading towards another episode, and I don't want her to harm herself.' He walks over to the fridge and scans inside, closing the door without taking anything out. 'I don't know what Khalid was thinking,' he says. 'But I don't blame him for getting out. Vanessa's—'

'Why are you so hard on your sister?' I shout. 'All she needs is people to have some faith in her.'

'Emmie, you don't know her.'

'You used to be close. She told me all about that. What happened?'

'That sister I was close to has gone. I've had to grieve for the relationship we had, and now the woman you know is like... someone different. I don't even know her.'

In some ways, I can understand this – but I know Vanessa can be helped if the Hollingers are willing to see past their bias. 'Maybe she's not the sister you all wished for – someone you can brag about to maintain the Hollinger reputation, but—'

'I don't care about all that,' Charlie says. 'Maybe I used to, but I'm also not the person I was.' He shakes his head. 'I told you I didn't want to move back here, but you pushed for it. Be careful what you wish for, Emmie.'

'I didn't want to throw your parents' kindness back in their faces,' I say. 'How would they have felt if we didn't accept the house? It was so kind of them to sign it over to both of us, especially as we haven't been together that long.'

'They would have got over it.' Charlie stares at me with cold eyes that make me shudder.

'Do you think I'm just going to ignore all your lies?' I say.

'That's all in your head,' Charlie says. 'Maybe you're as ill as Vanessa.'

My face burns with rage. 'Speaking of the house,' I say, trying to suppress my anger. 'It's in both our names, isn't it?'

'Course it is. Why? Are you planning how much you'll get when you leave me?'

I pull out my phone and show Charlie the picture I took of the title deed. 'Then maybe you can explain why only your name is on this?'

He stares at the photo, then turns away. 'Have you been going through my stuff?' He spins back around, his face flushing with anger.

'I was going through boxes to sort out what I could unpack. I can't help it if I just saw it in there. Maybe you should be more careful with important documents.'

Charlie's phone rings, but he ignores it. 'What difference does it make?' he says. 'We're living here together. It doesn't matter if the house is in my name. I just... panicked after what happened to us before. I didn't know if—'

'If we'd make it. You could have been honest and we could have talked it through. But this is just one more thing to show I can't trust you,' I say. My statement is risky – Charlie will surely end our relationship now, especially as the house isn't the legal tie I thought bound us together. But I won't let this end until I find out what happened to Sophie, and find a way to get Vanessa away from her family.

To my surprise, Charlie walks over to me and takes my hand. 'I love you, Emmie. Don't you know that? This is it for me. Us, I mean. It's all I want.'

The intensity in his eyes frightens me, and before I can respond, his phone rings again.

'I think you should answer that,' I say, pulling away.

Charlie sighs and takes his phone from his pocket, not even glancing at the screen before he answers. He falls silent while the person on the other end speaks. His face turns ashen. 'I'm coming,' he says, ending the call.

'What's happened?' I ask. What is it?'

He takes a deep breath. 'That was Myles. Khalid's dead. His body's been found in the woods.'

TWENTY-TWO
APRIL 2009

Sophie has come to realise that the thing about living a lie is that sometimes you forget what you're doing isn't real. The lines between reality and your fraudulent life become blurred. To the outside world, she and Charlie are love's young dream; only the two of them know the dark and twisted truth.

She lies on her bed, staring at the calendar on her wall, on which she's marking off the days until university starts. Everyone thinks she'll be going to the University of Surrey, so there'll be no need for her to move from Peaslake, but it's the offer from the University of Manchester that she's accepted. Medicine. A six-year course, that will take her far beyond this life, and far from Charlie. And nearer the time she will tell her mum why she has to get away from Charlie – and make her see that she and Orla need to leave with her. It cuts her up that she's keeping the truth from her mum, but she can't risk telling her now.

Sophie's also considered that her mum might not want to leave, and might insist on taking her chances with the fallout from Sophie leaving Charlie. But then who's going to help with Orla? If her mum won't come, then Sophie's sure she won't tell anyone where she is. *Tell them I'm missing, or that I've run away. Anything so that he doesn't come looking for me.* Because Sophie knows that she has done the one thing to Charlie that he can't handle and won't accept: she's unable to love him.

A knock on her bedroom door forces her back to the present. Her mum pokes her head around it, smiling. 'Someone here to see you,' she says. 'Shall I send him up?'

Sophie's stomach plummets. Charlie. She told him she needed today to study, but he doesn't care – Charlie will do whatever suits him, with no regard for who it affects. She's learned that much about him. Sophie's convinced he doesn't even like being in her company, but his need to control is too overpowering for him to let go.

Moments later, she's sitting at her desk, buried in schoolwork, when he comes in, clearing his throat.

Sophie looks up, and it's not Charlie standing there, but Liam.

'Hi,' he says, lifting his hand in a tentative wave. 'Haven't seen you around for a while. Hope you don't mind me turning up like this.'

On impulse, Sophie jumps up and rushes over to him, wrapping her arms around him and squeezing him tightly. 'I'm so happy to see you.'

Liam's eyes widen. 'Well, in that case, I'll stay away more often.' He smiles. 'Seriously, though, I was just giving you some space. Felt like you needed it.'

'Come and sit,' Sophie says, jumping on her bed and crossing her legs. 'Tell me everything. What's been going on? I haven't been able to hang around after school – Mum's working extra shifts and needs me to babysit more.' Sophie has lucked out there; it's the perfect excuse to avoid Charlie. His patience with babies is limited.

'Nothing much happening.' Liam pauses. 'How's it going with Charlie?'

Sophie tilts her head. 'Do you really want to know?'

'I don't care about Charlie,' Liam says. 'But I like to know you're okay.'

A wave of sadness flutters through Sophie. She'd convinced herself that Liam was some sort of stalker, when all along it was Charlie she needed to be wary of. 'Liam, I'm sorry,' she says.

He tilts his head. 'What for?'

'Never mind. Just know that I'm sorry.'

He shrugs. 'Okay, but whatever it is you're sorry for – one, you don't need to be, and two, I understand.'

Sophie wants to tell Liam how Charlie has backed her into a corner, blackmailing her into keeping up the appearance that they're having a relationship, but she holds back. Even though she trusts Liam, she knows how angry he gets about Charlie. He'll insist he tried to warn her by telling her about Andrea and the fire, and she doesn't want to hear that right now. She just wants to forget what's happening.

'I really don't trust Charlie,' Liam says. 'Sorry, but what kind of friend would I be if I didn't speak my mind about him. There's something not right about him. I worry about you.'

'I can take care of myself,' Sophie says.

Liam takes her hand. 'Don't I know it? But everyone needs a little help now and again.'

'I've just got to get through this term and then that's it. I'm out of here,' Sophie says.

'But you're going to uni in Guildford. You wouldn't have to move away.'

For a fleeting moment, Sophie's tempted to tell him her real plan for university, but, of course, she won't. She can't risk anyone finding out. 'Yeah,' she says.

Where's Charlie planning on going to uni anyway?' Liam asks.

'Law school in London. But he'll still be living here.'

Liam sinks back against Sophie's pillow. 'Hopefully it's nowhere near where I'm going.'

'Did you two really never like each other?' Sophie asks, lying back next to him. She's so comfortable in Liam's company, and finds him so easy to talk to that she can't imagine anyone not warming to him.

'Nope. You know when two people just instantly hate each other? That's me and Charlie.'

'So it was nothing to do with me, then?' Sophie smiles and nudges his arm.

Liam smiles. 'Think much of yourself?'

'Hey, you know I'm not like that. I'd just hate to think that you used to be friends until I came alone.'

'Well, rest assured we weren't. I like his parents, though. My mum and dad really get on with them. The Hollingers have always been good to my family. A couple of years ago the pub was really struggling. Edwin and Heather invested some money in it and helped Mum and Dad turn things around. It's been thriving ever since. Don't know how such a scumbag like Charlie—' He stops short. 'Sorry.'

'Don't worry about it.' Sophie recalls Charlie telling her what Heather really thought of her, how she doesn't believe Sophie is good enough for him, and she wonders if there are two sides to Heather. But she can't bring herself to believe this of Heather; it was just Charlie manipulating her, trying to make Sophie feel grateful that he stooped to her level.

She turns to Liam, with his warm, kind eyes, and she wishes she could feel something other than friendship. Things would have been so much easier if she'd started seeing him first, if she'd had those feelings when they went ice skating. Then she would never have let Charlie seep into her life.

Liam leans in towards her, and she knows he's about to kiss her. Sophie pulls back. 'Liam, I can't.'

'It's okay. I get it. Sorry.'

'You mean so much to me,' Sophie says, reaching for his arm. 'But—'

'I know – you're with Charlie.'

Sophie doesn't want to mislead him, to let him live in hope. 'Liam, it's not just Charlie. I just... I don't have those feelings for you. I love us being friends, and you mean such a lot to me. That's all it is, though. I'm so sorry.'

For a moment, Liam is silent, and his eyes seem to harden as he stares at her. 'It's fine. No big deal,' he says.

'But will you do me a favour?' she asks, more for Liam than for herself. 'Just lie here with me for a bit?'

There's no hesitation in his answer. 'Of course I will.'

Her mum calls to her from downstairs. 'Leaving now. Orla's having a nap.'

'Okay!' Sophie shouts, then she gets up and walks to the window, watching her mum walk down the road. And there, across the road, Charlie is watching the house. She veers backwards and shuts the curtains, fully aware that this will seem strange to Liam, and he could even misconstrue her actions. She should tell him about Charlie being out there, but she's too afraid about what Charlie will do. There's a chance he didn't see Liam arrive; he might assume Sophie's on her own and he was waiting for her mum to leave. And Sophie won't answer the door if he knocks.

'Are you okay?' Liam asks.

'Yeah. Um, I actually really need to get on with studying. Sorry. Do you mind?'

'Okay, I'll go.' He stands up, and Sophie can't bear the disappointment on his face.

She glances out of the window, relieved to see that Charlie is no longer there. Perhaps she only imagined it, anxious as she is by what he's doing to her, even if she's refusing to let it cripple her.

'Thanks, Liam. I'll message you later,' she says to Liam's retreating back.

Walking to the Village Stores that afternoon, Sophie contemplates what happened earlier with Liam. She could see how much he wants to be with her, and it's not fair for her to keep him around as a friend when he clearly wants more. And then there is Charlie, watching her flat from across the road. The sooner she's out of here the better.

'Hey, you look deep in thought.'

Sophie's head jolts up, and Vanessa is standing right there in front of her. She looks different, but Sophie can't pinpoint how. Perhaps it's because they've drifted over the last couple of months. Still messaging each other, but the dynamics of their friendship have changed, and Sophie doesn't know what's between them any more. Still, she'll be out of here soon – away from all the Hollingers, and away from Liam so he can get on with his life. She just needs to focus on that.

'How's it going with Caleb?' Sophie asks.

Vanessa nods. 'Yeah, good. We've got big plans for our life together, Sophie. Huge. I'm getting out of here soon. Caleb's nearly saved up enough for us to get somewhere, and I've been saving too. Did you know I've been working at the Hurtwood?'

Sophie frowns. Liam hadn't mentioned this. 'Really?'

'Yes. Hotel receptionist. I think they only gave me the job because of Mum, but I'm not going to turn down good money. It all goes in the Vanessa and Caleb fund.' She chuckles. 'What are you doing now, anyway?'

'I was just getting some chocolate. I'm craving sugar after studying all morning.'

'Are you babysitting later?'

'No. Mum has a rare evening off work.'

'Good, then you're coming with me. We're going into

Guildford to have some fun. Just us two. No boys, no parents. No worries. I feel like we've been... I don't know. Things are changing between us.'

Sophie can't help but smile. 'I've been worried about that too. Yeah, that sounds good. Count me in.'

Vanessa pulls out her phone. 'Just need to message Mum.'

Sophie notices that it's her iPhone again, the one with the scratch down the front. 'You found your phone?'

'What? Oh, yeah.' Vanessa slips the phone in her bag and grabs Sophie's hand. 'Come on then, let's shop till we drop!'

It's past ten p.m. when the girls get back to Peaslake, giggling as they jump off the bus, Vanessa laden with shopping bags. Vanessa had tried to buy Sophie some clothes, but she'd refused the offer, insisting she didn't need anything.

'Thanks for today – I really needed that,' Sophie says. It feels as though she's found her friend again, and that everything might actually work out. Maybe she'll even trust Vanessa with the truth about where she's going to university. But not yet. Sophie will see how the next few weeks pan out first. It still concerns her that Vanessa and Charlie have such a close bond.

'You're welcome.' Vanessa smiles. 'And you see those bags you're carrying for me? They're not mine, they're yours.'

'Vanessa, no! I can't.'

'Yes, you can. Why do you think I was making sure you loved everything I bought? We're the same size too, so... enjoy!'

Sophie hugs her friend. 'I don't know what to say. Thank you.'

'You know, it's so weird,' Vanessa says, 'but I feel like we're sisters or something.'

Sophie nods. 'Yeah – it does feel like that.'

'Hey, maybe we will be sisters-in-law one day. If you and

Charlie get married. How amazing would that be? Sophie Hollinger. I *love* how that sounds.'

Sophie forces a smile and tries to ignore the cramp in her stomach. 'Yeah.' But it's never going to happen, and she doesn't want to keep lying to her friend. 'Vanessa... I need to tell you something.'

Vanessa's mouth hangs open. 'No! He's already asked you? I mean, you're both a bit young, but who am I to stand in the way of true love!' She gives a twirl and takes Sophie's hand, trying to spin her around.

'No... no, it's not that. Can you just sit down for a minute?'

They both take a seat at the bus stop. The shop is bathed in darkness now, and Sophie's beginning to regret picking this moment to tell Vanessa the truth.

'This is really hard to talk about, but I need to tell you. I won't keep lying to you, despite what Charlie's threatening me with.'

The smile vanishes from Vanessa's face. 'Threatening you? What are you saying, Sophie?'

For the next few minutes, Sophie recounts to her friend all the details of Charlie's blackmail. Vanessa's face is unreadable, and Sophie knows this isn't a good sign. The silence is excruciating as she waits for a response.

'You are so fucked up, Sophie. Charlie would never do that. Never. He could have any girl he wants, why would he have to force you to be with him? And don't give me that shit about him wanting control.'

'That's true,' Sophie protests. She's given this a lot of thought, and it's the only thing that explains Charlie's actions. 'I think with your parents' overprotectiveness, he feels a bit powerless. And that makes him overcompensate in real life.'

'Don't give me that psychology crap. I won't let you talk shit about my brother.' Vanessa jumps up and rushes off.

'Please don't tell him I told you. Please, Vanessa.'

But Vanessa ignores her.

'I'm not the only one with secrets!' Sophie cries, desperate now.

Vanessa stops and turns around, but changes her mind and carries on towards the woods. And somehow, Sophie knows that this is the end of their friendship.

Wiping away tears that sting her cheeks, she begins the walk home, leaving behind the two bags Vanessa gave her. Her phone rings, and she snatches it from her pocket, praying it's Vanessa. But it's a number she doesn't recognise. She composes herself so she can answer. 'Hello?'

'Sophie? It's Liam's mum – Margot.'

'Hi Margot. Is everything okay?'

'No... not it's not, I'm afraid. I know he'd want you to know this. Liam's been attacked. He's in hospital.'

TWENTY-THREE

A police cordon surrounds a large part of the woods, and a white forensics tent has been erected under the trees. The dreadful scene sits incongruently beside the stark sunshine burning through the forest.

I stand beside Charlie, who is arguing with the uniformed police officer that he is as good as family to Khalid. Charlie's so used to getting his own way because of his family connections that this must be the first time nothing he says is working.

'Please stand back,' the officer says, ushering us away. We join Myles, who is further back from the police line, tapping on his phone. He gives Charlie a brief hug, then nods towards me. 'Horrible,' he says. 'Just shocking. Nothing like this has ever happened here before.' He slips his phone in his pocket.

'What happened?' I ask, as Charlie stays silent.

'Orla Bower found him. She was out walking and noticed him... It looked like he'd hanged himself but then the branch had snapped and he'd fallen to the ground. The rope was still around his neck. She didn't have her phone with her so she ran to the Village Stores to use Cassie's phone. I just happened to be there when she rushed in, so I heard it all.'

I turn back to the police tent, my body frozen despite the heat. 'What have the police said?'

'They won't tell us anything, even though I told them Khalid is a good family friend of ours. I can't believe he'd kill himself.'

Cold fear spreads over my body. 'Does Vanessa know?'

Myles shrugs. 'I told our parents, so I assume she knows by now. But she won't care – she hardly knew Khalid.'

Charlie and I exchange a glance, and I wonder if he will keep Vanessa's secret.

Charlie is silent, staring at the tent. He grabs my hand, and I let him; now is not the time to deal with what's going on between us.

'Why would he kill himself?' Charlie says, his voice barely audible. 'It doesn't make sense! He was happy with his life and his career – he had no reason to...'

'I think you'll find that many people who take their own lives suffer in silence before actually doing it,' Myles says. 'Their loved ones have no idea that they felt so desperate.'

I recall the conversation I had with Khalid when he dropped me home after the Hollingers' housewarming party. Those were not the words or actions of a man contemplating taking his own life. And his text message telling me he needed to tell me something urgently. *Is that the reason he's dead?*

Charlie squeezes my hand.

'I'm so sorry,' I say. 'I know how much he meant to you.'

A single tear tracks down his face, and he nods. 'I wish he'd talked to me,' he says. 'I know we hadn't been in touch for a while, but I would have listened.'

Myles wanders over to the police officer, and I wonder what he's asking.

'He might not have killed himself,' I say to Charlie. 'I know it looks that way, but we don't know for sure yet.'

Charlie turns to me, narrowing his eyes. 'What are you saying, Emmie?'

'I know we don't have all the facts yet, but I don't believe he did that to himself.'

He lets go of my hand. 'Emmie, you've got to stop this. You've become paranoid again.'

I turn back to the crime scene, where there's now no sign of Myles, and the police officer guarding the cordon stands with her hands on her hips, trying to disperse the crowd that has now gathered there.

'I need to go,' I say to Charlie. 'I don't like rubber-necking. Maybe you should go and check on Vanessa? You're the only one other than me who knows about her and Khalid. She'll need you.'

Charlie studies me for a moment before answering. 'I doubt anyone will be able to get through to Vanessa now. Not after this.'

I step inside the Village Stores, hoping Orla might still be in here. I know she's fond of Cassie, and often helps her out. But it's empty other than Cassie, who stands by the till, talking on her phone. She gives me a wave, signalling that she's almost finished, and by the time I've reached the till, she's ended her call.

'I can't believe it,' Cassie says. 'I keep thinking I should close the shop for a bit, out of respect for Khalid. Do you think I should? He's as much a part of this village as I am. Or he was, at least.' She sniffs and reaches for a tissue on the windowsill. 'At first I thought Orla was playing some kind of joke,' Cassie continues. 'But then I realised she's not that kind of kid. She'd never do that. Not after her sister.'

'Do you know where she is now?' I ask. 'I need to see her.'

Cassie throws her tissue in the bin. 'Is this about you

helping her? Lynette told me she'd responded to your ad. Glad it worked.'

I smile. 'Thank you. So, any idea where I can find her?'

'She stayed here for a while – I think it really affected her finding Khalid – I mean, she's only seventeen. Poor love. Anyway, she mentioned going to the Hurtwood to see Liam about something.'

'Thanks,' I call, already halfway to the door.

Outside, the sun blazes onto my skin as I rush to the Hurtwood. Khalid features heavily in my mind, and even though I didn't see his body, I can picture him now, just like I have an image of my dad that is buried deep in my mind. I need to know what Khalid found out. His words were a warning to me. *Am I going to end up like he has? Could this have been Charlie's doing?* I've never seen him displaying such emotion – but that could all be part of his act. If Charlie is capable of harming his closest friend, then there is no hope for me. The girl he met when she rode her bike into his car.

Liam's wiping down tables inside when I push through the door. 'Hey,' he says, his mouth twisting to the side. 'I heard about Khalid. I can't believe it.'

'He didn't kill himself,' I say.

'What? But I thought—'

'Just trust me. He messaged me last night saying he needed to tell me something urgent, and now he's supposed to have killed himself. Does that make any sense to you?'

'Well... no. But maybe he needed to talk to someone about how down he was feeling, and when he couldn't get hold of you—'

'He's hardly going to speak to a virtual stranger about his emotional state, is he?' I glance around to make sure no one can hear us. 'I barely know him, and you think he wanted to tell me all his problems?'

Liam chews his lip. 'I guess that doesn't make sense. But what do you think happened, then?'

'That's for the police to find out. Have you seen Orla? I really need to speak to her.'

He frowns. 'Yeah, she's here. She's upstairs with my mum. Mum's not in a good place with her dementia, and she seems to have really bonded with Orla, so she always comes to visit. Nice of her to give up her time like that.'

This is something Orla hasn't mentioned. 'Can I see them?'

'My mum?'

'Yes. Look, Liam, I know someone ran their car into me on purpose, and I think it's because I've been asking questions and looking into what happened to Sophie. Someone wants to silence me.'

He stares at me and doesn't say anything.

'I know it sounds far-fetched, but Khalid is proof of how serious this is. Someone knows what happened to Sophie. I think that might be what Khalid wanted to talk to me about. And if it's got anything to do with Charlie, then I need to know.'

Liam nods. 'Look, I suppose I could introduce you to Mum, but there's no telling how she'll react to you. And she doesn't remember anything, so there's no point asking her stuff about Sophie. She recalls things from her childhood, and that's usually with the help of photos, but not much else.'

'Thanks, Liam,' I say, already making my way to the door that leads to his parents' apartment at the back of the hotel.

We head up the stairs and through a narrow corridor, with closed doors on either side of it. 'Mum's at the end on the left,' he says. 'My parents don't share a room any more – Mum was getting freaked out in the night when she'd wake up and not know who was in bed next to her.'

'I'm sorry,' I say. 'But if you're the same age as Charlie and me, your mum seems too young to have dementia.'

'Early onset,' Liam explains. 'It was happening for years

before we realised what it was because she didn't seem old enough. The doctors put it down to menopause at first.' He sighs, then stops outside the door at the end of the hallway. 'This is it.'

I put my hand on his arm. 'I won't do or say anything to upset or unsettle her,' I promise.

Liam knocks on the door, and it's Orla's voice I hear, telling us to come in.

'Sorry to interrupt,' Liam says. 'Another visitor, Mum. This is Emmie, Charlie Hollinger's... partner.' He glances at me, then turns back to his mum.

She sits in the corner on an armchair, with a photo album open on her lap. Her short hair is curly and grey, and she's wearing pink lipstick, but no other make-up.

Looking up at me, her mouth slowly forms a smile. 'Come in, we were just looking at photos.'

So far, so good. I step inside the room, breathing in the strong scent of lavender.

'Emmie,' Orla says, rising from her chair. She walks across to me and lowers her voice. 'Have you heard?'

I nod. 'Are you okay? It must have been so hard finding Khalid like that.'

'It was horrible. I think I'm just trying to block it out. That's how I get through stuff.' She sighs. 'Margot was just showing me photos she took of the village,' she says, going back to her seat. 'When Liam was at school.' Her eyes flash me a silent message: *This is important.*

'I need to get back downstairs,' Liam says. 'I expect we'll get an influx of customers once the news spreads about Khalid.'

'Khalid Soto,' Margot says, shaking her head. 'Lovely boy.'

'Do you remember him, Mum?' Liam asks.

'Of course I do. He was always with Sophie, that girl you liked.'

Liam's face reddens. 'Yeah, anyway, I'll leave you to it.' He rushes from the room without a glance back.

Orla stares after him, her eyes wide. 'So, Margot, Liam liked Sophie, did he?'

'Oh, yes. He was besotted with her. Talked about her all the time. Not sure she felt the same. Not when she had Charlie and that handsome Khalid boy. He was a doctor, you know.'

'But Khalid wasn't seeing Sophie, was he?' I ask.

Margot frowns, her eyes narrowing. 'What was that?'

'We were talking about Khalid and Sophie,' Orla says. 'They weren't in a relationship, were they?'

'Who?'

Orla glances at me. 'Sophie? Remember her?'

'But you're Sophie,' Margot says. 'Why are you saying all this? What's going on?' She leans forward, then rocks back, repeating the gesture.

'Time for us to leave,' I say to Orla, nodding towards the door. 'We'll leave you in peace now, Margot. It was lovely to meet you.'

But Margot doesn't respond, and doesn't even look at us as Orla grabs her backpack and we leave the room.

Outside in the corridor, Orla stops and folds her arms. 'What was all that about? I was getting information.'

'Is that why you come to see Margot all the time, Orla? I totally get why you're doing that, but I'm not sure it's ethical. She's suffering from dementia. I think we have to find another way.'

For a moment I think she's about to object, but instead she smiles and pulls off her backpack. 'Good job I've got these, then.' She pulls out a notebook and flicks through it. 'There are seven of them.'

'What are they?' I say.

'Glad you asked. These are Margot Curtis's journals from years ago. *Before* she had dementia.'

'Journals?'

'Yep. She was looking for her photo albums just now, and when she pulled one out, all of these fell out of the cupboard. She told me she used to write down everything that happened in the village. Every day. When Liam was a kid. She was hoping to write a book one day about life in Peaslake. The side to the village that people don't see.'

Stunned by what I'm hearing, and what it could mean, I take one of the journals and flick through it. There are dates, times, seemingly every interaction Margot had with all the residents in the village. And when I flick through more pages, it becomes apparent that Margot was also a people-watcher, writing down her thoughts about everyone, unknown to them.

I look at Orla, who beams at me and takes the journal I'm holding from my hand, slipping it into her backpack.

'But we can't just take those.'

'We can – she's given them to me. Said she doesn't need them any more. I'm not going to argue with that, am I?'

This doesn't feel right, but if there's anything in there that might help us work out what happened to Sophie, then I've got to swallow my guilt.

'Better not let Liam see this,' Orla says. 'There's stuff in there about him too. We've hit the jackpot, Emmie!'

'Have you now?'

We look up to see Walter standing at the end of the hallway, leaning on his walking stick, watching us.

'Um, yeah, I won on a scratch card in the shop just now,' Orla says, shrugging. 'It's only ten pounds, but better than nothing.'

Walter shuffles towards us. 'My body might be decrepit, but there's nothing wrong with my mind, young lady,' he says, tapping the side of his head. 'Now, why don't you both come in the living room and tell me what's really going on? And what it is you've stolen from my wife.'

'Um, my mum's expecting me back,' Orla says. 'Can we do this another time?'

Walter raises his eyebrows. 'I hear there are a lot of police floating around outside today. Don't tell me I'll need to go and speak to one of them right now.'

TWENTY-FOUR

We follow Walter into the living room, a modern room with neutral decor and grey carpets, much like the rest of the hotel. We take a seat on the sofa while he closes the door, and Orla crosses her arms and rolls her eyes, while I fully understand why Walter is concerned about what we were doing.

'So, who's going to start?' he asks. 'I don't have long before I need to get Margot some lunch. She forgets to eat if I don't fix something for her. Can you imagine that? Forgetting to eat? Do you know how difficult it is for me to help her when she gets confused? And the two of you coming here, doing whatever it is you were doing, isn't helping.'

'I'm so sorry,' I say. 'But I think when we tell you what's been going on, you'll understand.'

Orla nudges me in the side, and I nod to her. 'We owe Walter an explanation,' I say.

'First, I think you need to tell me what you've got in your backpack, because when you came in, it looked empty. Now it's bulging.'

Orla hugs the bag to her chest. 'Margot gave them to me. I swear. I didn't steal anything.'

'And what exactly did she give you?'

'Show Walter,' I say to Orla.

With a heavy sigh, she opens the backpack and pulls out the journals, handing one to Walter.

He takes it and flicks through the pages with a sharp intake of breath. 'Jesus, I didn't know she still had these. I'd forgotten all about them.'

'So you know what they are?' I ask.

'A lifetime of thoughts and observations,' he says, almost to himself, running his hand over Margot's neat, rounded handwriting. He grabs his walking stick and crosses to the window, staring out at the lawn. 'She wanted to publish a book about life in Peaslake. A sleepy village.'

'She told us that,' Orla says. 'See, she knew what she was doing when she gave them to us. And it wasn't against her will or anything.'

Walter silently walks to an armchair and eases into it, wincing as he sits. 'But she stopped writing after Sophie went missing. I never understood why. Thought she was just too upset about something like that happening here. My wife grew up here, you see. Peaslake means much more to her than it ever has to me. Not that I haven't been happy here.' He begins to cough, letting go of his walking stick to cover his mouth.

I rush over to him and pick up his walking stick from the floor. 'Are you okay?' I ask, trying to recall if Liam mentioned what Walter's health issues are.

'Not really, but I appreciate you asking. I won't go into all the details of what's wrong with me. Probably easier to say what *isn't* wrong. But right now, all I want to talk about is what you want with my wife's journals?'

Orla glances at me, and I nod; this is her story to tell.

'This is about my sister,' Orla says.

Walter nods. 'Very sad business. I'm so sorry.'

'I should have had her in my life,' Orla says. 'We should

have been best friends, there for each other. I know she was a lot older than me, but that wouldn't have mattered, especially now.'

By laying it on heavily like this, I know what Orla's hoping to achieve, and judging by Walter's softened expression, it looks like it's working.

'I do understand,' Walter says. 'My twin brother died when we were kids. He was hit by a car. So I understand the sense of loss. But what's that got to do with my wife? And what do you want with her journals?'

'Someone knows what happened to Sophie,' Orla says. 'And if Margot was writing down everything she saw and every conversation she had with people, there might be something in her journal.'

'But the police interviewed everyone,' Walter says. 'They were here for weeks searching for Sophie. If Margot knew anything, then she would have told the police.'

'Margot might not have realised that something was relevant,' I say. 'She wouldn't have been looking for it when she was jotting down notes. And didn't a rumour start that Sophie had run away?'

Walter shakes his head. 'It feels like a violation,' he says. 'To let you have those books.'

'Please, Walter.'

'I don't know if I can,' he says, staring at his slippers.

'Why? Don't you want to know what happened to Sophie? Why she disappeared?'

'No!' he says. 'Because I'm terrified.'

I glance at Orla, who stares at Walter open-mouthed.

'I don't understand,' I say. 'What are you scared of?'

He doesn't say anything and buries his head in his hands.

'I understand,' Orla says, after a moment. 'You're scared because you think Liam might have had something to do with it. Aren't you?'

. . .

Outside, the stifling heat wraps around my body, threatening to suffocate me. Across the road, there are more police cars now, and two uniformed officers make their way out of the Village Stores.

Guilt bubbles in the pit of my stomach, even though Khalid's death has nothing to do with me, and I have nothing to feel guilty for.

'I thought Walter was never going to let us leave with these journals,' Orla says, handing me four of them. 'It was so good the way you convinced him to let us keep them. You really talked Liam up.'

It had been easy at first to persuade Walter that Liam would have had nothing to do with Sophie's disappearance, because I'm so convinced of Charlie's guilt. But the more I spoke, the more I began to question myself. I don't know Liam well enough to be sure about anything. But the goal was to get the journals with Walter's blessing, and that's what we got. Eventually.

'We can save time if we share the reading,' Orla says. 'I know what you said to Walter about Liam, but do you think Walter's right to be nervous that Liam could be involved?' She glances back at the Hurtwood.

'I don't think he'd just throw that idea around about his own son if it wasn't something that's played on his mind. But I suppose the parents of anyone who had any kind of relationship with Sophie might have entertained the notion.'

Orla frowns. 'But Mum said Liam really cared about Sophie. They were so close.'

I think about this. Sophie was close to Charlie, Liam, Khalid and Vanessa. But under the surface, it's possible that things weren't running smoothly between any of them. 'Hopefully Margot's journals will shed some light on things,' I say. But I warn Orla not to get her hopes up.

'Even if we don't find anything in them, I'm not giving up

on searching for my sister,' Orla says. 'Never. Anyway, got to go – I've got a lot of reading to do.'

Charlie's BMW isn't on the driveway when I get home, and I let myself in and double-lock the door. If he gets home and tries to get in, I'll tell him I locked it by mistake.

Exerting myself makes my body throb with pain, so I take some paracetamol and sit on the sofa, picking up the first journal, dated 2009, the year Sophie went missing. I read every page, immediately struck by Margot's attention to detail, and the way she was able to get people talking, even if they didn't realise she was hanging on their every word, mentally recording it for posterity. Adding her own take on all their actions. But there's no judgement in her words; somehow she manages to appear objective.

Until I get to the next page, dated July 2009 – a month before Sophie went missing.

I worry about the Hollinger girl. She's unpredictable, and I see how she influences people, especially that new girl, Sophie, who I can tell Liam's taken a liking to. He won't admit anything, but I see it in the way he looks at her, and watches her when she's not looking. But she's with Charlie Hollinger, so my son needs to back off a bit. You can't force someone to love you. And I can tell that Sophie adores Charlie.

They were all hanging out in the beer garden the other night. They thought Walter and I had gone to bed, but I couldn't sleep with all the noise, and once I'm woken up that's me wide awake for the next three hours. It felt like too much effort to read, so I peered through the blind. All the Hollinger kids were there. I say kids, but they seem to have morphed into adults over the half term. I suppose technically Vanessa and Myles are already adults.

I watched them for a moment. Myles drinking beer by himself at one of the tables. Charlie and Khalid engrossed in conversation on the patio. And further down the garden, Vanessa Hollinger and Sophie Bower looked like they were having an intense discussion. Vanessa was shaking her head, pacing up and down, her arms flapping by her sides.

I watched the boys to see if anyone noticed, or was even remotely interested in what the girls are doing, and only Liam was watching them. Eyes glued to Sophie Bower. My poor son. When will he learn that she just isn't interested in him?

I waited a few moments, then crept downstairs, to get a closer look at what all the youngsters were doing. It's important I know what goes on in Peaslake – the people are what make the history of this place.

I was in the kitchen, inspecting it to make sure it wasn't a huge mess, when the back door opened and Sophie Bower came rushing in. I slipped back behind the fridges, relieved that she didn't notice me. I've become adept at making myself invisible, and that night was no exception.

Sophie walked over to the bin and slipped something inside, then scurried back to the door, turning off the light as she left.

Of course I had to check the bin. And in it was a pregnancy test, the double pink line leaving no doubt as to why the girls were conferring so intensely.

Sophie Bower is pregnant.

I stare at the words, my breath catching in my throat. I should feel something – shock, fear, anger, anything – but I'm only numb. Sophie was pregnant with Charlie's baby. At only seventeen. Did he know? How did he feel about it? These are questions I burn to ask him, but he will never give me the truth. That, I will have to find out for myself.

Picking up my phone to message Orla, I'm startled when

the doorbell rings. I gather up the journals and hide them in the TV cabinet, then make my way to the door. It must be Charlie, and he'll be ready to question me about why he couldn't get in.

But when I throw open the door, a woman stands there, flashing me a badge. 'Emmie Jackson?'

I nod, trying to steady my breathing.

'I'm DC Stanthorpe. Can I talk to you?'

'Yes. Can I ask what about?'

'In connection with the death of Khalid Soto.' She pauses. 'We have reason to believe you were the last person to see him.'

TWENTY-FIVE

My throat constricts as I stare at DC Stanthorpe, who doesn't blink as she watches me, waiting for my reaction.

'He didn't kill himself, did he?' I say. My words sound alien, as if they've come from someone else.

'And what makes you say that?'

'Because I know he wouldn't.'

'Mind if I come in?'

I hold the door open, and DC Stanthorpe steps inside, glancing around. 'Just moved in?'

'Yes. Last week.'

She nods, seemingly satisfied with my answer as to why our house looks so bare and unfinished. 'According to my notes, you'd only just met him – so how can you be so certain Mr Soto didn't kill himself?'

'I can't be. But it doesn't feel right. So are you saying he did?'

DS Stanthorpe sighs. 'We can't say that for sure until we've seen the post-mortem results. We try not to make rash judgements. Shall we talk in the living room?' she says, pointing down the hall. 'Is it that door on the left?'

'Yes.'

'Lucky guess. Maybe that's a good sign for how this day will progress.'

Her overly talkative manner should put me at ease, but it only makes me more on edge. I need to get a grip – I haven't done anything, and I won't let this woman intimidate me.

DC Stanthorpe sits on the sofa, pulling out a small tablet. She's a tall woman, but I won't be intimidated by her sporty build, or the way her eyes probe me as if she can extract answers from me before I've opened my mouth to speak.

'I'm trying to get a picture of his last movements,' she explains, pushing her hair behind her ear. 'We haven't located Khalid's phone, but we have been able to access his call and message log, so we know that he called you last night. And told you that he needed to see you urgently. Did you get that message, Emmie?'

'Not until the early hours of the morning. I tried to call him back, but he didn't answer. I tried several times more and still no answer.'

'Yes, bit hard to answer when you're...' She stops herself and checks her notes. 'Yes, you and Vanessa Hollinger both tried contacting him numerous times throughout the night and this morning.'

I nod.

'We've spoken to Miss Hollinger. It took some doing to get anything out of her, but she told us that she and Khalid were in a relationship. Were you aware of that?'

'I knew about them, yes. But nobody else did.'

'All a bit strange, isn't it, that she'd keep it a secret. Especially as he was a close family friend. And she's a grown woman.' She checks her notes. 'Thirty-five.'

'You'd have to ask Vanessa her reasons,' I say. I'm not going to spoon-feed this woman Vanessa's personal history.

'Already have, but she won't say a word. Understandably,

she's very cut up about Khalid's death. But we will try to talk to her again later.' She taps something on her screen. 'So, if you could just run by me what happened last night.'

I take a deep breath and tell her about the Hollingers' housewarming party. How I wanted to leave early because of the pain I was in from being knocked off my bike, and that Khalid offered to drive me.

'Sorry to hear about your accident.'

I'm about to tell her it wasn't an accident, but she doesn't give me a chance.

'What did you talk about?' DC Stanthorpe says. 'When Khalid drove you home?'

'Mainly how my bike accident wasn't an accident. Someone deliberately drove into me.' I've said it now and won't take it back. It's only what I know to be true.

'What makes you so sure that's what happened?' she asks, looking up from her tablet.

Now that there's a police officer in my house, listening to my words, making a record of them, I can use it to my advantage. 'Because I've been asking questions about what happened to a teenager who went missing in 2009. Sophie Bower. She was only seventeen.'

Her eyes widen. '2009? That was before my time, but I do remember a call coming in about the case a few days ago. Something about writing in a basement.'

'That was me. I've been waiting for someone to get back to me, but no one has.'

'Because according to our records, there's no evidence compelling enough for us to come and look at your basement.'

'It's gone now anyway.'

'The basement's gone?'

'No, the carved messages. Pleas for help. From Sophie.'

DC Stanthorpe leans forward while I explain how the messages have vanished.

'I'll make a report of that,' she says. 'But I'm not sure what you expect us to do with messages we can't see.'

I pull out my phone and scroll to the photo I took.

She raises her eyebrows. '*Sophie was here*. Looks like something kids do to leave their mark somewhere. Not really proof of anything.'

'Can't you reopen the case?'

The police officer's eyes narrow. 'Sophie Bower was a child when she went missing. That means her case has never been closed. It might be dormant, but can be re-examined any time with compelling evidence.' She points to my phone. 'Which I'm afraid that is not. Especially if she spent a lot of time at that house. Did she?'

I nod. 'People don't just vanish without a trace,' I say, almost to myself.

'Er, I think you'll find that actually they do. Ask anyone who works in missing persons. Not everyone gets found.'

'I've been digging around, asking questions, and I think I've ruffled some feathers.'

DC Stanthorpe snorts. 'That's putting it mildly if you're claiming that someone put you in hospital.'

'Which makes me even more certain that Sophie Bower didn't run away.'

A moment of silence passes, and I can almost hear the detective saying she believes me, and that she's going to help me. But instead she shakes her head. 'Look, I need to work with facts, not theories or speculation. Bring me something concrete and I'll get the case opened up again, but until then can we just focus on Khalid Soto?'

'It's all related,' I insist. 'I'd talked to Khalid about Sophie too. When he left me that message, I'm sure it was about her. He needed to tell me something, and then the next thing I know, he's dead.'

'And you have no idea what he wanted to tell you?'

'No! I wish I did. But I feel like someone's trying to silence me.'

Her eyes narrow as she appraises me. 'So, after Khalid dropped you off, you didn't see him again that night? And as far as you know, he was heading back to the housewarming party?'

I nod.

'And he didn't come inside this house?'

'No. And I went straight to bed.' I contemplate whether or not to tell her that Vanessa turned up here in the middle of the night, but something stops me.

'Mind if I take a quick look around?' DC Stanthorpe asks.

'Why?'

'Just routine. You were the last person to see him, so we'd like to rule things out.'

Unsettled by her vague answer, I stand up to lead the way, but she holds up her hand. 'You're fine to wait here,' she says. 'I'll find my way around. Huge place, but I'm sure I'll manage.'

She leaves me alone in the living room, and I pull out my phone and send Orla a message.

I've found something in one of the journals. I'll come over in the next hour.

It feels like an eternity before DC Stanthorpe returns, smiling. 'Thanks for that. I'll let you get on, then.'

I see her to the front door, and when we get there, she turns to me, smiling again. 'It's more than likely we'll need to speak to you again. Might even have to be at the station, if that's okay?'

She must sense my unease as she quickly adds, 'As you're a key witness, that is.' She turns back to the door, then stops. 'Oh, my laces...' She bends down to tie her laces, then when she stands, her elbow knocks my bag to the floor, scattering its contents over the tiles.

'So sorry,' she says. 'Let me help you with that.'

She leans down again, just as a thin black wallet catches my eye. It's not mine, and Charlie's is brown leather. But I recognise it.

It looks exactly like the one Khalid pulled out of his pocket when he was giving me his phone number.

TWENTY-SIX

I slide my foot over the wallet, praying that DC Stanthorpe hasn't already noticed it. My heart thunders in my chest, and I'm sure my face has turned several shades paler. 'It's okay,' I say, holding my breath. 'I'll clear this up.'

She slowly rises, a frown replacing the smile she wore only moments ago. 'Are you sure? Happy to help, seeing as I'm the one who caused this mess.'

'I'm sure. It's fine.' I try to keep the urgency from my voice, but it's hard when my heart pounds so violently.

She stares at me, and for a moment I imagine her insisting on doing it, picking up my things while I stand by, unable to hide what's under my foot. I just want her out of here so I can work out what the hell Khalid's wallet is doing in my bag.

'Well,' she says, finally, 'if you think of anything that might seem important, or even anything that doesn't, please give me a call.' She hands me a card. 'You can reach me any time.'

I take the card and open the door, relief flooding through me when she says goodbye and steps outside.

Even though I want to slam the door shut the second she's outside, I make myself wait until she's turned away, her feet crunching on the gravel as she heads to her car. I pick up the wallet and rush back to the living room, watching her blue Mitsubishi disappear down the lane.

Only then do I rifle through it, pulling out credit cards and a driving licence, all of them belonging to Khalid. It's no accident it got in my bag, and it's only by luck that DS Stanthorpe didn't find it.

I try to recall every moment of last night, and I'm sure I didn't take my bag with me when Vanessa and I rushed to the Hurtwood. So whoever put it in there did so before or after that. It wasn't Khalid – I didn't take my bag to the Hollingers' house. Which means it could only have been Charlie or Vanessa. No one else has been in the house.

I don't know which option chills me more – at least with Charlie I already know I can't trust him. But I've chosen to put my faith in Vanessa, and believe in her when her own family won't.

My phone pings with a text from Orla, asking when exactly I'm coming. I reply, telling her I'm on my way, and then I order an Uber and wait outside, Khalid's wallet safely in my pocket.

Lynette answers the door, welcoming me inside the cottage as if I'm an old friend. In some ways, it feels as though I am – that we are connected in some way, because of Sophie.

'Orla told me you were coming,' she says. She lowers her voice. 'I know she seems okay today, but it must have shaken her up finding Khalid like that. I know if it had been me, I'd never shift that image from my head.'

'Yes, it must have been awful.'

'Before last night, I hadn't seen him for years,' Lynette says, 'but I remember him being a lovely boy. Sophie liked him a lot. Anyway, thank you again for everything you're doing for Orla.'

I swallow my guilt; I'm not here to help Orla, at least not in the way Lynette thinks. And when I break the news about Sophie being pregnant, it's going to change everything for both of them.

'You really don't need to thank me,' I say. 'I'm the one who should say thank you. For sharing your story with me, and for keeping me busy while I look for a new job. I've applied to the school, actually. Still waiting to hear if I'll get an interview.'

Lynette pats my arm. 'They'll be lucky to have you. You're a lovely person, Emmie. And that seems to be rare these days. Most people are just out for themselves.' She smiles. 'Can I get you coffee? Anything at all?'

'I'm fine, thanks. But actually, I'd like to talk to you and Orla together if possible? There's something I need to share with you both.' In the cab over here, I wrestled with telling only Orla what I found out. But she's seventeen – still a minor – and this concerns Lynette as much as it does Orla.

'Is everything all right? Is this about Khalid?'

'If you don't mind, I think it's best if I speak to you both together.'

Lynette's face seems to fall in on itself, a mixture of fear and annoyance. 'I'd better get her down, then.'

I wait in the living room while Lynette calls Orla down, preparing myself for what I'm about to tell them.

Moments later, Orla appears, her eyes narrowing as she silently questions what I'm doing. 'I thought you were coming for a session,' she says, glancing behind her at Lynette. 'Even though I really don't need them. But Mum said you want to talk to both of us.'

'We can definitely have a session afterwards,' I say. 'But there's something I need to tell you both first.'

Orla sinks onto the sofa with a heavy sigh, pulling her legs up and crossing them. 'What's up, then?'

Lynette sits next to her, and I choose the armchair, where I can sit across from them. 'I was talking to Margot Curtis earlier today, and she gave me her old journals.' I ignore Orla's eyes boring into me, and turn to Lynette. 'Did you know she was keeping journals for years about everything that happened in the village?'

Lynette frowns. 'No, I didn't. But I got on with Margot. We were quite friendly with each other. So sad about her dementia.' She sighs. 'No one gets through life without suffering, do they?'

I think of my dad, and how his murder shaped my life. It could so easily have been different, and I'd be someone else, living a life I can't possibly imagine. 'But somehow we find a way to carry on,' I say.

'What's going on?' Orla says. She's growing impatient, and I can tell she's itching to speak to me alone.

'This is really difficult to tell you,' I begin. 'And I'm not even sure it should be me who breaks it to you, but I discovered something about Sophie in Margot's journal.'

Lynette gasps, her hand folded over her mouth. 'What... what is it? Just tell me, please.'

I take a deep breath. 'It appears that Sophie might have been pregnant.'

The word hovers around us, cruel and full of unanswered questions. Lynette and Orla stare at me, then turn to each other.

'No,' Lynette says. 'She... she would have told me.'

'How do you know?' Orla asks. She seems to have recovered from shock and digested this news remarkably fast. 'You can't assume that. She was my age – we don't always share everything, Mum. And something like that is difficult to talk about.' Orla glares at me; she won't be happy that I didn't share this with her first.

'I want to see what you read,' Lynette says.

I reach into my bag and pull out Margot's journal, where I've stuck a Post-it note on the page Lynette needs to read.

Her eyes flick back and forth as she takes in Margot's words, and then she passes it to Orla, shaking her head. A tear trickles down her cheek, and I fight the urge to wipe it away. I've caused this pain, and now I wonder if I needed to share this information right now. But if it helps us find out what happened to Sophie, then Lynette will understand why I've done so. And she's her mother, she has a right to know.

'Margot never said anything,' Lynette says. 'Not even back then, when she was... okay. Why wouldn't she tell me?'

I shrug. 'Maybe because it doesn't look good for Margot that she was snooping around in everyone's business without them realising. According to Walter, nobody knew she was keeping all these journals. There's stuff in there about affairs and all sorts of things people wouldn't want anyone knowing about.'

Lynette takes Orla's hand. 'And what about the Hollingers? Is there anything about them?'

'Everything I've read shows them all in a good light.' Except Vanessa, but I don't mention this.

'Did... did Charlie know she was pregnant?'

'I don't know,' I say. 'But I'll find out.'

'That's if it was Charlie's,' Orla says, folding her arms. 'We don't know that, do we?'

'Who else's would it have been?' Lynette snaps. I've never heard her speak in anything other than a calm manner. And I'm surprised that she's so adamant when she was the one who told me she had an inkling that Sophie might have been seeing someone else.

'Forget I said anything,' Orla says. 'I'm going upstairs.' She storms off, with both of us staring after her.

'Do you remember when we spoke about Sophie – you told me you thought she might have been seeing someone else.'

'I don't have any proof of that,' Lynette says. 'It was just something that niggled at the time. But Sophie wasn't like that. She made a commitment to Charlie, and she wouldn't have done anything to ruin that.'

'But were you thinking of Liam?' I ask. 'I know they were close.'

'Yes, they were. But not like that. I was thinking of... never mind. What does it matter now?'

'Please, Lynette. This might be important. Who were you thinking of?'

She lowers her head, taking her time to answer. 'I was thinking of Khalid.'

My head feels like it's about to explode as I make my way upstairs, and I can't tell whether that's from my bike accident or from what Lynette has just told me. She has no evidence for her claim, but that doesn't mean I should dismiss it. Is that what Khalid wanted to tell me? But it makes no sense that he's dead because of it.

Orla's lying on her bed when I get to her room, staring at the ceiling. I knock, even though the door is wide open. She sits up and glares at me as I make my way to her bed and sit on the end of it.

'I know why you're angry with me,' I say. 'But I had to talk to your mum at the same time. You're a minor, Orla. I have to be mindful of that.'

'I know all that,' she says, rolling her eyes. 'But it's harsh. We were working together on this. You could have at least warned me that you were coming to talk to Mum as well. Ever heard of WhatsApp?'

I contemplate telling Orla that I was distracted by my visit from DC Stanthorpe, and Khalid's wallet turning up in my bag, but decide against it; Orla has no reason to trust me. 'Khalid's death has thrown me off course,' I say. 'He seemed a nice guy. And I was the last person who saw him.'

With a sharp intake of breath, Orla swings her legs around

so she's sitting on the edge of the bed. 'I didn't know that. What happened?'

I tell her he dropped me off at home, and that he left me a message saying he needed to talk to me urgently.'

'Woah, this is huge! Khalid might have found out something about Sophie, and now he's dead! We have to tell the police.'

'I pretty much have, and they don't seem to think there's compelling evidence to reopen the investigation. We can't prove anything yet,' I say. 'But we will. Listen, your mum just told me something downstairs that could change everything. She says she had a gut suspicion that Sophie might have been seeing Khalid. Has she ever mentioned that to you?'

Orla stares at me. 'No, never. Mum's always just gone on about how in love Sophie and Charlie were.' Her face creases. 'Maybe that was to shield me from the truth. But... there's something I've always thought about. This great love affair – sometimes I've wondered if it was Mum making it into something it wasn't.' She jumps up and closes the door. 'Put it this way – after Sophie's dad, Mum never found love again, and I know she wanted to. She met my dad, but he left her. No other relationship worked out for her either. I wonder if Mum was just pushing her big dream of finding the right man onto Sophie?'

'I guess she could have done that without realising what she was doing. But your mum isn't the only one around here who believed Sophie and Charlie were deeply in love.'

Orla nods.

'What I need to do now is speak to Vanessa.'

'Why?'

I tell her about Vanessa and Khalid. The police know now, so it won't be a secret for much longer.

'This just gets weirder by the second,' Orla says. 'What are we missing?'

This is exactly the sense I get. There's something lurking just beneath the surface of all this, and I have no idea what it is, or how to reach it. 'Can you check through the rest of the journals while I go and see Vanessa?' I ask. 'We've already found something in there – who knows what else we'll find.'

She nods. 'I'm on it.'

'Thank you.' I stand and walk to the door.

'Emmie?' Orla says.

'Yeah?'

'Do you think the baby's got anything to do with why my sister went missing?'

'I don't know, Orla. But I'm determined to find out.'

Downstairs, I pop my head around the kitchen door to say goodbye to Lynette. She's loading the dishwasher, and doesn't notice I'm there until I clear my throat.

'Oh, finished already?' she asks.

'I think we'll postpone today's session,' I say. 'Given the news about Sophie I've just broken to you both.'

'Sophie would have made an amazing mum,' Lynette says, closing the dishwasher.

I nod, and goosebumps sprout along my arms, even though shards of sunlight bathe the kitchen in warmth.

'Do you know what I keep thinking?' Lynette says. 'I was going over dates, and even if she'd just done a pregnancy test in July, there's no way of knowing how pregnant she already was by then. But I know there's no way Sophie would have had a termination. She would have asked me for help. And we already had Orla, so one more baby wouldn't have been too difficult for us to manage. I would have found a way for her to still go to university. She would have *known* that. And Sophie never gave in, never let life beat her.'

'What are you saying, Lynette?'

She grips the back of a kitchen chair, as if she'll topple over without support. 'I think someone didn't want her to have that baby. And when she didn't listen, someone made her disappear.'

TWENTY-SEVEN
APRIL 2009

Liam's sitting up in the hospital bed when Sophie gets there. Orla's in her buggy, but she's writhing around and grizzling, so Sophie takes her out and holds her. 'What happened?' she asks, sitting on the chair by Liam's bed. There are other people in the ward, so she keeps her voice low. It's hard to look at Liam – his face is barely recognisable under the tapestry of purple and black bruises.

'I was walking home from your place, and someone attacked me.'

Sophie's stomach wrenches. 'Did you see who it was?'

'No. They had a balaclava over their face.'

'Did they say anything? Did you recognise their voice?'

'You sound like the police. I told them I don't know who it was.'

But Sophie has a good idea. 'Where exactly were you?'

'I thought I'd cut through the forest.'

Again, her stomach twists. 'I'm so sorry this happened.'

'It's not your fault, is it?'

'What if it *is* my fault? When you were at my house, I looked out of the window and saw Charlie standing across the road.'

'You didn't say anything.'

'I know.'

'Well, what was he doing?'

Sophie feels as though the hospital walls are closing in on her. 'I... I don't know.'

'That's just weird,' Liam says.

'What if he saw you leaving and now he thinks there's something going on with us? And... that's why he attacked you?' The words lodge in her throat; she's learned that Charlie is a master manipulator, but she doesn't want to believe he's capable of a brutal attack like this.

Liam's eyes widen. 'Jesus, Sophie! I told you he was a nasty piece of work. Remember the fire he started at my ex's house? You should have told me he was outside your window.'

'I... I didn't want to worry you. And he'd gone by the time you'd left. I didn't think he'd follow you.'

Liam shakes his head. 'You have to tell the police, Sophie.'

'I can't. You don't understand.'

'Then help me understand!' he shouts, and the other patients turn to look at them.

'I can't,' Sophie whispers. 'I wish I could, but I can't.'

'Then *I'll* tell the police. I don't even have to mention your name, or that you saw him outside your house. I can make out I remember seeing him.'

'No, Liam, please don't.'

'Why are you protecting him?'

'I'm not,' Sophie protests. 'But think about his family. How powerful the Hollingers are. They'll find a way to get him out of this if he's arrested or charged, and then he'll make your life miserable. It's not worth it, Liam. And we don't know for sure it was him. You *can't* say anything. Please.'

Sophie hates herself for having to say all of this to Liam, when he's lying battered in a hospital bed. 'I'm sorry, Liam.' She stands and straps Orla back into the buggy. 'I have to go. I'm glad you're doing okay. Sorry.'

Heather opens the door when she gets to the farmhouse, smiling at Sophie. She looks lovely today, in a black wide-leg jumpsuit, and Sophie can tell she's just had her highlights done. No doubt in that expensive salon in Oxford Street. 'You're just in time!' Heather says. 'Ah, and there's little Orla. What a treat to see you both.'

'What am I just in time for?' Sophie asks, as Heather helps her pull Orla's buggy over the doorstep.

'I've made apple crumble, and you simply must have some – it's delicious. It was one of my mum's recipes, and we loved it as kids.' Heather leans down and strokes Orla's cheek. 'What a little angel,' she says.

'Yep, when she's asleep!' Sophie jokes. 'Um, apple pie sounds lovely, but I really just need to see Charlie quickly.'

Heather pats her hand. 'Just humour me – I've spent hours baking and no one's had any yet.'

'Maybe just a small piece.' Sophie follows Heather into the kitchen, and pushes Orla's buggy to the window.'

'I'm glad you have a healthy appetite,' Heather says. 'Not like my darling daughter. Speaking of Vanessa – have you any idea where she is? She's done another disappearing act and isn't answering her phone. But heaven forbid if I keep trying. I wish she'd just let me know she's okay when she's out and about.'

Sophie nods; she feels sorry for Heather – Vanessa really isn't fair to her – but she needs to find Charlie and have it out with him about Liam. She watches Heather as she cuts into the crumble – none of it's been touched until now.

Heather hands her the plate and watches her eat. 'I hope you don't mind me asking, but are you and Charlie okay? Everything going well?'

She finishes her mouthful. 'Yes... we're fine.'

'I'm so glad to hear that.'

'I'd better go and find him,' Sophie says, taking her plate to the dishwasher. 'That was delicious, thank you.'

'Why don't you leave Orla here with me. I'll give her a cuddle if she wakes up.'

'Thanks, Heather.'

Upstairs, Sophie rushes to Charlie's room and knocks, her heart racing. There's no answer, and after a moment, Sophie wonders if it's for the best that he's not here. Charlie won't like her confronting him about Liam's attack. Perhaps she needs to rethink this. Charlie doesn't care who he hurts.

She's about to go back downstairs when she hears Charlie's voice coming from Edwin's study at the end of the hall. She needs to let him know she's here – Heather's bound to mention it and then Charlie will wonder what she was doing. Inching towards the study, she sees the door is closed, so she stands and listens.

'Why do you need to know this?' Edwin asks.

'It's for my English homework, Dad. A creative writing piece.'

'Surely you can google it?'

'I have, but I just want to double-check. We can't trust Dr Google – you're always telling us that.'

Edwin laughs. 'True. Okay. Tell me exactly what you need to know for this story of yours.'

'I just need to know what pills my character could slip into someone's food to... you know. Hurt them.'

'That's a bit grim, isn't it?'

'It's just fiction, Dad.'

'Probably ketamine. Horse tranquiliser. Very deadly.'

Sophie can't breathe.

There is no creative writing homework.

Outside, while Orla screams to be let out of the buggy,

Sophie fishes her phone from her pocket, dialling a number and holding it to her ear.

'Can you meet me this evening?' she says. 'I need to talk to you. It's urgent.'

It's past eight by the time Sophie leaves the house. Her mum had got home from cleaning the hospital later than expected, and then she'd wanted to ask questions about Liam. Her mum likes him, Sophie knows that, so this was only to be expected. 'But you'd only just seen him. It's so awful,' her mum had said. 'Margot said it happened on his way home from here. I just don't understand who'd do that to him.'

Sophie had been vague in her answers, but she could tell her mum suspects there's more to this incident.

'Are you okay?' her mum had said when Sophie grabbed her coat to leave. 'You would tell me if you weren't, wouldn't you? If you were in any kind of trouble?'

'Yes, Mum – I would. Definitely,' Sophie had assured her, leaving the house before her mum could say any more.

Khalid's already found a table and is waiting for her in the beer garden. It's too cold to sit outside, but Sophie's happy to be in the fresh air – it helps to clear her mind.

'I've got you a lemonade. Hope that's okay? I've seen you drinking it a few times so assumed it would be okay.'

'Thanks.' She takes a seat and tries to get straight in her mind what she'll say to Khalid.

'I heard about Liam,' Khalid says. 'How's he doing? Can't believe someone did that to him. Did he see anything?'

'No. Nothing.'

Khalid nods. 'Well, hopefully the police will find out what happened.' He smiles. 'So you said it was urgent? Is this about me getting two marks higher than you in the maths test on Monday?' He laughs.

'No, this is serious, Khalid.'

'Sorry,' he says.

'No, no. Don't apologise. Look, this isn't an easy conversation to have. I'm worried. About Charlie. Please don't tell him I've spoken to you. Promise me.'

'Look, Soph – I know he's my best friend, but you're a good friend too. I can be loyal to both of you.'

'Okay, good.' Sophie takes a deep breath and tells Khalid everything she overheard this afternoon.

He listens without interrupting, drumming his fingers on the table, his eyes darting around the pub. 'We didn't have any English homework,' he says. 'And Charlie hates writing.'

Sophie nods.

Khalid frowns. 'You know Charlie's my best friend. We've been close since we were at nursery. Two years old. That's how deep our friendship is.' His hand stills and he smooths it over the table. 'But I don't like this. And... I know something's going on with you and Charlie. Something's wrong.'

Sophie stares at him. 'How did you—'

'Nobody else sees it, but I do,' Khalid says. 'I've known Charlie long enough to know there's something up. You can talk to me, Sophie. I like to think that we're friends, and whatever Charlie's doing – we can work it out ourselves. Maybe he needs help. I've actually started to feel like I don't even know him any more.'

Sophie doesn't trust people easily, but her instinct tells her she can confide in Khalid. Although she's already confided her suspicions to Liam, it might help speaking to someone Charlie trusts. 'There is some stuff going on with Charlie,' she begins. 'And I think he's the one who attacked Liam.'

Khalid's head tilts forward as he gapes at her, open-mouthed. 'I think you should tell me everything. I'm really worried, Sophie.'

So she does, and it feels good to let the words spill from her mouth, everything that's been happening with Charlie.

When she's finished, Khalid shakes his head. 'That's dark,' he says. 'Even for Charlie.'

'What do you mean *even for Charlie?*'

'It's hard for me to speak badly of him – his family mean a lot to me. But... I've always worried about him. Since we were kids.'

'You've seen it. That side to him that isn't... isn't right.' Sophie sighs. 'I can't explain what it is.'

'I think it's because he's out for himself. The only thing that matters to Charlie is Charlie. But that's one thing – researching lethal medications is another.'

Sophie studies Khalid. He's mature beyond his years, and she respects him. 'What are you saying?' she asks.

'I don't know. But I think you need to get away from him. There was this girl—'

'I know all about Andrea. Liam told me what happened with the fire.'

'I doubt he told you everything. She had to get away from Charlie. I think she was too scared to tell Liam this, but Charlie was harassing her – he wouldn't take no for an answer and refused to accept that she was with Liam.'

'I know,' Sophie says. 'It's why her family moved away.'

'I don't want to think about what might have happened if they'd stayed in Peaslake,' Khalid says. 'And I can honestly say that I'm not sure it's safe for any girl to be around him. After what you've just told me, I think you need to get as far away from him as possible.'

'I can't just disappear,' she says.

'But what if you could?' Khalid says. 'That might be the only way you'll escape from Charlie...'

And with those words, an idea cements itself in Sophie's head.

TWENTY-EIGHT

When I arrive at the Hollingers' house, I'm out of breath, a layer of sweat coating my skin. I would have had to wait half an hour for an Uber, so I stopped at the Hurtwood and talked Liam into lending me his bike. He didn't want to, but somehow I convinced him I'd be fine.

But now I know I've pushed myself too much, and every inch of my body burns.

I lean the bike against the wall and check my phone. There are several messages from Charlie, asking where I am. Telling me he's worried about me. Begging me to call him. I switch my phone to silent and shove it in my pocket.

Edwin answers the door, dressed casually in loose jeans and a T-shirt. He looks harried, but quickly recovers when he registers that it's me. 'Come in, Emmie. I'm afraid we're having a bit of a struggle at the moment. When the doorbell rang, I thought it would be the police again wanting to speak to Vanessa.' He lowers his voice. 'I don't understand it – Khalid took his own life – it makes no sense that they want to question Vanessa. As if she's guilty of something.' He sighs. 'Terrible business. Khalid was like a son to us. No, strike that – he *was* our son.'

'I'm so sorry,' I say. 'It's a heartbreaking time for you all.' I glance up the stairs, where I'm sure Vanessa will be.

'And I can't get hold of Myles,' Edwin says.

Heather appears from the kitchen, her arms folded across her stomach as if she's in pain. 'It's all terrible,' she groans. 'Everything's just... falling to pieces. And we were so happy to be back home. Now look what's happening! Poor Khalid. And Vanessa's in such a state – there's no getting through to her.'

Edwin rushes to her and puts his arms around her. 'It's okay, darling. Everything will be okay.'

He turns to me. 'And Charlie's been acting strangely. I feel like the whole family's falling apart.' He shakes his head. 'We had a peaceful life in Dubai, but for some reason we pined for this place. I'm tempted to put this house straight back on the market and get out of here.'

'It was me, Edwin,' Heather says, pulling back and dabbing her eyes. 'I talked you into coming home. You were happy in Dubai.' She looks at me. 'Oh, my – I haven't even offered you tea or coffee. I've made some cupcakes too. I'll be right back.' She disappears to the kitchen.

'I understand why you feel like this,' I say to Edwin. 'But remember, you wanted to come back. To come back home. I know this isn't Peaslake, but it's only a short drive away.'

'It's not me who pined for Peaslake,' he says, keeping his voice low. 'It's often the women who get their way in a marriage, isn't it? Wasn't it the same with you and Charlie moving here? Myles tells us Charlie wasn't keen, even with the offer of the house. Did he say why?'

'No. I just assumed he was happy living in London and didn't want our lives to change that much.'

He puts his hand on my shoulder. 'Well, I'm grateful to you that you've brought our son back home, where he belongs. I know Charlie can have his moments, but he's got a good heart.'

I can't listen to any more of this. Charlie is so skilled at hiding who he really is that even his own family can't see it. At least most of them. 'Can I see Vanessa?' I say, before I say something I'll regret.

Heather appears from the kitchen, holding a plate with a cupcake on it.

'That's kind of you, Heather, but maybe I can have it later? I just need to see Vanessa.'

'Oh?' Heather glances at Edwin. 'I really don't think she's up to seeing anyone at the moment. She's... in a bit of a bad state. We're devastated that she didn't tell us about Khalid. We would have been happy for her. Finally, a boyfriend we could approve of. But his death has sent her spiralling. The doctor's given her some anti-anxiety medication, but she's just not talking to anyone. Even us.' She glances at her watch. 'Where is Myles? He said he'd be here by now.'

'Still not answering his phone,' Edwin says.

I look towards the stairs. 'Would you mind if I just showed my face? I want her to know I've come to see her, even if she doesn't want to talk to me.'

Heather glances at Edwin. 'Well, you can try, but I don't think it will do any good. Hers is the door at the end of the corridor.'

As I make my way upstairs, I half expect them to follow me, but they don't, although I feel their eyes on me.

Vanessa's bedroom door is closed, and she doesn't answer when I knock. Slowly, I open the door and find her in bed. The curtains are drawn, casting an eerie darkness into the room. 'Are you okay?' I ask, stepping inside.

She doesn't answer, or even move. Her eyes remain fixed on the wall as if she hasn't registered that I'm there.

'Vanessa? Can we talk? It's really important.'

Again nothing.

'I know how devastated you're feeling.' I picture my mum, how I sat by her bedside, holding her hand as she passed away, losing her battle with breast cancer. It was a year and a half ago, yet the memory feels like a gaping wound. Death changes us irrevocably, and I have no doubt that Vanessa will bear more scars from this.

Slowly, she pulls herself up, hugging her knees to her chest. And finally, she stares at me with vacant eyes.

I sit on the floor beside the bed, mindful of invading her personal space. 'Vanessa, I found Khalid's wallet in my bag and I have no idea how it got there.' I choose my words carefully. 'Can you think of anyone who might have slipped it in my bag?'

Silence.

'And then the police came to question me because I was the last person to see him.' I draw in breath. 'Except I wasn't – the person who did that to him was.'

There's still no reaction, and Vanessa continues her blank stare. 'Khalid was about to tell me something, but someone stopped him. I need to know why. Let me help you, Vanessa. I see that you're not like Charlie. Is that why you drifted apart? Did he do something that damaged your relationship?' I'm flailing in the dark here, but I know I'm close to the truth. I let the silence float around us, praying she'll say something, but at the same time wondering if the Hollingers have been right about Vanessa all along. Right now it seems she's beyond any help I can give her, and I don't know if I can trust anything she's told me. All I know for sure is that she was seeing Khalid.

Seconds tick by and I realise I can't reach Vanessa right now, so I stand and tell her I'll give her some space.

At the door, I turn back. 'I found something out today,' I say. 'Sophie was pregnant.'

I let her sit with my words for a moment. 'And I think you knew it. You had an argument about it at the Hurtwood one evening. Someone found her pregnancy test.'

Vanessa stares at me, her eyes wild. 'Get the fuck out!' she screams. 'Get the fuck out!'

. . .

When I get home, the smell of cooking greets me at the door. Checking to make sure Khalid's wallet is still in my pocket, I make my way to the kitchen.

Charlie is standing by the hob, stirring a large pan. He turns to me and flashes a bright smile, as if everything is normal between us. 'I'm cooking dinner for you,' he says. 'I know I haven't been around much since we moved here. And things have been a bit... strained between us, but I want to put things right.' He puts the spoon down and comes over to me, wrapping his arms around me. They feel unfamiliar now, as if we haven't touched for months, rather than days. More likely it's what I've learned about him since we moved here that makes Charlie a stranger to me.

'You didn't have to do that,' I say, glancing at the hob. He's gone all out with this meal.

'I wanted to,' Charlie says. 'It's also helped take my mind off Khalid. It's really hit me badly. I just don't get why he'd do that.' He kisses me, then goes back to the hob. 'It's beef ragu. Is that okay? I know you used to like it when we first met, but I don't think we've had it for a long time.'

'No, we haven't.' It does smell good; I hadn't realised how hungry I was. 'The police don't think it was suicide.'

Charlie's hand freezes mid-stir. 'What?' Slowly he turns to me.

My legs ache, so I pull out a chair and sit at the table. 'A detective came here this morning to question me. I was the last person to see Khalid, as he never went back to the party.'

'I don't remember. I was so out of it. Not proud of that.'

'Well, apparently he didn't make it back.' Which means it's likely he died soon after he dropped me home. After his urgent phone call, but I won't disclose that to Charlie. 'I don't know how the police are so sure it wasn't suicide, but...'

'What a mind-fuck,' Charlie says, stirring the ragu. 'Why would anyone kill him? Was it a mugging?'

'Really?' I snort. 'And they thought they'd just make it look like he hanged himself?'

'Yeah, I know, that doesn't make sense,' Charlie says. He joins me at the table. 'We should never have moved back here. I was thinking—'

The doorbell rings, and Charlie stares at me, but I shrug. 'I'm not expecting anyone,' I say.

While he goes to get the door, I walk over to the hob, staring into the pan. In all the time we've been together, Charlie has rarely cooked. He's taken me out for dinner, or ordered us takeaways, but hardly ever this.

'Hello, Emmie.'

I turn around to see Myles standing in the doorway. Charlie brushes past him and rushes back to the hob. 'Myles just wanted to come and check how I'm doing,' he explains.

'What a terrible day it's been,' Myles says. 'Or week, I should say. How are *you* feeling, Emmie?'

'I'm fine,' I say, annoyed that he's interrupted something important Charlie was about to say.

'You're cooking?' Myles says to Charlie. Without being invited, he takes a seat opposite me.

'Yes. I'm looking after Emmie.'

'Now, this I need to sample. Enough for me too?' Myles asks.

'Afraid not,' Charlie says. 'And actually, Emmie and I could do with some time alone.' The tension between them is palpable, and I recall Orla mentioning the argument she overheard them having a few months ago. When according to Charlie, he never came to Peaslake.

Myles glances between us. 'I would have thought you have plenty of time alone together. Not like you have kids taking up all your time.'

'And how are your kids doing?' Charlie says, smiling.

Myles stares at the floor. 'That's low. You know how much my kids mean to me.'

Charlie turns back to the food, stirring it again even though I'm sure it doesn't need it.

'So sad about Khalid,' Myles says after a moment. 'I really liked him. You just never know what someone's going through.'

I'm about to correct him, but I don't bother; he'll find out soon enough, and I don't feel comfortable talking about Khalid to either of them.

'How about a coffee then before I go?' Myles says to Charlie. 'We could do with a chat about Vanessa. Mum and Dad really don't know what to do to help her. She can be so self—'

'If you don't mind, I'll leave you to it,' I say, standing and pushing back my chair. I won't sit here while they badmouth Vanessa, especially when she's not here to defend herself. 'Nice to see you, Myles.'

Leaving them to it, I head out to the garden, where it's far warmer than the stone-cold kitchen, even with the hob on high. I make my way to the summer house, glad to find it open so I don't have to go back in to get the key.

Inside, I collapse on the sofa, exhaustion overtaking me. I haven't spent any time in here since we moved, and it occurs to me that this is the only part of the house that doesn't need replacing. It's clean and modern, and I imagine the Hollingers barely spent any time in it.

I reach in my pocket for DC Stanthorpe's card, staring at it until the words blur. It is time for me to call her. Khalid's murder is proof that it's too dangerous for me to try and do this on my own, and I can't put Orla at risk either. I pull out my phone just as it pings with an email.

I don't recognise the address: allseeingeye@gmail.com, but the subject heading sucks all the air from my lungs: *Baby found in shallow grave in Peaslake.*

I open the email, but it's blank, and there's no attachment either. Before I can wrap my head around the strange email, the door slams shut and Charlie is standing there, staring at me. 'What are you up to?' he asks.

I shove my phone and the business card behind a cushion, aware that this makes me look guilty. 'Nothing. Just resting. I need it.'

Charlie walks closer to me. 'Yes, I'm guessing you do.'

My heart beats so rapidly, and my body feels as though it's on fire – I'm sure Charlie can see how nervous I am.

'Myles has just left,' he says. 'Shall we eat now? It's almost ready.'

'Actually, I'm not very hungry. But I'll have it later.'

He sits on the edge of the sofa. 'I've spent hours cooking that meal just for you. And you're happy for it to go to waste?'

'No, I just—'

'How long are we going to do this for?'

'What?'

'Cut the bullshit, Emmie. I *know*.'

I glance at the door, but with my injuries there's little chance I'll get past him. 'What are you talking about, Charlie?'

'I know who you are. And that our whole relationship has been a lie.'

TWENTY-NINE
JUNE 2009

Sophie has become adept at biding her time, waiting patiently to escape this nightmare she's in. And she's learned how to keep Charlie happy and unsuspecting. She sees him as much as she can, messaging him all the time as if she can't live without him. And she never mentions Liam's attack a couple of months ago, even though it's brought to the front of her mind whenever she's with Charlie. She's even tried to keep a distance from Liam, which she hopes he understands.

All of this is working. Charlie has no idea how she really feels, and this new dynamic has made him comfortable, so she no longer feels as though she's on a leash. But Sophie is no fool, and she doesn't stop watching him for a second, especially if he gets her a drink, or makes her any food.

This evening, all of his family are out, and she and Charlie are in his living room, stretched out on the floor, when she's hit by a wave of nausea. They've just eaten pizza, but it was a takeaway, and Sophie's had her eye on it since it was delivered. It tasted fine; surely she would have noticed if Charlie had slipped anything in it. Besides, part of her keeps hoping she got the wrong end of the stick when she overheard Charlie questioning his dad.

Without a word, she clamps her hand to her mouth and rushes to the bathroom, unable to answer Charlie when he calls after her.

Sophie feels slightly better once she's been sick, but as she looks in the mirror, a ghostly reflection stares back at her.

Charlie bangs on the door. 'Hey, are you okay? What's going on?'

And then it hits her like a tidal wave: Sophie can't remember the last time she had her period. She normally keeps track of it, but she's been so distracted with her exams that she hasn't been paying attention to her body. But she definitely hasn't had one since she started her exams in May. Possibly even before that. She buries her head in her hands – this is the last thing she needs. *Charlie's baby.*

'Sophie, talk to me.' Charlie pounds on the bathroom door again. 'I'm worried!'

'I'm okay,' she says. There is no way she'll tell him about this – he will make her get rid of it, she knows that as much as she knows her own name. He will never let a baby alter the course of his life. She opens the door and plasters on a smile. 'I think it's something I ate,' she says. 'Would you mind if I went home?' She nestles into him as she says this; she's worked out that physical contact with him softens the blow whenever she has to tell him something he won't be pleased to hear.

Charlie pulls back and stares at her for a moment, frowning, cementing in her mind that he's going to object. 'Okay,' he says, holding her tightly. 'I'll just have to miss you, then.' He kisses the top of her head. To the outside world, he behaves like the perfect boyfriend. 'See you tomorrow?'

'Yes. For sure.' It's all she can do not to run from this house.

. . .

Her mum's curled up on the sofa watching TV, her hands clasped around a mug of tea, when Sophie gets home. She looks content, and Sophie hasn't seen her so at peace for a long time.

Sophie stares down at her stomach, still flat because she can't be more than a couple of months gone. She should do a test, but somehow she can't face the thought of seeing those lines appear, of that white plastic stick spelling out her fate. She's fully aware this isn't healthy, but she wants to carry on as if nothing is happening.

Her mum looks up. 'Hi, love. Wasn't expecting you back so soon. Everything okay?'

Sophie's tempted to say what she thinks: *No, it's not. Charlie is awful and I think I'm pregnant.* Instead, she nods. 'Yep. Just really tired and wanted an early night.'

'I'm surprised you could tear yourself away from Charlie,' her mum says, smiling. 'I remember that feeling when I was with your dad. It makes you feel invincible, doesn't it?'

Even though this is not her experience, Sophie nods. 'Mum, are you happy here? I mean, I know you are, but is that because of Peaslake, or would you be happy anywhere?'

Lynette looks up, tilting her head to scrutinise Sophie. 'I love it here,' she says. 'I didn't think I'd ever get used to village life, and it took a couple of months, but I feel like this is where we belong.' She shrugs. 'I know life's still hard and I'm working three jobs, but I'm at peace with that. As long as I can provide for you and Orla, that's all I care about.' She smiles. 'So, to answer your question – I think my state of mind has got everything to do with being here. There's something about this place that makes me feel... myself.'

Sophie's heart sinks to have this confirmed, although it's what she already suspected. 'I love you, Mum,' Sophie says.

'Love you too. Now what's brought all this soppiness on? I don't think I've heard you say that since you were in primary school.' Lynette laughs.

'Just realised that I don't tell you it enough.' Sophie gives her mum a hug. 'Going up now. Night, Mum.'

In her room, Sophie starts a mental list of all the things she needs to do. She's got to make sure that she covers everything, leaving no trace of her here. And then she needs to find Caleb – he's the only one who can help her. She messages Vanessa, casually asking how she's doing. In less than a second, Vanessa is calling.

'Hey, you okay?' she asks. 'Hardly see you these days – you're always busy with my dear brother.'

'Yeah. Sorry,' Sophie says. 'I didn't mean for you to call – a text would have been fine.'

'Um, no, I couldn't. I need to talk to you. I was about to message you but then your text came through. It's like fate. We're connected, aren't we, Soph? No matter what.'

Sophie frowns, grateful Vanessa can't see her. 'Yeah. Course. What's up?' She prays this isn't about Charlie.

'I've found somewhere safer for Caleb to stay. Somewhere warmer. He can't stay in that tent, and it's taking him a lot longer than he'd thought to get together the money we need. But this place is closer to you than it is to me. So I was wondering if you could go and check on him? I've been calling him all day and he's not answering his phone. I'm worried. You know he has people who want to find him. People who... want him dead.'

'Yeah. Okay. Say no more. Where is he?'

'I've rented a garage, around the back of your flats.'

Sophie knows these garages but thought they belonged to the houses across the road. 'How did you—'

'Money talks, doesn't it? I offered to rent it from an elderly woman. Wasn't hard to convince her to let me have it. It's the one at the far end. Grey door. All the others are white.'

Sophie is stunned silent.

'Don't judge me – I'm giving her a good monthly price for it.

I'm doing her a favour – pensions don't go far, Sophie. Anyway, it's not for long. Caleb and I are determined to do this ourselves. I'm not asking my parents for any help. You should be proud of me.'

'Yeah, it's great,' Sophie says. 'But how can Caleb live in a garage?'

'Better than a tent, right?'

'I suppose.'

'So will you go, then? Now? Please, Soph.'

Sophie checks the time. Eight fifteen. Not too late. 'Okay, fine.'

'Thank you. You're the best friend anyone could ever have,' Vanessa gushes. 'Oh, I bumped into Liam Curtis this morning. He said he's inviting some people over to the Hurtwood for a barbeque, to celebrate the end of exams. And I think he wants to put the attack behind him and give people something else to talk about. Let's go together. I'll tell Charlie this is girl bonding time.'

Sophie's surprised that Vanessa is interested in going, but she can't be bothered to question her. 'Okay,' Sophie says, even though she doesn't really want to. But it doesn't matter – she's got an excuse to see Caleb now, and he's just the person she needs to speak to.

There's a code Vanessa has instructed Sophie to use when she reaches the garage. Knock four times, pause for a second, then knock three more. It all seems a bit over the top; Sophie can't see why she can't just call out to him that she's here. But Vanessa had insisted, saying it was her and Caleb's secret code so that he doesn't open the garage door for anyone else.

The door screeches open and Caleb stands there, his eyes wide when he realises it's not Vanessa. 'Sophie! How did you—'

'Sorry – Vanessa asked me to come and check on you. She can't get hold of you and she's worried.'

Caleb scans the garage area. 'You'd better come in,' he says, pulling her inside.

The first thing Sophie notices is how cold it is. They've had an early heatwave this June, but inside this place it could easily be winter. There are piles of boxes lined up against the back wall – which Sophie assumes belong to the elderly woman Vanessa is renting the garage from – and a strong musty smell. She feels sorry for Caleb having to live like this.

'Are you okay here?' she asks, stunned that he seems so relaxed about it.

'Better than dead in a ditch somewhere,' he says. 'Let's just say the tent wasn't safe enough. Sit. No chairs, though – only that.' He points to the grimy mattress on the floor and shrugs. 'Better than standing.'

Reluctantly, Sophie sits on Caleb's mattress, trying to ignore the icky feeling it gives her.

'Vanessa got me this,' he says. 'Said she couldn't stand the thought of me sleeping on the hard floor. Isn't that something? Trouble is, it's so filthy in here, so now it looks awful. It's only been a week. If you see her, don't tell her. I'll try and sort it out.'

'She really loves you,' Sophie says.

The smile vanishes from Caleb's face. 'Which is exactly why I have to leave her.'

'What? No, you just said you love her.'

'She deserves someone... easier than me,' Caleb explains. 'I come with so much baggage, and it's not fair on her.'

'Is that why you've been ignoring her messages?'

He nods, handing Sophie a can of Coke. 'This okay? It's all I've got. I'm starting to hate the stuff.'

'Plus, it's probably rotting your teeth,' Sophie says.

Caleb snorts. 'Think that's the least of my worries.'

'I need to ask you something,' Sophie says, taking the can and placing it on the floor.

'Go on.' Caleb's can hisses as he opens it, and he takes a long sip.

'I know this will sound weird. But do you know how I can get fake documents?'

He raises his eyebrows, staring at her for a long moment. 'What kind of documents are we talking about?'

'Everything I need to get a place at uni under a false name.'

'Woah, hang on a second. Why would you need to do that?'

Walking over here, Sophie knew he'd ask her this, and she thought she was prepared to answer, but now, having to reveal the truth about Charlie to this man she barely knows, she can hardly get the words out.

Caleb listens attentively, shaking his head when she gets to the part about Charlie asking his dad what pills could kill someone. 'Jesus. You think your life is in danger?'

'Possibly. But even if that's not what Charlie's intending, he made it perfectly clear that he'll ruin my mum's life if I leave him. Force her to leave the village when she's made it her home. Or get Orla taken away from us.'

Caleb mulls this over. 'So your plan is to disappear?'

'Yes. But I still want to go to university. I've worked hard to get good grades, and I've wanted to be a doctor since I was five. I'm not letting Charlie ruin that for me. Never.'

'Does Vanessa know?' Caleb asks.

'I can't tell her. Charlie's her brother. The less people who know, the better.' It's bad enough that Khalid will suspect what she's done as soon as she goes missing. She's just hoping he will keep silent.

'There's something else,' Sophie says. 'A bit of a hiccup in my life plan. I think I'm pregnant. And if Charlie finds out, then he'll make me get rid of it, but there's no way I could do that, no matter how hard it will be.' She feels tears threatening to fall and tries her best to stop them.

'I get it,' Caleb says.' Then he adds, 'I'd love to be a dad. It would give me a higher purpose than just myself. What could be better than that?'

Sophie nods. 'I'm sure Vanessa would love to have kids one day.'

He shrugs. 'Not sure she would. We've talked about it, and she's not against it, but I don't think it's ever been a goal of hers either. Anyway, that doesn't matter now. I've got to move on.'

'Nonsense!' Sophie says, surprised by her own vehemence. 'Do you love Vanessa?'

'Without a doubt. Never knew what it was until I met her. Corny as hell, I know.' He pauses, and Sophie notices his eyes glisten. 'But—'

'No buts, just fight for her.'

'Jeez, anyone ever told you how bossy you are? And I thought Vanessa was bad.'

Caleb is silent for a while, lost in his own thoughts, silently going over her story. 'If you're sure this is what you want,' he says finally, 'then I know someone who can help. We're talking passport, exam certificates. Any kind of ID. But it will cost you.'

Sophie nods. She's been saving up for years, without her mum knowing. Babysitting jobs in London, birthdays, Christmases – she's put aside all of it so she can help her mum and Orla if they ever need it. 'How much?' she asks, already fearing the answer.

'Not sure exactly. But I think we're looking at thousands.'

Sophie sucks in her breath; she doesn't have that much saved, and it will take years to get it.

'You don't have it, do you?' Caleb says, finishing his drink and crushing the can.

'No. Nowhere near.'

Caleb studies her. 'Then I'll help you,' he says, after a moment.

'I can't let you do that. That's money for a new life for you.'

'It's just money,' Caleb says. 'I've spent my whole life chasing it, and where's that got me? Has it made me happy? No. Has it made Vanessa love her family more because they're loaded? No. But look at you. You've got your head screwed on and you're a good person. Nothing to do with money. That's why I want to help you.'

Sophie can no longer hold back her tears; Caleb's kindness has rendered her speechless. 'Thank you,' she says when she's pulled herself together. And then she gives him a hug.

'I wasn't expecting that,' he says. 'Leave it with me. I'll need photos of you for the ID. Can you get those to me?'

Sophie nods. 'As soon as I can. This is urgent, Caleb.'

'I know,' he says. 'Your situation isn't good, that's for sure.'

He walks her to the garage door and pulls it up, shattering the silence of the night as it lurches open.

Outside, it's turned chilly, so she wraps her arms around her body. 'What shall I tell Vanessa?' she asks Caleb.

His mouth twists, and he lets out a sigh. 'Tell her you couldn't find me.'

THIRTY

As much as I've prepared myself for Charlie's lies, and the behaviour he exhibits towards me, the words he's just uttered are not something I ever thought I'd hear from him. *I know who you are. And that our whole relationship has been a lie.*

Again, I glance at the summer house door, but there are no options for me. My judgement day has come. And I have no plan for how to deal with this. My mind scrambles for answers, but the only thing I can hear is Charlie's voice telling me that he knows.

'I can see this is a huge shock to you,' Charlie says, casually folding his arms.

I don't speak – I can't. For a long time I've carefully plotted and planned all my words and conversations, so this unexpected twist has derailed me, and I feel as if I'm veering off a cliff.

With a heavy sigh, Charlie walks to the door, turns the key in the lock and slips it into his pocket.

He's planned this.

'I think you'd better start talking,' he says.

So I tell him everything. Because he already knows, and it will only make things worse if I lie.

A YEAR AND A HALF A AGO, LONDON

The Royal Marsden hospital feels like a second home. I know all the nurses' names, and I could navigate the corridors with my eyes closed if I wanted to. But, of course, I never do; eyes wide open at all times. After what happened to my dad, I will never be taken unawares.

I'm four minutes late today, and Mum will already be anxious, her mind conjuring up all kinds of horrific things that could have happened to me. 'I'm here,' I call, the second I reach the ward door, where Mum will be having her chemo. But there are only two patients hooked up to chemotherapy pumps, and my mother isn't one of them.

I step back into the corridor and spot Raquel, one of the nurses, walking towards me. 'Hi, do you know where my mum is?'

Creases form on her forehead and her mouth forms an apologetic smile. 'She's not having chemo now today, Emmie – she's been moved. I'm sorry, didn't anyone tell you?' She consults the tablet she's carrying. 'Um, I can get the doctor to speak to you.'

I'm the one who's anxious now. Mum needs her chemo – this isn't supposed to happen. It's keeping her alive. 'Can you just tell me where my mum is?'

She hesitates for a brief moment, then tells me to go with her. I follow her, focusing on the squeak of her shoes against the floor to try to drown out the voice in my head, one that's screaming that something terrible has happened. 'Is my mum okay?' I ask.

The grimace on Raquel's face tells me all I need to know.

'What is it?' I stop walking. 'Just tell me!'

'I'm so sorry. Your mum had some complications, and the doctors felt she was too weak to continue with her chemo. We think it's time to stop, and she agreed. I'm sorry if she didn't talk to you about that. We've had to refer her to the symptom control and palliative care team.'

I don't need her to tell me what this means. 'How long?'

'We can't know for sure, but it won't be more than a few days.' She tries to explain how my mum's body is packing in, her organs barely functioning. I can't listen; I only want to see my mum.

When I don't say anything, we continue along the corridor. My whole body feels numb, as if all emotions have drained away, leaving me an empty shell. In all the months Mum has been having treatment for her breast cancer, I've never let myself believe this would be the outcome.

Raquel stops outside a door. 'We've made her comfortable in a private room. You can stay as long as you want. Overnight if you'd like.'

I nod. 'Thank you.'

'I'll let Dr Ingrams know you're here. I'm sure there's a lot you'll want to ask him.'

She disappears, and I wait for the excessively loud squeak of her shoes to fade before I push through the door.

'Emmie,' my mum says, trying to pull herself up in the bed.

'You don't have to move,' I say, rushing over to her. There's a chair by her bed, so I sit down, taking her hand. I only saw her yesterday, but already she is frailer, as if her body has given up on itself. Or am I only seeing that now because of what I've just learned? 'Oh, Mum,' I say, bursting into tears, even though only moments ago I made a silent vow to be strong for her.

'I fought as hard as I could,' Mum says. 'But it's time to let go now, Emmie.'

I shake my head, though I know she's right. 'Please don't give up.'

'That's not what I'm doing, Emmie.' She rests her head against her pillow. 'I'm accepting it, that's all. There's a big difference.'

Her voice is dry and cracked, so I fill a cup of water from the jug on her side table and place it in her hand. She only takes a small sip.

'You have been the greatest blessing I could have hoped for,' she says. 'You and your brother.'

At the mention of Craig, I clutch her hand tighter. Mum rarely talks about him – it's too painful for her.

'I feel like I let him down,' she says. 'And I've carried that weight with me since he died.'

Only two months ago, while Mum was battling cancer. 'No, you didn't let him down,' I assure her. 'You did everything for him. For both of us. He made a choice to take his life – it's nobody's fault.'

'But it is someone's, Emmie. He was only sixteen – too young to have been so deeply scarred by life. He should have had coping mechanisms for when things got tough, but that was all taken away from him the minute he was born.'

I frown. 'It must have been hard for him, knowing he was given up by his birth mother. But he had you – and you gave him the best life you could. You made sure he knew you loved us both the same.'

'But it was never enough.'

I struggle to make sense of her words. Craig was a tiny baby when he was adopted – he wouldn't remember his birth mother.

'I wasn't going to tell you this,' she says, in a hoarse voice that must hurt her to speak. 'But I need to. Lies don't do any good, do they?'

'Mum, what is it?'

She takes her time to answer. 'There was more to Craig's adoption story than I told you both. Please don't hate me. I had good reason to keep certain things hidden. But then Craig found out. A few weeks before he killed himself.'

'What are you telling me, Mum? What did Craig find out?'

'His birth mum didn't just give him up for adoption when he was a newborn. She... she tried to kill him.'

The shock of her words snatches my breath. 'What... what happened?'

'He was found in the woods in a grave, partially buried – she must have heard someone and run off. If she'd finished burying him, he would never have survived.'

I can't find any words. 'And you found this out from the adoption agency?'

She lowers her eyes and grips the bed sheet with pale, bony fingers. 'No. Not exactly.'

'It must have been in the news, then. A terrible story like that.'

'No, it wasn't.'

'I don't understand.'

'It was a private adoption. And the woman with the baby was lovely. We met several times. She lived in Peaslake, a small village in Surrey. She told me she couldn't keep the baby.' She pauses for breath for several moments, but continues, determined to finish her story. 'She said she already had an older son and there was no way she could cope with a baby. But then, when it had all gone through, she came to see me and told me the truth.' Again, she pauses, rasping. 'She'd found that baby being buried in the woods. It was dark and she was walking the dog. She heard someone digging, so she ran towards them, but the person ran off. She was sure it was a female, though.'

I clap my hand to my mouth; I'm moments away from retching. 'But... why did she pretend the baby was hers?'

She closes her eyes and winces. 'She said she didn't want the baby to ever find out what his mother tried to do. She wanted him to have the best start in life, and not be defined by such a horrific act.'

We sit in silence for a moment, both of us lost in our own thoughts, and I picture Craig's face when he was happy. He could get whatever he wanted with that smile. He just never knew the impact he had on people, even at such a young age. 'But how did Craig find out?' I ask.

'I kept in touch with the woman. We often emailed, and we talked about it sometimes. Craig must have found my emails. He needed to use my laptop when his broke. He asked me about it, and I couldn't deny it. I didn't want to lie any more. But the truth sent him spiralling.' Tears slide down my mum's cheeks, and I reach for a tissue and dab them away. 'It's my fault,' she continues. 'But how could I have told him such a horrific story?'

I squeeze her hand and continue wiping away her tears.

'Not long before he died, he told me that all his life he'd had a little thought in the back of his head that one day he'd find his birth mother. He was convinced that because she'd be older now, and in a much better position in her life, that she'd be happy to see him. Finding out the truth destroyed all the hope he'd had. And I'm sorry I didn't tell you either. But you'd already suffered just knowing what happened to your dad in that basement.'

'Let's not talk about this now,' I say. 'It can't be undone. None of it matters now.'

She nods and exhales, as if she now has permission to be at peace. I hold her hand while she drifts off to sleep. And my eyes, too, start to close, so I don't notice when my mother is no longer there.

And it's too late for me to ask the name of the woman who found my brother.

THIRTY-ONE

After Mum's death, I go through all her papers and computer files but find nothing about the woman who took Craig to the adoption agency. I've always known her laptop password and she uses the same one for her emails, but when I check through them, there's nothing from anyone I don't recognise.

I learn all I can about Peaslake, that small village in Surrey Mum said Craig was found in, and using Google Earth, I zoom in on the forest, picturing the woman who wanted my brother to die there.

I've barely been out of London, but one weekend I hire a car and drive down there, just to see what it's like. I familiarise myself with the layout, storing it in my head for when I need it. The vast forest haunts me, but through my brother, I am linked to it now, so I will not walk away.

And still there is the unsettling question of who the mother is. I google news articles about Peaslake, and find one about a teenage girl who went missing at the same time. Sophie Bower. There's no mention of her being pregnant, but it's possible that if she was planning to do what she did, she wouldn't have told anyone. And her boyfriend was a boy called Charlie Hollinger. To this day, Sophie still hasn't been found.

The story refuses to leave my head, and I think about it constantly. It may or may not be linked to my brother, but I need to find out.

I learn all about Charlie Hollinger, a teenage boy at the time from a rich and powerful family who were loved in the community. And I know that if I'm ever going to find anything out, then I'll need to start with him.

Desperate for answers, for my dead mother and young brother, I become obsessed with Charlie Hollinger, a corporate lawyer in the city. In every spare moment that I have, I ride my bike to his offices, and sit and watch him from across the road. He is the person I need answers from, and I'm determined to find a way into his life.

The idea comes to me by chance, while I'm cycling home from his office one evening; it's funny how inspiration strikes when we don't expect it. There's a cyclist in front of me, riding too fast for these jam-packed roads. A double-decker bus swerves out, forcing him to veer into the oncoming traffic. It's a narrow miss, and the young male cyclist continues on, shaking his head as if he didn't just cause this. And a plan forms in my mind.

I do it the next day. It's a huge risk – and it could all go wrong, but I need to take this chance.

It's seven forty-five when Charlie Hollinger leaves his office and walks through the car park to his car. It's a shiny new BMW, and I feel bad that it's very likely about to get damaged.

He pulls out of the car park, and I'm there right behind him. Thankfully, he's driving slowly, the busy roads prevent any significant speed, and I take my opportunity when he stops at the traffic lights further along.

I glance inside his car, and see that he's looking at his phone, typing a message to someone. This couldn't be more perfect. I cross my fingers that the lights will change before he's finished on his phone.

They do. And Charlie Hollinger pulls off, his phone still in his hand. I aim my bike for his car, praying I'll make it out of this without serious injuries. I slam into his BMW, with an ear-splitting smash, and I'm catapulted too far into the air, across the bonnet of his car. I've underestimated the impact of this crash, but now it's too late.

I lie on the road in front of his car, fierce pain searing through my legs.

He rushes out of the car, leaving the door wide open, dropping to the ground by my side. 'Are you okay? I'm so sorry! Don't move – I'm calling an ambulance.'

But the pain is already fading, and I'm quite sure I haven't broken anything. 'No, honestly, I'm okay.' I gradually pull myself up, relieved that I can stand. But this has shaken me – I didn't plan for the impact to be so hard. And the damage to my bike is worse than I'd imagined. But I think of Craig, and I know that this is what I'm meant to do. 'My bike isn't okay, though.'

Charlie looks at the crumpled heap lying by his car. 'Jesus! This is awful. I... I wasn't on my phone – it literally just rang so I just looked at the screen.' *He's lying. I saw him typing on it.* 'Normally I connect it to the car system, but it hasn't been working.'

His rambling shows me how nervous he is – something I can definitely use to my advantage. I don't say anything, but stare at my bike.

'Listen, I'm so sorry,' he says, following the direction of my eyes. 'I can pay for a new bike for you. An even better one. I'll give you cash. Right away. No need for all the hassle of going through insurance, is there?'

'I loved that bike,' I say, and let the tears fall hard and fast.

'Listen, can we just talk about this?' he pleads.

I imagine begging isn't something this man is used to. More

likely getting his own way without any effort is the pattern his life has followed.

'There's a coffee shop around the corner,' he continues, when I don't respond. 'Let me just park my car back at my office and we'll go and keep warm while we sort this out. You must be really shaken up. I work literally two seconds from here. You could walk if you'd prefer not to get in my car. I would totally understand that.'

'Don't think I'll be walking with this pain in my legs,' I say, smiling. I want Charlie Hollinger to feel at ease with me. To feel as if I'm doing him a huge favour by not involving the police or insurance companies. Besides, I hadn't expected this; all I thought I'd get was his phone number and address – something to help me get closer to him so I can find out what happened to Sophie Bower and whether she's the one who tried to kill her own baby. My brother.

'Okay,' I say. 'Thank you.'

Charlie nods. 'Good. That's good.' He picks up the crumpled heap of a bike and manages to fit it in the boot of his car, then he opens the passenger door for me.

'Sorry your car got a bit damaged,' I say, pointing to the massive dent in the side.

'It's all right. I'm just glad you're okay. I'm Charlie, by the way.' He holds out his hand.

'Emmie.'

'Sorry we're meeting like this, Emmie.'

And he does look sorry, which makes me feel bad that I've changed the course of his day like this. Maybe even his life.

At the coffee shop, everything falls neatly into place, more securely than I could have imagined. True to his word, Charlie buys me an expensive new bike, ordering it on his phone right there with me. It's one I would never have bought for myself.

'Delivery to your address in five days,' he says. 'Will you manage without one until then?'

'Yes,' I say. 'I live close to my work, so not a problem.'

'What were you doing around here?' he asks.

'Had a training course,' I lie. 'That's why I was on my bike.'

He swallows my lie, and I think what a shame it is that we've met like this. He seems like a decent person.

It's not the end of things after the coffee shop. Charlie Hollinger and I have somehow connected, and we're drawn to each other, wanting to spend more and more time together, first in video calls, then in person. I know he's developed feelings for me, but it's not until two months after the accident that he asks if I'll go on a date with him.

My conscience tells me to say no, and that I could try to force a friendship instead, but being involved with him romantically will make things much easier. And quicker.

And then he's moving into my flat – I love my place and refuse to give it up for his excessively priced rented flat in Chiswick. 'Why don't you buy somewhere?' I'd asked him, before we'd got together. 'Surely you don't have to rent.'

'Too big a commitment,' he'd explained. 'I like to think that I can up and leave at any time.'

It was only later I found out that this had been Charlie's attitude to girlfriends too. One after another, an endless trail of relationships with no meaning. Faces soon forgotten about.

And Charlie thinks I am just another woman who will leech off him. That couldn't be further from the truth.

Over time, I learn about Charlie's wealthy family, and the close bond he shared with his siblings growing up in Peaslake, but never once does he mention Sophie Bower, or any baby left to die in the woods. I have to be subtle with my questioning, but even that draws nothing out of him. Which intrigues me even more, fuelling my desperate need for the truth. Charlie is too guarded, as if he's carefully selecting what he wants me to see.

Months pass, and just as I've got comfortable, sure that Charlie has fallen for me and I'm not just another woman to add to his long list of past relationships, we face a challenge that takes me by surprise.

Charlie gets nervous.

He's been so content with our relationship, and falling into a commitment he didn't plan for, that he's barely had a chance to reflect on what he's giving up to be with me. Until one day it hits him.

I know something's wrong when he walks in the door that evening. He barely looks at me, and there are anxious frown lines etched on his face. And when I try to hug him, he smells different, a mixture of alcohol and unfamiliar perfume.

'You're leaving,' I say, pulling away.

He misinterprets the fear in my eyes, assuming that I love him so much I don't want him to walk away. When the reality is that I'm wondering how I will get the truth about Sophie Bower out of him now. He might eventually be happy to talk to me if I'm his partner, but if I'm an ex-girlfriend, then he'll avoid me, like he does all the others – I know his style.

Charlie takes his time to answer, and I've been living with him long enough to know that I need to let him be, that forcing him to talk will only make him close down even more.

'I bumped into an ex today,' he says, still avoiding looking at me. 'We... had a drink. That's all. I didn't touch her or anything. But... it made me think. Not about her, but about me. Us, I mean. I... I'm not good with relationships. I start to feel... trapped.' Finally, he looks at me. 'It's nothing to do with you, please believe that, Emmie. Maybe I just need some space. To think things through.'

I walk over to him and put my arms around him, holding him close to me. 'It's okay,' I say, as if I'm soothing a child.

He pulls back and stares at me. 'You're really okay about this?'

'Love should have wings to fly,' I say, quoting something my mum used to always tell me. 'I will never force it.'

He buries his head in my neck and cries, so I stroke his hair and tell him it will be okay. But when his tears don't subside, I wonder if it's something else he's distraught about. When he finally gets up and heads to the bedroom to pack a bag, I have no choice but to start formulating a plan for how I will get what I need without Charlie in my life.

But three weeks after that night – three weeks during which I've made no headway – Charlie comes back to me, turning up at the pupil referral unit where I work. And just as silently as he left, he is in my life once more. Things are strained between us, no matter how hard we try to pretend nothing happened, but then an offer from his parents changes everything.

'This could be just what we need,' I say. 'A fresh start away from London. Our own house.'

'I do want a fresh start,' Charlie says. 'Just not there. I can't go back to Peaslake. Not

now. Not after all these years.'

But Charlie's parents are refusing to sell the house, insisting it should stay in the family, which only helps my cause. 'Myles is in Leeds, and they won't offer it to Vanessa,' he says, without expanding on why.

'I think we should take it,' I say. 'Once it's in our name, we can always sell it further down the line. They might not care by then. And I want to get away from that creep Gary next door.'

'I've dealt with him,' Charlie says. 'Hasn't he left you alone now?'

'But for how long?'

Charlie still won't be persuaded, so I try another tactic. 'I had a letter from the landlord yesterday. He's selling up and needs us out of here in the next two weeks.' Charlie will never ask to see proof; he seems to trust me. 'You've been so busy with work, I didn't want to worry you. I was planning to find somewhere else for us ASAP.'

'Oh, Emmie, please don't worry – we can easily find somewhere else.'

'There's something else... I found out today I've been made redundant.' I haven't planned to say this, but I need Charlie to see that we need to take his parents' house. And it's not too hard to make myself cry – all I do is imagine leaving the job I've loved for seven years, and a waterfall cascades from my eyes.

This seems to work, and Charlie holds me tightly, telling me maybe they could take the house after all, if it will make me happy. But the decision weighs down on him.

Everything has fallen into place, and soon we are moving to Peaslake, where I will find out how Charlie is linked to Craig's birth, and the shallow grave he was left to die in.

* * *

Charlie stares at me, his eyes full of vitriol. 'You made me think you loved me. And the whole time you set me up.'

'What did you do to Sophie? You knew she was having your baby, didn't you? Did you try to force her to get rid of it? Was it you who buried the baby in the woods? My brother! Sophie wanted to keep it, so you tried to kill it instead. What did you do to Sophie?' I have no evidence of this, but I don't want to believe Sophie could have done that to her baby without being pressured by someone.

'I don't know what you're talking about,' Charlie says, grabbing my arm so tightly it burns my skin. 'Did that hurt? Still in pain after your *real* bike accident? Or did you fake that one too?' He pulls me to the door and unlocks it, dragging me across the garden and shoving me through the kitchen door. I try to squirm away from him, to fight, but my body is weak, and Charlie easily overpowers me.

'I know how much you like basements,' he snarls. 'Maybe you need some time to think about what you've been doing.' He pushes me towards it.

I scan the kitchen, searching for anything I can use to defend myself, but there's nothing I can easily reach. My throat constricts and my stomach lurches; I know now that Charlie is a killer – he won't think twice about doing the same to me. 'Why did you do that to Khalid? He was your best friend!'

'Shut up! You need to stop talking,' Charlie demands. He shoves me into the basement, sending me hurtling down the stairs.

And then I hear the key turn in the lock, and I know that I will never get out of here.

THIRTY-TWO

I bang on the basement door until my knuckles bleed, but Charlie doesn't respond. I don't even know if he's still in the house, and there is no way to know what's happening outside these walls.

I look around me, and although the basement has been replastered and the floor redone, there's nothing in here – no food, nothing to sit on. Panic overwhelms me and I sink to the floor, pulling my knees up to my chest for comfort, and cursing myself for leaving my phone in the summer house.

Is this where Sophie ended up? All because she had a baby growing inside her that Charlie didn't want. The thought of it sickens me. Craig had his problems, but beneath that, he was a kind and loving boy. It was finding out about his birth mother and what she'd done that made him suffer the way he did.

With no phone or watch, I don't know how long I sit there, minutes blurring into each other, before I hear footsteps in the kitchen. The basement door opens, and Charlie stands there, holding out a plastic carrier bag. 'I've brought you some food,' he says. 'Thought you'd be hungry.' He sounds like the man he was when I first met him.

'How did you know?' I ask. 'When?'

'I could tell you,' Charlie says. 'But why would I give you that satisfaction after what you've put me through? For over a year! I loved you, Emmie.'

'Like you loved Sophie?'

He ignores me. 'And you've made a fool of me.'

I try to glance past him, but he's blocking the door.

'Here,' he says, handing me the bag. When I don't take it, he throws it on the floor by my feet.

'I don't want food,' I say. 'I just want to get out of here. Let me go and I'll disappear. You'll never hear from me again. I don't care what happened with Sophie, or—'

He steps inside. 'And you think I'll believe anything you say? After being lied to for over a year. You'll never let this go. Look at the lengths you've already gone to. All the lies and deception. The manipulation.'

'Not just me,' I say. 'What about your lies, Charlie?'

'Not telling you about Sophie isn't a lie,' Charlie says. 'Huge difference.' He steps closer to me, and I shrink back, aware of how vulnerable I am at this moment.

'You had a baby. I'd say that counts as a lie.'

Charlie shakes his head, but he looks unsure of himself. 'I would have known if Sophie was pregnant. And she wasn't.'

'You're lying. Covering things up to keep your family name untarnished.'

He grabs my arm, and I swing around, pulling away as forcefully as I can manage. Charlie reels back, then loses his balance, falling backwards down the stairs. I stare in horror, praying he's not dead, but then slowly, he moves, pulling himself up.

I take the opportunity and run from the house, as fast as my bruised and battered body will allow.

Outside, it's pitch black; Charlie had kept me locked in that basement for hours. I keep running, checking behind me to see if he's coming after me. But he doesn't. I don't let myself slow down or stop, though – Charlie will never let me go, not after what I know. I feel as though I have no more breath left when I reach the Hurtwood. The car park is empty, so I assume it's past closing time. With a quick glance behind, I reach the main door and push through it, surprised to find it open.

Liam is clearing tables, and when he sees me he rushes over. 'What's happened? You look—'

'Can you lock the door? Please. Just lock it!'

He stares at me for a second but then grabs his key from his pocket and hurries to the door. 'Emmie, what's going on? Are you okay?'

'No... I...'

He takes my arm. 'Just sit down.'

'Not here – can we go upstairs?'

He nods, and I follow him through the door at the back of the bar.

'My parents are asleep, so we'll have to be quiet,' he says, when we get to the living room.

While he fetches me a glass of water, I tell him everything that's happened, including how I came to be in Charlie's life. I'm taking a huge risk trusting him, but Charlie already knows, and it's likely he won't keep quiet, so it makes little difference.

'Let me just get my head around this,' Liam says. 'Your relationship with Charlie was never real?'

I shake my head. 'Not on my part, at least.'

Liam smiles. 'Well, isn't that karma for you?' He must notice the look of disapproval on my face and quickly backtracks. 'Sorry, I mean, yeah, he's got what he deserves, but this is awful for you and your family.'

'I'm the only one left of my family,' I explain. 'Which is why I need answers. My brother died because of the trauma of learning he was almost killed as a baby. I can't let this go, Liam. He was sixteen. And my mum gave him all the love she could, but it wasn't enough. I think that destroyed her.' I clench my hands to stop them shaking. 'You must have known about the baby? How did nobody here know Sophie was pregnant?' I don't mention the blank email I was sent with the subject heading about the baby being found in a shallow grave in this very village.

'No, I didn't know! Nobody knew. I swear to you. She must have hid it well. But I don't believe Sophie would have done that to her baby,' Liam says. 'Never. She would have found a way to look after her baby *and* go to university. Lynette would have helped her.'

'That's what I want to believe too,' Emmie says. 'Which means that Charlie must have done it. And if he's capable of burying his own baby alive, then what did he do to Sophie?'

Liam falls silent. 'I loved her,' he says. 'In a way that's different to how you might imagine. Yes, I was attracted to her, and if she'd wanted to be with me then I wouldn't have hesitated. But it was more than that. We had a connection far deeper than physical attraction.'

I study Liam; he's an attractive man, beyond just looks, and it crosses my mind that if Sophie was here now, then there's every chance she might have wanted more from him. My heart aches with sadness, even though I still don't know for sure that Sophie is innocent.

'She was young. Desperate. She had other plans for her life. People do rash things when they're trapped.'

'We're talking about murder,' Liam says. He will never see Sophie as anything other than perfect. 'But there's something more pressing to deal with. Charlie. Khalid's already dead, and clearly you're supposed to be next, especially now he knows that you never loved him. He's obsessive, Emmie. And although she never said it, I got the feeling that Sophie didn't want to be with him any more. But she was too scared to leave him.'

'We're missing something that's right in front of us,' I say. 'I just don't know what!'

'Can I say something?' Liam says. 'You won't like it, but I need to tell it to you.'

I nod, already preparing to defend myself.

'You could let this go. Get out of here before Charlie finds you. Never look back. Your mum and brother are gone now, and finding out the truth won't bring them back. It's not worth risking your life.'

'Don't you think I've thought about that? Every day since we got here I've wanted to run. But I will never give up, no matter what it costs me – I've already lost everything I cared about.'

Liam silently digests my words, then slowly nods. 'Okay. What can I do to help you?'

'Can I stay here for a bit? Just until I can work out what to do. Charlie won't look for me here, he doesn't even know we've been talking.'

Liam nods. 'Of course. But I really think you should go to the police.'

I think of DS Stanthorpe, and her business card shoved behind a sofa cushion in the summer house, along with my phone. Thankfully, Khalid's wallet is in my pocket, and I breathe a sigh of relief that Charlie won't come across it and take it to the police, who would find my fingerprints all over it. I open my mouth to tell Liam about finding it in my bag, but instinctively I freeze. I don't want him mistrusting me; I need him onside. While I'm staying here, I can find somewhere to hide it in the hotel.

'I *will* go to the police,' I tell him. 'But first I need to speak to Vanessa. I can't do that until Charlie's at work, though, in case he suddenly turns up at his parents' house.'

'I can try and figure out where he is tomorrow,' Liam says.

'And I'll need Edwin and Heather to be out of the house when I try to see Vanessa. They're so protective of her, and last time I could tell they didn't want me speaking to her.'

'I'll head over there in the morning and try to find out,' Liam says.

'But you'll need a reason to go there,' I say.

Liam smiles. 'Got one. A nice bottle of Dom Pérignon. Let's just say it's a housewarming gift from my parents because they couldn't go to the party.'

'Perfect,' I say.

'Come on, let me get you a room. You must be shattered. There's nothing more we can do tonight, and at least you'll be safe here. Charlie's not getting in this place.'

The room Liam's offered me overlooks the large beer garden at the back of the hotel. I stand by the window, staring out at the lawn. There are stake lights all around it, casting a white glow onto the forest beyond. The place where my brother was left to die.

Liam has made me a ham sandwich and put some fruit on a plate for me, but I leave it on the desk and climb into bed, every limb in my body screaming for respite.

I wake in the night, certain I heard a noise outside. Climbing out of bed, I check the room door is locked, then peer out of the window. There's no one there, though anyone could be lurking in the shadows. Charlie has made me paranoid, and I can't let him do that to me. I get back into bed and close my eyes, trying to drown out the warning voices in my head screaming that I need to get out of this place.

. . .

Sheer exhaustion allows me to sleep, and when slivers of sunlight force my eyes open in the morning, I groan as the events of yesterday come crashing back to me. Charlie knows everything, and locked me in the basement – probably in exactly the same way that he kept Sophie a prisoner.

Liam knocks on my door just after eight, and brings in a tray of breakfast. I stare at the toast and croissants, the steaming pot of tea, and although my stomach aches for food, my mind is repulsed by it. 'Thanks,' I say, putting the tray beside my untouched sandwich from last night.

'You should keep the curtains closed,' Liam says, crossing to the window and pulling them shut. 'People in the beer garden could see you, and we don't want anyone knowing you're here. I haven't told a soul – and I've registered you under the name Bella Holmes.'

I raise my eyebrows. 'Where did you get that name from?'

'A book I'm reading,' he says, grinning. 'Seriously, though, you need to stay in this room until I know where Charlie is and what his plans are. I still think you should go to the police.' He pulls something from his pocket. 'This is an old phone of mine. Still works. I've put my number in it so you can reach me anytime. I've put Vanessa's in there too. You can even use it to... I don't know... call the police?'

'Not until I've spoken to Vanessa. And Lynette. I need to tell them both the truth about who I am before they hear it from Charlie.'

'I do get all that, but like I said last night, don't you think your safety is more important right now?'

He's right. Which means I'm a prisoner in this hotel, dependent on Liam, a man I barely know. 'I'm not good at standing still,' I say. 'But if it makes you feel any better, I will stay here until you tell me it's safe to go and see Vanessa.'

'Let's hope it won't be long,' Liam says. 'And then you'll tell the police that Charlie locked you in the basement? Tell them everything he's done?'

'Yes,' I say. But how can I, when Charlie might have fabricated more evidence linking me to Khalid's death? 'Can you just be quick finding out where he is?'

'I'm already on my way.'

I watch Liam leave, and when the door closes, I realise that I'm just as trapped and powerless as I was in that basement.

THIRTY-THREE

Liam has given me some books to read, but I barely take in the words. Instead, I constantly check the time, minutes merging into hours with still no word from him. I try to call him, but it rings without him answering. And there's no message from him on the phone he's given me.

By two p.m., I can no longer ignore or dismiss the swell of fear in my gut that's bubbled in me since he left this morning. I have no idea where he is, but I'm sure he hasn't come back to the Hurtwood all day.

Slipping Liam's phone in my pocket, I open the door and peer outside. The corridor is empty, so I slip out and make my way downstairs; there's a door leading to the beer garden at the bottom of the stairs, so I can avoid the bar area.

I breathe in the humid summer air, feeling as though I haven't seen daylight for weeks.

Without my phone, I can't get an Uber, so I have no choice but to walk to Shere.

I'm still sore after my accident, and it takes me nearly an hour and a half, but when I reach the Hollingers' new house, I'm relieved to see their car isn't in the driveway, and neither is

Myles's. There's a chance that wherever they are, Vanessa could be out with them, but it's not likely, given the grief she's suffering after Khalid's murder.

I ring the doorbell and stand back to wait. Seconds tick by and there's no answer. Looking up at Vanessa's window, I see her there watching me, making no attempt to hide herself.

'Can we talk?' I shout up. I place my hands together as if in prayer. 'Please.'

She doesn't move.

I pull out Liam's phone and dial her number, and just as I hold it to my ear, I wonder how Liam had Vanessa's number. But she answers immediately, so I don't have time to dwell on that. 'What do you want, Emmie? Can't you just leave me alone?' Her voice sounds slurred, too slow, as if her senses have been dulled.

'Please, Vanessa,' I beg. 'I really need to talk to you. Can you just let me in? I won't stay long, I promise. And then you'll never have to see me again.'

There's a slow and heavy sigh. 'Mum and Dad don't want me talking to anyone.'

'Where are they?'

She hesitates before answering. 'London. Seeing friends. But I don't want—'

'Please, Vanessa. I need to tell you the truth.'

She falls silent, and I wonder if she's ended the call, until she finally tells me that she'll come down.

Her skin is pallid and her eyes red, underlined with dark circles. Her usually neat blonde hair is matted and she's wearing pyjamas. It's a heart-wrenching sight, and I wonder how much of it is down to grief, and how much is due to her former struggles. I can't let myself think like this; Vanessa is in pain, and she needs me to trust her.

'What do you mean, you need to tell me the truth?' she asks when I step inside and close the door.

'Can we go and sit down? In the living room?'

She shakes her head. 'No, not in there. My room.'

I don't argue with her; it's probably the only place she feels safe.

Upstairs, she climbs into bed and pulls the duvet up to her chin, drawing her knees up and gently rocking.

I perch on the end of her bed. 'Vanessa, I need to tell you something about me. And you may hate me afterwards for not being open about it, but that's a chance I have to take. I hope you won't, though. I hope you'll understand.' I take a deep breath. 'I'm in danger, and now I'm certain that Charlie wants me dead. Because I've been digging up the truth about what happened to Sophie.'

Vanessa's eyes widen and she stops rocking, staring at me as if she can't make sense of what I've said.

'Yesterday... Charlie locked me in the basement, and it's only by luck I got away. I've been hiding since then; it's a risk for me to even be here, but I needed to come and see you. I think Charlie killed Khalid.'

She gasps and starts rocking again.

'Khalid was trying to tell me something, and I'm sure it was about Charlie.' I move closer to her, try to reach for her arm, but she pulls away. I begin my story, telling her every detail of how my brother Craig was buried in the woods as a newborn, left to die by his own mother. When I've finished, a haunting silence hangs between us, and I have no idea what Vanessa will say, or if she'll even respond. Has she even heard what I've said? 'Vanessa? I'm sorry. But I had to find out what happened to my brother's birth mother. I think that was Sophie. I know this is a lot to take in. She was your closest friend, and it's going to be hard for you to believe she would try to kill her baby. But it looks like that's what happened.'

Vanessa rocks more violently now, and begins groaning. 'No,' she says. 'No.'

'But if it wasn't Sophie, then I think Charlie did it. The woman who found the baby thought it was a female running off, but she couldn't be completely sure. It was dark, and it all happened quickly. It could have been Charlie.' I pause to give Vanessa time to digest my words. 'I'm going to the police with this, but I wanted to warn you. Because it's not just the attempted murder of a baby, it's Khalid's death, and Sophie's disappearance too.'

Again, Vanessa groans, placing her hands over her ears like a child who doesn't want to be told what to do. She lurches forward and tries to grab my top, but I manage to pull back before she can get hold of me.

And then the door flies open, and Myles stands there, staring at us. 'What the hell is going on? Vanessa's not supposed to have any visitors.'

'I'm going,' I say, standing. I turn to Vanessa. 'I'm so sorry.'

But Myles blocks the doorway, pulling the door shut and standing in front of it. 'I can't let you do that,' he says, shaking his head.

My body feels as if it's on fire, and I try to push past him. 'Let me go, Myles.'

He grabs me and pushes me to the floor. 'Tell me what the hell you're doing here.'

I turn back to Vanessa, who's staring at Myles as though she doesn't recognise him, but she stays silent.

'I came to see how Vanessa's doing,' I say. 'That's all. So I think you should let me go now. Or do I have to call the police?'

'You're lying,' Myles says. 'Every word that comes out of your mouth is a lie. Charlie's told me everything – I know that you're a fraud, conning my brother into having a relationship with you so you can get close to our family.'

There's no point denying this if Charlie has told Myles everything. 'I just want to find out what happened to Sophie.

That's all. I didn't want to hurt your family. But I think Charlie killed—'

'Shut up!' Myles shouts, shoving me back. 'Jesus! You should never have come here, Emmie.'

'I'll leave,' I say. 'Right now. There's nothing else I can do here.' I make my way to the door, but once again Myles blocks me.

'It's too late,' he says.

Vanessa jumps up, rushing to Myles and ploughing into him. 'Let her go! This has nothing to do with her. It's all my fault! I'm the one who's a murderer!'

THIRTY-FOUR
AUGUST 2009

Sophie hasn't seen Vanessa since they argued at Liam's barbeque, and that was weeks ago. Vanessa is avoiding her, quickly disappearing whenever Sophie spots her around the village. Sophie tries to convince herself it doesn't bother her – she's moving on soon, and Vanessa will no longer be in her life – but the truth is, it stings.

Her mum calls to her from downstairs, telling her dinner is ready. The smell of chilli con carne drifting up the stairs makes her mouth water. Sophie heads to the kitchen, fully aware that she needs to pull herself together. There's much to be grateful for: Charlie has no idea that the time on their relationship is about to expire, and he's actually been quite decent over the last few months. Sophie has made him feel secure, and this has lulled him into a false sense of security. And right now, all the Hollingers are in Wales for a week, to stay in their holiday home near the beach. Charlie had told Sophie he wanted her to go with them, with that look in his eyes that dared her to object, but her mum provided the perfect excuse for Sophie to get out of it: she couldn't get a babysitter for Orla. Charlie couldn't argue with that.

All is well, even though Vanessa acts as if Sophie's got some infectious disease she doesn't want to catch.

After dinner, she sits with her mum on the sofa, pretending to be interested in the film they're watching. It's an old film, *Beaches*, about a strong friendship between two women, and all it does is remind Sophie of Vanessa.

Just before nine p.m., her phone rings. A withheld number. Hoping it's not Charlie, but knowing there's no one else it could be this late, she tells her mum she'll take it upstairs.

'Hello?' Sophie prepares herself to hear Charlie's voice, to tell him she misses him when the opposite is true.

'Sophie? It's Caleb.'

'Oh, hi.' It's been weeks since she's heard from Caleb, and she's begun to think he's given up on the idea of helping her. 'What number is this?'

'I'm at a payphone. By the shop. Just need to be careful. You okay?'

'Yeah, I am now that Charlie's in Wales.'

'Yep, I think that's turned out to be a good thing for both of us.'

'Is something wrong? You and Vanessa are okay, aren't you? I know you had a wobble a few months ago, but you told me you'd fixed things.'

'Don't worry – Vanessa and I are fine. We're better than okay,' he says, and she can almost feel the smile coming through his words. 'Can you meet me tonight? In half an hour? Your documents have arrived.'

A rush of adrenalin floods through her; Sophie's been waiting for this moment for months. 'Where?'

'Vanessa's given me her spare key to the farmhouse. That's what I meant when I said them all being in Wales has worked out for me too. She persuaded me to stay there while the house is empty. I tried to protest, but you know what Vanessa's like. She insisted. And actually, it's better than that garage. It's starting to feel a bit like a prison cell in there. So you'll meet me there, yeah?' There's urgency in his voice now, as if he needs to get off the phone quickly.

Sophie's not sure. It will feel weird going to the farmhouse without any of the Hollingers there. But she needs those documents. 'Yeah, I'll come. Did it all arrive? Everything we paid for?'

'Yep. Passport, exam certificates. The whole shebang. Worth every penny, I'd say. No one would ever know they're not real.'

'And it's got my new name on it?'

'Yep, you're now Scarlett Humphries. It actually suits you.'

Sophie knows this will take some getting used to, but it will be worth it. And then when she's settled into her new life and given it some time, she'll let her mum know that she's okay. She's already got a letter in her drawer, ready to leave on her mum's pillow. Short and sweet, but enough to make sure she doesn't cause her mum unnecessary pain:

> *I love you, Mum. I have to go, but I'll be back. I can't explain now, but I have no choice. Please don't worry about me – I am going to be fine. But please don't tell anyone about this note. No one. Tell everyone that you don't know where I am. Please, Mum. Soon you will understand. I love you and Orla xx*

Sophie spent so much time agonising over every word that she can recall each one of them without looking at it.

'Guess I should start calling you Scarlett,' Caleb continues.

'No, not yet. That's for my new life. Right now, I'm still Sophie.'

'I'm excited for you,' Caleb says. 'You deserve this.'

'And you and Vanessa deserve every happiness too.'

'Thanks,' he says, more quietly. 'Oh, yeah, one more thing. I've got a phone you can use. It's a spare phone I got Vanessa so she could message me without worrying someone might see it. Nobody would look for a phone they didn't know she had, would they? But we won't need it any more. She's going to tell her parents about me.'

This explains the other phone Sophie saw Vanessa with. 'That's great, Caleb. I'm really happy for you. See you in half an hour.'

'I'll leave the back door open,' Caleb says.

When the call ends, Sophie grabs her backpack. She'll need it to put the documents in. She closes her bedroom door, and at the front door, calls to her mum that she's just popping out.

Her mum comes into the hallway. 'You look lovely,' she says.

Sophie thanks her and rushes out, even though she's desperate to give her mum a hug. If she does, though, her mum will immediately sense that something is going on. Sophie has never been able to lie to her.

It's a warm evening, and the sky has a dark purple hue as Sophie makes her way to the Hollingers' farmhouse. She doesn't want to go through the woods at this hour, but it's far quicker, and she's impatient to get her hands on her new documents. Her ticket out of this place. At the edge of the forest, she hesitates as she flicks on the small torch she's brought with her. It's not that late, she'll be fine. She can do this.

With a deep breath, she scans the road to make sure no one is following her, then heads into the darkness.

Under her feet, branches and twigs snap and crunch, and she's grateful for the noise breaking the eerie silence. And if anyone is following her, she is bound to hear their footsteps. Deeper into the forest, her anxiety starts to heighten, and she breaks into a run, her stomach cramping as she sprints. She stops and places her hand on her stomach, doubling over to stop the pain.

She hears the snap of a twig, and turns around, peering into the darkness. Someone is out there. 'Hello?' she calls out, just to let them know she's aware of their presence. And then she runs again.

There are tears in her eyes by the time she reaches the edge of the forest and steps out onto the main road. She glances back at the forest, but there's no one there. She's certain there was, though, and wonders if someone who's after Caleb somehow knows she might lead them to him.

She hesitates for a moment, but then continues running again, determined not to stop even with the excruciating cramps in her stomach.

By the time she reaches the farmhouse, Sophie is convinced she was overreacting. There's nobody behind her; everything is fine. She opens the side gate, and makes her way to the back door. True to his word, Caleb has left the kitchen door open.

'Hello?' she whispers, stepping inside, her anxiety returning, making her palms sweat.

Voices drift from inside the house, and she can only make out who's speaking when she slowly opens the kitchen door.

She can hear Caleb's voice, coming from the living room. 'Please,' he begs. 'I'm telling the truth!'

Panic overwhelms her. Someone has found him – is this her fault? Did they follow her after all? But then how did they get in the house before her? She pulls out her phone, ready to call the police, but stops dead when she hears a familiar voice.

Heather Hollinger.

Screaming at Caleb.

But it can't be Heather; she's supposed to be in Wales.

When the woman speaks again, though, Sophie knows for sure it's her. She creeps along the hallway, grateful that the light isn't on. The living room door is ajar, and she flattens herself against the wall, a few feet away, peering inside.

Her breath catches in her throat when she sees that it's not just Heather in there, but Edwin and Myles too. Is Charlie also here in the house? And Vanessa? Was Charlie lying to her about them going away? But Vanessa never would have let Caleb come to their house if that was true.

'You're lying!' Heather screams. 'You piece of scum. You broke into our house and I'm calling the police right now!'

'Please,' Caleb begs. 'I promise you. I've been seeing Vanessa for a year and a half. All the times she's been out at night, it's been to see me.'

'He's lying,' Myles says. 'Vanessa would never—'

'Never what?' Caleb says. 'Be with someone like me? You don't know your sister, do you? In fact, none of you know her! You all make her life miserable. That's why we're getting out of here. She can't stand being around you any more. Being part of your family. In fact, she never could.'

Edwin rushes towards him. 'How dare you! You vile...' He turns to Heather. 'Call the police. Quick. I'm not listening to any more of this... this—'

Caleb lunges towards Heather, trying to grab her phone, but she pulls back and his body smashes into her instead. With a scream, she falls to the floor.

'I'm sorry,' Caleb says. He steps towards her, reaching down to help her up, but before he can, Myles is towering over him, clutching Heather's marble lamp in his hands. The one Sophie knows is a family heirloom and probably weighs as much as she does.

It seems to happen in slow motion: Myles smashing it into Caleb's head, the heavy *thunk* it makes as it crushes his skull, the shower of blood cascading over him, all over the floor, all over Heather. Caleb drops to his knees, then falls on his side by Heather's feet.

Sophie's not sure who's the first to scream – it could be Heather, or Myles, Edwin even. All Sophie knows is that *she's* screaming too, the sound piercing her own eardrums. And now it's too late for her to hide.

The Hollingers all turn to stare at her, and for a moment nobody speaks, all of them in a twisted and heinous tableau that none of them will want to remember.

Myles is the first to break the silence, sprinting towards her and grabbing her arm, shaking her as if she's a ragdoll. 'What the hell are you doing here?'

Sophie can't speak, instead she throws up, all over Myles's shoes. His eyes wild with disgust, he drags her into the living room.

'He... he broke into our house,' Edwin says, staring at Sophie, his eyes pleading with her. 'It was self-defence. He tried to attack Heather. He tried to kill her.'

'Liar!' Even though she knows he's dead from the state of his battered skull, she rushes over to check his pulse. Nothing.

Through a veil of tears, she turns to the Hollingers. 'You didn't even try to help him,' she screams at Edwin. She jumps up and pummels her fists against his chest. 'You're a doctor! You should have tried to help him!'

Edwin grabs both her arms and peels her off him. 'There was nothing I could have done,' he says. Sophie's never seen him look so ghostly. And it terrifies her.

'Someone call an ambulance!' Sophie shrieks. 'The police!'

Myles grabs her arms. 'He broke into our home, Sophie. Told hideous lies about Vanessa. He's probably been stalking her! And he was about to attack Mum. I had to do something!' He turns to Edwin, seeking reassurance from his father.

'He wasn't lying!' Sophie yells. 'He was Vanessa's boyfriend! They loved each other. And they were—'

'No,' Heather says. 'No...' But there's no conviction in her voice, not like before.

For a moment, all is silent, and Sophie pulls out her phone.

'Nobody's calling the police,' Edwin says, snatching it from her hand. 'Do you know what this would do to Myles? To his future? To the family? It would destroy us all. Don't you give a damn about Charlie?'

'Of course she doesn't,' Myles snarls. 'What the hell was she doing here?' He glares at Sophie, his fear now replaced with venom. 'Were you seeing that man?' He points to Caleb's dead body. 'That would fit, wouldn't it. You're both scum. Well-suited. I told Charlie a million times to stay away from you. And even after all those messages I sent you, you still didn't get it. He should never have been with you.'

'Myles!' Heather says, but her voice is barely above a whisper.

'What *were* you doing?' Edwin asks, walking towards her. 'You broke in too.'

'No, I didn't!' Sophie insists. 'Where's the sign of forced entry? Vanessa gave Caleb the key! How else would he have got in without damaging the house? Check his pockets – you'll find it in there!'

'Nobody's touching him,' Edwin commands.

Heather is crying now; the enormity of what her son has done must be crashing down on her. The realisation of how much trouble they're in. And Sophie's aware that when people are cornered, they do things they wouldn't ordinarily do. She glances at the door, then bolts for it, but Myles is too fast and grabs hold of her before she reaches it, twisting her arms back so that she can't move.

'Get off me,' Sophie screams, trying to pull herself out of his grip.

Sophie looks at Edwin, silently appealing to any sense of decency he might have, but he says nothing, watching them as he paces the room. 'We need time to think,' he says. 'Jesus, Myles. You'd go to prison for this. Your life would be over.'

'But it was self-defence,' Myles insists.

'No, it wasn't,' Edwin says. 'He was trying to help your mum, not hurt her.'

Blood drains from Myles's face. 'No, Dad, I—'

'Shut up!' Edwin yells. 'I need to think!'

And when Edwin stares at her, Sophie knows she needs to get out of here, whatever that takes. 'I won't say anything,' she says, speaking softly now. 'I'm leaving anyway. I'm going to university in Manchester. Please, just let me go.'

'She's lying,' Myles says.

'I promise you, I've been planning to leave all along. That's why I was meeting Caleb here tonight. He... he got me some new documents, so I can start a new life away from here.'

All three of them stare at her.

'What the hell are you talking about?' Heather says. 'Why would you do that?'

'Did Caleb have anything with him?' Sophie asks. 'A bag?'

Heather nods, and points to a black sports bag on the armchair. Definitely Caleb's; Sophie's seen it before.

'Open it,' Sophie says. 'That will prove I've been planning to leave.' She tries to wrestle out of Myles's grasp, but he only tightens his hold on her.

Edwin unzips the bag. 'What the hell is this?' He pulls out an A4 folder and opens it, pouring the contents onto the floor. A passport, GCSE and A level certificates, a national insurance card. He picks up the passport and flicks to the back page. 'Scarlett Humphries? What is this?'

'My new life,' Sophie says. 'I told you. Caleb was just helping me. That's why I came here tonight. To get these from him.'

Heather takes the passport from Edwin and studies it. 'Charlie doesn't know about this, does he?' Heather says. 'I know he doesn't. Why are you leaving? Why would you do that to him?'

Sophie could lie to them, make up some story that has nothing to do with their son, but she refuses to do that. 'Because of the person he is,' she says.

Again, they all stare at her as if she's just told them the world is about to end within seconds.

'You're lying,' Heather says. 'Why would you leave because of Charlie? After everything he's done for you. He loves you to pieces.'

'I told you all she wasn't good enough for him,' Myles says.

'Shut up, Myles,' Edwin commands. 'You've done more than enough! I suggest you keep your mouth shut. Don't say anything!' He continues pacing the room.

'You really don't know any of your children, do you?' Sophie says. 'You're so busy trying to protect your reputation, the precious Hollinger name, that you've never stopped to ask what they all really want. Or who they really are. What they like or don't like. They just have to conform to your expectations. You think overprotecting them is loving them, but it's *not*. It's the opposite.'

Sophie ignores the anger on their faces, and pushing aside the danger she's in, she tells them everything that Charlie has done to her, and everything that Vanessa feels about her parents. It doesn't feel good to say all this, and it comes as no relief, because all that matters now is that Caleb is dead, and Myles is a murderer.

When she's finished speaking – the whole time Myles still gripping her arms – her voice is sore and her tears have run dry, but she will never regret telling the truth. It's what they needed to hear.

Heather walks over to her, and for a fleeting moment, Sophie thinks the woman is going to hug her. But Heather raises her hand, smacking Sophie's cheek so hard it makes her head spin. 'You little bitch,' Heather says. 'I wish my son had never met you.'

All eyes are on her as Sophie tries to free her arms. But the painful sting in her cheeks is nothing compared to what Caleb suffered.

'What do we do now?' Heather says, crossing to Edwin, and placing her hands on his arms. 'What the hell do we do?'

They all turn to Sophie, a mixture of fear and hatred on all of their faces.

Finally, Edwin speaks. 'We need time to think. We can keep her locked in the basement until we sort out what to do.'

THIRTY-FIVE
AUGUST 2009

It's cold in this basement with its stone walls, and it feels like she'll soon run out of air, even though she knows that's not possible. It's past one a.m. now, and there are no sounds coming from the house. Sophie wonders if they've all left – and if their plan is to leave her to die here, but she's sure they wouldn't do that. Sophie doesn't want to believe that Heather is a bad person – she's a mum who just wants to protect her son. But Sophie knows that with no food or water, it's unlikely she'll last longer than a week.

Sophie's had plenty of time to think down here. And what she thinks about most is her mum and Orla, Caleb's smashed-in skull, and Vanessa and Charlie. Where are they? She's sure they weren't in the house; Vanessa would have rushed to Caleb's defence, and even though things have been rocky between her and Vanessa lately, Sophie still believes in their friendship, and that Vanessa would never let her family do this to her.

There's a shuffling sound upstairs, and after a few seconds the basement door opens, the silhouette of Heather standing at the top of the stairs.

Sophie scrambles up.

'Don't move, please,' Heather says. 'Stay right there. I just came to give you this.' She holds up a large bottle of water, and a carrier bag. 'I'll leave these here. And here's a bucket.' She reaches behind her. 'For... a toilet.'

'Please, Heather,' Sophie begs. 'Please let me go. I won't say anything to anyone. You have my word. I'm going to university in Manchester. I'll be out of your lives. You'll never see or hear from me again.'

'We can't take that risk,' Heather says. 'Edwin and I have worked too hard to let our lives crash down around us. I can't let Myles go to prison. You're not a mother – you wouldn't understand.'

Sophie's hand instinctively clutches her stomach. The cramping pains are still there, but her fear has overridden the pain, and she's barely conscious of them now. 'Please,' she begs again.

But Heather turns her back to Sophie, as if she can't bear to witness what she's doing to her. 'We have to go back to Wales now. We only came back because Edwin had an emergency at the hospital. Myles was kind enough to drive us because we'd only just got there and it's a long drive. I wish we hadn't let Myles bring us back.' She's mumbling now, as if she's talking to herself.

'Heather, *please*. What's going to happen to me?'

'I don't know,' Heather says. 'You've got water and some food. We need time to think about what to do. We've got to protect our son.'

'Please,' Sophie begs again.

Heather's hand reaches for the door handle, but she hesitates, standing still.

Sophie tries again, convinced now that she can get through to Heather, the woman who has always shown her such kindness. 'Please, Heather, just let me go home. To my mum. And baby Orla.'

Seconds tick by, each one of them laced with hope, but then Heather closes the door, without a glance back.

In the long days that follow, Sophie sings to herself to keep her sanity intact. She knows being locked in here will have a profound and traumatising impact on her, but she's determined to fight it with every inch of her being. *I will be okay. I will be okay.* She forces the mantra to play repeatedly in her head. And sometimes she talks to her mum and Orla too, has conversations with them where she tells them she's sorry for everything that's happened to her, for bringing this pain into their lives. Her mum will be going out of her mind. Sophie wonders if she will go through her things and find that note in her drawer. The one explaining that she is leaving and not to tell anyone that she's going. Tears gush from Sophie's eyes and soak her T-shirt. If her mum finds it, then she probably won't even call the police now, not if she thinks Sophie has deliberately gone, and certainly not when Sophie has begged her not to tell a soul. Instead, she'll be anxiously waiting for Sophie to make contact, and it could be weeks before she truly worries and tells someone.

Sophie loses track of the days, as if time no longer exists. Is it Monday? Tuesday? Or still only Sunday? There's no way for her to tell. But still, she refuses to let go of the tiny sliver of hope she's desperately clinging to. The hope that Heather, or any of the Hollingers, will come to their senses and let Sophie out of there.

The gush of blood comes with no warning, followed by an intense spasm of pain in her abdomen. Sophie stares down at the floor. She hasn't had a period for months, and now, in this horrible basement, it finally comes, and looks like at least four months' worth.

She searches the basement and finds a box of old clothes. She uses some to soak up the blood, and then changes into what must be a pair of Vanessa's old jeans. And then once again, all she has to occupy her mind is her thoughts. She vaguely wonders if she's still sane. Or perhaps she's already dead.

Sophie hunts through the boxes again, though so far she's found nothing but junk. Not a single thing that could help her break out of here. But it gives her something to focus on. She's pulling out some toys, throwing them on the floor – tidying them up afterwards will give her something to do – and there, in the middle of some Lego boxes, is a small screwdriver. Sophie laughs; a loud cackle that is clear evidence that she's gone mad. That tiny tool is not going to do anything. Still, she picks it up, and then tries to come up with ten new uses for it. Anything to keep her mind busy, to ward off atrophy, and to keep at bay the horror of her situation.

She sits on the bottom stair; it's where she's been spending a lot of her thinking time, when she's not trawling through boxes or sleeping. The food ran out ages ago, and it won't be long until she's dead, if she isn't already.

A pen, she decides, examining the small screwdriver. It could be used for writing. Sophie leans down and starts to carve into the bannister. *Please help me.* She hadn't planned those words, but clearly, they're at the forefront of her mind. No one will read her plea, she knows that, but it feels good to write it anyway. And then, just to spite them all, she fills the grooves with her blood from the pool on the floor.

She opens her eyes, disorientated. As usual, she has no idea what time of day or night it is, and her body clock is a disrupted jumble. She hears a noise and pulls herself up from her makeshift bed of old clothes, fully alert.

Silence.

She makes her way up the stairs, leaning her head against the door to see if she can hear anything else, but all is silent.

Sinking to the floor, she pulls the screwdriver from her pocket and rams it into the door, screaming into the empty void. Bubbles of panic, which so far she's done so well to keep at bay, form in her stomach, so she starts carving on the door. *SOPHIE WAS HERE.* No one will ever see it – who would ever notice the back of a basement door? But it stills the swell of panic, and gradually she begins to breathe normally again. It just needs blood. More of it this time. She doesn't know why; it's just something she's compelled to do.

Minutes later – or is it hours? Days? – Sophie hears footsteps. She rushes upstairs again, holding her breath. The door opens, and Heather is standing there, staring at her as if she's forgotten they've locked Sophie in this basement.

Overcome with weakness, Sophie drops to the floor. Heather crouches down and holds her tightly, like a baby, wiping away the tears that Sophie has held back since they locked her in here.

'It's okay,' Heather soothes. 'I'm here now. And I'm going to help you.'

Sophie hugs her, and for just a moment, with her eyes closed, Heather feels like her mum.

'Come on,' Heather says, easing her up. 'I've got you some food and some lemonade. And then I'm going to take you home.'

'Really?' Sophie asks, pulling back, staring at her without blinking. 'I'm going home?'

'Yes. I'm so sorry, Sophie. But I have to be careful. This isn't what Edwin and Myles wanted. I hired a car and drove back a day early. They think I'm visiting a friend of mine who lives in Wales. But don't worry, it will be a while before they realise what I've done.'

'Thank you,' Sophie whispers, clinging to Heather, tears soaking into her expensive blouse.

Heather leads her to the kitchen table and helps her sit

down, then she sets about getting the food onto plates. 'Is fish and chips okay?' I stopped on my way home.

It's her favourite, and despite her anger, she's touched that Heather remembered. 'How long have I been here?' Sophie asks.

'Six days.' Heather pauses, her hands resting on the fish wrapper. 'But it's probably best not to dwell on that. You've got your whole life to live, Sophie. University around the corner. You need to forget that you ever met Charlie. Forget all of us.' She opens the wrapper and places Sophie's fish on a plate. 'Here you go. Eat up and then we'll get you home.'

Sophie is ravenous, and wolfs down the food, while Heather pours her some lemonade and places it in front of her. 'Thank you,' Sophie says, with her mouth full of food.

'I really liked you, Sophie. I'm sad this all had to happen.'

Sophie nods.

There are tears in Heather's eyes, and she pulls a tissue from her sleeve and dabs them. 'What a mess we find ourselves in sometimes. Still, things always work out in the end, don't they?' She pushes the glass of lemonade towards Sophie. 'You need to be back with your mum, Sophie. That's where you should be.'

Sophie reaches for her glass, gulping down warm lemonade because her throat is parched. It tastes funny – stale and flat, as if the plastic has leached from the bottle, but she doesn't care.

'Good girl,' Heather says, taking Sophie's plate to the sink. Her tears have made a mess of her foundation, and Sophie thinks she must be crying because her son is a murderer. Heather begins to wash up, quietly humming to herself.

Sophie feels dizzy. She's eaten too quickly after having no food for days – that must be it. Then her throat starts to tighten, and she can't breathe. She looks at Heather, but she has her back to Sophie and Sophie can't form any words. Clutching her neck, she tries to haul herself off the chair, but she loses her balance and falls to the terracotta floor. Everything blurs, the shape of Heather's back merging with the sink until Sophie can no longer make out anything. The humming starts to fade, and all Sophie can hear is Heather sobbing.

Then everything is black and silent.

THIRTY-SIX
AUGUST 2009

Vanessa has hated every excruciating second of being in Wales. She's missed Caleb, and didn't feel right being so far away from him. But at least they're nearly home now – about an hour away, Myles reckons. He's driving them all home because her mum decided to visit a friend in Wales and took Dad's car. Her parents are acting really weird, but Vanessa doesn't have time to worry about their bizarre behaviour. What was the point of them all even going away? Some family holiday that turned out to be when she hardly saw her parents.

Her phone pings and she snatches it up, desperate to hear from Caleb. She hasn't heard from him since he messaged to say he was at the house and enjoying a life of luxury. She's sent him several since, but nothing, not even after the one warning him that her parents were on their way back and there's a chance they could stop at the house, even though her mum said they'd be staying in London.

Her heart races as she sees Caleb's name on the screen, and eagerly she opens the message, ready to devour his words.

I'm sorry. I can't do this any more. Please don't try to contact me. Being apart is the right thing for us. Please forgive me.

Vanessa stares at the words, reading them again, then once more. It doesn't make sense. They've been planning a life together – she knows Caleb loves her. She feels sick, and wants to tell Myles to stop the car, but they're on the motorway with nowhere to pull over.

She places her hand on her stomach, and feels the baby kicking under her baggy jumper. How could he do this to her when they were about to be a family? No one has noticed that she's been wearing oversized clothes all summer. She didn't want this baby – she's too young to make this life-changing commitment, but it had been Sophie's words at Liam's barbeque that had convinced her not to go through with a termination. And now Vanessa's going to be a teenage single mother because Caleb's got cold feet and wants nothing to do with her.

She hopes no one can see her tear-streaked face.

Vanessa's no expert, but when she feels a gush of water pass between her legs two days later, she knows the baby is coming, and there's nothing she can do about it. Thankfully, there's no one in the house tonight; her parents are at the opera in London, and Charlie's with Khalid somewhere, probably drowning his sorrows because he has no idea where Sophie is. Vanessa is sure she's far away from this poxy place, though. She was never at home here.

She gives birth to the baby on the bathroom floor, and the pain is unbearable, but she gets through it. And it's quicker than she'd expected. And now she is holding a wrinkled pink thing, a boy, whose ear-piercing wails make her want to run away from it. She wraps it in a small towel and holds it close to her to keep it warm. But she doesn't want to look at it – in case she sees Caleb in his face.

Eventually Vanessa forces herself to look at the shrivelled thing; it doesn't look like Caleb or her. But it must need feeding, and there's nothing she can give it. It's as if her brain is divided into two – one half knowing she could try to breastfeed and see if she's got any milk, and the other wanting to pretend it doesn't exist.

Caleb would know what to do. He would have made this experience a whole different thing, and then Vanessa might feel some joy holding it, instead of feeling as though it's nothing to do with her.

She's not sure how long she sits motionless on the bathroom floor, to the symphony of baby shrieks, but eventually she stands up and hunts for some scissors to detach herself from it. *You deserve better than me. You deserve better.*

She changes her clothes, then she puts on a coat and hides the baby under it. It's stopped crying now, and seems to have fallen asleep, but this brings no relief for Vanessa – she's sure this respite will be short-lived.

In the garage, she finds a small shovel and slips it inside a plastic bag, then leaves the house, grateful for the dark night sky that hides her from view.

The ground is hard, and it takes longer than she expected to make any headway. But finally she's dug deep enough and she opens her coat and lifts him out. Its eyes are closed, but it's squirming. Her tears splatter onto its tiny head, but she only feels numb, as if this isn't really happening to her, as if she's watching someone else carry out this heinous act. 'I'm sorry,' she says. 'I'm so sorry.'

She places the baby inside, and then picks up the shovel

again, not looking at what she's doing. She definitely can't look. Mud flies around her as she continues to cover the hole, and then she hears shoes crunching on twigs. Gasping, Vanessa grabs the shovel and runs.

And all she knows is that she will never be the same.

THIRTY-SEVEN

'I tried to kill my own baby!' Vanessa screams. She sinks to the floor. 'It wasn't Sophie – it was me who buried him in the woods!'

Myles stares at her, his mouth hanging open, and I, too, am speechless.

'But Sophie was pregnant,' I say, when I recover from the shock of her declaration. 'The baby was Sophie's.'

She shakes her head. 'No, it was mine. I was the one who was pregnant, not Sophie. She begged me to keep it when I told her I wanted to have a termination, and we fell out because of it. But in the end I didn't go through with it. I just kept thinking it would go away, that I wasn't really having a baby.'

Myles walks over to her, and places his hand on her arm. 'Vanessa, this isn't making sense. You've never had a baby.'

'Yes I did!' she screams. 'None of you noticed I was covering it up with big, baggy clothes that summer.'

'But... whose was it?'

'My boyfriend's. Caleb. And I got my head around it and was finally happy, but then Caleb left me. With a text message.'

'No,' Myles says. 'No. We would have noticed if you were pregnant.'

I stare at Vanessa and Myles as they speak, still in shock that I got this so wrong. What else have I been wrong about? All I know is that I can't trust any of the Hollingers. 'You know what happened to Sophie,' I say to Myles; even if she wasn't Craig's mother, I still need to know what happened to her. Lynette needs to know. 'Charlie killed her, didn't he? And Khalid found out. Did Charlie kill him too? You're covering for your brother! You need to stop and tell me what you know. It's over – I've already told the police.'

His face drains of colour. He has swallowed my lie about the police. 'Charlie didn't do anything... You don't know what you're talking about!' Myles shouts. 'You should have stayed away from our family. We were fine before you came along.'

'No, we weren't!' Vanessa shrieks. 'None of us has ever been fine! We've never been free to be ourselves.'

Myles swipes her face, knocking her backwards so her head smacks against the wall. I rush towards her, but he grabs hold of me and I can't wrestle out of his grip. 'I'm fine with who I am,' Myles says. 'I'm proud to be a Hollinger, even if you're not.'

Vanessa clutches her head but pulls herself up. And in that moment, seeing the mask of pure evil on Myles's face, and his aggressive manner, I wonder if Myles knows where Sophie is. 'Do you know what happened to Sophie? Is that it? How else could you be so sure it wasn't Charlie?'

He doesn't answer but lunges towards me, grabbing me by the neck, tightening his grip. Vanessa jumps up and tries to pull him off, kicking and punching him like a feral creature.

She screams at me to run, but I hesitate. 'Go! He won't hurt me,' she screams. 'Just get out of here!'

I bolt for the door, slamming it behind me to slow Myles down – I know he'll come after me, and I hear the door being thrown open. I stumble down the stairs but quickly pick myself up, and Myles is right there at the top. With strength I didn't know I was capable of, I make it to the door and rush outside, where Myles's red Audi is parked on the driveway.

Shouts and screams come from the house – Vanessa shrieking at Myles, and then the front door flies open and she's there, throwing something at my feet.

I look down and see it's a car key.

'Myles dropped it – just go!' Vanessa yells.

Jumping in the car, I slam the door shut and lock it, just before Myles slams into it, pounding on the window. 'Get the fuck out!'

I start the engine and reverse; Myles clings to the bonnet, refusing to let go. Suddenly I brake and he thumps to the ground. Everything falls silent, and I'm about to open the door, terrified that he's dead, but then he picks himself up, slamming into the car again, hollering that he'll kill me.

Slamming my foot on the accelerator, I screech down the road, only slowing when I've put some distance between me and the Hollingers' house. But my breathing still comes in fast bursts, my pulse refusing to steady.

There are things I need to get from the farmhouse, so I never have to come back to this place; everything I own is in there, and I need to call the police. I can't prove anything, but I can tell them that Myles just attacked me, threatening to kill me. Surely that will be enough to make them investigate him.

I reach the farmhouse, hoping Charlie will still be at work, but I freeze and stop the car when I see he's outside, arguing with someone. As I get closer, I see that it's Liam, who pushes Charlie backwards, yelling something at him.

I stop the car, but stay inside with the doors locked. They both turn to look at me, and Liam runs over, Charlie following closely, trying to pull Liam back.

'It's okay,' Liam says. 'The police are on their way.'

'What the hell are you doing in my brother's car?' Charlie shouts. 'Where's Myles?'

I roll the window down a fraction so they can hear me. 'He tried to attack me! At your parents' house. Vanessa helped me get away. I was asking him about Sophie and he... he lost it.' I turn to Liam. 'I think Myles knows what happened to her. Or he...' I stop. 'What are you doing here?' I ask Liam.

'He caught me following him.' Liam glances at Charlie. 'He... he told me all kinds of lies about you. And I found this on the doorstep.' He holds up Khalid's wallet.

'I've never seen that before,' Charlie insists. 'I don't know anything about it!'

'You're lying!' Liam says. 'We'll let the police sort it out.'

Charlie turns to me. 'Fine with me. I'm sure they'll be interested to know what Emmie's been doing. How she coerced me into a relationship under false pretences.' He stalks back to the front door and sits on the doorstep.

'It's no more than you deserve,' Liam says. 'After how you treated Sophie. I know she didn't really want to be with you. You had some kind of hold over her. She might not have admitted it, but we were so close – I could tell something was off about your relationship.'

As I listen, it occurs to me that Charlie isn't running. If he was guilty of anything, then surely he'd want to avoid the police. It makes no sense that he's standing there, listening to everything Liam is throwing at him.

'You were always jealous of me being with Sophie,' Charlie says. 'You didn't just want to be her friend. You can't stand the fact that she chose me.'

'You're wrong,' Liam says. 'Yeah, maybe I did love her, but that love I had for her meant accepting her choices. I was fine with her not being with me. I just knew you weren't good enough for her.'

I open the car door. 'What happened to Sophie?' I ask Charlie. 'The police are going to look into it now. She was a minor, so the case has always been kept open. It will all come out.'

'I've just asked him that, and Charlie said he didn't kill Khalid,' Liam says. 'And he said he's got nothing to hide, and that he's sure they'll be interested to know what you did to him.' Liam shakes his head.

'I did what I had to for my brother.' I climb out of the car. 'But I got it all wrong. Sophie wasn't the one who abandoned him in the forest. It was Vanessa.'

Charlie walks over to us.

'Stay back,' Liam warns.

'I'm not going to hurt Emmie,' Charlie says. 'The police can sort her out.' He doesn't look at me as he speaks.

'You locked me in the basement,' I say. 'For hours. And you expect me to believe that you're harmless?'

Without warning, Charlie springs forward and grabs my arm. 'I don't know what happened to Sophie! I didn't kill her, or do anything to her.' There are tears in his eyes, and for the first time, I believe they are genuine. His words hang in the air around us. And he sounds like the man I first met, who was invested in our relationship; a relationship he thought was real.

'If it wasn't you, Charlie, then I think it was Myles. At the very least, he knows something.'

Charlie stares at me. 'Why would he do anything to Sophie?'

'I don't know! Nothing about this makes any sense. But the way he was just now... he would have killed me. I'm sure of it.'

'You're delusional,' Charlie says. 'You've become so obsessed with Sophie's disappearance that you're looking everywhere for something that isn't there.'

'Khalid found something out and he wanted to tell me. Myles could have—'

'Don't talk about my brother!' he yells in my face.

'Back off!' Liam says, standing between us.

'Did you see Myles at the housewarming party after I left?' I demand

Charlie stares at me. 'I don't know! I was drunk. I can't remember.'

'So, he could easily have slipped out.'

Charlie's phone rings, and he fumbles in his pocket and pulls it out. 'Vanessa,' he says. 'I can't really—'

He stops, his eyes widening, and I can hear Vanessa's voice through the phone – loud and frantic. And then she falls silent.

'Is she okay?' I yell, grabbing his arm. 'What's happened to Vanessa? Has Myles hurt her?'

Charlie takes his time to answer, clutching the phone to his chest. 'No,' he says. 'But...' He stares at me, then Liam, glancing between us before he can form any words. 'Vanessa's just told me where Sophie is.' He sinks to his knees.

For a moment I'm too stunned to speak, and everything seems to slow down. 'Where?' I shout, when I recover from shock. 'Where is she?'

He looks up at me with bloodshot eyes. 'The summer house.'

'How can she be in the—'

And then realisation slams into me, weakening every limb in my body. The summer house was newer than the rest of the house – the Hollingers must have had it put in years later. But I need to hear this from Charlie. 'What exactly did Vanessa say?'

I can tell he doesn't want to tell me. 'Please, Charlie. I'm begging you. What happened?'

But when he finally speaks, it doesn't make sense. 'The summer house was built not long after we got back from Wales. After Sophie went missing. My parents never talked about having one before, but suddenly it was being built. For us,' he says. He buries his head in his hands.

'Are you saying that Sophie is buried under the summer

house?' Liam shakes his head. He stares at the farmhouse as if he'll be able to see through it. 'No... no...'

Charlie doesn't speak, and his silence tells us everything. In the distance, I hear the faint blare of police sirens.

'Vanessa killed her?' I'm almost afraid to hear the answer.

A car pulls up, but it's not a police car, it's a white cab. We all turn to stare as Myles gets out and makes his way towards us.

Liam rushes up to him. 'The police are coming. I'd think very carefully about what you do next if I were you.'

But Myles ignores him and heads straight towards Charlie.

Charlie lunges towards him, shoving him to the ground. 'Vanessa's already told me, but I want to hear it from you! What the hell did you do? Tell me!'

Myles cowers on the ground, holding up his hands. 'It wasn't meant to happen... She shouldn't have been there. She had no right to be there.'

'What the hell are you talking about?'

The police sirens draw closer.

'No,' Charlie says, burying his head in his hands. 'You wouldn't have said a word if Vanessa hadn't just threatened you with a knife. You must have thought she wouldn't think twice about slitting your throat!'

But as I listen to this, stunned silent, I don't believe Vanessa would have hurt Myles – she just wanted the truth from him.

'Where is she?' Charlie says. 'What did you do with Sophie?'

Myles pulls himself up and looks towards the road, then back at the house. 'Under the summer house,' he mumbles, sinking to his knees.

'But you couldn't have known your parents were going to get a summer house,' I say, still confused. 'When the builders came, they would have found Sophie's body!'

Charlie's eyes widen. 'Dad's friend built it. For free!' He shakes his head. 'I asked Dad why they weren't using our normal builders.' He stares at Myles. 'He said this person wanted to repay him for saving his life when other doctors told him he was inoperable. It all makes sense now. It's sickening! He took ages building it as he was doing it all himself. Usually Mum likes things being done quickly, but she never once complained about how long it was taking, even though I could tell it was stressful for her.'

Myles stays silent.

'Heather and Edwin had to have known,' Liam says.

Charlie leans down, his face close to Myles's. 'Is this true? Tell me Mum and Dad didn't know!'

Again, Myles doesn't speak, and Charlie's face drains of colour. He pulls himself up. 'When Sophie went missing, Mum and Dad were really weird around me. Every time I came in the room they would fall silent. As if they'd been talking to Myles and didn't want me to hear. Is this why, Myles?' He kicks Myles's leg.

'We don't know anything for sure,' I say, placing my hand on his arm. 'And it's for the police to find out now.'

'I was never good enough for her,' Charlie says, through loud gut-wrenching sobs. 'I never deserved her. I thought I could make her stay with me...'

I don't want to hear anything Charlie has to say about Sophie. Not now. Because I'm sure that whatever happened, it can all be traced back to him. 'I need my phone,' I say, nausea rising in my stomach. 'Please, Charlie, give me my phone.'

Without a word, Charlie reaches into his pocket and places it on the doorstep, still avoiding looking at me.

I snatch it up and scroll through it. There are several missed calls, all from Orla, and a ton of messages begging me to call her. There's also a voicemail. I hold the phone to my ear and listen.

'Emmie, where are you? Really worried now. Please, please call me. I've finished reading Margot's journals and ... it was

Margot!' My heart almost stops. 'It was Margot who found the baby!'

I listen to her message again. It's almost too much to process alongside everything else I've learned today. Margot saved my brother's life, and blessed my mum with the second baby she was desperate for. My heart aches with sadness for all of them. And most of all for Sophie, who just wanted to start her life, and didn't deserve to become entangled with the Hollingers.

The police car pulls up, and DC Stanthorpe steps out of the car. But this time, I'm relieved to see her. There's a lot she needs to know, and then I can put Peaslake, and the last year and a half behind me.

'How did you find out about me?' I ask Charlie. 'How long did you know?'

He stares at the ground. 'I liked you the minute I met you. When you were lying on the ground after your bike hit my car. But if I was getting into a relationship with you, then I needed to be sure about you. I hired people to look into you. They found a witness who could have sworn you hit my car on purpose. But I thought you were just after me for my money. I had no idea about all the other stuff until you confessed it to me in the summer house.'

I stare at him, my mouth hanging open. I can't take any more lies. 'Why did you lie about Sophie's carving in the wood? It was you who got rid of it, wasn't it? And you deliberately arranged for the builders to destroy the basement.'

Charlie hangs his head.

'Why, though? Did you know what Myles had done?'

'No. But I... I didn't want it all being brought up. I wasn't exactly kind to Sophie. I wanted to forget it all, and you just kept going on about it. But I did the basement for you. I knew you didn't like it... after your dad...'

I shake my head and turn away.

Charlie pulls me back. 'Just tell me something. Was none of it real?'

There are many things I could say in reply. I could tell him about all the times I almost forgot how I'd manufactured our meeting. That when we were alone together, and I wasn't thinking of my mum, or Craig, or how I could get information from Charlie, it did feel real. How I often mused that if we'd just met by chance, I would probably have fallen for him. But I could never let Charlie under my skin, to dilute my desire for the truth.

I don't answer, but lean towards him and kiss his cheek. He can make of that what he will. I won't ever look back.

THIRTY-EIGHT
TWO MONTHS LATER

Two months ago, I thought I would never set foot in this place again. But here I am, back in Peaslake, parking outside Lynette's cottage. I let myself in through the narrow side gate, as instructed, and find Lynette and Orla in the back garden, making the most of this September heatwave.

They both jump up from the table, rushing over to me with smiles I don't deserve on their faces. Lynette throws her arms around me. 'I don't know how to thank you,' she says.

'I haven't done anything,' I say, feeling awkward now that they both know the truth about me, and that I lied to them.

As soon as Lynette lets go of me, Orla hugs me. 'It's good to see you, Emmie.'

'Come and sit,' Lynette says, taking my arm and leading me to the table. 'I've baked some cakes.'

We sit at the table, basking in the sun, but somehow my body feels cold. I can't help thinking that it might have been better for Lynette to have lived in hope of one day seeing her daughter again. But looking at her now, she does seem to be at peace.

'I still can't believe they found another body buried with

Sophie,' Orla says. 'And he was Vanessa's boyfriend. That's so twisted. It's always in films or TV shows, isn't it – people burying someone in their back gardens – but I never thought anyone would actually be crazy enough to do that.'

'I don't think the Hollingers were crazy,' I say. 'I think they were desperate.'

'It shocked me when I found out he was Vanessa's boyfriend,' Lynette says. 'Poor girl. And her own brother doing that to him and Sophie. I just can't understand why.'

'He's changed his story now,' Orla says. 'None of the Hollingers are speaking about it or admitting what happened, but the parents definitely knew.'

No doubt gossip has been rife around here, and I'm only glad I haven't been here to hear any of it. It doesn't matter – all of the Hollingers are as guilty as each other.

'It doesn't change anything, knowing exactly what happened,' Lynette says. 'It won't bring my Sophie back.' Her eyes glint with tears.

'At least it doesn't seem like Charlie and Vanessa had anything to do with it,' Orla says. She looks at me as she says this, and I'm sure she's wondering how I feel about Charlie now.

Lynette pours me coffee, and pushes the plate of cupcakes towards me. I take one and place it next to my mug.

'You could have told us the truth,' Lynette says. 'We wouldn't have cared. You were trying to find out what happened to Sophie – it doesn't matter what your reasons were. And we only know the truth now because of you.'

'It wasn't me who got to the truth, though,' I say. 'Vanessa did that by herself.'

'But everything you did led up to that point. You were the catalyst. Thank you, Emmie.'

I take a sip of coffee; I can't accept their gratitude, but I know they still want to offer it. 'I still don't know who sent me that email I got mentioning the baby in the woods. I can only guess it was Margot. She was the only person who knew the full details of what happened to Craig.'

'She definitely has moments of lucidity,' Lynette says.

'How is Vanessa?' I ask. It's not common knowledge that it was Vanessa who tried to bury her baby, and I will never mention it – she's already suffered enough. But I'm sure Lynette must have worked it out once she found out it wasn't Sophie who was pregnant.

'She actually seems to be doing well,' Lynette says. 'Can't understand why she'd stay in Peaslake, but she told us she wanted to be here. Close to... Sophie and Khalid. And Caleb.'

'I'm sorry I thought Sophie was pregnant. That must have caused you untold pain.'

Lynette shakes her head. 'I didn't believe it anyway. I knew my daughter. And I know she would have told me if she was pregnant. There was no doubt in my mind about that. Being a single mum meant we had such a strong bond. I was her everything, and she was mine, until Orla came along. But Sophie helped me raise Orla. I wouldn't have managed without her, and she knew that I would have done the same for her.' Lynette looks away, staring at the pretty rose-covered pergola.

I glance at Orla, wondering how much of what we discovered she has shared with her mum.

'Mum knows about Margot's journals,' Orla says.

'I can't believe Margot saved your brother's life,' Lynette says. 'And she never said a word to anyone about what she'd found in the woods.' She pauses. 'There's another reason I knew Sophie couldn't have been pregnant,' Lynette says. 'I... I wasn't exactly honest either.'

Orla leans forward, frowning. 'Mum, what are you talking about?'

Lynette reaches into her pocket and pulls out a folded piece of paper. 'I found this in Sophie's drawer, after she went missing.' Tears that weren't there a moment ago trickle down her cheeks. 'Sophie wrote it.' She hands me the note, and I take it, suddenly feeling cold again.

> *I love you, Mum. I have to go, but I'll be back. I can't explain now, but I have no choice. Please don't worry about me – I am going to be fine. But please don't tell anyone about this note. No one. Tell everyone that you don't know where I am. Please, Mum. Soon you will understand. I love you and Orla xx*

'So, she was planning to leave,' Lynette says. 'And I never told the police. I wanted them to keep looking for her, and I knew that if they saw the note, they'd assume she was a runaway. But I don't understand why she was leaving. What would make her do that?'

'I don't know,' I say, even though I'm convinced it was something to do with Charlie. All of the Hollingers seem to be tainted by violence and death. And not as victims. 'But maybe we have to let ourselves be okay with not knowing.'

'I know it's about the Hollingers. It has to be. Everything is about them.' Lynette dabs her eyes with a napkin.

'I'm meeting Vanessa this afternoon,' I say. 'She messaged me and asked if we could meet up.'

'And are you okay with that?' Orla asks, folding her arms. 'I wouldn't want anything to do with any of them.'

I think about this for a moment – I've been tempted to ignore Vanessa's request to see me, but she is as much a victim as Sophie and Caleb. And Khalid. None of the Hollingers have admitted to his murder, but it was very likely one of them.

'It's something I need to do,' I say, shifting in my seat. As much as Lynette and Orla are making me feel welcome here, I am an intruder in their lives. Vanessa is the one I have a forced bond with, because of the baby she tried to murder. My brother.

'How's your final year of A levels going so far?' I ask Orla, desperate to change the subject. I pick up a cupcake and bite into it, hoping it will distract me from feeling so uncomfortable.

'Yeah, it's going well.'

'Can't believe she'll soon be off to university to study medicine,' Lynette says, a mixture of pride and sadness in her voice.

Orla reaches across and hugs Lynette. 'My sister's dream.'

'But is it what *you* want to do?' I ask.

'Definitely,' Orla says. 'I can't imagine doing anything else.'

'I wish you could have known Sophie,' Lynette says. 'You're both so different, but so alike too. It's strange. You remind me of her. Not how you look, but... just how you are.'

I smile, and wonder if this is why Charlie fell for me. Did I remind him of Sophie too?

'And you?' Lynette continues. 'How have the last couple of months been for you?'

'I start my new job next week,' I say. 'And there's more focus on animal therapy, so I'm really excited.' I don't mention that the email from the school in Peaslake inviting me for an interview still sits in my inbox. I'd received it the day after the police dug up Sophie's and Caleb's bodies. I never once considered taking that job, but for some reason haven't deleted it, even though the job will be long gone by now, and I will never leave London again.

For another hour, I sit with Lynette and Orla, and we talk about the future, none of us mentioning the Hollingers again. And when I tell them I'd better get going, Lynette immediately offers me more tea. 'Won't you stay a bit longer?' she asks.

'I'd love to, but I need to get going,' Vanessa will be waiting.

'Will we see you again?' Lynette asks, as they walk me to my car. 'Talking to you somehow makes me feel that Sophie's still here.'

I'm stunned and flattered by her words, and it takes me a moment to respond. 'I don't think so,' I say, because Lynette has already spent too long living in hope.

. . .

Vanessa is unrecognisable. Her long blonde hair now sits above her shoulders, and it's dark now, a reddish-brown colour that suits her. She's wearing a floaty white summer dress with thin straps, and she seems to stand taller now, as if the emotional pain she's carried with her all this time no longer cripples her. I find this surprising, given what her family has done. I would have assumed it would only make her worse.

I walk up to the entrance of the church, where, in a few minutes, we will visit Sophie's and Caleb's graves.

'Emmie!' Vanessa walks up to me and wraps her fragile arms around me. She smells of perfume; bothering to wear it is surely a sign that she's beginning to heal.

As I approach her, I'm surprisingly nervous, even though, clearly, she's happy to see me. 'You look well,' I say.

'Thank you.' She touches her hair. 'I'm really trying to make a fresh start. It... hasn't been easy.' She links her arm through mine and we follow the path leading to the cemetery at the back of the church.

'Are you sure you're ready for this?' I ask.

Vanessa nods. 'Yes, now that you're here with me. I couldn't do it before.'

She'd told me in her message that she'd missed Sophie's funeral – she was in too much pain and not able to face saying goodbye to her friend. And Charlie had moved back to London straight away, cutting off everyone in his family. And with Myles awaiting trial for three murders, Vanessa has lost both of her brothers.

'There it is,' Vanessa says, pointing to a fresh gravestone, bunches of lilies and roses resting against it.

I lean down and place the flowers I've brought on it – chrysanthemums and carnations, because I've heard they do well outside. Vanessa does the same with hers – an extravagant bouquet of pink roses. 'They're meant to symbolise friendship,' she says. 'And I've never had a friend like her.' She sighs. 'Shall we sit for a bit?' she says, pointing to a bench near the back wall of the church. 'You don't have to rush back to London, do you?'

Although I want to leave – being here makes me feel as though I'm slowly suffocating – I give in to the pleading look on Vanessa's face. 'I'll stay for a bit,' I say.

We sit on the bench, and Vanessa pulls her sunglasses over her eyes. 'I had a call from the police today,' she says. 'They found Myles's DNA on Khalid, under his fingernails.' She lets her words sit for a bit, giving me time to process what this means. Khalid must have tried to fight back. It makes me sick to think about it. 'What I can't get my head around is why. What did Khalid know? Why did he have to be silenced?'

I've given this a lot of thought, and the only conclusion I can reach is that Khalid must have got back to Heather and Edwin's house and had an interaction with Myles. I have no idea how that might have led Khalid to call me with his urgent message, but it's the only thing that makes any sense.

'At least we know it wasn't Myles who drove into me,' I say. A few weeks ago, the police found a stolen car in Guildford that had been involved in an accident, and there were traces of my bike paint on it.

'I heard that was a teenager,' Vanessa says.

I nod. 'He stole his mother's car, and when he lost control and ploughed into me, he was too afraid to stop.' It doesn't make Myles any less of a monster, not after all the things he *did* do.

'At least that's one thing the Hollingers aren't responsible for.' Vanessa stares at the floor. 'Me included. I'm no different from them, am I? I tried to—'

'It's probably best not to dwell on that,' I say.

'My baby would have died if Margot hadn't been walking the dog that night and decided to cut through the forest.'

I don't say anything; the truth is I can't make excuses for

Vanessa, even though I know she wasn't in her right mind. The devastation of Caleb leaving her without warning and the fear of raising their baby alone was enough to tip her over the edge. Her family are also responsible for what happened to my brother.

'Have you been okay?' I ask.

She shrugs. 'I was never close to my parents. Or Myles. Charlie was the one I had a bond with. That's why it almost destroyed me when I thought he might have done something to Sophie. Every day I thank God that it wasn't him. I don't think I'd be okay if it was.'

'Have you heard from him?'

'We've spoken on the phone a few times, but I think he finds it hard to talk to me now. Maybe I do too. I think we just need a clean break. For a while, at least.' She smiles.

We sit in silence for a moment, and I focus on the birdsong.

'I'm planning to go to America,' Vanessa tells me. 'Maybe take a road trip. It won't be the same without Khalid, but... I think it will be good for me. Away from my parents. Doing it alone.'

I nod. 'That's a great idea,' I say.

'What about you?' she asks, lifting her sunglasses a fraction to study me.

'Throwing myself into work. London life again. It suits me much better.'

'Yes, I can see how all the smog and car fumes would be preferable to this.' She gestures around her, and I find myself smiling.

And then she talks about Sophie until I feel like I know that seventeen-year-old inside and out. And like Lynette said, I can see myself in her.

'I need to tell you something,' Vanessa says, when we fall silent again.

My pulse quickens. I'm not ready for any more shocks.

'I was the one who put Khalid's wallet in your bag.'

I stare at her. 'I don't understand.'

'I found it in my bedroom. And I panicked. Myles must have put it in there. I'm sorry – I didn't know what to do. I wasn't trying to frame you, I just... I don't know what I was thinking.'

I study Vanessa's face, searching for any hint of a lie. But the effort of trying to decipher her is too much. 'It doesn't matter,' I say. 'Anyway, I'd better go. There's someone else I need to see before I go back to London.'

Vanessa raises her eyebrows. 'Liam, by any chance?'

My cheeks feel hot. 'Yeah. I thought I'd say goodbye to him.'

Vanessa smiles, but doesn't say anything.

I stand, and pull my car key from my pocket. 'Keep in touch,' I say to Vanessa.

And I mean every word.

A LETTER FROM KATHRYN

Thank you for picking one of my books to read. *Sophie Was Here* was an absolute joy to write from the moment I typed *Prologue*. This story flowed like never before and I really feel as though I went on a journey with my characters. If you as a reader feel just a fraction of that, then I've done my job.

Back in 2014, when my first novel was published, I never imagined I'd be on my sixteenth book. In my twenties, I used to browse bookstores and be in complete awe of the amount of books Stephen King had written (I still am in awe of him, of course!). Fast forward, and it's an utter privilege to have been able to do this for over ten years. As long as you keep wanting to read my books, I will keep writing!

I hope *Sophie Was Here* runs deeper than psychological suspense, and that at its heart, it's about the complexities of families and relationships. The shades of grey that mean being human isn't just always as straightforward as being good or bad. Many times throughout writing, my heart broke for Sophie, Emmie and every other character.

It's ultimately a dark story, but no matter how dark the path gets, I always believe in shining a light on the strength we find in ourselves – and in others – when we need it most. I hope this story makes you feel something, whether it's fear, shock, or even a quiet moment of reflection.

Most of all, I hope this book gave you space to escape for a little while. In a world that never seems to slow down, stories remain a powerful way to pause, feel and connect.

If you enjoyed *Sophie Was Here*, it would mean so much to me if you could take a moment to leave a review. Reviews are vital for helping books find new readers, and I truly appreciate every single one.

Want to stay up to date with my latest books? You can sign up for updates here:

www.bookouture.com/kathryn-croft

If you'd like to, please also feel free to connect with me via my website, Facebook, Instagram, or X. I'd love to hear from you!

Thank you again for all your support – it is very much appreciated. And enjoy whichever book you're reading next!

As Stephen King said: 'Books are a uniquely portable magic.'

Kathryn x

www.kathryncroft.com

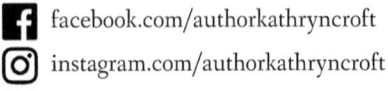

facebook.com/authorkathryncroft
instagram.com/authorkathryncroft
x.com/katcroft

ACKNOWLEDGEMENTS

Writing a book is always a journey – usually a long, perilous one! I start with huge excitement – that *I've got this!* feeling – then by mid-point I'm seriously questioning my life choices! But still I continue, until finally I stumble across the finish line with a mixture of exhaustion and relief. Luckily, I had some incredible people (and possibly too much caffeine) to help me get there.

Lydia, my wonderful editor – thank you for your fantastic idea for this book – I hope I did it justice. Once again, you've knocked this book into shape and helped me see things I was too stuck in my head to see! And thank you for your humorous editorial comments – they really do take away the pain of structural edits!

Maddy, my fantastic agent – I feel so privileged to have been part of your agency for over ten years now – where has that time gone?! Thank you for still believing in me, for fighting for me, and for putting up with my many annoying emails!

My family – I'm sorry I'm always holed away writing and for constantly saying, 'As soon as this book's finished, I'll have a short break.' I'm beginning to realise I don't actually know how to have a break! But thank you for being there, and making sure I do actually step away from my computer now and again!

Jo Sidaway and Michelle Langford, my police pals – thank you for once again checking that my police procedure isn't ridiculous. And thank you for the laughs!

And of course, my readers. Whether you picked up this book on a whim or have been waiting for it, you're the reason this story exists. Thank you for giving my words a home.

PUBLISHING TEAM

Turning a manuscript into a book requires the efforts of many people. The publishing team at Bookouture would like to acknowledge everyone who contributed to this publication.

Audio
Alba Proko
Melissa Tran
Sinead O'Connor

Commercial
Lauren Morrissette
Hannah Richmond
Imogen Allport

Contracts
Peta Nightingale

Cover design
The Brewster Project

Data and analysis
Mark Alder
Mohamed Bussuri

Editorial
Lydia Vassar-Smith
Imogen Allport

Copyeditor
Angela Snowden

Proofreader
Lynne Walker

Marketing
Alex Crow
Melanie Price
Occy Carr
Cíara Rosney
Martyna Młynarska

Operations and distribution
Marina Valles
Stephanie Straub
Joe Morris

Production
Hannah Snetsinger
Mandy Kullar
Ria Clare
Nadia Michael

Publicity
Kim Nash
Noelle Holten
Jess Readett
Sarah Hardy

RAISING READERS
Books Build Bright Futures

Dear Reader,

We'd love your attention for one more page to tell you about the crisis in children's reading, and what we can all do.

Studies have shown that reading for fun is the **single biggest predictor of a child's future success** – more than family circumstance, parents' educational background or income. It improves academic results, mental health, wealth, communication skills, and ambition.

The number of children reading for fun is in rapid decline. Young people have a lot of competition for their time, and a worryingly high number do not have a single book at home.

Our business works extensively with schools, libraries and literacy charities, but here are some ways we can all raise more readers:

- Reading to children for just 10 minutes a day makes a difference
- Don't give up if children aren't regular readers – there will be books for them!

- Visit bookshops and libraries to get recommendations
- Encourage them to listen to audiobooks
- Support school libraries
- Give books as gifts

Thank you for reading: there's a lot more information about how to encourage children to read on our website.

www.JoinRaisingReaders.com

www.ingramcontent.com/pod-product-compliance
Ingram Content Group UK Ltd.
Pitfield, Milton Keynes, MK11 3LW, UK
UKHW010019020725
6674UKWH00002B/196